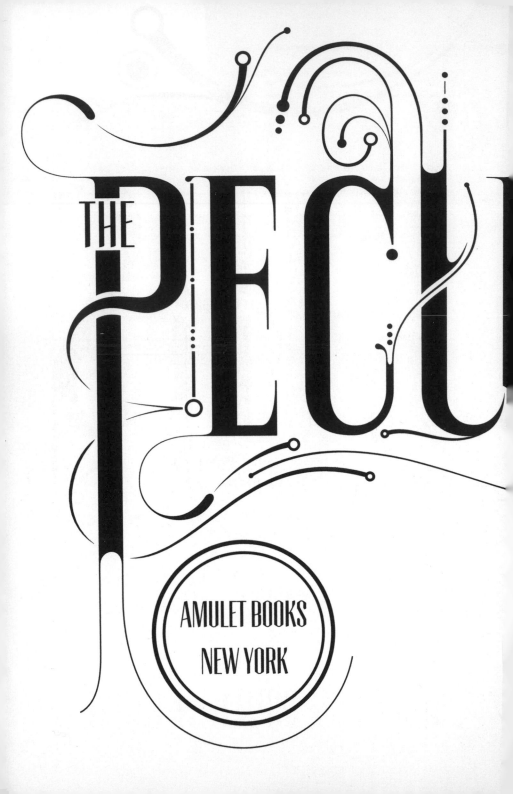

THE PECU

AMULET BOOKS
NEW YORK

LIARS

MAUREEN DOYLE McQUERRY

The Library of Congress has catalogued the hardcover edition of this book as follows:

McQuerry, Maureen, 1955–
The Peculiars / Maureen Doyle McQuerry.
pages cm
Summary: Eighteen-year-old Lena Mattacascar sets out for Scree, a weird place inhabited by Peculiars, seeking the father who left when she was young, but on the way she meets young librarian Jimson Quiggley and handsome marshall Thomas Saltre, who complicate her plans.
978-1-4197-0178-8 (hardback)
[1. Adventure and adventurers—Fiction. 2. Identity—Fiction.
3. Abnormalities, Human—Fiction. 4. Goblins—Fiction.] I. Title.
PZ7.M24715 Pec 2012
[Fic]—dc23
2012000844

ISBN for this edition: 978-1-4197-1206-7

THE ART OF BOOKS SINCE 1949
115 West 18th Street
New York, NY 10011
www.abramsbooks.com

FOR DENNIS

CHAPTER 1

A PHYSICAL EXAMINATION RAISES THE QUESTION OF GENETICS

LENA AT EIGHT YEARS OF AGE

"There's no mistaking what your father was, not when you've got feet and hands like those." Nana Crane grabs my hand in her own plump one. She runs her finger with the emerald ring down the length of my palm. I try to pull away. She pinches my hand tighter. "Goblin phalanges. The hands and feet don't lie, child. It's in your genes."

"But Poppa doesn't have hands and feet like these!"

Nana Crane's ring glints in the light. "No, he doesn't. His are small. Everything about him is small, especially his heart. I always knew there was something peculiar about him despite his talk of being from the East." She drops my hand and stares into the middle distance. Her chin quivers. "Not every goblin has them, but it's a sure sign. Just like those feet. You're bound to be just like him."

It scares me when she talks that way about Poppa. Inside the ugly specially made shoes, I try to curl my stiff toes to make my feet as small as possible, feet that are so long no regular shoes will fit them. I am tired of the doctor prodding and poking at my tender feet, then speaking as if I weren't in the room.

"The girl has the signs of goblinism. There's no denying it, even though not many people can recognize the syndrome anymore." Dr. Crink looks at my mother over the edge of his glasses. "She displays three readily identifiable characteristics to the trained eye: elongated hands and feet, soft fleshy soles, and precocious intelligence. If you're worried about what other people will think, don't. Hardly anyone but a few old doctors has seen anything like this in their lifetime. Most doctors would say these hands and feet are a defect of birth."

A small gulping noise. Mother is having trouble speaking.

"When you find them clustered like that"—the good doctor shrugs his beefy shoulders—"it points in one direction. Of course, only time will tell about the other, less obvious, characteristics."

I sit on my hands. They splay under me like giant spiders. Mother has always said that they are piano-player hands. That I have an advantage any pianist would envy. I can easily span more than an octave, but practice makes my fingers ache. I know I will never be more than a middling pianist.

"And those characteristics?" Now that her voice returns, it is hardly more than a whisper.

Dr. Crink continues as if he didn't hear her. "You're sure that no one in your family has displayed these traits?"

"No one."

"Your husband's family, then?"

"I've never met them, but my husband has normal hands and feet."

The doctor writes something on a clipboard. "I'd like to meet with him."

"My husband is no longer with us."

He looks up, removing his glasses. "He is deceased?"

Mother's face blooms pink. "No, he left us several years ago."

She now has the doctor's full attention. "Left, eh? Describe him to me, please."

I remember Poppa's quick laugh, the funny faces he made, the way he used to sing to me when I cried. And I remember the other things: flashes of anger that could sear me to the bone.

"My husband is a short man with a quick wit and good business sense. He can be very charming."

"Charming, is it?" The doctor raises caterpillar eyebrows. "And does he drink?"

Mother's lips pleat into her face. I know that look. She won't say another word.

"Loyal." He shook his head. "Silly woman. We're talking about a genetic disorder. In mixed marriages—cases like these—we wait and see which traits are dominant."

"Surely, environment can—"

"There is no question of nature versus nurture. Science shows very clearly that development is all in the genes. Mr. Mendel proved it with peas." He tears a piece of paper from his pad. "Here are the other things you should watch for."

. . .

And they had watched. Lena's feet grew longer and the soles softer. Her hands spidered out like daddy longlegs. Her grandmother monitored her for wild thoughts, a keen interest in money, and for a temper she did her best to hide. And Lena had watched herself.

Lying in her bed at night, her heart pounding, she wondered if her thoughts were too wild, if goblin genes would overtake her while she slept. She imagined running away on a belching steam train or fording streams on the back of a fat elephant while its leathery trunk swung like a pendulum. In her dreams, Lena rose and fell with the swell of waves, captaining a ship, sea spray salting her hair. When she had these dreams, she knew that goblinishness was taking hold, growing from a seed buried deep inside her. No other girl could have such wild imaginings and, try as she might, she couldn't tame them. And the truth was she didn't try very hard.

Every morning she checked the mirror with dread, expecting a face she didn't know. She wanted to be anybody other than her father's child.

A SHORT AND UNSATISFACTORY LETTER FROM HER FATHER DELIVERED BY HER MOTHER ON THE OCCASION OF HER EIGHTEENTH BIRTHDAY

"Sit down, Lena. I have one last gift for you."

Puzzled, I look at my mother. She had already given me the new Wilkie Collins novel I'd been wanting and a short green velvet jacket. Now I notice her hands trembling, and the telltale flush of her face.

"Best get it over with, Rose," Nana Crane urges from her chair by the fire. "It's past my bedtime, and I want to see what the fool had up his sleeve this time."

"Your father left you a small inheritance and an envelope to be opened on your eighteenth birthday." My mother places two envelopes side by side on the tea table next to the bone-handled letter opener. Poppa's script, sharp and vertical, runs across the front of both envelopes. With my own hands trembling I slit open the larger of the two envelopes.

Inside, there is a paper wrapped around a slim stack of crisp, new bills. Not a fortune, but enough. Enough to finance my plans.

"Well, what will you do with it?" Nana Crane's eyes glitter like a bird's.

5

"Go to Scree." When I finally say the words aloud, I realize I have opened a box that cannot be closed again. I think of Pandora.

"Oh, my dear!" Mother wails.

And then louder and sharper, Nana Crane's voice: "Of all the foolish nonsense! You will not set foot in that wild place."

"I've been thinking about it for a long time. I have to go." I'm watching Mother's face, knowing my words will hurt and hating myself for them.

"Just like her father. It's her goblin blood calling her home." Nana Crane barks a dry laugh. "What's in the other envelope?"

"I'm not going to open it yet." The envelope is clenched in my hand. "I expect it's a letter." Better to read it in private, without

Nana Crane's eyes on me, without Mother's tears. I rewrap the bills in their paper and slip them back into the envelope.

"No good will come of this." And leaning on her cane, Nana Crane makes her way to bed.

A log pops in the fire. I stay seated in the dim parlor with Mother, both envelopes buried now in the pocket of my skirt.

"Scree's the place where they send criminals. They say the forests are filled with hideous things. Why would you want to go to such an uncivilized place?" Her voice quavers.

I count the furrows on her forehead. It's the first time I've disobeyed her openly.

"Because I have to know if Nana Crane is right, if I am part goblin. If there really are such things as Peculiars." Now it's my voice that stumbles. "I can't keep living this way, wondering what I am, what I'll become. Besides, it's the kind of place Poppa might have gone. Maybe I'll find him there."

"I've reassured you over and over again: You're a perfectly normal girl, despite your poor hands and feet." She puts her arms around me to offer comfort the way she did when I was little. For a minute I lean into her warmth. Her voice drops to a whisper. "No matter what Nana Crane says, your father is not a Peculiar. He's from the East, which explains some of his unusual ways . . . although it doesn't excuse abandonment."

For the first time I hear the strain of bitterness in my mother's voice, the words stretched tight as a wire. "Don't look for him, Lena. He's not worth the risk."

It's almost dawn before I'm alone in my room. I rip open the envelope.

Lena,

It appears that I have no talent for ordinary life. I'm hoping you do and that you take after your mother. Things will go easier with you. There are many rumors you will hear told of me. Some of them may be true. I've left you something to help you get by. You'll know what to do with it. Don't let anyone tell you different.

Your father,

Saul Mattacascar

I can't help but notice that he had signed his full name, as if writing to a stranger.

I tuck the envelope of money under my chemise in my dresser. Then I read the short letter once more, trying to decipher a hidden meaning. What was he? Did he know I'd break my mother's heart? Each carefully formed letter was as sharp as the quills of a porcupine, bristling across the page. If I touched them, they would prick, draw blood.

PASSENGER TRAIN FROM THE CITY TO KNOB KNOSTER

She was more than the sum of the crimes of her father. Or so Lena had told herself every time Nana Crane got that gleam in her eye, rattled her knitting needles, and reminded her of Father's indiscretions, of which there seemed to be no end. She was still telling it to herself now, at eighteen, in the Pullman car of a passenger train where, beyond the blue brocade curtains, the arms of trees waved her on through billows of steam. A pot of tea steeped on the table, a familiar comfort for an unfamiliar journey.

Lena was the last passenger in her car. The rest—mostly businessmen in their starched collars and bowler hats, and harried parents taking sticky-faced children to autumn festivals in the country—had disembarked at the various small towns strung along the rail line. She recited their names: Middleborough, Tropolis, Banbury Station. Only three stops left before the end of the line, three stops that would take several hours. Finally, Lena could stretch out her legs, which she had kept tucked under the seat until the last passenger left, and loosen the laces of her handmade boots. How she hated them! Good alligator hide, the cobbler had assured her, never wore out.

The scenery had become progressively wilder as the train made its way north from one town to the next. Each pair of towns had been farther apart than the last two, with small forests and hummocky fields in between. For the first hour she had stared out the window, never turning to the novel on her lap. She had always lived in the City. Open fields and forests were as foreign as brocade curtains and the cut crystal lamp swaying above her head. She pulled off her gloves and flexed her fingers. When she was younger, her mother had cut the fingertips from regular gloves so that they would fit her hands.

As the train slowed, the walnut-paneled door slid open and the conductor strolled in. "Approaching Northerdam, miss," he said around the ends of his blond waxed mustache. "And I've brought some biscuits for your tea."

He shot a second glance at her gloveless hands. Almost everyone did. But to his credit, he made no comment, merely nodded and passed on to the next car.

CHAPTER 2

LENA MEETS A MAN OF SCIENCE

LENA REMOVED A MAP FROM THE LINING OF HER DRAWSTRING purse and smoothed it across the marble-topped table. She had traced her route with a thick black pen months earlier. Three more towns to the borders of Scree, where the train line ended—and most roads did too. Knob Knoster, the first stop on her own journey, was the last town, a mere outpost that jutted into the sea on a knob-shaped projection of land. She had circled the name and then drew a line north. Not thirty miles beyond the town was the border of Scree behind its hedge of forest and shale. No one knew much about what went on beyond the borderland, other than the government's official statements: an undeveloped land, rich in natural resources, home to small numbers of indigenous Peculiar people. Lena had read every report she could find in the library.

"Scree's been declared *terra nullius*."

Lena jumped. She had been so absorbed in her map that she hadn't heard the conductor enter the car again.

"A 'land belonging to no one.' Just got it over the telegraph last night."

He paused to look over her shoulder at the map.

"Excuse me if I'm interfering." His mustache twitched. "But the government has sent in the military to colonize the land and keep order. Most of it is now officially a penal colony. No one's there but misfits, political enemies, and aliens." He considered a minute. "And a few profiteers. Of course, there's the indigenous folks, but I don't know what they're considered. Superstitious people say Peculiars live there."

Lena worked hard to keep her face blank at the mention of Peculiars.

"There are not even any reliable roads. Can't see why a young woman would be interested in a place like that." He refilled the water in her teapot.

Lena quickly refolded the map. Her hands were trembling. "I am traveling to Knob Knoster to see my mother's cousin."

The conductor wiped the spout of the silver serving pot with a white towel. "Beg pardon, miss. It's just that your map shows Scree and—"

"And I am a student of geography. The land interests me." Lena turned her face to the window.

"Yes, miss. Let me know if you need anything else, miss."

Lena heard him leave, but she did not turn her head. A lone woman traveling to Scree for any purpose was sure to draw attention and arouse suspicion. No woman in her right mind would consider such a notion. Nana Crane had made sure Lena understood that. Tales of murders and enchantments, unrest and unsavory politics filtered their way beyond the borders and into the City. Everyone knew someone who knew someone who had heard a story about Scree and its inhabitants. And Lena, thanks to her grandmother, had heard them all.

The train slowed to rest in a valley after lumbering up Jackson Grade and then racing down to Northerdam. It belched great sighs of steam in satisfaction. Lena drained the last of the tea from her cup. Nana Crane would have insisted on reading the leaves, and Lena purposefully gave them a poke with an index finger to rearrange her fate. She flexed her fingers; they were sore. They often were. The doctor had said it was the extra knuckle. The walnut door slid open again, and, without looking up, Lena sighed, then politely asked for more biscuits.

"I'm afraid I haven't brought any with me." It was not the voice of the blond conductor. It was a younger voice, but a man's voice all the same. She looked up slowly as she slipped her hands into the folds of her skirt.

"Jimson Quiggley, without any biscuits." He removed his hat. His curly black hair immediately sprang out, glad to escape the confines of such a hat. "May I—that is, unless you don't want company?"

She didn't want company. She had been relieved when everyone left. Why was this man—well, he was really not much older than she was—getting on the train so near the end of the line? She could hardly ask him. She smiled thinly.

"Of course. Lena Mattacascar." She nodded. She was not about to offer her hand to this stranger in a cheap suit. Despite being strictly middle class, Lena's mother and Nana Crane had been very particular about the cut and quality of cloth in Lena's few traveling garments.

"That's good. I walked through the cars until I found someone to sit with. It's better than traveling alone. Did you know there are only a few stodgy sorts left in the front?" He spoke quickly, all in one breath. Lena found it annoying.

"Not many people travel this far north." She wanted to put her map back in her purse, but to do that she would have to remove her ungloved hands from the fabric of her skirt.

He plopped down in the seat across from her; stretched his long legs, and carefully placed his dreadful little hat on the seat beside him. It was amazing how much a hat could tell you about someone, Lena thought. Either his taste was bad or it was the best he could afford.

The train lurched to wakefulness, shuddered once, and let out a loud snort before resuming its lumbering gate.

"We're headed out to the coast now." Jimson had his nose pressed to the window. "That's my sister Polly. She rode with me to the station." A pretty black-haired girl with a toddler at her side waved a handkerchief at the train. "And my nephew, Gelft." With two fingers he stretched his mouth wide and waggled his tongue back and forth at the little boy on the platform. "He couldn't wait to see the train. We took one of those new steam wagons to the station! Holds eight people and doesn't need a horse at all because it has a sixteen-horsepower, two-cylinder motor. All run by steam!"

Lena tried not to laugh. It seemed Jimson was as excited as Gelft. "I've never been in one," she said. "But I've heard they're very noisy."

"Noisy? That's the sound of progress!" Jimson kept his face pressed to the window as he waved to his nephew.

While Jimson was distracted, Lena quickly stuffed the map back in her purse and pulled on the constricting black gloves. "You should always wear black, dear. They will make your hands look so much smaller," the glover had said when Lena had eyed a lavender pair with beading. She drew her feet back under the seat, making sure the hem of her skirt shielded them from view. Jimson, she noted, was traveling with a book, Mr. Darwin's latest.

"Where are you going?" Jimson removed an orange from his bag and began to peel it with a pocketknife. Peels fell in curls on the table, and the smell of orange filled the car. Lena's mouth watered.

"North."

"Well, of course you're going north. That's the only direction this train is headed, isn't it? Let me guess, then. Cloister." It was the next stop en route. "You've got a sister who is a nun and you're going to visit her. Unless you're planning to become a nun yourself?"

Lena colored. It was not polite to talk about religion. "No, I—"

"Good thing, because you would have to cut off all that hair. How long is it anyway?" He gazed admiringly at her thick black braid that disappeared behind one shoulder. Unbound, it came to her waist and in some way made up for her miserable hands and feet, but she wasn't about to tell him that.

"I'm traveling to Knob Knoster."

"What—Knoster? On the borderlands? Me too." When he smiled, it was with his whole face, not just his mouth.

Lena couldn't help herself; she could feel a real smile stretching around her faux one. He paused with a slice of orange suspended midway to his mouth. What if he offered it to her? She'd have to reveal her hands. Lena swallowed and clenched her right hand into a fist.

"What are you going to do in Knoster?"

Lena had rehearsed an answer to this question; it was to be expected. Still, she wound one ankle tightly around the other in the shadows under her seat where no one else could see. "My mother's cousin lives there."

It just happened that her mother really did have a cousin living in the closest town to the borders of Scree. But Lena had no intention of visiting her. She had the cousin's address written on a scrap of paper buried deep in her drawstring bag, along with the address of her real destination, a boardinghouse— Miss Brett's. It would be temporary lodging while she made her plans and gathered supplies. The fewer people who knew about her intentions of traveling into Scree, the better. So she had never bothered to contact Miss Amelia Crane to let her know she was coming. But she kept the address just in case her plans didn't work out.

Jimson wasn't really interested in her answer anyway, Lena decided. He just wanted to tell her about why he was traveling to Knoster, and she was happy to let him talk.

"I'm going for a job. I'm going to be a librarian."

Lena looked up, past his lively blue eyes and dark brows to the top of his curly black hair. Then she looked down over the shiny knees of his gray suit to his gleaming black shoes. His feet, she noted, were much smaller than her own. Nothing in what she observed made her think of the word "librarian." Everything about him was too wild—as if his body could barely contain all the life in it. "My mother is a librarian" was all she could think to say. "A children's librarian." She slipped her hands under her thighs and nodded for emphasis.

"Is she?" Jimson was leaning forward in his seat, his elbows resting on the shiny knees of his suit. His long face was earnest and close enough that Lena noticed a faint dappling of freckles across his nose and cheeks. "What exactly does she do?"

"Excuse me?" It was a very peculiar question, coming from this non-librarian-looking librarian.

"As a children's librarian, I mean. I know she must catalogue books and research things for people with questions and check out books—" Here his voice faltered. "I'm kind of new at this, see. I've never really been a librarian before. I've been working in my father's store selling farm implements and hating it."

Lena tried to cover her surprise. Most librarians had training. Just two years prior, the first library school had opened in the City. "Well, she does check out books and research things, but she does much more than that. She recommends books, she orders books, and every Saturday afternoon she holds a story time for children." Lena found that it was difficult to keep her hands still as she talked. She could feel them fluttering under her thighs as if they had a life of their own. "Didn't you get your librarianship degree?" Her mother was always scornful of librarians who worked without a degree.

"No, I . . . er . . . I took some classes for librarians, though." She noticed a flush of red spreading up his neck, fanning out across his cheeks. "I'd just started taking classes and saw the advertisement. I never thought I'd get the job. But I've always loved books, and every summer I've worked in the local bookstore for a few weeks."

That's pathetic, Lena thought. He has no real experience at all. She rearranged her feet under the seat and tried not to think about stretching out her legs.

"I'm to be head librarian for the Beasley Collection." He sat up straighter. "I was as surprised as anybody when I got the job." The orange was mostly gone now, but Jimson held out the last two sections to her. "Please, have one."

The smell was wonderful. She'd have to take her gloves off to eat; no one with any manners ate an orange with gloves on. "No, no thank you. That's wonderful that you got the job. What's the Beasley Collection?"

"Never heard of Mr. Beasley's library?" Jimson popped the last two sections of the orange in his mouth at once. "It's huge. I've never seen it, of course, but I've heard about it. He's a collector of rare books and artifacts."

Why would Jimson, who seemed to know very little about being a librarian, be put in charge of a collection of rare books? Lena wrinkled her brow. "Do you know anything about book conservation?"

Jimson rubbed a hand across his face. "Well, I, er—"

Before he could say more, the conductor stepped into their car. "Dinner will be served in the dining car in twenty minutes."

Outside, the October sun dipped below the Coast Range. The conductor lit the gas wall sconces before shuffling on.

"Are you going to dinner?" she asked to cover Jimson's embarrassment. She was right. He obviously knew nothing about book conservation either.

"No, I'm saving my funds until my first paycheck. My sister made me sandwiches." He gestured to the small satchel he had set on the seat beside him.

Lena had planned on the dining car. She had never had dinner on a train before, and now that she was spending the little inheritance left to her by her father, she felt that she wanted to have the full experience of eating on a train. But she didn't want to appear rude, either. She needn't have worried, because Jimson was already asking his next question.

"Story time . . . I don't suppose I'll be doing anything like that, since this is a private library rather than a public one. What's it like?"

"You've never been to story time?" Lena's hands were beginning to itch in her black gloves. She rubbed them across the nap of the seat. "I used to go all the time when I was little. My mother would turn down the gaslights until the room was shadowy. We would scrunch in close on the floor." Lena closed her eyes. "I used to close my eyes and listen to all the breathing around me while we waited. No one talked. She always cleared her throat as if she was about to say something very important, and then she opened the book." Lena opened her eyes and looked up. For a few moments, she had been there again—a small girl in the middle of the crowd, trying to hide her long feet and hands under the puddle of her skirt.

"It sounds like it was grand. Too bad I won't have the chance." He reached into his satchel and pulled out some squashed bread.

If she was going to make it to the dining car in time for the early serving, it was time to take her leave. But how to get up gracefully without questions about her hands and feet? When she was younger, she had joked that she was still growing into them, but now, at eighteen, she wasn't growing anymore. Besides, all the old jokes had long since worn thin. She would just brazen it out.

She stood and smoothed her gray traveling skirt, cut extra long to cover more of her feet, and gave a tug to her tailored green jacket. "I'm going to dinner now." She threw her shoulders back and lifted her chin.

"Well, enjoy it, and I'll see you after."

Lena couldn't tell if his response was a statement or question. She didn't look at his eyes. Sometimes it was better not to know where people were looking. Her first step caught the hem of her dress. She stumbled, throwing out a hand to steady herself. The china teacup shot across the table and thumped on the carpeted floor. Her hand was splayed in plain view on top of the table.

Jimson leapt to his feet to retrieve the cup. "It isn't broken, not even cracked," he declared.

Lena snatched her hand back to her side. Perhaps he hadn't noticed. "It was so clumsy of me."

"Could've happened to anyone." But he didn't meet her eyes. Instead, he was staring at her black-gloved hands, which hung like two giant spiders by her sides.

CHAPTER 3

AN ENCOUNTER WITH
A CRIMINAL AND A GUN

BOWLS OF ROSES WERE SET IN THE MIDDLE OF EACH TABLE. Cut crystal glasses winked in the candlelight. Only six other passengers were enjoying the dining car. Lena, still trembling, chose a small empty table and sat with her back to the door. This way she could watch everyone else. Secretly she liked to imagine other people's lives. The elderly couple was Jack Sprat and his wife. The words of the old nursery rhyme rang in her ears: *Jack Sprat could eat no fat; his wife could eat no lean; and so betwixt the two of them they licked their platters clean.* The two businessmen were bankers or financial types who took fishing holidays and long lunches. A missionary sent to convert the heathens of Scree, Lena thought, as she glanced at a thickset woman with a stern jaw and two red poppies on her hat. Then there was the reedy man with the newspaper. Now, he was interesting. Perhaps a detective watching the men in business suits from behind the raised page.

She picked up the menu and gazed at the two choices of entrée: roast beef or lamb in a sauce she had never heard of. She sat up straighter. It was elegant, eating in a dining car with silver and crystal glasses as the day dimmed. A white-coated waiter poured water in her glass just as the train slowed, a great belch of steam fogging the window. It must be Cloister. Lena decided on lamb, closed the embossed menu, and looked out over the platform. A tall nun and her companion—a bandy-legged little man—were the only ones boarding in the early dusk. The nun was broad-shouldered and a full head taller than the young man at her side. Perhaps it was her brother collecting her for a visit home. Did nuns get visits home? Lena's knowledge of nuns was slight. The nice thing was that they were hidden away from the world. Her own family was Episcopalian. Lena had briefly considered converting and joining a convent just to escape the curious remarks about her hands and feet. But a friend once told her that underneath their habits, nuns were entirely bald, and Lena had put the idea aside.

She peeled off her gloves and laid them beside her on the tufted seat. Then she buttered and bit into a flaky white roll. The nun and the wiry, red-haired man came through a door that opened straight into the dining car. Trying not to stare, Lena watched them from the corner of her eye. Nuns must get tired of people staring at them in their long black habits. She knew exactly how they felt. The red-haired man talked animatedly to the conductor while the nun stood silently holding her valise. The nun's head was bent, her face obscured by the shadow of her wimple. What would it be like to believe in something so strongly that you gave your life to it? That was something Lena couldn't imagine. Her eyes lingered on the nun. Something was wrong. The nun stood as if she was tense enough to spring. Her empty hand at her side was balled into a fist. Lena's own shoulders tensed. The back of the nun's hand was covered with thick dark hair. The nun was a man—she was sure of it.

As if her thought had been spoken out loud, the nun suddenly dropped the valise. From the depths of her habit, the nun drew out something that gleamed in the gaslight. A gun! Lena had only seen pictures of them in books. Her hands grew moist. The gun was pointed straight at the conductor.

The red-haired man spoke. "Give us the prisoner, or we shoot the passengers." His voice was high and reedy as he drew out his own revolver with one hand. With the other, he jerked the emergency brake, preventing the train from leaving the station. The two businessmen gawked with their cheeks bulging. The lone man dropped his newspaper, pages drifting to the floor, while a low moan escaped from the lady with her husband. Only the woman with poppies on her hat looked unperturbed and raised a curious eyebrow.

"Now. And I mean it. One of 'em will go first." He swung the revolver in the direction of the low moan, pointing it at the elderly couple.

Meanwhile, the nun kept a gun pointed at the conductor,

whose mouth opened and closed like that of a fish. Lena could see a film of sweat shining on the conductor's brow. He inched slowly toward the door to the next car, with the nun following, gun cocked.

"That's right. Lead the way, old man."

"Now, see here—" But before the conductor could complete his sentence, the red-haired man lunged toward the elderly couple.

Lena braced for a shot. Instead, the man slammed the butt of the revolver against the elderly man's head. A sharp crack of metal against flesh and bone.

His wife screamed.

At that precise moment, the engineer swung through the door. "Who stopped this train?" Bellowing, he crashed straight into the conductor and the nun. They staggered. The gun went off. The wild shot sent a bullet through the paneled wall, leaving a hole to the outdoors. People shouted and the woman continued to scream.

Lena found herself under the table, peeking out from beneath the hem of the white tablecloth. She could see the black edge of the nun's habit just a few feet away. If she could grab an ankle, she might tip the man off balance. Creeping forward as far as she dared, Lena grabbed for the black-socked ankle just below the hem of the habit. From another car Lena heard a second shot. And then everything was chaos. Her fingers closed on empty air. She could hear feet running, muffled cries, and someone quite nearby swearing a steady stream. The black edge of the habit was gone. Then all was quiet.

Lena inched forward on her knees. The gray fabric of her skirt balled up and caught underneath her. She tugged it free. Her armpits felt damp, and a trickle of sweat ran between her shoulder blades. Moving the tablecloth just a fraction of an inch, she peered out. The car looked deserted except for the woman stroking her husband's head. A trickle of blood ran from his ear. Were the other passengers hiding under tables the way she was?

The door swung open. Drawing back, Lena smacked her head on the edge of the table. Pain flared.

"The criminals have left the train." In his blue uniform with polished brass buttons, the conductor stood wide-legged in the middle of the aisle. "A doctor is coming to examine your husband, madam."

Amid rustles and grunts, diners appeared from under tables.

"I am sorry to report that the pretenders have escaped with a prisoner we were transporting to Scree. There will be a short delay, and then we will be able to resume our journey. I am most terribly sorry for the inconvenience." But his last words were lost in a jumble of voices and the arrival of a short, stout man with a medical bag.

"What prisoner? Why didn't we know a prisoner was on board?" A voice rang out above the others. It belonged to the lady with the flowered hat.

The conductor turned. "Trains to Knob Knoster sometimes carry prisoners bound for Scree. A federal marshal and deputies are on these trains."

"Obviously incompetent. You'll be hearing from my lawyer." One of the businessmen was brushing himself off. His face was a pasty gray, his breathing ragged.

"It's the first time a prisoner"—losing his composure, the conductor floundered for words—"has been . . . abducted."

"What was his crime?" the woman persisted.

"Madam, this one was a bad sort: forgery, stolen goods, a web of crime. A real goblin, he is."

CHAPTER 4

A LAWMAN'S QUESTIONS

JIMSON SNORTED. "MY FRIENDS AT HOME WILL NEVER BELIEVE
this. A prisoner escaping! Gunshots! And I missed it all. I
heard something, but it just sounded like a series of pops.
Wish I'd been in the dining car!"

Lena had just finished describing the ordeal, and she was
still shaking. For the first time she was grateful for Jimson's
company. Now that all the excitement was over, she found it
rather thrilling herself. Her appetite had disappeared along
with the prisoner. She'd made her way back to her car as
soon as they were allowed to move about. Every square inch
had been thoroughly searched. Deputies with their guns
prominently displayed swaggered up and down the length of
each car, reassuring the few passengers who hadn't been in the
dining car. Jimson had been briefly questioned. He seemed to
find that terribly exciting, Lena noted.

"And 'goblin.' It's just an expression for anyone who's up

to no good. You don't think there are real goblins, do you?" Jimson's blue eyes were glinting. "You can't believe those old superstitions."

"Well, the conductor called him 'a real goblin.' He said he was involved in a web of crime."

"Have you ever seen a goblin?" Jimson persisted. "Outside of a book, I mean?"

Lena shook her head. She wished he would drop the subject of goblins. It made her stomach feel sick. And it reminded her of her hands. Jimson had been staring at them when she left, so why hadn't he mentioned them? She was prepared for the usual questions, the usual jokes. Perhaps he'd forgotten all about them in the excitement.

"Exactly my point. Science will overcome all this superstitious nonsense once and for all. Then only uneducated people will believe clap like that. You do know about the scientific method, don't you?"

When she didn't say anything, he continued. "It's an empirical method of inquiry. There would have to be observable evidence of goblins. It's all in Pierce."

"Of course I've heard of the scientific method, but I'm not sure it works for everything." Lena bent to loosen the laces on her boots so he couldn't read her face. She found his supercilious tone grating. "Besides, how would you know if you'd seen a goblin?"

"Well, he'd look different—small and kind of craggy would be my guess. But it doesn't matter, because there are no such things. Goblins are supposed to be Peculiars, right? Only superstitious, unenlightened people still believe in them or in any Peculiars. They're old wives' tales—like fairies. A successful, practical man needs solid, practical scientific knowledge. And I intend to be a successful, practical man."

"Some educated people think Scree has Peculiars as well as convicts." Lena deliberately folded her hands in her lap.

Jimson leaned forward but kept his eyes averted from her hands. Lena noticed for the first time that his nose was slightly lopsided, giving him a roguish air. "People—even some educated people—are afraid of what they don't know. That's why fairy tales fill the forests with all kinds of monsters. I've been hearing the rumors of Peculiars my whole life. There's no such thing; evolution wouldn't allow for it. Rumors of Peculiars are an excuse the government uses to control people. Just like sending convicts to Scree. It's not as much about getting them out of our country as it is about getting cheap labor to colonize new territory and exploit the natural resources there. We want Scree's coal."

The train suddenly shuddered to life. Darkness had crept in slowly while they had waited. Now the gas lamps bathed the car in warm gold. Lena knew that most educated people were like Jimson. They believed that "goblin" was just a way of labeling undesirables, that real goblins no longer existed, if they ever had. Goblins and other Peculiars were inventions of fairy stories to keep children behaving themselves. Maybe they were right. Maybe there were no Peculiars. Maybe her hands and feet were merely an accident of birth and nothing more. Her grandmother and the doctor didn't think so, but they were old and superstitious.

The rush of adrenaline was gone, and she regretted that she'd walked away from her dinner. It might be too late to find food when they reached Knob Knoster. Lena reached for the novel she had left on her seat when she went to the dining car, but the tufted red bench was empty. Then a dreadful realization hit. Her drawstring purse was gone as well.

She groped on the shadowy floor beneath her seat. Her fingers found the spine of her book. She drew it out and set it on the seat beside her, her heart hammering in her chest, and bent again to search the floor. Most likely, the bag had slid from the seat along with her book. Had she remembered to take it with her to the dining car? She couldn't recall. She'd left in a hurry, worried about her hands. On her hands and knees now, she crawled under the table.

"What are you looking for?" Jimson's face appeared next to hers in the shadows.

"My bag. It must have slid off the seat." Her words were coming out in funny little gasps. Most of her money was in the bag. The rest she wore against her ribs—pinned into the lining of her chemise. Her carefully planned map, the address of the boardinghouse where she planned to stay that evening, everything—gone!

There was very little room for two bodies to maneuver in the cramped space under the table and between the seats. They bumped heads twice and one of Jimson's sharp elbows jabbed her in her ribs. When she had covered every inch of floor, Lena crawled out and back to her seat. Her braid had come partially undone, and wisps of hair tickled like spiderwebs against her face.

"Is there anywhere else it could be?" Jimson's face was pinched with concern. "Maybe you left it in the dining car?"

"I'll go and look." She smoothed her hair, forgetting momentarily about her hands. This time she noticed Jimson staring openly. She dropped them quickly to her sides and asked, "Has anyone been in this car besides you?"

He shrugged his shoulders. "Just the conductor and deputy while I was here, but I left for a few minutes to refresh myself. Anyone could have come then." He continued staring at her hands. "Are you a pianist?"

There was no point in asking why. Lena just nodded, and for the second time that evening, stood abruptly and made her way to the dining car.

The next passenger car was identical to hers. The curtains had been drawn against the night and only three people sat in the entire car: the silent man who had been reading the newspaper at dinner and the Jack Sprat couple. It was a domestic scene. The man was wearing a bandage on his head and his wife was pouring him a cup of tea. Glad to see that he had recovered, Lena hurried past. There were no passengers in the dining car. Fresh silver gleamed on tables. There was no sign of the previous disorder. Lena hesitated only a moment, and then hurried toward the table where she had been sitting. Nothing.

"I'm sorry. The dining room is closed for the evening, miss." A waiter spoke to her from a corner table, where he was engaged in conversation with one of the deputies.

"I was just looking for my purse. I thought maybe I'd left it here."

A bear of a man with a handlebar mustache and sandy hair rose from his seat. A badge gleamed on his chest. "And did you find it?"

Lena shook her head, afraid to speak in case her voice quavered.

"I'm sorry to hear that. I'm Marshal Saltre. Were you in

here when the, eh, incident occurred?"

Lena nodded, wishing he would let her escape before she began to cry.

"I wonder if you wouldn't mind my asking you a few questions, and perhaps you could describe your purse for me as well."

What choice did she really have? Lena sat down in the chair he pulled out for her. He smelled of something spicy— cologne, perhaps. From his pocket he pulled out a small notebook and flipped through the pages. Up close, Lena realized that he wasn't as old as his commanding presence made him appear.

"Let's start with your name, then." He looked at her expectantly from under shaggy brows. His eyes, Lena noticed, were pale and intense, as if a fire quickened behind them.

"Lena Mattacascar."

"Well, now, that's something." He frowned, looked up, and then looked back at his notebook. He fired the next questions, one after another. Routine questions about what she had seen and what she had done. Lena found that she could answer them clearly and concisely. Even from under the dining table, she had been observant. A few times, he grunted in response. That was all.

Then he asked for details about her missing purse. He didn't look up again until she had finished her entire account.

"And did you notice anything at all when the nun first came into the car?"

"I knew something wasn't right. And then I saw the nun's hands. They were a man's hands."

His eyes, pale blue under the bushy sandy brows, sought her own. "Ah, very observant. And something you would be particularly aware of, no doubt." He looked pointedly at her gloved hands. Lena balled them into fists. "Mattacascar is an unusual name. I knew of a man once named Saul Mattacascar. My father tracked him for years." The marshal's voice was mild. "Could it be that you're related to him?"

Lena's heart was hammering so hard that she was sure the marshal would hear it. "My father's name is Saul."

"Is that so?" Fire danced in his eyes now. "Would you know where I could reach him?"

"I—no—I mean . . . I haven't seen him in a while."

The marshal nodded his head as if satisfied. "Just how long a while would that be?"

"He left home when I was five."

"So, the stories were true. Old Saul vanished. And he had a daughter." He exhaled noisily. "Have you heard from him recently?"

"No." Her voice was low now and she was thinking furiously. "How do you know of him?"

"Everybody in my line of work knows Saul. I grew up on stories about Saul. My own father died when I was twelve. Let's say there's some unfinished business between my father and your father. But I find it hard to believe even a man like Saul wouldn't be in touch with his own daughter." As he fastened her with his eyes, his mouth quirked into a smile. A dimple flashed. His voice softened. "Come now, tell me the truth."

Lena could smell coffee on his breath as he leaned forward. She curled her fingers. "It's true. I haven't heard from him."

"Your mother, then—has she heard from him?"

"No." His eagerness unnerved her.

He closed the notebook with a snap and put it away. "And you're traveling to Knob Knoster on the borderlands. That's not where most attractive, respectable young ladies want to go." The marshal's inquisitive eyes traveled slowly down from the crown of her head to her waist.

As if her legs had turned to water, Lena rose shakily. "I have a cousin there." She tried to sound like it was a family trip and nothing more. What unfinished business did this man have with her father?

The marshal ran his index finger across his wide mustache. "And her name is?"

"Amelia Crane. She's my mother's cousin." Would he try to find her there?

"That's all for now, Miss Lena Mattacascar. Let's hope you take after your mother."

CHAPTER 5

REVELATIONS

JIMSON WAS DOZING WHEN SHE RETURNED AT LAST, STILL SHAKING, to their passenger car. Not only was her purse missing, but now the loss was compounded by her unsettling conversation with the marshal. She looked at Jimson. His lips were parted, and his head slumped against the curtained window. Was he handsome? She couldn't decide. What would Emily, her one friend from school, say? She would say that his nose was lopsided and that his chin was too sharp. But she'd like his eyes, as thickly lashed as a girl's.

Lena buried her face in her hands. There was almost no chance the marshal would retrieve her purse; she was sure of it. What had her father done to be known by the man, to make his eyes burn with such intensity? When she looked up, her eyes sloppy with unshed tears, Jimson was sitting upright watching her.

"You didn't find it." It was a statement rather than a question.

"No."

"Have you talked to the conductor?"

"I talked to a marshal. He questioned me about the shooting in the dining car."

Jimson quirked an eyebrow. "And?"

"And nothing. He doesn't have any idea where it is. He says that the train was in so much chaos that anyone might have taken it."

"Can you do without it? I mean, do you have enough to get by until it's found?"

Lena bit her lip to keep from crying. "For a few days, maybe, but there were other things—addresses, and a map, some private papers . . ." Her voice trailed off, and she stared at the brocade curtains.

"I'm sure Mr. Beasley would be willing to—I could help you out if you need anything."

"Thank you, but I'll be fine." Her voice was cold. She couldn't risk becoming dependent in Knob Knoster. It was only a launch point for her quest. But now she would be seriously hampered by her lack of funds. How would she afford to purchase the things she needed for the journey into Scree?

Jimson was looking at her with perplexity, and Lena realized that he had asked her a question.

"I'm sorry. I didn't hear you."

"I asked you about your hands. Were they burned?"

"Burned?" The question caught her by surprise. "Why would you think they were burned?"

"Because you keep them covered all the time. But perhaps it's just to protect them. You said you are a pianist."

Not many people asked about her hands or feet directly. They stared. They whispered. They made sideways remarks: "You must be quite artistic." Or they asked jokingly if she planned to grow into her feet the same way a puppy grew into oversized paws. Not many had the gumption to ask her a real question. It was always easier to joke than to be sincere. She admired Jimson's directness.

"No, they're just rather . . . long." Her face flamed.

"But that's good for a pianist, isn't it?" He looked genuinely puzzled.

"I didn't grow them this way to make me more accomplished at the piano."

Soft light flickered in the car. The brocade curtains had been drawn against the dark. They were entering a deeper dark now, the first of three tunnels blasted through rock.

"Each finger has an extra knuckle. I was born that way. That's the only reason I'm a pianist. I thought I'd better put them to use." She feigned a laugh as if it didn't matter and splayed both hands on the table, exposing their full mannerist length.

Jimson didn't laugh or make a smart comment; he seemed genuinely curious. "You were born that way?"

She nodded. "A disorder, an accident of birth."

"They're so thin. Do they hurt?"

"Sometimes, but not much."

The chandelier overhead cast shadows across her gloved hands. When Jimson looked up, his blue eyes were also shadowed.

"May I see them? Without the gloves?"

Again, Lena was surprised by his directness. Coming from anyone else she would consider it rude, abrupt. What did it really matter here in this car, hurtling through the dark? The worst that could happen, the very worst, was that she would see the revulsion in his face. She'd seen it in people's eyes many times before, but it was never something she grew used to. This time she felt reckless. What he thought wouldn't matter. In another hour, she would never see him again.

"All right." She didn't meet his eyes as she deliberately rolled the black fabric of the glove down the length of her left arm. In the gaslight, her skin was moon-pale and smooth. The gloves had protected her hands not only from prying eyes but from the scorch of sun as well. Hesitating at the wrist, and then with determination, she peeled the fabric from her palm and down the length of her fingers until the pale pink skin of her hand lay bare. Only then did she look up to read his expression.

Jimson's eyes rested on her hand. His lips were slightly parted, as they had been in sleep. His gaze was so intense, she curled her fingers.

"They all bend? Each joint, I mean." His voice had a breathless sound.

"Of course they bend," she snapped. "They work like normal hands."

"It's just that I've never seen anything like it. They're amazing, so long and delicate."

Lena checked to see if he was mocking her. But his face was serious, reverential almost.

"They're ugly. 'Goblin phalanges,' my nana calls them." Why did she say that? An almost imperceptible sob escaped her lips. She had come to terms with her differences long ago. She tugged the covering back over her fingertips.

"No, they're not. Ugly, I mean. And you don't have to do that. It must be annoying to have to wear gloves all the time." He leaned back against the seat and looked her full in the face.

"It is. They itch and they're hot in the summer. But I don't like having to explain my hands to everyone. I don't like people staring."

He nodded as if he understood. "I won't mention your hands again, unless you do. Take both your gloves off. I won't even look." He closed his eyes.

"We'll be to Knoster soon, and then I'll just have to put them on again." But the offer was tempting, and Lena peeled the gloves from her right hand as well as her left. She flexed her fingers, then leaned her head back against the seat. But she kept her feet hidden in the shadows.

When the train stopped an hour later, Lena was startled awake. Her mouth was dry and her head felt thick. Her bare hands were curled in her lap. Across from her Jimson was brushing off his ridiculous hat. Hurriedly, she yanked on her gloves and smoothed wisps of her hair behind her ears. Then she remembered her purse. It was gone. Her head ached. There would still be enough money for a few nights' lodging, she calculated, but not enough to purchase the supplies she needed. Not enough to hire a guide. She stood and buttoned her green jacket. At least she could remember the address she needed—Miss Brett's for Women, 22 Thistlewaite. Only blocks from the train station, according to her lost map.

"I suppose your cousin is meeting you." Jimson was standing at her side, his black curls poking out from under the unfortunate hat. "Here. I wrote down Mr. Beasley's address in case you need anything. Perhaps I can see you again?"

The conductor interrupted before Lena could answer. "Good evening. I hope you enjoyed your trip." Lena nodded her thanks while trying to keep her feet from poking out too far from beneath her gray skirt.

As the train doors slid open, the smell of the sea rushed to greet them.

CHAPTER 6

KNOB KNOSTER BY THE SEA

A HANDFUL OF PEOPLE HAD COME TO MEET THE PASSENGERS AT THE station in Knob Knoster, but none had as strong a presence as the sea. As Lena took the conductor's hand and stepped from the train, she stepped into a sea-claimed world. She could smell it. The very feel of the air was different—moist and salty. She ran her tongue across her lips, tasting the air. In the distance, she was sure she could hear it calling her, a deep rumble of longing.

Knob Knoster, built on a knob of rocky coast that projected into the sea, had once been a wealthy seaport. The train station was an aging dowager, spotted and faded but still clinging to a gilded past. The building itself was flourished with cornucopias and buttresses, but blue had faded to pale gray in the sea air and the gilt trim had flaked away in patches. Three buggies, with flickering side lights, waited at attention to collect passengers. Lena noticed the two businessmen climb into one conveyance while the Jack Sprat couple were greeted by an elderly couple and whisked away. The lone businessman appeared not to be a detective after all. He was met with joyous cries by a round wife with three children at her side.

From the third carriage a wizened man stepped down. He limped his way toward Lena and Jimson.

"Where's your cousin?" Jimson turned to Lena after scanning the crowd.

"She must be late." Lena pretended to search in the distance. If only Jimson would leave now, before she made her solitary way to Miss Brett's.

"No, *we're* late." Jimson looked at the brass clock on the peak of the station house. "Very late. Perhaps she's come and gone."

Lena moved to collect her plaid bag from the pile the porter had unloaded onto the wooden platform. "I'm sure she's only delayed. Don't worry about me. I have your address."

"Mr. Jimson Quiggley? I'm Arthur, come to collect you for Mr. Beasley." White muttonchop sideburns bristled from the man's weathered cheeks.

Jimson directed the small man to his two bags. "I don't feel right going off and leaving you alone in a strange town," he said. Lena noticed how he jutted his sharp chin forward. Stubborn, she thought.

How was she going to get out of this? The platform was becoming quickly deserted. The woman with the poppy hat was embracing another woman of her same type. Two missionaries, Lena was sure, bent on saving the lost souls of Scree. Jimson showed no signs of moving on.

Toward the back of the platform, Lena spied an older woman in a knitted shawl. In a desperate move, she raised her arm and called out. The woman looked up. Lena grabbed her satchel and plunged forward in her direction. As she did, she called back over her shoulder, "Good-bye, Jimson. Good luck being a librarian!" And she marched toward the startled woman, who was still considering Lena, trying to decide if she knew her or not.

As she approached the woman, Lena realized that she must work for the station. An apron with the railroad insignia was fastened around her ample middle, and a broom and dustpan rested nearby against the side of the station house. She must be taking a break from work, Lena thought. From the top of the cupola, the gears rotated hands across the face of the great brass clock. Nine chimes rang out. Lena looked over her shoulder. Jimson was talking to the man with a limp as they walked toward the last of the carriages. The train shuddered and groaned to wakefulness.

One last passenger remained on the steps, ready to disembark. It was the marshal. His hand resting on the doorway, he scanned the dispersing passengers. Even from a distance, Lena could feel his eyes fasten on her. He stroked his mustache and then, nodding, descended the steps to the platform. Marshal and platform disappeared behind a cloud of steam as the train crept out of the station.

Lena turned away, glad to be blocked from his view. She smiled at the puzzled station worker. "I beg your pardon. I mistook you for someone else."

The woman nodded toward the station house. "I suspect your ride's waiting inside for you. If he's still here, the train being so late." She picked up her broom and returned to work.

But Lena, clutching her plaid bag, walked briskly away from the station toward the road winding up the hill. Gas lights dimly lit the deserted streets. If she could manage to follow the route to Miss Brett's as she remembered it from her map and didn't let the darkness confound her, she should be fine.

Lena recalled Jimson's face. He had looked sad and maybe a little angry at being dismissed so easily. It gave her a pang, but it couldn't be helped. She had waited too long for this journey to begin. Deep inside, a small seed of excitement was stirring, beginning to sprout.

Happy that she'd packed light, Lena trudged uphill. The grand train station was at the base of the town, near the harbor. Few of the roads in Knob Knoster were straight; most were hilly, and all led to the harbor, one winding way or another. From the look of things, it was a town that closed up early. No lights shone from the windows of shops or restaurants, but a warm glow shone in windows of the clapboard houses. They were not aligned in straight rows like the houses at home but were perched at strange angles along the street to gain the best view of the harbor. It looked to Lena as though a giant had tossed them about like random dice. Most were tall and narrow, wearing widow's walks like crowns.

The wind whistled in Lena's ears, and for once she was glad of her gloves. The small pools of light from the lamps did little to make her way easier. She reminded herself repeatedly that this was a great adventure that she was starting on. Being afraid never aided in any adventure that she had read about, and she had read all the adventures she could find in her library. It was an advantage of being a librarian's child—there was never any shortage of books.

The cobbled streets were uneven, and more than once she stumbled over a raised cobble or on the crumbling edge of the wooden walk. And all the while the sea remained her constant companion. It chortled and murmured, beckoning to her as she trudged along.

Her memory of the map led her correctly at last to Miss Brett's on Thistlewaite Street. Number 22 was a long-legged house with a small bay window facing the street, an iron gate, and a front porch large enough for one chair. A brass plaque by the door read MISS BRETT'S FOR WOMEN. Before ringing the bell, Lena reached inside her waistcoat, the green velvet one she had received for her birthday, the one that matched her topcoat, and made sure that the money she still had left was safe.

The woman who answered the bell showed no surprise to see a young girl alone on her step well after nine at night. She stood ramrod straight and had a porcelain face and a hooked nose that gave her a patrician air. Lena was a great observer of noses, and this one was worth remembering.

"I'm Lena Mattacascar, and I'd like a room, please."

The woman stepped aside so Lena could come in and closed the door behind her before speaking. She held out her hand. "Lila Brett. I've a room available for the rest of this week, but I'm full up after that. You do have money, don't you?" And without pausing for answer, she continued, "I provide breakfast every morning at seven a.m. Hot chocolate and biscuits every night. You don't have any men with you, do you?"

After reassuring Miss Brett that there were no men at all in her life and that she did have money, Lena was shown to a small room near the top of the house, a room that didn't look like the setting for the start of a great adventure. It was plain and sparsely furnished, with an iron bedstead, a pine wardrobe, and a single chair. But Lena had read enough books to know that adventures could start in the oddest of places. She removed her gloves and unlaced her boots, pulling her feet free. The soft, fleshy soles were sore, as they often were. It seemed nothing could toughen them up—not massages and not walking barefoot, which only bruised the tender skin. Her feet had stopped growing when she was twelve years old, but still they were longer than the feet of most men, and narrow as a girl's wrists. Lena's toes had always reminded her of wrinkled caterpillars. If only she could wiggle them as easily as other people could, she might be able to relieve the stiffness, but only the first joint moved; the rest were as unyielding as rusty hinges. Lena hobbled to the window and slid it open. The sound and scent of the sea crashed in. She unpinned her remaining money and her father's letter from her chemise. If only she had kept everything there all along rather than in her bag, she wouldn't be in this predicament. Tomorrow, she told herself, she would make discreet inquiries. Perhaps she still had enough money to hire a guide into Scree, someone who was not afraid of Peculiars.

CHAPTER 7

MISS BRETT'S FOR WOMEN

DEEP BOOMS AND SHARP CRIES. STRANGE SOUNDS ERUPTED IN Lena's dreams. She bolted up from her bed, heart hammering, and found herself in a strange room filled with gray light. A cool, thick fog had crept in through the window and with it the lonely boom of a foghorn warning ships off the rocky coast of Knob Knoster. Hungry gulls screamed and squabbled for breakfast, and Lena realized that if she didn't hurry, she would miss hers. Miss Brett had said seven a.m. With no time to bind her hair in a braid, she ran her tortoiseshell comb through the knots and pulled on a pair of pale thin gloves.

She was the last guest to arrive in the small dining room. There was only one seat empty, next to an old lady with a horn in her ear, which suited Lena fine. Perhaps there would be little conversation about her hands. As expected, no one else in the breakfast room was wearing gloves for the meal. Lena hoped that the pale color she chose would draw little attention and that anyone who did notice would be too polite to remark on them.

At the next table, Lena recognized her companion from the train—the lady with the firm jaw and red poppies on her hat. She was wearing the same hat, Lena noticed, not even removing it for the meal, as would have been proper. The woman next to her, the one Lena had seen at the station, shared the same thick profile. A pink carnation blossomed on the front of her stiff black dress. Lena smiled at the ladies in recognition, but they were too engaged in conversation to notice her.

The china teacups were delicate, covered with a pattern of blue forget-me-nots. Lena reached a trembling hand for the teapot. Her fingers wrapped around the thin handle. With practiced concentration she maneuvered the teapot with only one hand, steadying her cup with the other. Her long fingers made it much too easy to drop one of the tiny cups. By the time she had poured her tea and reached for a roll, a thin trickle of sweat had run between her shoulder blades.

"It's the fog, Mrs. Fetiscue." Poppy Hat's voice carried across the room. "It would drive anyone mad." She lowered her voice. "It's a cover for evil."

"Once," her companion replied, "the fog didn't lift for three weeks. Imagine that, Mrs. Fortinbras. You couldn't hardly tell if it were day or night. That's when the lot of them came slinking over the border. Killed a family in their own beds and then disappeared back to where they come from."

"Evil, Mrs. Fetiscue, pure evil. I don't know how a God-fearing woman like yourself could have lived here so long."

"You know, sister, that ever since our husbands died—God rest their souls—I've counted you as my closest friend and ally. It's how I've bore living in this heathen place."

Mrs. Fortinbras leaned across the table and patted her sister's hand. "There is no friend like a sister, Mrs. Fetiscue. I'm glad to have been some encouragement."

By now everyone in the room was listening. Miss Brett entered from the kitchen carrying a steaming tray of eggs. "The fog is natural to all sea towns."

"It's wicked!" declared Mrs. Fetiscue. "People do things under the cover of darkness they would never do in the light of day. Fog provides them the same benefit."

Mrs. Fortinbras nodded so vehemently that her poppies shook.

"Are you saying the people of Knoster are wicked?" Miss Brett set the tray of eggs down with a thump.

"No more than the average. But living so close to the borders of a land thick with heathens . . ." Mrs. Fortinbras's voice trailed off, but the point was clear. "My sister and I are traveling into Scree to convert the heathens. We'll have to get used to such things."

Miss Brett peered down the length of her nose.

Lena couldn't help herself. "Do you believe there are Peculiars in Scree?" she asked.

"Oh, there are Peculiars, all right. But we won't be

concerning ourselves with them, dear. Peculiars do not have souls. Nothing to convert."

The rest of breakfast continued with subdued conversation. As soon as she could politely escape the dining room, Lena fled. A strange hollowness had filled her at the missionary's words. Perhaps this is how it feels to be soulless, she thought. Could one feel a soul? Lena concentrated very hard, focusing her attention on her rib cage. Surely that was where the soul would be encased. Nothing, except the anxious fluttering of her heart.

Lena tried to put her unease aside. It was time to be businesslike, time to focus on the reasons she had stopped

in Knoster. She drew a thick shawl over her fitted jacket and took her second-best purse out of her luggage—the first-best having been the one lost on the train. As she prepared to leave, she had two purposes in mind. The first was to stand on the shore and touch the sea. The second purpose required more courage: Find a reliable guide into Scree, one whom she could afford now that her circumstances were considerably reduced.

All roads in Knoster wound down to the harbor. Foghorns beckoned, and Lena kept a good pace, although thick fog still obscured most of the view. Tall, crooked houses brooded like ghosts over the cobbled streets. Miss Brett had predicted the fog would burn off before noon and then Lena would be able to see some of the glories of Knob Knoster. The promise of a steam carousel near the boardwalk quickened Lena's steps.

Once Knoster had hopes of becoming the major port city in the West. Trade boats arrived from across the sea. Whalers set forth on the spumy waves, and a fishing fleet flourished. Miss Brett's father once owned a large fishing boat with a crew of twenty. But it had proved difficult to transport the necessary supplies for a town into Knoster. Train tunnels had not yet been excavated through the basalt cliffs, forcing the price of goods higher. And then there had always been the rumors.

As the coastal town mushroomed, news of its superior harbor drew investors despite the high cost of supplies. But then animals began to disappear: a merchant's horse, the dairy farmer's best milk cow, neighbors' dogs. Then a handful of the new citizens of Knoster gave credence to rumors about the wild lands to the north. Old stories of Peculiars resurfaced, and with the rumors fear blew in like a persistent wind. People saw Peculiars in every misfortune. The final blow came when the Whittlestone Mining Company withdrew its plans for a base of operations in Knoster. The new and still fragile economy collapsed. Houses were sold cheap, farms abandoned. Only the hardiest people remained, along with a few eccentrics who found that the isolation of Knoster suited them.

Now only a small fleet of fishing boats and whalers remained, and every year their numbers grew smaller. The weather and tides were too capricious to allow them to compete with those from more southerly ports.

The town had a faded glamour. The opera house, still the largest building in town and the only one made out of brick, had once offered performances by the likes of Ida Fincher, the Western Star. It was now reduced to a glorified grange, advertising town hall meetings and displaying a tattered poster for a salon steam carousel known as the Pleasure Dome. On the poster, men, women, and children rode on painted wooden ponies or pigs while others glided in gold-leaf gondolas circling a carousel organ. Lena stared at the poster for a long time. She had always dreamed of riding a carousel pony.

Like the poster, everything in Knoster had grown tattered with time. Nothing could stand up against the relentless salt wind. That wind was stirring now. Lena watched the fog swirl in tendrils across the sky. The dampness made her hair curl, and beads of moisture clung like tears to her lashes. Her anticipation quickened with her pace. She had never been to a beach before. As she wound her way down the hill, the train station appeared suddenly on her left, and she heard more distinctly the slap of water and the roar of waves. Dark pilings pierced the fog, and she set them as guideposts to the harbor. Suddenly, the sidewalk ended and stone crunched beneath her feet.

As a child, Lena had pored over pictures of tropical beaches in faraway lands, beaches where sand lay smooth and warm as a blanket. Those were not the beaches of Knob Knoster. She sifted crushed rock, bits of shell, and glass through her fingers. Everything around her was muted in shades of gray—water, sky, and land. She breathed in the distinctive smell of fish and tar. Waves licked the stony shore of the harbor and crashed against the riprap of a jetty. And Lena found that she was listening, as if the wild call of the ocean was familiar. It filled her with strange longings for adventure, longings Nana Crane would say no civilized girl should ever have. Her heart beat faster. Lena tried not to listen, afraid the ocean might call her name.

She was not sure how long she stood in the harbor listening, and not listening. It was long enough that the sun began to fight its way through the remnants of fog. And with the sun, the wind whipped in, salty and sharp. And the landscape emerged. Lena was surprised to see she wasn't alone on the harbor beach. A wizened man with a pipe in his mouth stood looking out to sea not more than a few yards away. Not wanting to disturb him, Lena averted her eyes and looked down at the ground around her feet, hoping to discover shells. She jumped. Instead of shells, strange brown snakes crisscrossed the rough beach. Long and bulbous, they sprouted tufts of green hair but lay completely still. Lena bent closer. Cautiously, she poked at one with the pointed tip of her alligator boot. It didn't move.

"Bull kelp." The man wore a squashed bowler hat and mumbled his words around the pipe between his lips. "Some folks say it's mermaid whips, used to tame the sea horses." His laugh was rusty, creaking like something exposed too long to the sea air. From under the hat deep-set eyes twinkled. "Not from here, are you?"

Lena shook her head and recovered her voice. "No, it's my first time at the ocean."

"Thought so." He nodded and chewed his pipe.

The man, Lena noted, was barely taller than her shoulder. He looked like one of the craggy boulders come to life. "Do you live here?"

"Came here with my father's fishing boat 'fore this town was anything at all, and I'm still here now that it's nothing again."

"You're a fisherman?" She could see five or six boats bobbing not far offshore now that the fog had cleared.

"Used to be." He rubbed his hand across the stubble on his face. "Now I just help out on the boats, some."

Lena thought quickly. If he'd been here that long, he might be just the person to ask. "I want to hire a guide. Perhaps you could tell me whom to talk to?" She wasn't prepared to reveal too much about her reasons for coming to Knoster.

"Fishing guide? That's the kind of guide most tourists want." He squinted out toward the open water.

"No, a travel guide." Lena scuffed the toe of her boot in the grainy sand. "I'm not really a tourist. I need a guide into Scree."

The man turned toward her, his furrowed face scrunched tightly as a raisin. "You don't look the type to have business in Scree." He sucked his pipe thoughtfully as his eyes traveled from the pointy toes of her boots to her dark, windswept hair.

Lena attempted to appear dignified. "Nevertheless, I am here on business. And I'm willing to pay."

Overhead a seagull whirled and screeched as it dropped a

clamshell to smash against the rock. In a sharp dive the bird dropped and swallowed the exposed animal in a gulp.

"They're clever that way," said the man. "Know how to get what they want." He tapped his pipe against his leg and pulled out a pouch of tobacco. He took his time refilling the pipe. Lena waited.

"Looks like you know what you want too. Name's Milo. If we're going to talk business, we'd best introduce ourselves." He shuffled toward her and extended a brown-clawed hand.

"Lena Mattacascar." She held out her gloved hand, which he took and shook without comment.

"Well, Lena Mattacascar—it just so happens you asked the right man. There's only two folks I'd trust to take me into Scree. Two folks who really know the land and can help you find whatever it is you're looking for." He paused, waiting for her to say just what she was looking for. When she didn't, he continued. "And I suspect it's not the usual tourist curiosity. But it'll cost ya."

She nodded.

"Margaret Flynn—you can find her down at the Parasol." He nodded toward the row of shops lining the harbor. "And Mr. Tobias Beasley. But he don't do that kind of thing much anymore. Lives in a big house outside of town."

Lena started at the name Beasley. "Is that the Mr. Beasley with a library?"

"You've heard of him. Yep, that's him, all right. Used to be a practicing medical man. Gave it up a few years back. But I can say this for him: He helped out some of those poor folk living in the forests up there. A shame the way they been treated. Beasley and Flynn're both strange folk, I won't deceive you. But they know things about Scree others don't." He turned back toward the sea, nursing his pipe, hands buried deep in his pockets.

"Thank you. Thank you very much." Lena looked up the narrow harbor lane, wondering just how far it was to the Parasol. "There's one thing more."

"Go on."

Lena could feel her face turning red. "Does Knoster still have the Pleasure Dome?"

Milo nodded. "Fancy carousel. Still runs on the weekends, hoping to draw in tourists. Not far from the Parasol. You can't miss it. The front's covered with cupids and doodads."

"You've been very helpful, Milo."

"Not often I get to help folks looking to go into Scree."

Lena wasn't sure, but she thought she caught the muttered words "a fool's errand" as she walked away.

EAVESDROPPING
LENA AT FIVE YEARS OF AGE

Late at night. Banging on the front door. I sit up in bed, and in the darkness there are shadows cast from the gas lamps outside my bedroom window. Creeping into the cold of the upstairs hallway, careful to avoid the squeaky floorboard, I seek out the listening grate. All day Mother's been sharp, hardly talking, even when she tucked me into bed. And there had been no story.

Nana Crane watched with her birdlike eyes but held her tongue. I haven't seen Poppa for two days. I wonder where he's gone. But I'm afraid to ask.

I can hear the bolt slide open on the front door and the mumbling of a male voice. Is it Poppa? No, another man's voice. Mother invites him into the parlor. Good, I can hear the words more clearly when they come from the parlor. It's freezing outside. I put my ear to the grate and wrap my icy feet in the hem of my nightgown.

"Your husband's down at the precinct in lockup. Started a fight in a bar last night and gave a fellow a nasty blow to the head. Sent the gentleman to the hospital. Far as anyone could see, it was unprovoked. Same thing last month, Mrs. Mattacascar."

Mother's words are too low to hear. I wonder what a precinct is.

"I understand, ma'am, but bail's going to be larger this time. Here's what the judge has ordered."

Papers rustle.

"I'll pay it, of course, I'll pay it. First thing in the morning."

In the morning, before I finish breakfast, Mother hurries out. Nana Crane pours a glug of tea into my mug of milk.

"Your father has bad blood. Nothing your mother does can change that."

I stir the milk, wondering what makes some blood bad.

CHAPTER 8

THE MARSHAL AGAIN

ALONG THE HARBOR ROAD A HODGEPODGE OF SMALL SHOPS AND eateries were clustered close enough together to hold each other upright. Unlike the rest of the faded town, these shops were painted bright blues and corals, deep greens and sunflower yellows. It's alive here, Lena thought. I've found the heart of Knob Knoster. Two men gutted and sold fish from a cart while an opportunistic cat slunk nearby, waiting for breakfast.

She inhaled the smell of chowder and frying fish. Shops were just opening for the day. Most were trinket stores that sold shells and models of whaling ships, snow globes with models of the gilded opera house inside, and fancy silver spoons with a fishing boat riding atop the handle. She imagined what type of shop the Parasol might be and pictured the store where her mother bought gloves and hats—a milliner or a dress shop.

She did not expect the Parasol to be a tearoom and public house, but that's what it turned out to be. And one block behind it, Lena could see a gilt sign announcing the Pleasure Dome. Her foot tapped with excitement. But first things first.

The Parasol was one of the largest buildings on Harbor Row. It was painted a garish green. A purple sign above the door showed the black outline of a woman's face peeking out from under the edge of a ruffled parasol. In the window, a hand-lettered sign read OPEN. When she entered, Lena found herself standing in a small room with eight tables. Only one was occupied, by an elderly woman and a small boy. A larger sign reading PUBLIC HOUSE pointed through an adjoining doorway toward the back of the building. It was clear that the public house was the larger of the two establishments. She hesitated just inside the door until a girl about her own age came out bearing a tray with a teapot and cups.

"Excuse me," Lena said.

"Be with you in a minute. Got some customers ahead of you." She gestured to the open tables. "You can sit anywhere you like."

Perhaps I should take a table and buy something, Lena thought, if I'm going to ask questions. She sat down at the nearest table and waited. When the waitress finally made her way to the table, Lena saw that her face was a star map of freckles; even the backs of her hands were dotted with the sandy spots. This girl couldn't be Margaret Flynn.

"Do you want anything with your tea?" She handed Lena a sheet of paper with a selection of breads, scones, and muffins neatly listed.

"No, just the tea will be fine. I came here really to talk to Margaret Flynn." Lena watched the girl's pale eyebrows rise in her freckled face.

"Are you a friend of hers?"

"No, but I have a business proposition to discuss." Lena folded her hands in her lap, noting that the girl was staring at them.

"She's the owner. I'll see if she'll talk to you. She's in the back."

"Tell her it's about Scree," Lena added as the girl hurried off through the open doorway.

From her table by the window Lena watched the activity on Harbor Row. She could see the edge of the long wooden pier and two old men, knobbly as pelicans, who were leaning over the edge with fishing poles. The morning sun warmed her face. She wondered if Jimson had begun his work in the library—and if he'd be dismissed once Mr. Beasley discovered that he knew nothing about libraries.

The waitress returned with a pot of tea and a rose china cup. "She's coming," the girl muttered before bustling back to the kitchen.

Dressed in purple silk with an impressive girth not even her corset could tame, Margaret Flynn commanded the room. Her large breasts flourished over the plunging neckline of her dress, and although bustles had fallen from fashion a decade earlier, Margaret Flynn still wore one, sashaying grandly as she entered the room. A mound of gray hair was held in place with a silver comb.

"What's this talk about a business proposition and Scree?" Her voice was as large as she was, and Lena shrank a little in her chair. "You don't look the type. Too pale-faced and puny for most men's taste."

She loomed over Lena, who shrank even deeper into her chair.

"Men like women with a little flesh on their bones . . . Though you do have good hair and your eyes aren't half bad," she added grudgingly.

"I don't understand." Lena felt that her voice sounded as pale and puny as Margaret Flynn's description of her.

"Working girl looking for a business proposition. I sent a trainload of them up to Scree last spring." She pulled out the chair opposite Lena and edged her bulk down into the seat.

Slowly, Lena began to understand. "Oh. Not *that* kind of business."

"Pity. Some men have a taste for the exotic." She nodded toward Lena's hands.

Burning with embarrassment, Lena buried her hands in her skirt. She tried to keep her voice level. "I need a reliable guide into Scree. I was told that you would be one of the best there is."

Margaret Flynn's muddy eyes widened. "One of the best! Why, I know Scree better 'n anyone. Know the good and the bad. I traveled up there with my first husband. He was a miner. We crossed the country one side to the other. The things I saw . . ." Beads of perspiration dotted her forehead, as if the memory required a great effort. "After he died, I earned an honest living as a working girl. The men up there"—she leaned across the table, and Lena was unable to take her eyes from the mounds of flesh that threatened to topple from her dress—"the men up there are hungry." She gave Lena a broad wink. "Then I took up guided tours. Took folks into the wild places no one else would go. People'll pay a lot of money to catch a glimpse of Peculiars." She fanned her face. "Married a customer of mine and we came to Knoster. A whaling man. Left enough money for me to buy this place when he died."

Behind Lena, the door opened and a breeze ruffled the back of her hair.

Lena nodded and tried to sort out her thoughts. Questions burned her throat.

"What business could a girl like you have in Scree?" Margaret asked, but her eyes were no longer on Lena's face. She was looking at a point behind Lena's head.

Lena felt a presence at her shoulder.

"Miss Mattacascar, you're headed to Scree? And here I thought you were staying in Knob Knoster with your mother's cousin." The voice behind her was familiar and this time oozed charm. "I hope you don't mind if I join you and Maggie. Why would a young lady such as yourself want to go beyond the borders?"

With one finger, Margaret scrubbed a bit of lipstick from a front tooth and smiled as the marshal pulled up a chair. "Thomas Saltre, I didn't know you were in town."

Lena went cold, then hot. He was looking at her with a

question on his face. His eyes fastened to hers. She had to think quickly. "Curiosity, I guess. I've heard that there are good business opportunities there and thought that since I'm so close I'd go. I might never have another chance . . ." Her voice faltered, as if it had run out of steam. Sweat prickled beneath her arms.

"Wouldn't be looking for anyone in particular, would you?" His voice was mild, but underneath, it was as sharp as a razor. A dimple winked on the left side of his mustache. Lena could see why Margaret Flynn was preening.

"Who'd she be looking for in Scree? 'Less it was a husband." Margaret looked over her shoulder. "Ruby, bring my gentleman friend some tea and a plate of cakes."

The freckle-faced waitress, who had been hovering within earshot, leapt and scurried back to the kitchen.

"To tell you the truth, my guiding days are over. Used to ride a horse, hike for miles." She laughed. "I'm citified now. But I can draw maps. Tell you where to go, what to watch out for. But I wouldn't recommend going. Things are restless in Scree since they sent all those convicts there."

Lena glanced up. The marshal's light eyes under the sandy eyebrows were assessing the situation. She was sure of it. She quickly looked down again. The waitress brought another pot of tea and an assortment of iced cakes. The girl looked curiously at Lena now, lingering longer than she needed to pour a cup of tea.

"I can tell you who to talk to, help you out a little." The

marshal's voice was gentle now, like the lap of waves in the inner harbor.

"Now, don't be sending her to Beasley. He's odd. Rumors are that he—"

"Thank you, Maggie, for your hospitality, but I can't stay." The marshal swiftly and effectively cut off Maggie's words. She shut her mouth with a snap.

"I need to escort this young lady back to her cousin's domicile. It's so easy to get lost in unfamiliar territory." He gallantly stood and came around to pull out Lena's chair.

Lena hesitated, but it seemed she had no choice.

"I'll be back later for the cakes and anything else you have." He winked and dipped his head.

Margaret Flynn beamed. "This is all on the house, honey," she said to Lena. "Any friend of Thomas's is a friend of mine. Thomas, you see that she doesn't go places she shouldn't."

He fit his thick hand across the small of Lena's back and gently nudged her forward. "Oh, I'll look after her. You can be sure of that."

The wind from the sea caught Lena's protests and sent them spinning into the sky as they walked out of the tearoom. Firmly, the marshal steered her out onto the pier.

"I've a little proposition that I think will benefit us both, Miss Mattacascar. But it's best to talk about such things in a place where we can have complete privacy."

The pier was built of thick cedar planks faded by years

of sun and salt. Wide cracks let her see between the boards as they walked, and her stomach lurched as the shore gave way to a rush of blue. She had never stood over water before. They passed the two fishermen still angled over the side of the pier watching their lines bob in the water. Black cormorants perched like carvings on pilings, and seagulls wheeled overhead. No people strolled the far end of the pier. Alone now with the birds, they walked toward the pier's end.

The wind stung Lena's face and made her eyes water. She clutched her shawl more tightly across her shoulders while strands of her black hair whipped out behind.

"I think this is far enough." The pressure on her back eased. He smoothed his mustache with two fingers. "Miss Mattacascar, I want you to talk with Tobias Beasley. Ask him about being your guide into Scree. It would be a favor to me." His smile was heartbreaking.

"Why should I? Why should I help you at all?" She dared not look at his eyes, soft now and inviting.

"Because, Miss Mattacascar, it would be beneficial to us both. You have your own reasons for wanting to visit Scree. I need to know what Tobias Beasley is up to. And I believe that it would behoove you to help me. Your father, Saul, is a wanted man, is he not?" He dropped her father's name casually like a rock into a pool. The surface rippled.

She was trapped. She did want to find the man who had so casily abandoned her and her mother. And she certainly didn't want the marshal finding him. Most of all she needed to discover if Peculiars really did exist.

The marshal's familiarity put her on edge. How old was he anyway? It was difficult to tell, but Lena guessed he was in his mid-twenties. Young to have so much responsibility. "How would this help me?" Lena worked to keep her voice level, thinking that she could never tell him the real nature of her quest.

He smiled his slow, thin smile. "You mean besides distracting me from the case of a missing felon? I'd find you a reliable guide into Scree, Miss Mattacascar. If you still decide to go, I wouldn't stop you."

A felon? She had not heard her father called a felon before. Was that worse than a convict? She didn't know. "What would I have to do?"

"Keep an eye open at Beasley's house. Your father isn't the only man I'm interested in. See if Beasley is doing anything illegal." The marshal took her hand and pressed it between his two strong ones. "Answer a few questions for me. May I call you Lena?"

She nodded.

"You'd be helping your country, Lena, not just me." His dimple flashed with his smile. "Margaret is right—Beasley is odd. But she doesn't know the half of it. Beasley is up to something wicked." He paused and searched her eyes, still firmly clasping her hand in his. "When I have the information our country needs, you'll be free to go."

The sun had finally bested the last of the fog. All around her, the sea called in its innumerable voices. She was standing on the edge of the world as she knew it with a man who confused her, one she didn't know if she could trust. What if he was right? Perhaps Beasley was wicked. She could help, make up for some of the trouble her father had caused and get a reliable guide into Scree in the bargain. That would please the marshal. She looked into his pleading eyes. Her answer seemed as inevitable as the tide.

CHAPTER 9

MR. BEASLEY'S LIBRARY

THREE MILES OUTSIDE OF TOWN, NORTH ALONG THE COAST ROAD.

The directions had been short and simple when the marshal had given them to Lena the previous day.

"You'll see the house clinging to the cliffs. There's a long track leading to it, bordered by a row of poplars. I'll have a coach drop you near the track. It's best if he thinks you came on your own."

"But what pretense do I have for showing up uninvited?" Lena had worried her lower lip between her teeth as she and the marshal had stood out on the pier.

"You're your father's daughter. I'm sure you'll think of something." Thomas Saltre had laughed, and only when they had turned and started back to town had he dropped her hand.

Lena had another dilemma as well, not one she chose to share with the marshal. (Even now that she knew his full name, she could not think of him as anything other than "the marshal.") Her problem was that she would soon have nowhere to stay. Her room at Miss Brett's would be taken over shortly by a dowager from the southland. And Lena's limited resources would not permit a stay at the one hotel in Knoster. She was in a pickle, as her mother used to say.

For some inexplicable reason, she had not mentioned Jimson Quiggley to the marshal. It would be natural for her to pay a call on her companion from the train, especially since he had so kindly offered her assistance, should she need it.

So the next morning she dressed carefully, braiding her long black hair and pinning the braids across the crown of her head. Her other traveling suit was still fresh—a fitted jacket with a skirt of dark blue to match her eyes. It had been made by Nana Crane. The skirt was just long enough to be fashionable but short enough not to get caught in the doors of a coach or train. She selected her one pair of kid gloves, saved for the most special of occasions, whose leather was soft and buttery against her skin. Then, with mixed feelings, Lena set out for Mr. Beasley's house.

The coast road north beyond Knoster was a seldom-used route. Most people heading to Scree preferred the newer and more direct inland road. Even the train turned inland at Knoster, chugging its way to the northern border crossing one day each week with its burden of convicts, suspected Peculiars, and opportunists. The coast road embraced the rocky shoulders of cliffs that dropped to pocket beaches. A few farms dotted the outskirts of Knoster, where mainly pumpkin and lettuce were grown, and Lena saw globes of orange in fields of green that tumbled toward the sea. This new world was a riot of color so different from the muted gray of her city. Lena absorbed it all as she leaned forward, peering from the confines of a Concord coach. She had been deeply disappointed to be seated inside the coach rather than riding with the driver on his bench outside. She had read Mark Twain's account of his overland journey in *Roughing It*—"a-top of the flying coach, dangled our legs over the side and leveled an outlook over the world-wide carpet about us for things new and strange to gaze at. It thrills me to think of the life and the wild sense of freedom on those fine overland mornings"—and had been fully prepared to experience the same thing herself, but it was not to be. The marshal had tucked her securely inside the coach and said that she would hear from him soon. She didn't bother to ask where or how. She was happy to escape his robust mustache and prying eyes.

Even though she was inside the coach, she couldn't help but feel some of Twain's "wild sense of freedom" as she rode into a new adventure. But the ride ended quickly, at an imposing row of poplars that bordered a gravel track that led toward the cliff's edge and the sea below. A few hundred yards down the track was Beasley's house, and Lena was glad to stretch her legs. She had seen glimpses of the building as they approached—cupolas and towers, sharp roof angles, and the wrought-iron railing of a widow's walk. But she was not prepared for Mr. Beasley's house in its entirety.

It clung like a limpet to the edge of the cliff and was tall and gray-shingled with white railings and trim. The architecture had followed no particular style—a cornice here, a bay there, a swooping roofline that looked as if it might take flight. There was an old-fashioned garden that had run amok on the south side of the house and also a small apple orchard, beyond which Lena could see a weathered railing to a staircase that dropped over the edge of the cliff. On a point of the roof, a copper horse, tinted green by the sea air, danced crazily in the wind. Several other brass fixtures that Lena didn't recognize spun furiously.

She lifted the brass knocker and mentally rehearsed what she would say. But the woman who opened the door never gave her a chance.

"All vendors use the back door." She was tall and angular and stood with her hands on her jutting hip bones. She glared at Lena.

"I'm not selling anything. I'm here to see Mr. Beasley and Jimson Quiggley."

The woman looked her up and down. "You're not here about the bicycles? Or the hair tonic?" She peered around Lena as if she was expecting to see someone with her on the step. "All by yourself, then? What's your business?" She thrust her neck forward, like a chicken, Lena thought. Next thing she'd be strutting and clucking.

"I'm a friend of Mr. Quiggley, and I have a business question for Mr. Beasley."

"I'm not sure I should bother the gentlemen if you can't tell me more—"

"Tell you more what?"

Lena recognized the voice immediately. Jimson's head appeared behind the housekeeper's taut gray bun, and his eyes grew wide with surprise or pleasure as he gazed over her shoulder. "Mrs. Pollet, this is my dear friend Miss Lena Mattacascar. I think we should invite her in, don't you?" His eyes twinkled in the way Lena remembered from the train.

Mrs. Pollet sniffed, but her expression softened when she looked at Jimson. "She could have said so in the first place." She backed away from the door just enough to give Lena room to slip inside. As she scooted past, Lena realized that the housekeeper was half a head taller than Jimson.

Jimson was around Mrs. Pollet in a flash, taking Lena's hand in his and pumping it up and down. "How have you been? Are you still staying with your cousin? Did they ever find your purse?"

Lena could hardly answer one question before he was on to another. She found herself smiling at Jimson's lively face. The entryway itself confused Lena even more. It was like no foyer she had ever seen. The ceiling was two stories above her and painted to look like the night sky, except where a window in the painted sky let in a patch of real blue with clouds scudding by. The wall in front of her featured brass instruments, some with dials. There was a barometer, a compass, a thermometer, and others she couldn't identify.

Jimson was still talking. "You have to see the library and meet Mr. Beasley."

Lena dove into the rushing stream of words. "What did she mean about bicycles and hair tonic?"

"Oh, Mr. Beasley ordered a bicycle from Mr. A. A. Pope and Company. It was supposed to be here last week. Hair tonic . . ." His forehead dissolved in wrinkles as he thought. Lena had forgotten how open Jimson's face was. It held none of the marshal's secretive intensity. "I'm not sure about that one. But you have to come see what we have here."

He's only been here a couple of days, and he's already talking as though he owns the place, Lena thought enviously.

"Come with me. Mr. Beasley's a great inventor, a man ahead of his time. But first tell me everything you've been doing."

Lena was surprised how comforting it was to be with someone familiar, someone who made her feel safe. This time Jimson really did pause to listen, asking her just a few astute questions about her days in Knoster. Lena left out all mention of the marshal except to say she had met with him once and that he had failed to find her purse. She even confessed that she was now staying at Miss Brett's rather than with her cousin.

As they talked, Jimson led her through a series of hallways toward the library.

"How have you gotten on with your library work?" She hoped he'd managed to satisfy Mr. Beasley.

"Perfect. His library is the most amazing place, nothing like any library you've ever seen. It doesn't matter that I don't have all the regular librarian training, because everything here is so different. Being a quick learner is more important than knowing all the answers." He winked at Lena and then stopped abruptly and changed direction. He led her down a short hall to a door that opened out onto a patio overlooking the cliff. In the middle of the patio there was something that appeared to be a large cauldron with a mirror. It was enclosed in glass.

"What is it?" Lena edged closer to the device, but her real interest was in looking over the rail to the rocks and sea below.

"Mr. Beasley's converting solar power into steam energy. The sun reflects off the mirrors and makes the water boil."

"You can do that on a stove," Lena remarked.

"This is on a much larger scale, and it doesn't take wood, coal, or oil to power it. Mr. Beasley predicts coal will run out eventually, and then where will we be? Industry requires steam. This"—he gestured toward the cauldron—"can produce enough steam to power an engine. It could power an electricity generator, or perhaps a smaller one could power a motor vehicle."

He looked as pleased as if he had invented it himself, Lena observed. "What happens when the sun isn't shining?"

"Even on a cloudy day you get some energy. Ultraviolet makes it through the clouds; it just isn't as efficient. You're right, though. It works best in a climate with lots of sunny days. Mr.

Beasley's always experimenting. He's even working on a flying machine. He's a true man of science."

Jimson led Lena on to the library, chuckling when he heard her sharp intake of breath. The doors, with their massive metal mechanisms of revolving gears and rods, were unlike any Lena had ever seen. "Why, they're like machines or sculpture!"

"The inner sanctum . . . the holy of holies. Welcome to the library." Jimson gave a short bow.

As unconventional as the doors was the library itself. It was far more than a collection of books. It was more like a cabinet of curiosities, a museum of the strangest sort. Rich leather-bound volumes lined walls on shelves that reached twenty feet to the ceiling. Prized artifacts filled display cases. Unlike the dim, marble-floored building where her mother worked, this library was filled with filtered light from long windows. On top of a glass case a collection of small volumes glowed red, blue, and green.

"They're real jewels," Jimson informed her, "rubies, emeralds, and sapphires. Mr. Beasley says they were made by Mr. Sangorski and Mr. Sutcliffe. And this book is the oldest book of medical illustrations ever written."

A narrow gallery halfway up the wall supported a rolling ladder to reach the higher books. Any unused wall was covered with maps—mostly of continents Lena had explored only in her imagination. Many were marked with little flags that Jimson said showed places Mr. Beasley had visited as a medical doctor and as an explorer. And then there were the display cases. The room was filled with variously sized oak-and-glass cases, each carefully labeled with a brass plate. Lena stepped close to the nearest one. Inside on a purple velvet background was a spear with a long blade on one end. Attached to the shaft just below the blade was what looked like all the hair from a horse's tail. Lena read the brass plate: THE SOUL OF GENGHIS KHAN. She looked up at Jimson.

"It's a *sulde* from Mongolia. A warrior ties the hair from the tails of his best horses on his spear and keeps it outside his tent. It's kind of like his name card, but Mr. Beasley says they believe it's even more than that. It's his identity, and when he dies it becomes his soul. This one belonged to Genghis Khan, one of the smartest men who ever lived, Mr. Beasley says."

Lena was reminded of the missionary ladies at Miss Brett's, proclaiming that Peculiars had no soul. "But it's not really a soul."

"Well, our vicar in Northerdam would agree with you. Besides, science hasn't proved we even have souls."

"But it hasn't proved that we don't." Again Lena felt hollow inside and she wondered if it was because she was different from everyone else.

"Mr. Beasley collects all kinds of wonders from his travels. In this case"—Jimson led her by the arm to a very small glass case on the top of a low bookshelf —"we have a pipe made from the femur of a Chinese pirate." Lena recoiled, but he held her arm more tightly. "It isn't so bad. Take a look."

She peered into the case. A long and delicate pipe lay on a bed of satin. It was carved with strange vines and yellowed at the mouthpiece. "How does he know it was from a Chinese pirate?"

"Because he got it from a Malaysian pirate who had lost an ear in the battle."

A sudden whizzing noise flew by her ear. Lena jumped. For the first time she noticed a series of glass tubes suspended overhead crisscrossing the library.

"They're pneumatic. It's the way Mr. Beasley sends requests from his study." Jimson walked to a large desk and opened the end of the tube and removed a copper cylinder from which he extracted a folded sheet of paper. "He wants his copy of Swinburne's *Poems and Ballads*. He's a great fan of poetry."

Lena watched openmouthed as Jimson rolled the ladder to an upper shelf, climbed up, and returned with a book in hand.

"I don't know Dewey's decimal system yet, but I'm working at it. I know most modern libraries are using it now. Come on. It's time I introduced you to Mr. Beasley."

CHAPTER 10

AN OFFER

MR. BEASLEY'S STUDY WAS SEVERAL DOORS DOWN FROM THE library, on the side of the house that faced the sea. Jimson rapped on the dark paneled door and waited until a deep voice asked him to enter.

One wall of the study was mostly windows, with a view of the sea stretching into eternity. The rest of the room was dark-paneled and dim, and from the depths of that dimness a man arose.

"Here's your book, Mr. Beasley. I have a friend visiting—the girl from the train, Lena Mattacascar."

Had he been talking about her? Lena suddenly felt flustered. She looked up into the face of a very tall, mostly hairless man. She tried hard not to stare, but it seemed impossible. Above his gray eyes two brown arching lines had been neatly drawn where eyebrows should be. The rest of his face was smooth—there was no stubble of beard. And the top of his head was crossed lightly with only a few strands of pale hair.

"I'm delighted to meet you. Tobias Beasley at your service." He extended both of his large hands and enclosed her right hand. When the fingertips of her pale butterscotch glove extended well beyond his, his eyes lit with interest. But he said nothing other than "Welcome to Zephyr House."

She remembered the marshal's words—*He's up to something in that strange house of his, and you're going to help me find out what it is*—and shivered. "Thank you. Jimson has already shown me the library. It's amazing."

"It is wonderful, isn't it? But you must be tired after the drive out here, and I suspect Jimson didn't think to offer you any refreshment. I'll ring for Mrs. Pollet. We'll have tea."

He ushered them over to chairs by the large mullioned windows, and Lena found herself looking out over the endless blue sky and the sea. The way they merged into one gave her a strange feeling in the pit of her stomach.

"Jimson told me that your mother is a librarian. Does she use this new Dewey decimal system? I'm having Jimson re-catalogue all my books using it."

"That's not how the books are arranged now, but the librarians have been talking about it. I remember my mother coming home and complaining about the new system."

Mrs. Pollet strutted into the room with a tea tray loaded down with sandwiches and cups and a steaming red teapot. She wiped her hands on her apron and looked at Lena skeptically, as if she blamed the girl for this disruption to her household routine. "Will there be anything else, Mr. Beasley?"

"No, Leticia, this is more than enough. But would you ask your husband to check the water levels of the Aeolipile?"

She nodded and hurried off.

"Jimson also showed me how you are converting water to steam using solar power. Is that the Aeolipile?" Lena asked.

"No, the Aeolipile is something else altogether. It's sometimes referred to as a 'Hero engine.' It's a demonstration of how steam can power a device. It's a two-thousand-year-old invention and not very practical. But I'm hoping to modify it. The house is full of experiments." Mr. Beasley leaned forward to pour them each a cup of tea. "Coal won't be around forever. We'll use it up eventually, just as we will oil. But steam—that's the true wave of the future. What we need are more ways to generate steam power that don't depend on resources that will disappear."

"But aren't there coal mines all over Scree?" Lena tried to direct the conversation toward the land to the north.

"Yes, right now Scree is full of coal. But it won't be forever; it can't be. So while we're busy exploiting the land, someone needs to be researching the next step. That's the problem with engineers. They can be shortsighted."

"Mr. Beasley has all kinds of inventions. I only showed you one." Jimson lifted the top off a sandwich to inspect the filling inside. Chicken salad seemed to please him, because he took a hearty bite.

"Steam will change lives, Lena," Mr. Beasley continued. "For example, look what steam has contributed to the medical profession. We still struggle with believing only those things we can see. That's why no one paid attention to Joseph Lister when he said that something called bacteria was killing patients and that we needed to use steam to sterilize medical equipment—even the sheets the patient has been lying in. This is a new age of science."

Jimson's eyes never left Mr. Beasley's face. "'Science dogs his every footstep, meets him at every turn, and twines itself around his life.' That was in a copy of *The Naturalist* magazine. Mr. Lockyer said it."

"See how fortunate I was to find Jimson?" Mr. Beasley beamed, and Jimson flushed. "But what brings you to Knoster, Miss Mattacascar?"

Lena twined her own feet around the clawed feet of the reading chair and smoothed the wrinkles from her blue skirt. "I had hoped to go to Scree. I came prepared to hire a guide and buy provisions, but an unfortunate incident on the train—"

"Her bag was snatched."

"Makes it more difficult now. I would still like to go to Scree after I've earned some money." She looked up and found Mr. Beasley regarding her thoughtfully.

"Why Scree?"

She had thought out her explanation carefully. "I've always been interested in it, and my father had some business dealings there when I was younger. I guess I just want to see the place for myself."

"Scree is not a journey to be undertaken lightly. You're right to want a guide and to count the cost of provisions. The land belongs to no one. That's what our government claims, even though there have been indigenous people there for thousands of years. If we didn't look at it as unclaimed land, we'd have a difficult time justifying our actions there." His forehead creased with concentration and his painted eyebrows dove down to his nose.

"Several people mentioned that you are an expert on Scree and might be the perfect guide," Lena ventured.

Jimson's eyebrows shot up.

"Whom have you been talking to?" Mr. Beasley's voice grew more cautious.

"I met a man named Milo by the pier, and I also talked to Margaret Flynn." She was careful to omit mention of the marshal.

Mr. Beasley's mouth twitched as if he was about to smile. "Margaret Flynn was a fine guide in her day. She's seen more than most people have in a lifetime, but I can't imagine her leaving the comforts of her business now. And Milo, he's one of the old-timers."

"I didn't know you'd spent time in Scree," Jimson said, sounding rather left out.

"Most of my money came from my father's mines in Scree. They are what have allowed me my freedom to travel and experiment. I know Scree well." He ran his finger down the bridge of his nose, considering. "Where are you staying now?"

"I'm at Miss Brett's."

He nodded.

"But I've only a few more nights there, and then she has the room rented. My resources are such that I hoped you might be able to suggest some part-time employment while I find alternate lodging and make arrangements for Scree." Lena felt as if she was asking too much. She caught Jimson's eye, and he smiled reassuringly.

"Well, if your mother's a librarian, you must know books. Jimson has a huge job ahead of him and could use an assistant. I could pay you a small amount and provide you with room and board while I consider your proposition." His eyes lingered just a moment too long on her hands, and Lena slipped them between the folds of her skirt.

"That would be very kind." She found her heart was hammering in her chest. A place to stay and a small salary. The marshal would no doubt be pleased.

Jimson looked delighted. His eyes danced. "I suppose she *could* help me out with the cataloguing—as an assistant."

"Is it a deal, Miss Mattacascar?" Mr. Beasley extended his large hand again, and Lena was forced to remove her gloved hand from the folds of her skirt. He took her hand very gently in his. "An extra joint?" He looked truly interested rather than disgusted, but still Lena blushed.

"Yes, I was born that way."

"And your feet?"

She wondered how he knew to ask. Slowly she unwound them from the legs of the chair. Mr. Beasley peered down intently, as did Jimson.

"Specially designed boots. I suspect your feet discomfort you at times, Lena. I've seen these traits before . . . Shall we expect you tomorrow?"

Lena appreciated his sudden turn of conversation, even though she longed to know where he'd seen such traits before. "Yes, I'll be here tomorrow. And thank you."

He waved her thanks away. "I'm grateful Jimson found you. A librarian's daughter! That pleases me."

Mrs. Pollet's husband, Arthur, drove her the three miles back to Knob Knoster in a buggy. The trees were dressed in autumn finery, and she enjoyed the ride, but she knew that by the end of the month nights in Knoster would be cold with the wind off the sea. She needed to reach Scree before winter, when travel would be almost impossible over the unpaved, snowbound roads.

By the time she arrived, it was late afternoon. She had arranged to meet the marshal at the Parasol. He had promised to buy her dinner, but Lena knew that his real interest was in what she might have discovered at Mr. Beasley's house. The problem, she reflected as she made her way to the tearoom, was that she liked Mr. Beasley. Instinctively. There was nothing about her initial impression that had made her wary. It would be difficult to think of him engaging in devious work. Eccentric, maybe—she thought of his eyebrows—but not devious.

The sun was sinking by the time she pushed open the door of the Parasol. Marshal Thomas Saltre was already waiting to greet her. He stood up as she came in. Lena noticed that he had slicked down his sandy hair and waxed his mustache. He wore a frock coat with a low-cut vest and looked as respectable as any businessman out to dinner.

"Miss Mattacascar, I have a table for us here in the tearoom."

Lena was glad he had reserved a place in the tearoom rather than in the dark and noisy public house. She was tired, and gratefully accepted the offered chair at one of the small tables in the back of the room.

"I hope you enjoyed your visit to Mr. Beasley's house. I hear it is an interesting place."

"It is. Mr. Beasley is very"—she searched for the right word—"inventive. And his library is the best I've seen. You've never been inside his house?"

The marshal's face clouded. "Alas, I've never had the opportunity. My father knew Beasley, though, when he was a younger man traveling the world. I met him first when I was four or five years old."

Lena wanted to ask him how his father knew Mr. Beasley, but the same freckled young waitress who had served her the day before arrived at their table.

"We have two dishes," she announced. "Mutton or pork. Same as in the public house tonight. Soup's oxtail or barley, your choice."

Lena settled on barley soup followed by a dish of roast pork. This would be the first proper dinner she'd had since arriving in Knoster. She felt quite grown-up dining in the tearoom with a gentleman.

"Did you notice anything unusual in the house? Perhaps you could describe it to me."

He doesn't waste any time, Lena thought. She did her best to describe the eclectic building, with its many balconies and cupolas. But it was only when she began to describe the solar generator that his interest perked up.

"What does he use it for?" the marshal asked around a sloppy mouthful of roll.

Lena averted her eyes in distaste. "I don't really know. I got the feeling that it was just to show that it could work. Everything in the house is unusual. It would help if you told me what you want me to look for."

"I don't want to bias the witness." He smiled, charming and urbane once again. "Just tell me everything you notice, just like you are doing now. Lena, you're my eyes inside that place."

As they were finishing their dinner, Lena told him the most interesting news of all. "Mr. Beasley has offered me a job and lodging until I can save enough money for Scree."

The ends of the marshal's waxed mustache curved upward and he ran his hand through his oiled hair, creating a forest of spikes. "That's good news—very good news indeed. Better than I could have hoped for. But I shouldn't expect less from such an intelligent and charming young lady."

Lena blushed. "I doubt that I'll be coming into town very often. Most of my work will be in the library."

He looked pensive. "At least let me promise you a visit to the Pleasure Dome?"

Lena tried to keep the excitement from showing in her face. She didn't want the marshal to think she could be so easily bought. Besides, she had not yet asked the one question that compelled her visit.

"In fact," he went on, "it is open this evening. The carousel shuts down when the summer crowds disappear. I have to admit a fondness for it myself, but I hate to go alone. This may be one of our last opportunities?" He phrased his statement like a question and shot Lena a beseeching look.

"Well, I suppose I have the time." Lena bit the inside of her cheek to hold back a smile.

The marshal pulled back her chair and took her arm.

Like much of Knoster, the Pleasure Dome had seen better days. The sea air had faded the gilt sign, and one of the cupids had dropped his bow. But the organ music was lively, and Lena could hear it from out on the street.

"Steam carousels are quite popular in Europe. Knoster is lucky to have even this small version. Now, shut your eyes." The marshal patted her hand and waited for Lena to follow instructions. He led her through the painted wooden door. Music surrounded her.

"You can open them now."

Lena gasped. In the center of the building was a rotating platform. Horses, ponies, pigs, and gondolas in bright colors circled around a large pipe organ. A handful of men and women rode in the gondolas, and a scattering of children rode the painted animals. A center pole painted blue with silver stars supported the draped fabric of the ceiling. The marshal followed Lena's gaze. "The pole in the middle is a chimney so that the smoke and steam can escape. The steam engine is under the platform." He turned to Lena, searching her face with his pale blue eyes. "Shall we ride?"

Lena could only nod. A bright yellow horse with a wreath of red roses around its neck caught her eye. But maybe she would have to sit in a gondola like the other adults.

"I prefer the animals, myself," the marshal said as he paid for their tickets. "As soon as it stops, we'll claim our mounts. Unless you'd prefer a gondola?"

"Oh no, a horse is fine with me." Lena watched for the yellow horse to circle around again.

When the music stopped, the marshal placed his hand under her elbow. "Choose your animal and I'll help you up."

Lena walked directly to the yellow horse. She noticed that even the littlest girls rode sidesaddle. She tried to place a foot on the narrow wooden stirrup, but her long foot slipped. In one swift motion the marshal put his hands around her rib cage and lifted her onto the horse's back as if she were no more than a child. Lena gripped the brass pole with both hands and then bent to smooth her skirt over her legs.

The animal next to the horse was a blue pig with an apple in its mouth. The marshal looked at it skeptically. "Not my first choice, but it will do." He threw one leg over its saddle just as the music began again.

The platform rotated. The horse bumped up and down. Lena was flooded with happiness. The platform rotated more slowly than she expected, but it didn't matter. She was riding a carousel. "This is wonderful!"

Next to her the marshal bobbed up and down on the blue pig. "I'm happy to show you a good time, Miss Mattacascar. And I do think it would be beneficial if we could meet on a regular basis."

A flush spread across Lena's cheeks. Why did the man confuse her so? Feeling cheered by a good meal and the carousel ride, she smiled and nodded.

"I shall devise a way to communicate with you, so that you can report back on any strange happenings at Beasley's."

Again Lena nodded. She couldn't imagine that there would be much to report. They circled the room a fourth time. The question she had been avoiding all evening niggled at the back of her mind, burrowing like a worm into her pleasure. She would wait until the ride was through.

When the organ stopped and the platform stilled, the marshal helped Lena from the horse. His hands were strong and warm. She couldn't resist giving the shining yellow neck a pat.

"I'm afraid I must see you back to Miss Brett's now. I need to make an early start tomorrow."

Reluctantly, Lena allowed herself to be led outside away from the color, the bright lights, and the music. She cleared her throat. "Thank you for this evening. I've always wanted to ride a carousel."

The marshal nodded. "The pleasure has been all mine. It isn't often I get to spend an evening in such charming company. The life of a lawman can be quite lonely."

Lena glowed under his approval. They walked a few moments in silence. "In what capacity did you know my father?" The question popped out more easily than Lena expected, but she found that her heart was beating very fast. She squeezed her hands together as they walked.

The marshal continued along in silence for some time, his hands clasped behind his back. "It's not necessary for children to know everything about their parents. It's enough to say he was a wanted man."

"But I'm not a child any longer and—"

"No, Miss Mattacascar, you definitely are not."

Again Lena found herself blushing.

"Perhaps we will speak of it at some future time. I wouldn't want to be accused of giving you bad dreams."

Infuriated, Lena felt all the excitement of the evening drain away. He was treating her like a child, no matter what his eyes said. The mournful boom of the foghorn punctuated the marshal's attempts at conversation. Lena walked in silence.

As they approached Miss Brett's porch, the marshal put a hand on her arm and stopped. "Let's leave it at this, Miss Mattacascar. Your father was trouble from the day he was born. He could also charm the skin off a snake. You are well rid of him. We can't choose who our folks are, but you can help me with Beasley, who is likely of the same ilk. Think of it as your duty. I'll be in touch." He lifted one of her long hands to his lips and stopped just short of kissing it.

Lena's breath caught.

With a bow, the marshal disappeared down the foggy street, leaving Lena seething, sad, and utterly confused on the doorstep.

Once in her room, she filled a basin with warm water to soak her aching feet. While her feet soaked, she wrote a postcard with a picture of the opera house to her mother and Nana Crane, describing Knoster the best she could, telling them about the magical carousel and that she had found a temporary job as a librarian. She knew that would please her mother.

When she was finished writing, she lay back across the bed. What had her father done? The question was an itch she couldn't keep from rubbing. She had a right to know. And how dare the marshal say her father was trouble since the day he was born! Why, the marshal hadn't even been alive then!

Mr. Beasley would be sending a buggy for her right after

breakfast. She packed her few things, making sure to again fasten the last of her money and the letter from her father to the inside of her chemise. Then she readied herself for morning.

She didn't like being in the role of a spy, but what if Mr. Beasley was breaking the law? What would Jimson say if he knew? She was surprised by how good it had been to see him again. It was nice to see a friendly face. Her thoughts wandered, and she slept.

EAVESDROPPING
LENA AT FIVE YEARS OF AGE

Darkness. I jerked to wakefulness. Mother was screaming. I clutched Rudy, my stuffed dog, to my chest. "It's all right, Rudy. You're safe with me."

"What have you done, Saul? What did you do?" Mother's voice rising in octaves.

"Be quiet or you'll wake the neighborhood!" Poppa's voice, slurred, sharp.

"Because if it's what I've heard, I'll leave you. And I'll take Lena, and you'll never find us again."

"Don't listen to the old cow. What's in the past has nothing to do with you and Lena."

There was a long wail like a teapot come to full boil. I covered my ears, Rudy fell into the covers, but still I could hear the cry.

"Shut up or I'll—"

Then I couldn't hear anything more, because I was crying. The next day Poppa got me out of bed, whistling "Camptown Races" while he made breakfast.

"Your mother's not feeling well today. Another one of her headaches. I thought you and me could go out to the park, grab a bit of sunshine."

"Don't you have to go to work?"

"I'm taking the day off to spend it with my favorite girl."

It was nice to have Poppa all to myself. Last night's terrors were gone, and I tied a fresh red bow around Rudy's neck.

CHAPTER 11

A MEDICAL CONUNDRUM

LENA WAS DELIGHTED TO BE TRAVELING THE COAST ROAD AGAIN.
The sun had shown up for her journey, making everything

look fresh and new. She had her very first job and felt that
she was well on her way to being an independent woman. It
was amazing how the promise of employment could lift one's
spirits, Lena thought. Even her vague unease about spying
on Tobias Beasley had evaporated with the sun. If there
was anything strange going on in Zephyr House, she would
discover it. The view from the two-person buggy was better
than from the confines of the coach. Arthur Pollet was a quiet
man, and Lena was able to revel in the passing landscape and
the salt wind in her face.

This time Mrs. Pollet greeted her with a curt nod and then
led her up the polished stairway to a second-floor bedroom
that Mr. Beasley had set aside for her. The room looked out
over the apple trees just beyond the kitchen garden. If Lena

stretched far enough, she could catch a glimpse of the sea. Unlike the simple room at Miss Brett's, this room was filled with heavy furniture made out of dark wood. A four-poster bed commanded the space. Against one wall was a wardrobe with a mirrored door that would easily hold her clothes. Its feet were cleverly carved lion claws. A small ladies' desk and chair sat under the window. Lena assessed her reflection in the long mirror, wondering if she looked the part of an assistant librarian. Her hair was wound in a braid and pinned tightly to the crown of her head. She wore her long gray traveling skirt and a striped high-necked bodice. Professional, Lena thought, just like something her mother would wear to work at the library, but a little more modern. She smoothed charcoal-gray gloves over the length of her fingers and exhaled slowly. It would be important to notice even the smallest details as she made her way to the library. Feeling like a detective, she tucked a small notebook and pencil into her pocket and retraced her steps to the main hall.

Lena soon discovered that the layout of Zephyr House was arranged in wings along the cliff's edge. She was in the main wing now, and she knew that the library sprawled to the north. If Mrs. Pollet hadn't met her at the foot of the stairs, Lena realized, she would have had no idea how to find her way there.

"Mr. Beasley is not at home at the moment. He told me to take you straight to young Jimson in the library. But I expect you to learn your own way about before long."

"I'm sure I will. I'm usually good with directions."

But Mrs. Pollet, her long neck thrust forward, had already steamed ahead down a corridor that ran along the sea-facing side of the house. They passed the balcony where Jimson had shown her the solar machine and an assortment of other doors, mostly closed, that Lena longed to open. She saw nothing at all remarkable beyond a large gray spotted cat with one green eye and one blue. The cat joined their procession to the library, keeping step by their side like a dog.

"What an extraordinary cat!" Lena bent to scratch its chin, but it kept its distance, tail in the air.

"That's Mrs. Mumbles. She has the run of the place and can do no wrong—according to Mr. Beasley. Can't abide cats myself; they give me the willies."

The cat gave her pointed shoulder a shake, and again Lena was reminded of a chicken fluffing its feathers. Mrs. Mumbles continued to pad with them right to the entrance to the library.

Without Jimson's chatter, Lena was able to fully appreciate its bronze glory. There were two doors, each standing at least twelve feet tall. What caught her eye was the magnificent mechanism that spanned the doors. Gears and rods of polished brass covered the surface. In the very center of one door was what appeared to be a ship's wheel made of highly polished wood. When Mrs. Pollet used both hands to turn the wheel, it rotated easily. Along the perimeter of the doors small bolts withdrew with a series of clicking sounds. Lena was mesmerized, but Mrs. Pollet and Mrs. Mumbles took it in stride, sailing through the open doors and into the library. Lena drew the notebook from her pocket and made a quick notation. Was this something the marshal would be interested in?

"She's here, Mr. Jimson. And I hope she's of some use to you." Mrs. Pollet looked Lena up and down as if she was quite sure she wouldn't be, and then she left.

Mrs. Mumbles stayed behind, leaping lightly onto a low bookcase and turning around once before settling into a contented ball of fur.

"Lena!" Jimson's voice came from the top step of the rolling library ladder, where he sat with a large leather-bound volume open on his lap. "You won't believe what I've found. Be right down."

While Jimson backed down the ladder rungs, Lena looked around in alarm. The library had been upended. Stacks of books were perched on every flat surface, the lopsided piles threatening to tumble and knock over one of the hand-carved chessboards or bury the display of Pygmy blow darts. "What's happened?" she asked nervously, turning in a circle to survey the entire room.

"I'm just rearranging things according to Mr. Dewey's system. It is rather a mess, I suppose." Jimson looked at the teetering towers of books and scratched his head. "But look what I've got here!"

Lena climbed over a short stack of magazines, trying her best not to knock against any of the precarious piles as she made her way to the base of the ladder. Jimson had a smudge of gray dust across his cheek, and his hair was in disarray, as if he'd been running his hands through it all morning. "What is it?" she asked.

"It's a book of maps by a fellow named Johnson. They're from all over the world. This one is of Holland and Belgium."

Lena peered over his shoulder. The maps were depicted with considerable detail and color. The map was dated 1867, and an ornate border ran all around the edge. "It's beautiful."

"I've always wanted to see the world, but this might be the closest I ever come." He looked around the library. "I'm really glad you're here. This organizing business is harder than I thought it would be."

"Especially if you open every book you need to catalogue. Maybe we should start with one section at a time, with one category of book."

"I knew you'd be worth your weight in gold!" Jimson closed the atlas with a snap. "I've got all the instructions copied over here somewhere." He sorted through the stack of papers blanketing his desk. "By the way, Mr. Beasley had a desk brought in for you." He gestured toward a beautiful little walnut desk across from his.

Lena was inordinately pleased to have her own desk. She ran one gloved hand across its smooth surface and sighed. The lack of clutter on its surface was calming.

"And one more surprise!" With a flourish, Jimson lifted the cover off a gleaming black Sholes and Glidden Typewriting Machine. "It types both uppercase and lowercase. We're to do all the labels and files on it. And Mr. Beasley's modifications will make it easier for you—for anyone." A slight flush spread up his neck.

There had been a typewriter at the library in the City for a brief period of time, but it typed only uppercase letters and was so loud that it couldn't be used when there were patrons in the building. The keys stuck more than they worked, and it was returned within a month of purchase. But this one was nothing like that. There were no decorative decals on the body. The body itself was larger and more open, and brass pistons and valves rose from behind the keys.

"See, a boiler in the basement provides steam to this outlet. This tube connects the machine. It takes hardly any pressure at all to push the keys." Jimson looked at Lena's hands. She didn't care how the machine worked; she was itching to try it.

"It would probably work best without your gloves."

Lena hesitated and looked up at Jimson's encouraging eyes. She remembered ungloving her hands on the train and how Jimson had studied her long fingers with such intensity. Now, in the daylight, the intimacy of that moment was gone.

Laughing, Lena elaborately tossed each charcoal glove across the empty surface of her desk. She wiggled her fingers, relishing their freedom. Then she gently tapped the keys. They responded to the lightest pressure, and she imagined her fingers flying across the letters.

By noon they had made some progress using Lena's suggestions of working with one category at a time. Because it took her so long to find letters on the keyboard, the process of typing was much slower than she had imagined. The machine wasn't much quieter than the older model, but the keys responded so easily that Lena decided it would become useful once she had had time to practice. Jimson, she concluded, was enjoyable to work with and quite fast as long as he could keep from inspecting every book he handled. And he kept her laughing.

Mrs. Pollet brought them lunch on a tray—sandwiches and small cakes with a pot of tea. She left them with dire warnings of what would happen if a crumb or sticky finger left a mark on any book. Mrs. Mumbles uncurled herself and came to investigate, sniffing delicately at the sandwiches and then turning her nose up and flicking her tail in disgust. She rubbed against Jimson's trouser leg, and a deep rumble started from somewhere within the depths of her gray fur. It was unlike any cat purr that Lena had ever heard. It was the sound of muttered words.

"Like a person mumbling something you can't quite catch," she said as she looked down at the arched back of the cat.

"Exactly. That's why she's called Mumbles." Jimson stretched out and leaned back until his chair rested on two legs. "You've made quite a difference, Miss Mattacascar. Anyone would think you'd worked in a library before."

"I guess it comes from being a librarian's daughter. I always loved the way everything was ordered on the shelves. After the patrons went home, when my mother was finishing up her work, I'd put the returned books back on shelves.

It was almost as if I could hear the books whispering their stories to one another. I told my mother that and she just looked at me like she didn't understand, but it was my favorite time in the library." She didn't add that many nights she had worried that this was a goblin thought invading her rational mind.

"I used to work in my father's store, and I hated it," Jimson replied. "He sold farm equipment mostly, but also all kinds of dry goods. In the back he had an old globe that no one ever bought. What I'd do when everyone was gone at night was I'd spin that globe, close my eyes, and drop my finger on it. Whatever country my finger was pointing to when it stopped, that was where I pretended I'd explore. And now I've made it as far as Knob Knoster."

"So you didn't want to be a storekeeper?" Lena blew gently on her tea.

"Thought I'd die if I had to. But all I've got are sisters, so it was expected that I'd take on the family store. I'm not a merchant. I can't see spending my whole life in Northerdam." He dangled a bit of string in front of Mrs. Mumbles, who gave it a few swipes with her paw before retreating and deciding it was time to groom her fur.

"So how did you get away?"

"It wasn't easy. My father made a deal with me. If I agreed to marry Pansy, then he would let me go."

Lena set her teacup down with a clatter and tea sloshed into the saucer. "You're engaged?"

"Technically, I suppose so." Jimson chewed his lower lip. "She's our family's ward, a friend of my sister Polly. Her parents died, and we took her and her twin brother, Randall, in a few years ago because they had no other relatives."

"But do you want to marry her?" Lena was not at all in favor of arranged marriages. And her chest felt strangely constricted.

"Well, I suppose that I'll have to marry sometime. And it's a long way in the future. She's pretty, and she's nice enough." He shrugged, but Lena noticed that he didn't meet her eyes.

"That's not how I would want someone to feel about me if I was going to get married."

"Don't be overly romantic. You've read too many books. Most marriages are just a business contract anyway. It's for the survival of the species and society."

"That's a horrid way to look at it." Lena stood up. Why did she feel so angry? "I don't think Pansy would look at it like that."

"I don't see why it should upset you. You don't even know her. Besides, if I marry Pansy, Randall can take over the store. There's nothing he likes more than counting money, and it would remain in the family, so to speak. That's how the deal works. The store has always been in the family. Father knows I have no interest in it. When Pansy and I are married, Randall will be my brother-in-law as well as the family's ward. Of course, it would be even better if Randall married one of my sisters. I know how my father's mind works. And then I would be free to do something more interesting, like seeing the world."

"Does Pansy want to see the world too?" Lena's voice ratcheted louder and she tried to soften it.

"I never talked to her about it. But girls generally aren't interested in things like that." He looked truly puzzled, Lena thought.

"Perhaps you should ask her. She should have some say in her life, don't you think? I'd like nothing better than seeing the world, and as far as I know, I'm a girl."

"Not an ordinary girl."

"What do you mean by that, Jimson Quiggley?" She could feel the heat rise in her face. She could picture Nana Crane smiling smugly and nodding in agreement with Jimson.

"I didn't mean . . . I didn't mean . . ." He cast a desperate glance at her hands and feet. "I just meant that you're nothing like my sisters or Pansy. All they talk about is marriage and clothes. You have some peculiar ideas."

That was the very worst word Jimson could have chosen. Lena slammed a typing machine key so hard that she winced. Maybe it was only goblin women who were restless and wanted to see the world. She didn't know.

"I didn't mean 'peculiar' in that way. You know I don't even believe in that nonsense. It was supposed to be a compliment."

Lena clenched her jaw. "I think we had better get back to work."

Jimson seemed only too happy to escape back into books.

A chill had entered the room. Lena felt it working its way up the back of her neck. The camaraderie, so easy before, was now off balance. Why should she care what Jimson did? She was there to get a job done, and it wasn't her business to tell him how to live his life. Pansy . . . What kind of a name was that?

At his desk, Jimson worked steadily, sorting through books, whistling a tuneless song.

The sun was slanting toward the west when Lena noticed the whistling had stopped. A cramp ran from her shoulder to her neck from hunching over books. Her fingers had grown numb from the typing machine. Looking up, she saw Jimson slowly turning the pages of a loose-leaf sketchbook. He ran his hand over his face and let out a low whistle. "Lena, look at this."

She was glad to get up, glad to have an excuse to talk to Jimson again, but her feet were stiff and she stumbled with the first few steps.

The sketchbook contained ink sketches of people, each carefully labeled. They looked like the medical drawings in her doctor's office. One page was given over to a sketch of the arm, hand, and fingers with each bone meticulously identified. But other drawings were more disturbing. There was one of a person the size of a child with a large head and full beard labeled CLINICAL DWARFISM, APRIL 3, 1859. The next showed a tall, exceedingly thin woman sketched from the front. To Lena's embarrassment, the woman wore no clothes. On the same page, the woman was also shown from the back.

From each shoulder blade hung what appeared to be a small crumpled leaf. In the same neat hand ANNUNCIUS SYNDROME was carefully labeled and underneath it was dated October 12, 1862.

"What's attached to her back?" Lena pointed to the crumbled growth. "They look like shriveled wings."

"I don't know. These all look like some kind of medical drawings." Jimson flipped forward a few more pages. "It's Mr. Beasley's writing. These must be his drawings."

"Well, he used to be a practicing physician," Lena said.

"I know. He still helps out some poor folk that come around. But have you ever seen anything like these? They look like something out of nightmares or old fairy tales." He pointed to a sketch of a boy with a forked tongue.

Lena's heart beat faster. She had never seen anyone who looked like any of these drawings, but what if . . . The thought was unbearable. She grabbed for the sketchbook, jerking it out of Jimson's hands. Loose pages spilled out.

"Hey! What are you doing?" Jimson looked at her in surprise.

"I—I—I just . . ." Lena had no idea what to say. She had reacted without thinking. What if they were medical drawings of Peculiars? Somewhere in the collection there might be a sketch of a goblin, a goblin with extremely long hands and feet. She riffled quickly through the pages. There were a few more technical sketches of the throat and palate, of the neck, but they were all on normal humans. There were too many sketches. She needed time alone with the sketchbook to look through it thoroughly.

"Why did you do that?"

"I've always thought that, maybe one day, I might be interested in medicine." It wasn't a lie, exactly. She *was* interested in medicine. Perhaps the interest had come from so many doctor visits when she was young. "I've thought about becoming a doctor."

Jimson's eyes widened. "Well, that's interesting. I never would have guessed it." He moved to her side and stared down at a sketch of the pharynx. "Now, this is scientific. The rest are just monsters from fairy tales. We'll have to ask Mr. Beasley about it."

Lena snapped the cover shut. "Oh, no. We don't want him to think we've been going through his personal papers."

"He left the sketchbook right here in the library."

"We don't know if he did it on purpose. Perhaps it was just misplaced. I'll put it on the library table, so he sees it first thing." Anything to keep Jimson from looking through the rest of the sketches until she could see what else was in there. Besides, wasn't this just what the marshal was hoping she'd find? Proof that Mr. Beasley was studying Peculiars? "No one wants employees who are snoops." She didn't meet Jimson's eyes.

He ran his hand through his hair. "You're certainly acting strange today."

Lena straightened her shoulders and bit back a response just as the mechanism on the door slid open.

CHAPTER 12

AN ILLUMINATED TEXT

MRS. MUMBLES ARCHED HER BACK AND RAN TO THE DOOR,
tail held high, as if she were expecting this visitor. The gangly
form of Mr. Beasley appeared with a wooden box carried
reverently in his large hands. The cat wound herself about his
ankles so that he stumbled his way into the room.

"Mumbles!"

She meowed in protest at his clumsiness or at the sound
of her name, Lena wasn't sure which. Then the cat began a
stream of steady mutterings.

Mr. Beasley carefully set the box on a long table. "How's
work progressing?" He eyed the piles of books and nodded
approvingly at several sections neatly labeled and shelved.
"She's just what you needed, Jimson. Too big a job for one
person. How have you got on, my dear? Is your desk adequate?"

"It's perfect. And the typewriter is"—she had trouble
thinking of an appropriate adjective—"remarkable."

"It is quite a nice little invention—much better than the earlier model." He plinked a key. "I've been to Cloister and brought back something rather special for our library." His face was pink with excitement. His penciled eyebrows danced. "Go ahead, but open it carefully. Put these on first." He opened the drawer of the library table and pulled out a pair of thin white gloves, which he handed to Jimson. Lena noted that they would be too small for her gloved hands. "This box is rosewood; and the design, mother-of-pearl."

Both Jimson and Lena bent over the gleaming wood box. It was not much bigger than a jewel casket. The lid was in two sections and was held together by a brass clasp set as a branch on a vine of glowing white. Mother-of-pearl, like the inside of the shells that washed up on the shore at Knoster, Lena thought. Jimson undid the clasp and opened the lid. He reached in and removed a red leather book. Lena caught her breath. The cover was overlaid with a delicate tapestry of mother-of-pearl as fine as spiderwebs and was held in place by a thin brass frame. Even Jimson's fine hands looked large and clumsy as he carefully opened the cover and the first pages rustled. The pages were a fine onionskin, covered with writing Lena couldn't read. Shoulder to shoulder, she and Jimson hovered over the small book. Each page was bordered with flowers and animals in the glowing colors of jewels.

"It's illuminated," Lena said breathlessly.

"One of the finest illuminated texts I've ever seen," Mr. Beasley added. "The text is Latin."

"But why did they give it to you?" Lena could never imagine parting with such a beautiful book, even if she couldn't read a word of it.

"The sisters believe that it would be safer with me for the time being. Jimson, please put it in the case by the Khan's soul for now and be sure it is locked. I've asked Mrs. Pollet to serve us dinner on the terrace. I'll expect you both in fifteen minutes." He scooped up Mrs. Mumbles and strode from the room with the cat riding his shoulder. She looked at Lena with a smug smile; Lena was sure of it.

"Does he often travel to Cloister?" Lena asked, thinking of the escaped prisoner from the train and the man disguised as a nun who had helped him. This would be something to add to her notes.

"He has been lately." Jimson, still wearing the white gloves, placed the volume tenderly into the glass case. "It's called *A History.*"

"Do you read Latin?" She tried but failed to keep the surprise from her voice.

Jimson shrugged. "Just a little. I used to be an altar boy."

"But I thought you didn't believe in religion." Lena finished sorting the papers on her desk into piles.

"My family does. Gone to church my whole life. Marx calls religion the opiate of the masses, and I think he's right." He locked the case and put the key on the ring in his desk. "Let's go eat. I'm starving."

Lena patted her braids. She would have liked to have had

time to clean up before dinner, but it wouldn't do to keep her employer waiting. The sketchbook of medical drawings lay on the library table where Mr. Beasley would find it. Before he did, she would need to go through it carefully.

Lena thought again of the strangely clinical drawings, and of Mr. Beasley's frequent visits to Cloister. Perhaps the marshal was right: despite his friendly personality, Mr. Beasley might be someone worth watching. After dinner she'd write up notes of what she had observed so far and decide how much to share with the marshal. And once everyone was in bed for the night she'd pay a visit to the library and finish looking at the sketchbook. But the thought made her feel vaguely guilty. Mr. Beasley had been nothing but good to her so far.

The terrace extended from the back of the house in an arc that followed the rim of the cliff overlooking the sea. It was a wide patio of brick and grass, perched high above the water. An ornate iron railing was the only thing to keep one from tumbling down the jagged rocks to the sea below. Lena made sure to keep her distance from the edge.

She was tired. The light was that particular gold of October, and the air was sharp enough for a wrap, but the crash of waves against basalt cliffs was soothing—enough to make her eyelids heavy. The three of them sat around a teak table, and Mrs. Pollet brought them steaming bowls of soup brimming with sea creatures. The shrimp reminded her of giant insects, and she wondered what else lurked beneath the thick broth.

Jimson looked at her with a twinkle. "It's bouillabaisse. Haven't you had it before? It's a staple of coast towns."

Mr. Beasley poured himself a glass of wine. "I would like to propose a toast, to my two librarians, the Dewey decimal system, and the end of autumn's glories." He held his sparkling glass high in the air. Lena and Jimson raised their glasses as well.

They kept no wine in Lena's house, and she took her first sip gravely, once again feeling tremendously grown-up. But the taste wasn't what she expected from the rich ruby liquid. Instead, it was slightly sour, and when she tried to disguise her expression behind a napkin, Jimson caught her eye and winked.

"Tell me about your day," Mr. Beasley said, and then he listened attentively as they told him about what they had catalogued and how they had shelved the books. Lena waited for Jimson to say something about the sketchbook, and when he didn't, she felt her shoulders relax.

Then Mr. Beasley entertained them with stories about life at Cloister and about the large vegetable gardens and horse stables. "The sisters are quite progressive when it comes to medicine. They have a great deal of knowledge about herbal medicines, and they've been using chloroform to do some simple surgeries on animals."

"On animals that have been injured?" Lena asked.

"Well, yes, on injured animals. But they also do a bit of research to better understand how treating animals might be transferred to human beings. For example, say an animal has an internal injury. If we learn how to treat that on an animal, then perhaps we can transfer that knowledge someday to humans."

"That's exactly what we should be doing." Jimson finished his last bite of custard. "It's a perfect example of evolution at work. We use our intelligence to combat disease, and gradually the human race becomes stronger."

"But what if the research doesn't work the same way on animals as it does on people?" Lena thought about her own hands and feet. "They are different species."

"Not so different as you might think. What makes us uniquely human?" Mr. Beasley asked.

"The fact that we can use tools," Jimson was quick to say.

Lena spoke quietly, remembering the missionaries to Scree and Nana Crane's view of the world. "Well, I've heard it said that it's because we have a soul."

"No one has ever observed a soul. There is no proof that a soul exists. What would be its purpose?" Jimson seemed eager to bait her.

Lena glared at him. "No one has ever proved that it doesn't exist either."

Mr. Beasley seemed to be enjoying the discussion. Lena watched his large hairless hands become animated as he talked. "Disproving is often more difficult than proving. Aristotle defined the soul as the core or 'essence' of a living being. And Aquinas believed that the soul is immortal. Put those two thinkers together and you have that which makes each of us unique, outliving our bodies. It's an interesting thought. It makes sense, doesn't it, that there is more to any of us than meets the eye? What would you say, Jimson?"

"I'd say that we can't know anything without it being observable, otherwise it's all guesswork."

"Spoken like a true scientist! And what about you, Lena?"

Lena slipped a little lower in her chair and pleated her large cloth napkin with her fingers. "I don't know. But I've always wondered what a soul feels like. What I mean is, can you tell you have one by the way it feels?"

"You don't feel something missing when your tonsils are gone, and you don't feel your liver inside of you. If there was such a thing as a soul, I don't think it would have any feeling at all," Jimson said.

"Speaking of the tonsils—"

The discussion changed tack then like a sail following a change in the wind. Mr. Beasley described the process of the new tonsillectomy surgery being performed now and how it prevented infections of the throat. When Mrs. Pollet arrived, bearing hot water for tea, the sun was setting in a golden wash over the sea. Lena had never imagined that she would be sitting in such a wonderful place having a conversation with two such interesting people. Contentment was not a familiar companion. Even here on Mr. Beasley's terrace, her fears found her and coiled at her feet ready to strike. She felt a sudden and sharp longing for her small parlor at home, for her mother reading out loud, and even Nana Crane rattling the familiar knitting needles. She looked from Jimson's lively face to Mr. Beasley and wondered if she would always be apart.

CHAPTER 13

A CRIMINAL ENDEAVOR

LENA WAITED UNTIL IT WAS JUST PAST MIDNIGHT AND THE HOUSE was quiet. She had written a long letter to her mother and Nana Crane, describing the wonders of the library and the house perched on the cliff by the sea. She had also carefully taken notes on all that she had observed since arriving. She had been sure to include Mr. Beasley's visit to Cloister and the beautiful red book he brought back for the library. She might or might not share these notes with the marshal. Perhaps it would be best when she met him the next day to offer just a few tidbits of information. She was still finding it difficult to believe that Mr. Beasley could be anything other than kind.

Sitting on the edge of her new bed, Lena willed her heart to slow down. All right . . . it was time. She visualized her path down the long hallways and stairs to the library, where the sketchbook waited. If anyone discovered her, she could claim that she had lost her way in the big house and that she was just looking for something more to eat—although that would be difficult to believe after the supper they had consumed on the terrace. Perhaps she should say that she couldn't sleep and was looking for something to read. She wrapped a shawl around the shoulders of her muslin nightdress and slipped out of the bedroom.

It was silent in the hallway, save for the distant sounds of the sea. Moonlight shone in through an uncurtained window, making it easy for Lena to see her way to one of the many staircases. She was barefoot, hoping to pass silently as a shadow. There was no light shining under Jimson's door, and she breathed a sigh of gratitude. Even the smooth wooden treads of the stairs were uncomfortably hard on her tender soles. Lena always had to pay extra attention descending stairs. The length of her feet was greater than the width of any tread, which made it easy to stumble.

She froze as a clock chimed 12:30. Only two hallways more to the library. All around her were the sounds of an old, comfortable house at night—the sighing of joists settling, pipes creaking like old bones. Lena moved more quickly now, following the hallway runner. A few gaslights turned low still flickered, but she tried not to gaze into the shadows, knowing how her imagination often betrayed her. As she rounded the last corner, she heard a voice. She drew close to the wall. Perhaps Mrs. Pollet was still up and talking with Mr. Pollet. The voice came closer down the hallway, moving toward her. Lena's mouth was dry. Should she return the way she had come? Her heart sped. The voice stopped. Perhaps she had been discovered? Then something warm brushed against her ankle and ruffled the hem of her nightgown. Mrs. Mumbles. Lena exhaled. "Oh, you scared me," she chided the cat in a whisper. The cat yeowed. "Be quiet!" Lena set the code on the lock. She turned the wheel of the library door. All the bolts and gears clicked into place. The door swung open.

Moonlight bathed the library in a cold blue glow. It was not the same place Lena had worked in happily by day. She hurried to the table, the cat at her heels. The door slid shut behind them. The sketchbook lay where she had left it. Lena hesitated. Perhaps the best thing would be to take it with her. Mr. Beasley wouldn't miss it for one night, especially in the library's current state of disarray. Then she could look at it in her room, away from the cold blue light of the library, and, if she decided, she could show the marshal actual evidence of Mr. Beasley's interest in Peculiars. But that was the problem. Mr. Beasley was a gracious employer. It was difficult for Lena to imagine that he had any ulterior motives. She snatched up the book before she could change her mind and tucked it under the edge of her shawl. She'd return it in the morning.

Before she left, she crept over to the case that held the beautiful red book. Jimson had set it open to a page where a vine and morning glories wound around the text. A small brown rabbit was hidden under the vines at the bottom of the page. If only she could read the words! Mrs. Mumbles leapt on top of the glass, and Lena tickled her under the chin. The cat lifted her soft white throat appreciatively. Then together they crossed to the enormous doors.

"Not a word, Mrs. Mumbles, to anyone, or I won't scratch your chin again."

Lena entered the code, again unlocking the door, and turned the wheel. With a satisfying click the mechanisms released. As she reset the lock, something nearby hissed. She froze. A shrill whistle like a teakettle pierced the dark. She was bathed in a cold sweat. Mrs. Mumbles sat just inside the library, her tail switching back and forth.

"Come. Now," Lena demanded.

The cat looked at her.

Lena bent to her knees. "Come here, kitty."

Mrs. Mumbles retreated farther into the library.

Lena heard footsteps. Perhaps the whistle alerted Mr. Beasley that someone had broken into the library. She let the door close, trapping Mrs. Mumbles inside, and ran blindly down the hallway. Any minute now Mr. Beasley or the Pollets would appear—Leticia tall and spectral in her nightdress, Arthur small and bustling at her side—and demand that she explain herself. Her breath came in ragged gasps. There were footfalls on the stairs. Lena turned doorknobs and ducked behind the first door that opened. If they found her, she would be searched, and when they found the sketchbook, she would be sent packing in disgrace.

She backed into something tall and hard. It clattered to the floor. Tears streamed down her face. The noise would surely give her away. Lena curled into a ball on the floor and waited for the inevitable. But no one came in. There were murmurings in the hallway and the sound of doors opening and closing, but no alarm was raised.

She waited hunched on the floor a very long time. The voices and footsteps were gone. The dark was silent once again. She carefully straightened. Her legs were numb, and her face was streaked with tears. As quietly as possible she righted the metal shield. She had stumbled into Mr. Beasley's weaponry room. Ghostly outlines of suits of armor surrounded her. Lena grasped the sketchbook tightly in one hand and pulled open the door.

The hall was empty. She could see the flight of stairs leading to her hallway just a few feet beyond. What would happen in the morning when Mrs. Mumbles was discovered in the locked library?

Lena fled up the stairs and to the safety of her room. She dove under the covers and burrowed down deep, pushing the sketchbook under her pillow. It took a very long time for her to fall asleep, and when she did, she dreamed she was pursued by a suit of armor, the face mask opening and closing as puffs of steam billowed through the mouthpiece.

Jimson had already finished breakfast and was about to leave for the library when Lena arrived in the dining room. She was ready for accusations, but Mr. Beasley was not at breakfast.

"Good morning, sleepyhead! Stay up late writing to your family?"

All awkwardness from the previous day had vanished. His hair was more tousled than usual, but his face looked cheery enough. He was, Lena thought, one of those dreadfully cheery morning people, while she couldn't think until she'd had a cup of strong tea.

"Bad dreams. Has Mr. Beasley been at breakfast?"

"No, but then he's often up and out early."

Jimson, Lena realized, was staring at her in a strange way.

She wore her hair down this morning, held back only with a wide blue ribbon. Yesterday's tightly wound braids had given her a headache.

"What are you staring at?"

Jimson colored and looked away. "You look good even first thing in the morning," he muttered.

Flustered but pleased, Lena asked, "Did you hear something in the middle of the night like a whistle?" It was best to know where things stood. Had the whole household been alerted?

"No, slept straight through and didn't hear a sound. What kind of a whistle?"

Lena poured tea into a china cup and added a glug of cream. "Like a teapot's whistle, sharp and shrill. I thought it would have woken the whole house!"

"Like this?" Jimson disappeared around a corner. Lena heard a door opening and closing. The shrill of a whistle made her jump.

A moment later he was back.

"Yes, just like that!"

"It's one of Mr. Beasley's new toys. He rigged up a steam-powered ringer just to see if it could be done. It's only on the side door by the garden. He told us all to ignore it if we heard its whistle because it was just his little experiment. Sometimes he gets deliveries late at night when there's something important expected. That must be what you heard."

Lena carefully spread marmalade to the edges of her toast and avoided Jimson's eyes. "Does he have other devices like that around the house? I'd have an alarm on the library if it was mine."

"Not that I know of. The library is alarmed, but only if someone enters without the code. Don't worry, you're perfectly safe here."

Lena smiled. Let him think she was worried about her safety. "That's good to know."

Mrs. Pollet bustled into the dining room with the morning's mail on a small silver tray. "A letter for you, Mr. Jimson."

She handed him a thick cream envelope addressed in a loopy hand. Jimson quickly stuffed it in his jacket pocket.

Probably Pansy, Lena thought, surprised that the idea made her feel cross.

"Mr. Beasley said to tell you that he had a late night and that he's got some work of his own today. He hopes he'll be down to see you at dinner. Has anyone seen Mrs. Mumbles? She didn't show up for breakfast."

Lena choked and shook her head.

"Probably off catching mice" was Jimson's flip reply.

Mrs. Pollet muttered to herself.

"I won't be at dinner tonight, Mrs. Pollet. I'm meeting someone in town." Lena realized that getting away discreetly might be harder than she thought. But at least this would show Jimson she had other interests than the library.

Jimson frowned. "Meeting your cousin, I suppose."

Lena didn't contradict him. "Mr. Beasley did say our evenings were free to do with as we pleased." She got up to carry her plate to the sideboard. Her feet felt as if they had been pummeled after her barefoot travels the night before.

Jimson looked at her with concern. "You're limping."

"It must have been all those times up and down the library ladder yesterday."

"Well, you rest your feet today. I'll do the climbing. I'll see you in the library in a little while." He left whistling, with one hand in the pocket where he'd put his letter. Perhaps he's gone off to read it in private, Lena thought, and then was annoyed at herself for wondering.

On a laurel bush outside the window a spider had strung an intricate web. It was hung with a sparkling drop of dew. It reminded Lena of a delicate necklace with a single jewel. She gazed at it, hoping to slow her anxious thoughts. Mr. Beasley had had a late night. She was sure she'd heard voices. Perhaps he knew all about her midnight visit to the library and was waiting to confront her later. Breakfast sat heavily in her stomach. She checked the clock. There was just time to look through the medical drawings if she hurried, and then she could return the sketchbook before Jimson noticed it was gone. If she didn't hurry, she wouldn't be the first to the library to liberate Mrs. Mumbles.

CHAPTER 14

THE NATURE OF PECULIARS

LENA REMEMBERED THE ILLUSTRATIONS IN DR. CRINK'S OFFICE. She had spent years contemplating them while waiting on the examination table for the doctor to measure her stretching hands and feet. The skeletal system and circulatory system gave multicolored peeks into the body. Femur, tibia, ulna, twenty-three tiny bones in the hand—they had all fascinated her, all but the chart with an illustration of a child spotted with raised smallpox lesions. That picture she avoided altogether.

Sitting on her bed now, she flipped through the pages of illustrations in Mr. Beasley's sketchbook and held her breath. Her hands shook. The sketches spanned years of his medical practice, detailing observations of the human body. Most could be found in any illustrated medical text, but not all. There was the tall woman with the small misshapen growths labeled ANNUNCIUS SYNDROME. Lena stared at it for a long time. What must it feel like to have tiny shriveled wings growing from your shoulder blades? Had they always been that small, or had they once unfurled like the giant wings of an angel? Even though the year and page number were carefully recorded under each sketch, the illustrations were not in chronological order. They appeared to be in disarray, as if the pages had fallen from the sketchbook many times before.

Lena sorted through the first few pages and found what she was looking for: a handwritten table of contents for the sketchbook. She let her eye skim the page. Between "gangles" and "goiter," she found the word she had been both searching for and dreading: "goblinism." She made a careful search for the page but found nothing. Page 43 was missing, or perhaps had never been completed. Would it show hands and feet like hers or something else entirely? She punched her pillow in frustration. It would be better to know the truth.

What if the illustration had been completed and was lying loose on the library floor or buried in a box with other books and papers? She remembered Mr. Beasley's casual comment when he noticed her hands and feet: "I've seen these traits before." Where had he observed hands like hers, in his practice or in Scree? If there were others with hands and feet like hers, perhaps Dr. Crink was right. Perhaps it was a latent characteristic of goblinism. Unless, of course, it was merely a chromosomal abnormality that other people shared.

Lena thumbed back to the sketch of the woman with wings. Where had Mr. Beasley observed such a person? And the boy with the forked tongue? She shuddered. It was impossible to think that she might be like one of them—a freak, Peculiar, a nonperson with different genetic makeup from the rest of the human race. She pressed the cover closed. Jimson must not look at the sketchbook again. She would have to search for the missing page and perhaps find a way to speak with Mr. Beasley about it privately. He would be able to tell her what was wrong with her body. But could she trust him?

Tonight she would meet the marshal in town. She'd tell him about some of what she had discovered in Mr. Beasley's house, about his visits to Cloister, about the strange artifacts in his library. But she wouldn't mention the sketchbook—not yet, not until she discovered what Mr. Beasley knew about people like her. Meanwhile, she would keep the sketchbook.

Lena checked the clock. It was time to be in the library. If asked, she would tell Jimson that she had delivered the sketchbook to Mr. Beasley's sitting room, where he would find it when he returned. She slipped it under the pillow on her bed. It wasn't a lie exactly, she reasoned. She would return it to Mr. Beasley as soon as she had talked to the marshal and was better able to assess her employer's character.

Lena reached the library before Jimson. Mrs. Mumbles was waiting by the door, eager to be let out.

"You dreadful cat. Why didn't you come when I called you last night?"

The cat merely looked at Lena reproachfully with her strange mismatched eyes, whisked her tail, and scooted through the door in search of her breakfast. When Jimson arrived, his chipper spirits seemed to have soured slightly, and Lena wondered if it was the contents of the letter that had changed his mood. But it was impossible for Jimson to remain out of sorts for long. It took only the discovery of a book with illustrations of shrunken heads to revive his spirits, and the morning passed quickly, followed by a brief lunch served by Mrs. Pollet right in the library.

"Mr. Beasley doesn't usually allow any food in the library," she reminded them, just as she had the other day. "Make sure you don't touch any of the curiosities with food on your fingers."

"Mrs. Pollet, I am a trained librarian. I love books like my family. Of course I would never consider dirtying their pages with particles of food," Jimson replied, disguising a smile. "And you did warn us last time."

"We'll be very careful. Thank you for the sandwiches," Lena said.

"Well, then." Mrs. Pollet sniffed. "I've made molasses cookies. Don't eat too many."

Lena wondered if Leticia Pollet wasn't growing just a tiny bit fond of both of them.

For someone who had never had much experience lying, Lena felt that she was doing a decent job. Not that she condoned lying, but if one had to, it was important to do it well, she thought. She left both Jimson and Mr. Beasley with the impression she was meeting her cousin for dinner without having deliberately misled them. She just never corrected their presuppositions. The marshal had promised to send a cab for her, and, just as promised, at six p.m. a gleaming black horse and cab arrived at Zephyr House. Lena had pulled her hair up in a twist and polished her alligator boots. She checked that the sketchbook was still safely under her pillow, and with a notebook and pen in her purse set out for Knoster.

The carriage lights flickered against the early dark. Lena could feel the damp chill from the sea and this time was glad to be in the confines of the carriage. The lights of Knob Knoster twinkled on the hillsides, and Harbor Row welcomed her after the ride through the dark and empty countryside. The driver took her to the Parasol, which boasted a lively crowd and music from the speakeasy, while the tearoom was all but deserted. As planned, Thomas Saltre was waiting. He rose to meet her and pulled out her chair.

"Miss Mattacascar," he said with a slight bow.

Lena found that she was trembling. Now that she was here, face-to-face with the marshal, all her noble plans seemed foolish. What business did she have passing on any news about her employer, who had shown her nothing but kindness?

"You look quite glowing. The sea air must be doing you good." The marshal eased his way back into his chair. Again Lena was aware of his powerful build. How out of place he seemed in a tearoom. "I've already asked Maggie to bring us some clam chowder, specialty of the house tonight."

"Thank you." Lena's voice floated, pale and thin even in her own ears.

"I trust you've brought me some information about Zephyr House?" The marshal flipped open a small notebook and removed a pen from his breast pocket.

Lena described the magnificent library in detail, becoming more and more animated as she talked.

At first the marshal made a few notes, but as she talked on, he laid his pen aside. "I can see that the job suits you, but I really need information about Mr. Beasley. Not just about his library."

"He's an inventor and believes steam is the energy of the future—"

Again the marshal cut her off. "Anything suspicious that you've noticed? I hear that for the average citizen it is almost impossible to enter Scree these days." He looked at her from under his thick brows.

Lena hesitated at the implied threat. What information could she offer as a bone to satisfy his curiosity? She would throw out an offering. "Well, I am in the library all day, so I don't know what is going on in the rest of the house. I do know that Mr. Beasley frequently travels to Cloister. In fact, he brought back an illuminated book for the library."

Now Thomas Saltre sat forward in his chair. "Cloister, you say? That's very interesting. We have a man watching the sisters there. Progressive lot of subversives. Remember the man who helped the convict escape the train?"

When Lena nodded, he continued. "The man was dressed as a nun. Don't be thinking he took that costume without the sisters' permission. They've been helping criminals all along."

"If you know that, why hasn't anything been done?"

"Because that's just the beginning. It's not only criminals they're aiding and abetting, it's Peculiars too." He leaned farther forward, and Lena could see the hairs on his mustache bristle as he spoke. His voice dropped to a thick, conspiratorial whisper that made her feel she was receiving privileged information. "There's also rumors of medical experimentation going on—unnatural acts. I wouldn't be surprised if Beasley wasn't up to his eyeballs in whatever it is. He used to be a medical man, you know."

Lena tried to swallow, but a piece of bread seemed lodged in her throat. She reached for her glass of water. "What sort of experimentation?"

"Let me ask you a question. What kind of a man would give up a successful medical practice to live in some godforsaken place unless he was a man with something to hide? A man up to no good? Did you ever think of that? I don't know if Tobias Beasley is performing medical experiments on Peculiars along with those unnatural sisters or if he's taking money from Peculiars and helping them disappear across the border. Either way, whatever he's doing is illegal."

"But his money comes from coal mining. His father owned mines in Scree." The marshal's questions unsettled her. The images from the medical sketches were still fresh in her mind.

The marshal leaned back and shot her a long look. "Do

you know that for a fact? Why would a man with a library like his hire a boy like Jimson Quiggley, who doesn't know the first things about libraries?"

Before she could stop herself, Lena rushed to Jimson's defense. "He's smart and a hard worker, and he knows a great deal about science. How do you know about Jimson, anyway?"

Thomas Saltre batted her question away as if he were swatting a fly. "For that matter, why do you think he hired you?" And he let his gaze linger on her gloved hands.

Lena slid them under the table so he would not see them tremble. Once again the marshal felt dangerous, his usual charm gone.

"All I'm saying is that you need to be very careful. A man like Beasley is smart. There's no telling what he'd stoop to. You're providing our country a great service, but you mustn't hold back information out of loyalty. I'm here to help you in whatever way I can."

But Lena barely heard his last words. She was thinking of the sketchbook, of the missing pages, of her own hands and feet, and of the strange noises she had heard at night.

At the end of the uncomfortable meal, Margaret Flynn joined them. This time she was wearing a garnet necklace, and there was a plum feather in her hair. "How are you, missy? Has Thomas got you working for the government?" Then she bellowed her brash laugh. "Don't let him alarm you. He's a serious fellow—all work, all the time." She looked at Lena fondly. "Wouldn't I have liked to have a daughter like you! I would have called her Daisy, but providence didn't see fit . . . Can I get you two anything else?"

Lena, who was looking for a means of escape, used this as her cue. "No, I really must get back to Zephyr House. Mr. Beasley will worry if I'm late." She stood up.

The marshal did as well. "I'll have the cab return you. And Lena, what you do for me, you do for your country and for your father. Speaking of your father, I have some news." He hooked his arm through hers as he escorted her to the door of the restaurant. Lena could smell his spicy aftershave. "One of my contacts says that he met with your father in Scree last spring. He's been working in the mining industry. You might also be interested in this." He reached inside his suit jacket and removed a folded paper. "A little advance notice. These flyers will be distributed in population centers by the government next week." Lena unfolded the plain white paper and read silently while the marshal waited.

Regarding the Nature of Peculiars

There live among us members of the Peculiar race, who, because of inborn differences, are not fully human.

- They exist without souls.
- It is in their nature to choose evil over good and strife over harmony and to infect civil society with wild and subversive behaviors.

- If left unchecked, they will erode the fabric of our society.

Therefore, all who are determined by blood or behavior to be of the Peculiar race will be taken into custody and transferred to Scree, where they may live among others of their kind.

Because many Peculiars bear no specific identifiable marks designating them as such, it is important that citizens be vigilant. Citizens who suspect the presence of a Peculiar are encouraged to report the individual to their local authorities without delay. All reports will be held in confidence, so that citizens may perform their national duty without fear of recrimination.

We are committed to keeping our borders safe. The government has provided military guards along the borders of Scree. Persons wishing to travel to Scree for business must be able to show documentation proving their identity and business plans upon entering and leaving Scree.

Lena's hands grew cold and her mouth dry. She looked up. "I thought you'd want to know. Travel into Scree grows more difficult all the time without the right connections. And I'd hate to have anything happen to you." The marshal caught her eyes and held them long enough to make Lena's heart thump. He brushed her cheek with one hand. "Take care of yourself. I'll be in touch."

Thomas Saltre stepped back and gave Lena a final long look. Then he strolled off into the night, leaving her staring at his retreating muscular back, still feeling the warmth of his touch on her cheek. She refolded the flyer and tucked it into her purse.

During the bumpy ride back to Zephyr House, Lena attempted to sift through thoughts that shifted like sand. Her father had been seen in Scree. Did that mean that the marshal would now hunt him down there? A strange longing filled Lena, as if her heart had been scooped out and hollowed. It was more pressing than ever that she get to Scree. She imagined herself confronting the man who had left her so long ago. What would she say? But her heart gave no answer.

She leaned back against the tufted seat and closed her eyes. Everything the marshal had said about Mr. Beasley aligned with what she knew. What if he was doing some type of experimentation? And yet she couldn't reconcile that idea with the man she knew. On the other hand, hadn't Mr. Beasley himself said that we're all more than meets the eye?

Tonight the marshal had at first been all business, fierce in his determination. But then . . . his hand on her cheek. And now this terrible flyer. She buried her face in her hands. How long before someone suspected her? Could even the marshal protect her then?

CHAPTER 15

A TRAGEDY IN THE ORCHARD

A WEEK PASSED. EVERY DAY LENA WAITED FOR NEWS OF THE flyer to reach Zephyr House. It was difficult to concentrate. More than once Jimson asked her a question and Lena found that she had no idea what he had said.

The first storm of the season battered Zephyr House. Rain lashed the windows. The sea grew angry and took on the color of iron. Lena spent the days alone, working in the library. One morning Mr. Beasley dragged Jimson off early to work on one of his pet projects—a flying machine based on research by Stringfellow and Cayley. She was surprised how slowly the time passed without Jimson's enthusiastic chatter. At first she was delighted. Jimson's absence gave her time to search the library for the missing goblin sketch. But as the day wore on, Lena became more and more discouraged. Despite her best efforts, she found no trace of the missing paper. The marshal's words had kept her awake for many nights, and she nodded off several times over her work.

The evening proved no better. Even though they all ate together, Jimson and Mr. Beasley were deep in conversation about the lightest materials for fabricating the boilers necessary for steam-powered flight. Mr. Beasley believed that he had discovered a way to circumvent the problem. Lena watched the two heads bent over diagrams—one dark and curly, the other pale and bald—and felt lonely.

The next morning the storm was a memory. Broken limbs and a litter of golden leaves were the only reminders of the wind's fury. The air shone fresh-washed, and for the first time in many days Lena's heart lifted. Jimson was still busy with Mr. Beasley, but she was determined to remain cheerful and finish cataloguing artifacts. As she considered how to categorize Pygmy blow darts, under *B* for blow darts or under *P* for Pygmy, Mrs. Pollet erupted into the library, eyes wild and arms flailing like the long blades of a windmill.

"Where's himself—Mr. Beasley?" she sputtered.

"He's in the study with Jimson. Is something wrong?"

A wail burst from Mrs. Pollet's throat as she ran from the room. Lena, tripping over an agitated Mrs. Mumbles, followed. They ran down the hallway to the heavy oak doors, and, without pausing to knock, Mrs. Pollet burst through with Lena at her heels.

Jimson was standing on a stepladder, balancing a long metal blade as Mr. Beasley carefully weighed it. They looked up in unison as Mrs. Pollet called out, "Arthur's fallen from the roof. Come quick now!"

Arthur Pollet lay crumpled on the ground like a branch the wind had discarded. His right leg was bent in a way no leg should be able to bend, and his face was ashen. He did not open his eyes when Mr. Beasley gently called his name and put an ear to his chest.

"He's breathing regularly, but it seems the fall has knocked him out. We'll need to devise a litter to carry him into the house. From where did he fall?"

Leticia Pollet pointed upward and all eyes followed. "He was trimming a branch that broke in the storm."

Sure enough, a broken branch lay across one of the gables of Zephyr House. And the twelve-foot ladder lay toppled nearby.

"Lena, find something to cover him with to keep him warm. Jimson, come to the workshop with me and we'll get some poles and canvas."

After Arthur had been safely transported into the house and placed on a bed in the first-floor bedroom, Mr. Beasley sent Jimson and Lena out while he inspected the patient. Lena went to the kitchen to make tea for Mrs. Pollet, and Jimson followed.

"Do you think he'll be all right?" Lena busied herself heating water so Jimson wouldn't see her eyes tearing up.

"Of course he will. Mr. Beasley knows what he's doing."

"But his leg looks so awful and—" Her voice cracked.

"A break can heal, and he's strong . . . Lena, there's something I want to talk to you about."

She looked up at the urgency in his voice just as Mrs. Pollet came into the kitchen muttering, "He's sent me away as if he thinks I'm in the way."

"I'm sure that's not it. Mr. Beasley is probably just trying to spare your feelings. Here, I've made you some tea." Lena poured a cup and added a generous spoon of sugar. For all her height, Leticia Pollet seemed a shrunken woman. Her shoulders hunched forward, and Lena could see the sharp outline of her shoulder blades poking up through the fabric of her dress. Jimson pulled out a chair for her while Lena buttered a scone she had warmed.

Mr. Beasley, sleeves rolled to his elbows, appeared at the kitchen door. "Lena, I could use your help."

Reluctantly, Lena followed him to the bedroom. Perhaps she was not cut out for medicine after all.

"The break is bad and needs to be set. It will take two people. Thank goodness the man is unconscious. That way he won't remember the pain."

Lena blanched. "But I don't—"

Mr. Beasley cut her off. "Jimson told me you're interested in medicine. This is a useful technique to learn."

Arthur Pollet looked small and pale on the big iron bed, his white muttonchops bristling against colorless weathered cheeks. Mr. Beasley positioned Lena at the top of Arthur's femur. Lena could hardly bear to look at the twisted leg. "I'm going to pull from the ankle to straighten the leg out so that it heals properly. Your job is to hold the leg as tightly as you can."

Tentatively, Lena placed both hands on the old man's muscled thigh.

"You'll have to grip harder than that." Mr. Beasley put his own hands over Lena's and squeezed firmly to show how much force was needed.

If she hadn't been holding tight, the leg would have jerked from her hands. Lena heard a tremendous snap but saw nothing because her eyes were squeezed shut at the last moment. When she opened them, Arthur Pollet's leg was back in normal alignment and a trickle of sweat was making its way down Mr. Beasley's face. Mr. Pollet thrashed about on the bed and then lay still, breathing regularly.

"I couldn't watch," Lena confessed.

Mr. Beasley ran a hand over his bald head. "The leg is the least of his worries."

"What do you mean?"

"He hit his head, and with a head injury you can never tell what will happen. We'll just watch and wait. I suspect he's broken a few ribs as well. I'll need to talk to Leticia, but there's no need to alarm her yet."

They returned to the kitchen, where Jimson had managed to calm Mrs. Pollet and was buttering himself a scone.

Mr. Beasley placed a large hand on Leticia's shoulder. "His leg is aligned now, but he needs plenty of rest. The next day or two will be critical as we see how that head wound develops."

"Critical? What do you mean?" Her dark eyes looked fierce, but Lena noticed her lips tremble.

"Jimson, perhaps you and Lena could finish his work in the garden? Cut off the damaged tree limbs and gather up the debris. There won't be many days left to get ready for winter."

Glad to have something constructive to do, Lena and Jimson retreated to the yard to pick up branches and stake damaged plants. It felt good to be in the sun after so many days cooped up in the library. Mrs. Mumbles accompanied them to the yard, rubbing between Lena's legs until she shooed her out of the way. Offended, Mrs. Mumbles ignored them altogether and went off in search of rodents in the tall grasses. Lena inhaled deeply. "I helped Mr. Beasley straighten the leg. It was awful."

Jimson nodded. "I've never much cared for blood and guts, myself. It always makes me hurt just to look at it."

Lena went on to describe the process in detail, but Jimson seemed distracted, as if he was only half listening. He grabbed a handsaw and began sawing some of the larger limbs into small pieces.

"Do you believe in angels?" he asked without looking up.

"What?" Lena paused, her arms full of twigs. "Is that what you wanted to talk to me about earlier?"

He nodded. "Angels. I don't believe in 'em. But I'm quite sure I saw one—yesterday, when I was on the roof. Here, hold this." He gestured to one end of a large twisted branch.

She dropped the branches into the wheelbarrow and steadied the limb as Jimson began sawing. "Explain what you just said to me."

"Yesterday, when I was up on the roof landing where Mr. Beasley's got the flying machine, I saw someone on the widow's walk. I took a second look because I couldn't imagine anyone being out in the storm. It wasn't raining yet"—he snapped the branch in half—"just winding." He paused. "You'll think I'm crazy. There was a lady looking out toward the sea. I could see her profile. And on her back was . . . a wing." His eyes caught Lena's. "At first I thought it was a trick of the light, but it was a wing, all right."

"Are you sure it wasn't just a shawl caught up in the wind?"

He shook his head. "I'm sure. It was gray, I think. But you couldn't mistake the shape of it. And when she turned, I saw another one coming out of her left shoulder blade." He reached behind Lena and poked her back. "Right here." After a pause, he continued. "They were big, like an eagle's wings."

Heart hammering, Lena thought of the drawing of the Annuncius syndrome in the sketchbook. But the wings in that picture were small, shrunken things—nothing like an eagle's wings.

"Do you think I'm losing my mind?"

Lena smoothed her skirt under herself and sat on the grass. "No, I don't. Here, there's something I want to show you, too." She pulled the now-crumpled flyer from her skirt pocket and smoothed it flat on the ground.

Jimson squatted beside her and read it quickly. He gave a derisive laugh. "The government's trying to pull the wool over our eyes," he declared. "Set people up as scapegoats to blame whatever goes wrong in society on them. No one will believe this stuff."

"But what if it's true? What if the woman you saw—and the drawings in the sketchbook—what if they're all true? What if there *are* Peculiars and Mr. Beasley is experimenting on them?" A gust of wind blew her hair free from its twist, and strands caught like webs across her face.

"But there are no such things as Peculiars. There couldn't be. It's all superstition and—" He lowered himself the rest of the way to the grass.

"Just for one minute consider that you might be wrong, Jimson Quiggley. What if it *is* true? You're always saying that we have to consider the evidence. And according to this"—she shook the flyer in her hand—"you usually can't tell by looking at someone."

"And now I've seen a lady with wings." He pulled up a blade of grass and chewed it thoughtfully. "If Peculiars exist, they'd be a dying race. They'd be genetic variations—part of a group who evolved differently from everyone else. But this piece of propaganda doesn't prove anything. It will just have people turning in the neighbor they don't like. It's dangerous to think that way."

"What Peculiars have in common could be on the inside, too. Maybe they're all compelled to do horrible things." Lena tucked the flyer away. Clouds scuttled across the sun. She shivered. Overhead a seagull screamed.

Jimson stood and brushed off his pants. Then he offered

Lena a hand and pulled her up. "Lena, what's frightening you?"

Jimson's eyes were kind. She wanted to tell him about her fears, but she shook her head and turned away when her eyes filled with tears. Anytime now she, too, might do something dangerous and unpredictable.

"You're right. We have to be objective and consider all possibilities." Jimson spoke to her back. "We can't just speculate; we need evidence."

Lena ran a gloved hand across her eyes and turned back to face Jimson. "How do we find the evidence?"

"We start with the winged lady. We won't ask Mr. Beasley. We'll just do a little exploring on our own." He wrinkled his brow. "She was someone I've never seen before. I didn't even know there was anyone else staying here. But then, I'm beginning to suspect there are lots of things we don't know about Zephyr House."

CHAPTER 16

EXPLORATIONS

JIMSON WAS AS GOOD AS HIS WORD. THAT NIGHT AS THE CLOCK struck one o'clock, when the house was groaning with sleep, Lena made her way down the hall to the first floor, where Jimson waited. She had dressed in layers to keep out the chill, but still she shivered.

Jimson had come prepared. A black cap was pulled low over his messy curls, and he wore a long black coat that Lena had never seen before. He held up an ornately cast brass cylinder with a reflector on one side and a clamp on the back. "It's a bicycle lamp," he whispered theatrically. "The light shines out here. The clamp holds it onto the bicycle." He tapped the part Lena thought of as a reflector. "It's fueled by kerosene, so you can ride at night."

"We're not taking the bicycle, are we?" Lena's heart beat a little faster.

"Of course not, but we might need some light, especially

when we go outside; there's no moon. It's the only thing I could find right away."

Lena wrapped her arms around herself. "What exactly are we looking for?"

"The winged lady . . . and anything else that we might find."

"But we can't just go opening doors."

"Of course we can. We'll be like Stanley, exploring uncharted territory, looking for Dr. Livingstone. See here, I've sketched a map." Jimson unfolded a drawing of Zephyr House. "I've never been in this whole wing of the house. If she's here, I bet that's where she'll be. The problem is that to get there, you have to walk right by Mr. Beasley's door, unless you enter from the outside. We should go out through the back terrace. That way no one will hear us."

In the night nothing was the same. Darkness transformed even the most familiar objects into something sinister. Lena was glad that this time she had Jimson with her, and she felt a thrill as they moved silently down the corridor toward the door that opened on to the terrace. From the corner of her eye, Lena caught a glimpse of something moving. She reached out and silently grabbed Jimson's arm. He stopped without a word. She looked again, and the thing she glimpsed took shape . . . her own form caught in the hall mirror. Her shoulders lowered; she took a deep breath. In moments they would be on the terrace.

That's when the screaming began. At first Lena thought

it was the whistle she had heard when she had gone after Mr. Beasley's sketchbook. But it wasn't. It was a woman's scream, high-pitched and horrible. Lena crouched, covering her ears. Jimson nudged her into the deeper shadows of a corner. His voice was in her ear. "Stay still. I can't tell where it's coming from."

A door banged open in the distance. Running footsteps across the stone floors. A light bobbed outside the terrace door. A lantern. For a moment Lena saw a face pressed against the window glass, heard someone rattling the lock. She knew that face! It was the redheaded man from the train, the man who had been with the nun, one of the men who had helped the prisoner escape. The face was gone as quickly as it appeared. Lena's breath came in gulps. She pressed her mouth against Jimson's ear. "Did you see him? It was the man from the train!" But Jimson shook his head. He had been looking back down the hallway where they had heard the sound of running footsteps.

The screaming had stopped, but Lena was sure she could hear a woman sobbing. The sound of voices, men's voices, muted. She felt as if she had been frozen in the dark corner forever. A gaslight sputtered to life, bathing the hall in light. Mr. Beasley stood wrapped in a peacock-blue dressing gown.

"Jimson, Lena, I see you were awakened too." He rubbed his hand across his face. There was something different about him, Lena thought. Then she realized what it was: His painted eyebrows were missing, and their absence gave him a curiously blank look. He didn't seem to notice that they weren't dressed in nightclothes. "It's Mr. Pollet. I'm afraid he's dead. The blow to his head was as bad as I thought. Leticia is taking it very hard. I've given her something to help her rest."

Jimson recovered first. "Is there anything we can do, sir?"

"There's nothing more to be done until morning."

Lena was still trembling from her view of the redheaded man at the door. "Mr. Beasley, there was a man on the terrace. I think it was the same man I saw on the train."

At first Mr. Beasley acted as if he hadn't heard her. He cinched the belt of his dressing gown tighter. "I'm going to the kitchen for some warm milk; milk is a great soporific." He met Lena's eyes. "I can't imagine what a man would be doing out and about on our terrace at this hour. Why don't you come and have some milk with me? Perhaps Jimson will go out on the terrace to investigate, seeing that he is already equipped with one of my bicycle lanterns." It was the only mention he made of their dubious appearance in the hallway. He turned and walked past them toward the kitchen wing.

"You shouldn't have said that," warned Jimson. "If something strange is going on, we don't want to put Mr. Beasley on guard. Are you sure it wasn't just a reflection or something?"

"That man helped a prisoner escape from the train, a Peculiar. He's obviously dangerous. And I *did* see his face at the door."

"I'm just saying that things look different at night. I'm going out on the terrace, as Mr. Beasley suggested. But if it was your man from the train, I'm sure he's gone by now."

"I'm going with you. I'm not about to go off to the kitchen for warm milk." Lena's face burned. "I know what I saw."

Jimson merely tipped his head and walked off. Lena followed.

The air was chill with damp wind off the sea. The lamp sputtered to life and Jimson held it high as they paced the stone terrace from one end to the other. The dim light cast flickering shadows against the imposing walls of Zephyr House. There was nothing to be seen, only the black night without moon or stars. The darkness was accompanied by the crash of waves far below.

"It doesn't prove anything," Lena said.

"No, it doesn't. There's no more proof than when I saw a woman with wings." Jimson lowered the light.

"But we both know what we saw."

Jimson looked at her over the lantern. "It would be nice if someone else could observe it too. See the south wing, by the orchard?" He pointed. "I've never been in there. It's where I was hoping we could explore tonight. The widow's walk is on the south end of the house. The woman I saw could have gotten there if she had access from a door on the third story." The wind blew the tails of his long coat out behind him. "But with Mr. Beasley up and all, I guess it will have to wait."

Lena thought about Leticia Pollet's cries. "I haven't

even taken a minute to feel sorry about Mr. Pollet; I've been so busy worrying about the red-haired man." She looked in the direction of the sea, but it had been swallowed by the dark.

"You're right. It's terrible. Arthur was a good man. And Mrs. Pollet will be lost without him."

"Jimson, what if we're both right? What if the man from the train *and* the winged woman are both hidden here somewhere?"

The light from the lantern ravaged Jimson's face with shadows. "Then I'm sure Mr. Beasley has a rational explanation for it all."

But Lena thought again of the marshal's words and wasn't at all sure.

Jimson was standing next to her, so close that she could hear his breathing. "You forgot your gloves."

Lena looked at her hands, ghostly in the lantern light. Somehow under the cover of dark, the gloves hadn't seemed necessary. Jimson tentatively reached out and gently placed one long spidery hand in his open palm.

Lena flinched.

"They're so beautiful, so fragile."

She found it difficult to catch her breath, but she didn't withdraw her hand. No one, besides her father, had ever called her hands beautiful before.

"Are there other people with hands like yours?"

"I think so, but I've never met anyone."

He turned her hand over, palm up, and ran a finger down the length of it, to the tip of her index finger. Lena watched his face, but his eyes were hidden in pools of shadow.

"Jimson, my doctor told us that my hands and feet . . ." She couldn't continue.

Jimson curled his hand over hers. "Go on. Your hands and feet what?"

She took a deep breath. "That my hands and feet are part of a syndrome that is rarely seen anymore. He said they were old signs of . . . goblinism."

The word hung between them. Lena was acutely aware of Jimson's warm hand wrapped around her own. She was acutely aware of his silence.

"He said that? Then he's nothing more than an old quack! You don't believe that, do you?"

"I don't know—"

"What did your parents say?" His voice was angry now. His grip on her hand tightened.

"My father left when I was five, and Nana Crane, my grandmother, always called him a goblin. He"—she searched for words—"had a difficult time."

"'Goblin' is just an old slang term. You know that. Anyone who's a troublemaker used to be called a goblin. So your grandmother didn't like your father."

Lena pulled her hand back and let it fall. "It's more than that. Dr. Crink agreed that he probably is a goblin. He said most people don't recognize the signs anymore, but he still

does. Don't you see what that means? I might be half Peculiar."
She was glad that the dark hid her flushed face and wet eyes.

"No wonder you're so worried about them." Jimson set the
lantern down and placed his hands on her shoulders. "Lena,
your mother must have known about your father. You are not
half Peculiar. You might not be like any girl I know, but—"

She cut him off. "My mother never says much about him.
But I've heard that he's done some terrible things."

"What kind of things?"

"I don't know. I don't want to talk about it." She felt a
desperate need to flee, but Jimson's grip was warm and
steadying.

And then in the silence, Jimson chuckled. The noise
startled Lena. She pulled away.

"It's nothing to laugh at. I may be just like him."

"I'm sorry. It's just that you, of all people . . . You're so
proper, so polite, and you're worried that—"

"No. Stop. You don't know what I'm like on the inside. You
can't know what it's like always wondering. I need to know."

A rectangle of light flooded the terrace. Mr. Beasley's
head protruded through the door. "I assume we're safe? No
intruders? Come in, then. I've got some warm milk ready for
both of you."

CHAPTER 17

A DISTRESSING DISCOVERY

DESPITE THE WARM MILK, LENA HADN'T SLEPT THE REST OF the night. She arose with a thundering headache to a gloomy household. As she pulled on a pair of black gloves, she rebuked herself for the previous evening. She had revealed too much. Now Jimson would see her as a freak or more likely a seriously deluded person. Not that it mattered—she couldn't afford to let Jimson or anyone else derail her from her quest. She bundled her thick hair into a loose bun and in deference to Leticia Pollet draped her black silk shawl across her shoulders.

Mrs. Pollet seemed to have caved in on herself during the night. Red-eyed and silent, she insisted on serving tea over Mr. Beasley's protests, claiming that work made things more bearable. Lena slipped into a chair at the far end of the breakfast table, avoiding Jimson's eye as she remembered the touch of his finger running the length of her palm. Mr. Beasley, eyebrows carefully in place once more, informed them that the funeral was set for two days hence, when Arthur Pollet's brother would arrive. He asked Lena and Jimson to take over Arthur's job of harvesting the small orchard until he could hire someone else. Meanwhile, he would drive Leticia Pollet into Knoster to make the funeral arrangements.

"Work in the library will have to be temporarily suspended until we get through the next week. Apples need to be picked and the squash harvested before the first hard frost. Jimson, there are ladders in the shed and buckets as well."

Jimson seemed eager to ignore Lena. "I'll go and get started, then." He drained his teacup and left the table.

In the kitchen Lena tied one of Mrs. Pollet's well-worn aprons over her own plain dress. Since she would be working all morning in the orchard, she was glad that she had dressed sensibly and chosen her practical dress. Her home in the City had only window boxes to cultivate and a small square of lawn off the back steps, which her mother called a handkerchief garden. She hoped that Jimson would know what they were supposed to do.

The leaves of the apple trees were gold, and scarlet fruit hung heavy in the branches. The hedge of sumac lining the orchard burned red. It was as if the entire world had caught fire overnight. The orchard was small, only thirty trees on the south side of the house. Jimson had already set up a tall picking ladder at the base of a tree.

"There are buckets and boxes in the garden shed. Come help me carry some out."

The shed was long and low, built of miscellaneous woods. The one window let a little light into the dimness. It seemed to function as a workshop, a gardening shed, and a place to store odds and ends. A workbench ran the length of one wall. An assortment of tools hung neatly above it. At the far end of the shed a jumble of discarded items had been dumped in a hasty pile—an old wooden birdcage, a bicycle wheel, numerous broken crates—all ready for the incinerator.

"That seems to be the gardening section," Jimson said, pointing to a short wall where hoes and rakes hung above shovels and hoses. There was a tall stack of wooden crates on the floor beneath. "It's quite a place, isn't it?" Lena could hear the delight in his voice.

"Well, it's interesting. I suppose those are the boxes we use? I've never done any gardening or orchard work before. We live in the City."

"Don't worry. My mother has always had a huge vegetable garden. Some years it was the only way to feed all of us. And we have fruit trees too—apple, plum, and peach. I'll climb the ladder and wear the picking apron. Then you can fill the crates."

Lena had made her way over to the jumble of discards. "This must be where everything from the house ends up. Look, there's even an old child's wagon."

"Help me with the crates, Lena. We'd better get started."

At the bottom of the pile something white and soft gray caught her eye. She bent down. Then tugged away several of the discards. "Jimson, come here! There are feathers and blood!"

Two severed wings the size of an eagle's had been buried under the pile of discarded items waiting for the incinerator. Cartilage protruded from the end of the feathers, which were discolored with the rust of blood. Lena felt her stomach heave. If the sun had not filtered through the window at just the right angle, she might never have noticed them.

Jimson poked them with his finger and whistled. "Looks like a big bird was killed."

Lena's throat grew tight. "Or something's happened to your winged lady." Again she thought of the drawings in Mr. Beasley's sketchbook and of the marshal's words.

They were both quiet, and then Jimson spoke. "We can't go jumping to conclusions. It's a pair of severed wings, but we can't assume what they're from. But it looks like Mr. Pollet had a pile ready for the incinerator."

"I'm going to take some feathers." Lena gathered a small clump in her gloved hands and put them in the oversized pocket of the kitchen apron. "Now what do we do?"

"Nothing for the moment. I don't know enough about different kinds of birds. I think we'd better get to work." Lena could hear the uncertainty in his voice. "Keep your eyes and ears open. I'm going to do some investigating later."

"Not without me, you're not!"

Jimson shot her a look she couldn't read.

In silence they carried stacks of wooden crates and placed them next to the ladder. Lena inhaled the smell of apples and damp earth.

"You get the lower branches. I'll get the higher ones."

Lena started to protest, but Jimson looked pointedly at her feet.

"Go ahead then."

The rhythm of picking apples, dropping them one by one into the basket on her arm, and then dumping the basketload into a crate, was soothing. But all the while Lena was conscious of the clutch of feathers in her pocket. She looked up through gold leaves burnished by the sun. "I don't think we can wait. We need to find your winged woman and make sure she's all right. I have an awful feeling that there's something terrible going on here."

"It could be a coincidence. Things aren't always what they seem. That's one of the principles of science." Jimson sounded as if he was trying to convince himself. "But you're right. We need to keep searching. I just can't believe Mr. Beasley's up to no good, no matter what the evidence says. Lena, let's promise we won't do anything until we talk to each other first."

By noon Lena's arms ached. Six wooden crates were full to overflowing with apples. She looked down the row of trees and realized that they had barely made a start. Jimson had been humming quietly, not his usual talkative self, but then Lena barely felt like talking either, the weight of their discovery subduing her.

Just after noon Mr. Beasley returned in a cab with Leticia Pollet and another passenger.

"It's time to take a break for lunch," Mr. Beasley called

in their direction. Lena hardly dared look at him, but she recognized the passenger who climbed from the car. It was Milo, the man she had met on the beach. "I've brought someone to help us. He's willing to help with the apple harvest."

"We met when I first came to Knob Knoster," Lena said.

Milo was wearing the same cap and the same coat with baggy pockets that she remembered from their previous meeting.

"Ah, the young miss that wants to go to Scree."

"So you've met Lena." Mr. Beasley gestured toward Jimson. "And this is my librarian, Jimson Quiggley."

Milo nodded. "Pleased to meetcher."

Mrs. Pollet insisted on serving lunch, again over Mr. Beasley's protestations. It was a hearty soup she had made earlier in the week. Her severe black dress made her face even paler. Lena noticed that her eyes were dry now, but she was still silent.

"Looks like the mail's come." She carried the day's correspondence in on the silver mail tray. "A letter for you, Mr. Jimson."

Lena couldn't help noticing that the fat letter smelled decidedly like perfume.

"And a letter for you as well." Mrs. Pollet placed a slim envelope at Lena's place. Lena snatched it up, hoping it was news from home. Instead, the return address, lettered in a cramped hand, was that of her cousin. Lena took a last spoonful of soup.

"Please excuse me. The soup was wonderful, Mrs. Pollet. Just what we needed after working in the orchard all morning." She left the rest of them at the kitchen table and made her way to her room.

Her gloves were dusty from the work in the orchard, and she gratefully peeled them off. Then she stretched her fingers wide, trying not to think of Jimson's words as he held her hand in his own. What business did an engaged man have, talking like that? Then she undid the laces of her alligator boots, still damp from the orchard grass, and rubbed her tender feet. Using a brass letter knife, she sliced open the thin envelope and unfolded the single sheet. The same cramped writing. She quickly scanned the closing. The letter wasn't from her cousin at all. It bore the signature of Thomas Saltre.

October 25, 1888

Dear Lena,

I would appreciate the chance to speak with you in person two days from now. My job requires that I leave town for several days. I would like to see you before I leave. And I am sure that you will have information that will be beneficial to us both. Please meet me on the pier at 3 o'clock.

Your servant,

Thomas

Lena folded the letter and returned it to the envelope. She retrieved her purse from the dresser and removed the contents of her wallet. She had saved every penny of her salary since starting work at Zephyr House three weeks prior. The amount was meager, but Mr. Beasley had provided a small advance so that she might purchase necessities. A few weeks more and she would have enough to purchase supplies for Scree. The marshal had promised her a guide if she supplied him with information. Perhaps the marshal would take her himself. She rested her chin on her steepled fingers. Staying in this house any longer than necessary was unthinkable. She would be sorry to leave Jimson, but he had his Pansy.

She pulled the sketchbook out from under her pillow and riffled through the pages, hunting for the Annuncius syndrome. There were the wings protruding from shoulder blades, just as Jimson had described them, just as she had found in the refuse pile of the garden shed. No, she couldn't leave until she found the woman. She looked down at her hands and feet. She might be next. It was time to show the sketches to the marshal, no matter what Jimson thought. In another hour she would be needed back in the orchard. She lay on her side, curled in like a comma, and slept.

"My father was a fisherman. He loved the ocean. But Mother, she loved the land. I been working on both land and sea as long as I can remember." Milo picked apples at a steady clip and talked just as steadily. "Zephyr House used to be a working farm, but that's long before Tobias Beasley came and added all these curlicues and doodads to it. Used to be the old Guthrie place. One of the few families round here that had nothin' to do with fishing or whaling. They're the ones planted this orchard. Mostly Baldwins and Belmonts, from the look of it."

"So, what happened to the Guthries?" Lena found Milo's stories a good distraction. They made the work go faster. On the other hand, she couldn't talk to Jimson about searching for the winged woman.

"They got gold fever—every last one of 'em."

"You mean they took off for the California gold rush?" Jimson asked from somewhere up in the leaves.

"No, I mean they headed north to Scree."

"But Scree doesn't have gold, does it?" Lena took a bite of a large red apple and let the sweet juice wet her mouth and throat.

"Scree has more resources than most folks know. It's got the richest coal and copper mines anywhere. There's always been rumors of other veins as well. Gold ore for the taking, and silver mines. 'Course most of the land was undeveloped, and no one really knew for sure what was up there. Looks like this crate is full. Mind you keep the ones that are too bird-pecked out. Leticia can use 'em for pies."

"So, did the Guthries find gold?" Jimson heaved the ladder to the next tree.

"If they did, I never heard about it. They never came back. Old man Guthrie had three sons. All of 'em redheads, just like him. They went off together, along with Mrs. Guthrie. The youngest boy was still in knee pants. House finally went up for auction, and that's when Tobias bought it. Not many folks would walk away from property like this unless they made their fortune or unless sumthin' unfortunate happened to 'em."

"You've been to Scree, haven't you?" Lena asked.

"Ah-yuh, but it's been a long time. Scree was just Scree then. It wasn't protected by our gov'ment." Milo gave a dry bark of a laugh.

"What was it like then?" Lena asked.

"It wasn't as empty as the gov'ment would like you to believe. Scree's a beautiful place, wild and full of life. The folks that lived there liked it that way. Adventurers came north to make their fortune, like Guthrie and his sons, and developed large mines, but there's always been mining in Scree. The native folks were mining long before we showed up."

Lena craned her neck to look up at Milo, who perched like a gargoyle on the top rung of a ladder. "What kind of native folks?"

"Folks we might find a bit peculiar. Now the gov'ment's making them work like slaves in their own mines. Ain't right . . . ain't right a'tall."

CHAPTER 18

LENA SPIES A WINGED GIRL AND MAKES A PACT

THE FUNERAL WAS A SMALL AFFAIR, CONDUCTED AT THE EDGE OF a cliff facing the sea. Leticia Pollet had insisted that her husband be buried on Mr. Beasley's land because it was the place where he had been happiest.

The sky, Lena thought, was too blue for a funeral, the sun too mellow, and the entire world too alive to commemorate death. Arthur's younger brother, Edwin, had arrived from the Middle West and stood awkwardly next to Leticia, his head crowned at her chin. His pale wrists jutted from the cuffs of an ill-made suit, and he wore shiny spats. Arthur and Edwin had not been close, Leticia had informed them, but Edwin was Arthur's only living relative—a banker, never married and terminally shy. He kept his chin down, his eyes focused on some imaginary spot beyond the open grave. He looked, Lena decided, as if he might bolt at any moment.

The only other guests were Milo and the Crimptons, an elderly brother and sister from Knoster who had known Arthur from a time before his life at Zephyr House.

As the minister droned a reading, Lena let her eyes roam and her thoughts wander. It was the first time she'd been to a funeral. Jimson had been to two, each time for a grandparent. He wore the same poor traveling suit Lena had scorned on the train. Here on the edge of the world with the sea as backdrop, it didn't look half so bad, she decided. She could feel him next to her, and a glance from the corner of her eye showed him leaning in to catch the minister's words. Mrs. Pollet was still and dry-eyed—a tall, gaunt crow in an open field, sheltered on one side by Mr. Beasley's large and comforting presence and on the other by the nervous Edwin Pollet.

If anyone had asked Lena how she felt, she wouldn't have been able to answer. She didn't feel much at all. She was sorry for Mrs. Pollet and she would miss quiet Arthur, but she had no overwhelming feelings of grief, and this troubled her. Perhaps she was like Nana Crane's description of her father: small-hearted and unfeeling.

The casket was plain pine, topped with a wreath of chrysanthemums because Mrs. Pollet said they were Arthur's favorite flower. Mr. Beasley had asked permission to plant a sapling apple tree on the grave because Arthur had taken such care of the orchard. Lena listened as the minister in a long, dark robe read from the Bible. As the hopeful words washed over her, a movement just on the edge of the field caught Lena's attention. A young woman, half hidden by a narrow poplar, stood perfectly still. She reminded Lena of a deer caught on the road, intent, every muscle alert to danger. Lena nudged Jimson. He frowned in her direction.

"Look over there, by the poplar row," she whispered.

The young woman was tall and angular. Her hair was the color of wheat, and the wind tossed it about her face.

Jimson hissed in her ear. "It's her! The woman from the widow's walk."

"What?" Lena jerked her head around in surprise.

That was all it took. The woman, like that startled deer, fled. Lena watched her retreating wingless back.

"I must have been seeing things." Jimson ran his fingers through his hair until the curls stood out in wild peaks. "I would have sworn she had wings." He spoke quietly so no one else at the small reception would hear him. The guests were huddled in the parlor of Zephyr House and speaking in hushed voices. "I think it was the same woman, but she was far enough away that it wouldn't be easy to tell."

Lena took a bite of apple crisp drenched with clotted cream. "Remember that the wings we found were severed. She might have had wings at one time." She licked the edge of her spoon. "She didn't want anyone to see her. She ran as soon as she saw me looking at her."

"I'm going to find her and talk to her this afternoon. Do you want to come with me?" Jimson asked.

Lena looked down at her empty plate. "I have an errand to run in town. I told my cousin I'd meet her for tea." If Jimson saw her eyes, he'd know she was lying.

"Lena, remember we said we wouldn't do anything without telling the other person first? Well, I'm telling you now. I'm going to try and find her and put an end to all this speculation."

Lena nodded. "I'd better clear the dishes. I don't want Mrs. Pollet to have to do anything today." If she didn't busy herself with a task, she was sure Jimson would be able to read her mind.

By early afternoon Lena had managed to escape the small reception at Zephyr House and boarded a coach into Knoster. The sketchbook and a clump of feathers were stowed in a large satchel she'd found in the library. It was just before three o'clock when the coach stopped near the pier and Lena climbed out.

The marshal was waiting on the pier, as he had promised. He was looking out to sea, his shoulders hunched and forearms resting on the worn wooden railing. Lena was able to observe him for a moment before he saw her. He was strong and handsome, but she realized for the first time that his real appeal came from the force of his charm. With the sea as background, he looked smaller, less intimidating. But then, the ocean could make anything look insignificant, she thought. The water was choppy with whitecaps, and a stiff breeze was blowing in from the west, sending the seagulls spiraling toward shore. Lena gripped her handbag tighter. It was time to tell the marshal what she knew.

He saw Lena when she was a few feet away and turned toward her. His blue eyes looked washed out, deep-set in their tiredness. "Lena." He tipped his bowler, then took it off his head completely before the wind sent it flying. "I'm so pleased you could join me. Shall we stroll?" Without waiting for an answer, he tucked Lena's hand over his arm and led her into the wind.

"As I told you, I'll be leaving town for a few days. I confess I'll miss having the opportunity to meet with you. You give me something to look forward to." He cast her a sideways glance. "I'm depending on you, Lena, hoping that you have something to tell me that might help me with my investigations. There are so few people I can trust completely. I know I can trust you."

Lena had to lean in to catch his words before the wind swallowed them. She felt the warmth of his body, the strength of his arm, just as she felt the weight of the sketchbook and feathers in the satchel. Still, she didn't speak.

"I went to Cloister. You were right. Beasley's got something going on there. Those sisters know a damn sight more than they'll say. Pardon my French, Lena."

"Did you find anything, Thomas?" She spoke his name hesitantly.

He squeezed her hand. "I found a pretty suspicious-looking fellow in that infirmary of theirs. Of course, I wasn't allowed to examine him, and they had some clever story about why they had a man all tucked up in one of the infirmary beds. He was a Peculiar, all right. I could positively smell it."

Lena shivered at his last words, and the marshal drew her arm closer. Perhaps Mr. Beasley was doing medical experiments with the help of the sisters. It was now or never, Lena thought. "I did find something at Zephyr House you might be interested in." Her heart pounded so loudly, it was a wonder the marshal could hear her words.

They passed an elderly couple strolling arm in arm. The marshal nodded at them, then bent his head close to Lena's. "Wait till we get to the end. It will be more private." They strolled to the pier's end. "Now, what have you got for me?"

Lena opened the satchel and drew out the small sketchbook. "I found this in the library. It's a book of medical drawings. The ones you might be interested in are in the back, but we need to be out of the wind before I can open it." She rummaged in the bag again. "And these feathers." As she spoke, the wind whipped several from her hand and spun them out over the water.

"Ah, my dear girl! We mustn't lose the evidence!" The marshal hurried her back to the Parasol. She could hear his breathing as they walked, eager and labored, like someone who couldn't quite catch his breath.

The tearoom was filling up primarily with ladies seeking the comfort of afternoon tea out of the wind. The marshal and Lena chose a back table. Lena flipped the book open to the strange sketches of Annuncius syndrome and of the boy with the forked tongue. The marshal pulled out a pair of spectacles Lena had never seen him use before and bent low over the pages.

"Hmm, Peculiars. There's no denying it. We had a boy who tried to saw the wings off his own back about a year or two ago. He was half dead by the time we found him, died soon after. I kept the story quiet. He was the only one I've seen like that in my lifetime." He looked up and folded his glasses. "You said Beasley made these sketches."

"Yes, I believe so." Something was constricting her throat. She took a swallow of tea. Then she drew out the rest of the feathers, spreading them on the table. "We found these, part of a severed set of wings in the garden shed, near the incinerator."

"By all that's holy!" The marshal looked as if he'd just won a prize. His mouth rode up to meet his mustache and his eyes burned. "So he's got one out there, does he?"

"And I think I saw the man from the train. The redheaded one who was with the nun."

"You have just done your country an honor, Lena Mattacascar. Even an old reprobate like Saul should be proud of you." He ran his fingers through his mustache. "And you have proved my opinion of you: intelligent *and* comely."

Lena found she couldn't meet his gaze. Blood was flowing to her face. The marshal reached out and brushed a stray lock of hair away from her eyes, letting his finger rest on her cheek. "Now, I need a little more evidence than a pile of feathers. Here's what I plan to do. I want you to ascertain just where he's holding the Peculiars. Soon as I get back, I'll do a raid on Beasley's place. Four days from now, October thirty-first. Don't worry. You'll be protected. Don't know what a crazy character like Beasley might do when he knows we're onto his scheme."

Lena's heart faltered at the word "raid." "And Jimson will be protected too? He's been helping me with gathering evidence."

"Jimson." The marshal snorted. "He's just a boy who doesn't know what he's gotten into. But Jimson too, if he cooperates. This will be purely a rescue operation. We'll get those Peculiars out of there and off to Scree before Beasley can do any more harm."

Lena felt the knot in her chest relax. The marshal had everything under control. Whatever Beasley was doing, he wouldn't be allowed to hurt anyone, even if they were Peculiar.

"I'll get word to you as soon as I return."

Lena nodded, feeling certain that she had made the right choice.

The walk up to Zephyr House was hidden in shadow when Lena returned from Knob Knoster. The sky was clear, and the poplars were silhouettes against a fading twilight. There would be frost by morning, and within a month the snows would begin in earnest. Lena pictured the marshal sweeping down like a storm on Zephyr House, pounding on the door, a small army of federal officers rushing through the corridors searching for Peculiars and their grateful cries at being rescued.

She pictured Mr. Beasley, his painted eyebrows raised in mock surprise. All along he must have known it would come to this. Then she pictured the marshal offering to be her personal guide into Scree. Twenty-five or -six, she decided, was the perfect age—just old enough to give a man maturity and experience.

When she pushed open the door, she could hear chatter coming from the dining room. She returned the satchel to her bedroom, then walked into the dining room with her scarf still wrapped around the neck of her dark wool jacket.

"Lena, you've made it back in time for supper. I hope your cousin is well," Mr. Beasley said. Lena nodded.

Jimson caught her eye and winked. On his right sat Edwin Pollet, stiffly formal, and across from Jimson was the round little minister who had presided over the funeral. And to his left, Leticia Pollet sat in somber black.

"The Crimptons are serving dinner tonight to give Leticia a rest. Come have a seat, Lena. In the midst of all this sorrow, I've a piece of good news to share."

Bewildered, Lena unwound her scarf and removed her jacket, then accepted the chair next to Mr. Beasley. On his other side, Milo was appreciating a glass of good wine. When she had left, they had just finished a funeral; now Mr. Beasley looked as if he would burst with excitement, and Jimson kept watching her as if he had something important to say. The knot re-formed in Lena's stomach as she looked from Jimson to Mr. Beasley.

"I've made a discovery that may change the future of air

travel. Titantum! It has a greater strength-to-weight ratio of any other known metal. In other words, anything fabricated from titantum will be incredibly strong, and sufficiently light!"

Jimson leaned toward Lena. "The boilers! We can make the boilers from titantum! You can make the entire ship from titantum!"

"*If* we can keep the metal uncontaminated during the welding process."

The minister looked slightly befuddled and even more confused when Leticia Pollet stood and proposed a toast to titantum and Mr. Beasley's incredible discovery. It must have been the strangest funeral reception he had ever taken part in. The Crimptons brought in fish and baked ham. Leticia alternated between guest at the table and running out to the kitchen to help with the next course. In his excitement, Mr. Beasley shouted at Edwin Pollet about the undiscovered wonders of steam-powered flying machines. Surprisingly, the minister had once conducted a service in a dirigible and was able to entertain them all with the story.

This is probably just the type of reception Arthur Pollet would have enjoyed, Lena thought. Then her thoughts drifted to the marshal, and her contentment vanished. Who knew what suffering might be going on in other rooms of this house while they enjoyed themselves around the table? She studied Jimson's animated face. She would tell him tonight and confess what she'd done. He'd applaud her courage and initiative.

"And did you hear, Lena, that we are to be graced with a

visit from Jimson's fiancée?" Mr. Beasley was looking in her direction, his cheeks rosy from wine, one eyebrow painted slightly higher than the other.

Lena snapped back to the conversation. She looked at Jimson, who seemed to have shrunken just the slightest bit. "Pansy's coming?"

"Day after tomorrow. She arrives on the one o'clock coach."

The dinner lasted well into the evening, after which Mr. Beasley proposed cigars in his study for the men. Lena was left with Leticia and Mrs. Crimpton. The two were talking, over tea and cakes, about people Lena had never met. She excused herself to wash dishes in the kitchen. She dropped her gloves on the counter, ran the hot water, and hoped that Jimson would appear before long. Even in the warm kitchen she could feel the cold seeping in around the windows. Outside, the moon glittered, hard and bright as a penny.

She was drying the last cup and saucer when Jimson came into the kitchen, trailing a waft of cigar smoke. "I didn't find her."

"Who—Pansy?"

"What are you talking about?" He leaned in closer. "The wingless lady. I went to the south wing of the house and searched. Most of the doors were locked. But I did find something I should tell you about."

Lena took her time folding a dishtowel, laying it just so on the counter. She would tell Jimson everything as soon as he was done.

He dropped his voice. "I tried every door on the first floor. Those that weren't locked opened to rooms that were empty or looked like they'd not been used in years."

They were sitting at the scarred old kitchen table now. Lena had wrapped her gloveless hands around a mug of hot tea, but still she felt chilled to the core.

"Just before I was ready to give up and move on, I heard a dreadful banging. I opened a door into a laboratory filled with test tubes and instruments. There were two long padded tables with manacles on each end. They must hold the hands and feet. It looked like an operating room."

Lena gripped the mug more tightly. "What was the banging?" She wasn't sure she wanted the answer and had a strong impulse to cover her ears.

"In the middle of the room was your red-haired man. He was wearing a mask and heating something that he gripped with iron tongs, and then he would bang away at it. His shirt was off and sweat was pouring down. I don't think he saw me. It was like a scene out of a horror story. Did you ever read Shelley's *Frankenstein*?"

"Of course I've read *Frankenstein*. But what was he doing?"

"I don't know, but the worst of it was all the surgical tools laid out." Jimson shuddered. "I'm going to talk to Mr. Beasley."

"You can't!" Lena almost knocked over her mug of tea. "There's something I have to tell you."

She recounted her meetings with the marshal, describing his suspicions that Mr. Beasley was experimenting with

Peculiars, and the marshal's desire to free them. "After we found the wings, I couldn't wait any longer. I showed him the sketchbook and told him about the lady you saw with wings."

But Jimson didn't praise her ingenuity. Instead, his face grew very white. "You *what*? You told him without us talking to Mr. Beasley first? I thought we had a deal—we'd talk to each other before we did anything."

At first Lena cowered under his disapproval. Then she felt a spark of anger ignite, and the flames filled her until her body shook. "It's better than doing nothing, Jimson Quiggley. I can't stand by and let him hurt people, even if they are unnatural. What good would it do asking someone who is in the business of deception? He's lied to us from the beginning. At least I did something!" She pushed away from the table.

The more she raised her voice, the quieter Jimson's became. "You have to give Mr. Beasley a chance. I admit it looks bad, but you can't turn on someone without hearing his side of the story. Now I've got three days to sort this mess out."

"What do you mean *you* have three days?" Lena grabbed her gloves and balled them in her fists. Her voice was loud and rough.

"Well, I can't very well trust you!" Jimson slammed the kitchen door, and the blast of cold air caught Lena full in the face.

CHAPTER 19

PANSY DEMPLE

WHEN PANSY DEMPLE ARRIVED AT ZEPHYR HOUSE, SHE CAME in a Cuthbert coach, which dropped her right at the front steps. Lena had been working and saw the arrival from the library window. She hadn't spoken to Jimson since their argument in the kitchen. All morning he'd picked in the apple orchard with Milo, and neither of them had appeared at lunch. When the coach arrived, Mr. Beasley stuck his head in the library door and invited her to come greet Pansy. Lena was not in the mood to greet anyone but put her work down and followed Mr. Beasley.

The first frost had killed the potted flowers on the steps. Their blackened leaves drooped sadly. If Arthur Pollet had been there, Lena thought, they would have been replaced already with stouthearted golden chrysanthemums. This was a bleak welcome for any guest. The air was sharp, and Lena paused on the front steps, glad for the warmth of her winter tweed jacket over her gray skirt. Her breath exhaled in a puff of white.

Jimson was helping Pansy from the coach, as Mr. Beasley hovered nearby. She extended a small white-gloved hand. Her jacket and skirt were pale blue and tailored. A small veiled hat rested on a cluster of bright yellow curls. She stepped onto the gravel drive with a dainty booted foot, a foot so small it barely protruded from beneath the ruffled hem of her skirt. Lena folded her arms across her chest, hiding her hands in her armpits. She looked down at her ink-stained gray skirt and saw feet that stuck out like two reptiles' snouts beneath the hem. It was going to be a very tiresome day.

"Lena, come and meet Pansy. Pansy, Lena is my other librarian." Mr. Beasley smiled up at Lena as she stood frozen on the steps. There was no recourse but to descend the steps, hoping she wouldn't trip over her own large feet, and meet Pansy Demple face-to-face.

"I am charmed to meet you." A dimple winked fetchingly in one cheek, below eyes like violets.

"It's nice to meet you as well."

Jimson, Lena noticed, did not catch her eye; in fact, he was doing everything he could to avoid her glance.

"In his letters, Jimson has said some very nice things about your work. My, this is the most unusual house I have ever seen." She used one hand to hold her hat to her head as she looked up at the staggered roofline.

"I'll get your bags, Pansy, and Mrs. Pollet will show you to your room. I hope your journey wasn't too strenuous." Jimson gathered her leather traveling case in one hand.

His voice was so formal that Lena had a strange desire to giggle, but she strangled the laugh before it could escape. "Yes, not discommodious, like our journey with an escaped convict on board," Lena said. "Did Jimson tell you there were gunshots and a man dressed as a nun? Well, I'd better get back to work in the library, but I'm sure I'll see you later."

Lena fled back up the steps, longing for the comfort of the library. What had possessed her to say those things to Pansy? She paused just inside the doorway, listening as Pansy exclaimed in shock. Perhaps Jimson had left out that part of his adventure when he invited Pansy to the wilds of Knob Knoster, she thought with satisfaction.

Then Pansy's voice floated through the open door. "Jimson, what's wrong with that girl? Her hands and feet are grotesque."

Lena felt something inside her shrivel. She had heard those words so many times before, but never, ever at Zephyr House. She straightened her spine, preparing to walk down the long corridor to the library, but she couldn't leave—not until she heard Jimson's response.

"Lena's a fine librarian, Pansy. Her hands and feet can't be helped. You'll like her when you get to know her."

A fine librarian? Is that all she was? Jimson could have Pansy Demple, with her dainty hands and feet. Lena, a fine librarian, had her own work to do, and the first thing was to examine the book from Cloister. She marched down the corridor.

Alone in the library, Lena slid open the small drawer in Jimson's desk where he kept the keys to the glass cabinets. If she kept working, kept focused, she would not hear the echo of Pansy's words.

She unlocked the cabinet. Even when set next to the other books bedecked with precious stones, the book from Cloister gleamed. Besides the magnificent illuminations, what else could this book contain that would make it safer here than at Cloister?

Lena rubbed her gloves on her skirt to make sure that they were clean. She shot a look over her shoulder and, assured that no one other than Mrs. Mumbles was watching, picked up the book. The intricate mother-of-pearl inlay still made her catch her breath. Her long fingers delicately turned to the title page that Jimson had translated from the Latin: *A History*. But a history of what? If only she had attended the type of school that taught Latin.

If she couldn't translate, then the pictures would have to do. In the midst of flora and fauna there were small people as well. A man and woman standing among flowers and trees, animals . . . each picture was so intricate she could gaze at it forever. She flipped more pages. The man and woman were hunched together, their faces contorted, the woman's mouth open in a scream. Lena turned to the next page. The flowers, trees, and animals were gone. The man and woman had covered themselves with leaves; they were alone. A sudden chill; she knew this story. The story progressed. The man and woman were tilling the land; they were surrounded by children. Lena bent close to examine the detail. In the woman's arms was an infant, an infant with disproportionately large hands and feet. Lena almost dropped the book.

The family grew; there were animals again. Lena searched the minutiae of each drawing, looking again for the child with hands and feet like hers. What had happened to that baby?

A murmur from behind made her freeze. But it was just Mrs. Mumbles twining herself about Lena's legs. Lena looked at the brass clock on the wall, the one that showed the time in London and India as well. It was later than she had thought, and there was still more that she had to do before they were all summoned to dinner. Heart pounding, she carefully locked the book back in its case and returned the key to Jimson's desk.

Jimson had described walking to the end of the first-floor corridor trying various doors. Lena hoped that Jimson was absorbed now with his Pansy. Mr. Beasley should be in his study, and Mrs. Pollet busy in the kitchen with dinner preparations. Lena considered. She should take something to protect herself. The brass letter opener was sharp enough to slice her finger. She slipped it into the waistband of her skirt and pulled her tweed jacket down over the bone handle. With Mrs. Mumbles at her feet, she made her way quickly to the south wing.

Lena remembered Jimson's description of banging and

heat. But she heard nothing as she walked, as silently as possible, down the carpeted hall. Stopping outside the last door, she felt her own heart banging, her breath tight. She swallowed and pushed open the door.

It was a laboratory, just as Jimson had described, gleaming with instruments. On an examination table in the center of the room a woman was hunched forward. Her naked back was turned to Lena, and along her back ran two ragged scars. A growth protruded just below the shoulder blade on the left side. Mr. Beasley, his back also to Lena, rested one hand on the woman's sharp shoulder. In his right hand he held a syringe.

Before Lena could cry out, Mrs. Mumbles streaked across the floor and jumped daintily onto the examining table. Startled, Mr. Beasley and the woman turned to find Lena standing in the doorway, the brass letter opener clutched in her gloved hand.

"Mrs. Pollet!" Lena cried.

"Ah, Lena . . . Not how I planned to introduce you to my work." Tobias Beasley's voice was smooth and reassuring, his painted eyebrows raised in a question.

Leticia Pollet's face was pale, her eyes wide with terror. She uttered a guttural sound. Lena looked at the letter opener in her hand. How silly she had been to think that she could do anything! She turned and ran.

Panic propelled her through the south wing and back into the main house. Jimson was not in the kitchen, nor was he in the library. Down the long corridor of the north wing, doubling back toward the kitchen, she saw no one. The image of Leticia Pollet's scarred back and agonized face drove her on. There was a flicker of motion on the terrace. Lena called out. Jimson and Pansy walked arm in arm, oblivious to her cries. Pansy turned to look up at Jimson and laughed, a head-back, full-throated laugh. In another wing of the house, in another world, Mr. Beasley was about to do something dreadful to Leticia Pollet.

Lena threw open the terrace doors. "Help! Mrs. Pollet is the winged woman, and Mr. Beasley is doing something unspeakable right now!"

Pansy looked at Lena with her mouth slightly open, her perfectly arched brows drawn together in a V.

Jimson dropped her arm. "What? The woman I saw was not Mrs. Pollet. You saw her too—at the cemetery. Mr. Beasley's in the laboratory now?"

"Yes, he's holding a syringe, and her back is covered with horrible scars!"

Even before Lena finished the sentence, Jimson was running full-tilt toward the south wing with Lena at his heels.

"Wait!" Pansy hoisted her skirt with one hand and followed. Lena could hear her voice floating from behind. "Jimson Quiggley, you wait for me!" But there could be no waiting now.

Jimson burst through the laboratory door seconds before Lena. It was empty. Mrs. Mumbles slept curled contently on the examination table. As the adrenaline left her body, Lena began to shake.

"What is this place? What are you two doing?" Pansy peered through the doorway. Her yellow curls had come unpinned and tumbled down around her small face. She was breathing hard, and a bead of sweat shone on her upper lip. "Somebody please tell me what's going on."

Lena still found it difficult to speak. Her words came out in gasps. "They were here. Mrs. Pollet was sitting on the table. Her back was bare, and there were two long scars and something growing from them. Mr. Beasley said, 'This isn't the way I wanted you to find out.'" To her embarrassment, Lena began to cry. It wasn't a ladylike cry, but great sobs that shook her body and made her nose run.

"Lena, don't." Jimson pulled a wadded handkerchief from his pocket. "I believe you. I just can't make sense of it all."

She dabbed at her eyes and blew her nose.

Pansy possessively clutched Jimson's arm. "I think it's time you explained what's going on here."

Jimson looked at her blankly as if he had only just realized she was there. "I wish I knew."

CHAPTER 20

MORE REVELATIONS

JIMSON ESCORTED PANSY TO HER ROOM, PROMISING TO RETURN with a cup of tea to settle her nerves. "This must all be a terrible shock for you, especially when you're still tired from your travels. I'll bring you some tea and tell you everything that's been going on."

Lena dismissed them both with a snort. What was Jimson thinking? They needed to find Mr. Beasley now and confront him before he could do any more damage. Thank goodness the marshal had a plan in place.

The first person she found was Milo. He was in the kitchen, adding dried basil from the garden to a simmering pot of stew.

"Where's Mr. Beasley?" Lena's face was pale, her lips set in a thin, determined line.

"He's making a call. Mrs. Pollet isn't feeling well at all and I'm—"

"I saw what he was doing in the laboratory." The picture she was trying so hard to forget was seared to her brain. "He was doing something to Mrs. Pollet. Her back was all scars."

Jimson appeared in the doorway. Lena turned her back to him.

Milo wiped his hands on a towel and replaced the lid on the great iron pot. "Mr. Beasley is a medical man. His way is to help, not to harm. It's that oath they make them all take."

"But I saw him—saw him with a syringe." Lena couldn't keep the panic from her voice.

"Without Tobias Beasley, Leticia Pollet would be working in the mines of Scree along with her daughter, the one that's left."

"Her daughter?" Jimson was at Lena's side. "Does she have a daughter here?"

Milo shook his head. "I thought you all knew about the goings-on at the house. Thought that's why you came." He looked pointedly at Lena. "Tobias Beasley has been helping Peculiars escape a life in Scree."

He continued. "Leticia has sump'n rare, I can't remember the fancy name. Folks don't see it much anymore. But she growed wings. Mr. Beasley does this operation that cuts them off and then has to treat her every six months or so or they'll grow back. Her daughter's got the same thing. The wings don't come till adolescence, so Leticia brought her here to get help."

Lena, feeling that the world was spinning, leaned on the wooden table. "You said 'the one that's left.'"

"Ay-yuh. Leticia and Arthur had another daughter, Arabelle. Arthur isn't—wasn't—a Peculiar. They thought they stood a chance for a normal life, but when the first daughter, Arabelle, reached twelve or thirteen, the wings sprouted and the family got sent to Scree. Then the other girl, Merilee, showed signs of the same problem. That's when they escaped and came here. Merilee's fifteen now and just had her wings removed."

"That's who I saw on the widow's walk? I'm not crazy after all."

Lena could see the relief in Jimson's face.

"How did they know to come here?" Lena's heart was racing.

"The word gets spread to those who need it. Zephyr House's always been a sanctuary of sorts." Milo nodded toward Lena. "You can see how I thought you were needing a place to go, what with the new decrees and all."

Lena's thoughts collided. This was not the story the marshal told. And Milo suspected that she, Lena, would be in need of help as well.

A sharp intake of breath made them all turn to the doorway. Pansy, violet eyes wide, pale brows drawn to a point, stood with her arms crossed. "I heard what you said. That's illegal. Helping Peculiars is against the law. Everyone knows they're not human. They're dangerous." She looked at Lena and one corner of her bowed lips turned up. She drew back. "You're a Peculiar?"

"Pansy, that's enough." Jimson's voice was firm. "We have no scientific proof that there even are such—"

Lena cut him off. "I think we're beyond that discussion now. What else could account for a woman who grows wings? What further proof do you need?" Panic beat in her rib cage like a frantic bird, trapped. It was as if she were listening to someone else's voice. She looked at Pansy, and the strange voice continued. "Maybe I am a Peculiar. Maybe I'll cut your heart out right here in the kitchen and add it to the stew."

Jimson took a step toward Lena.

Pansy cowered behind him.

"Did you know my father is a goblin? He was in jail as much as he was at home."

"Enough!" Tobias Beasley stood in the doorway, his shirtsleeves rolled up to his elbows. His eyes burned.

But the strange voice inside Lena could not stop. "Is that why you hired me? So you could observe my hands and feet? Can you cut off a joint so I'll look 'normal' like her?" Sobbing, Lena gestured toward Pansy. "But it won't change who I am, will it?"

"Lena—" Jimson's voice was soft and controlled.

Pansy began to cry.

When Leticia Pollet entered the kitchen with a young woman by her side, Lena ran.

She ran down the front hallway and out the door, grabbing her scarf and purse on the way. She heard Jimson behind her. Heard him call her name and Mr. Beasley say, "Give her time."

What she wanted was not time but distance, distance from them all. She couldn't think. Her head wasn't working right. Panic continued to beat its wings, clawed at her rib cage. At the end of the drive she passed a cart headed in the direction of Knob Knoster.

Again her own voice surprised her, this time with its steadiness as she inquired politely for a ride. When the farmer delivering a load of autumn vegetables to town agreed, Lena clambered up onto the wagon seat. She would leave them all behind. But unfortunately she could not escape herself.

The cold came creeping in from the sea. As she walked along the streets of Knob Knoster, Lena wound the plum scarf her mother had knitted more tightly around her neck. She had no destination in mind, except being away from Zephyr House. Everything she had ever heard about Peculiars was jumbled now in her head. There were so many voices she couldn't silence. She remembered the doctor warning her mother about wild thoughts and reckless actions. When she thought of her father, the pain was visceral, starting somewhere near her breast bone and emanating out: his gentleness with her, his hot bursts of anger, the whispered rumors. The marshal's voice was among the crowd, convincing her that Peculiars had no place in society, that it was better for them if they were with their own kind. And Pansy's words came back with a sting: *What's wrong with that girl?* Lena couldn't pretend any longer; she was her father's daughter. But what did it mean to be Peculiar? Why had he left her to figure it out on her own?

With hands stiff from the cold, she ducked into the first lighted doorway. Knoster Dry Goods. It was a blessing to be inside where it was warm. Lena worked her fingers, clenching and unclenching them until feeling returned, but her mind was still numb. Bolts of fabric lined one wall—winter weights, tweeds and brocades, supple wools. Drawers of buttons and threads. Beyond were rows of canned goods. The bird in her chest had stilled, was preening its feathers and waiting. The marshal's plan had seemed the logical consequence, a way to stop Mr. Beasley from doing the unspeakable.

But what if Milo was right? What if Mr. Beasley was *helping* Peculiars? The marshal would raid Zephyr House either way; helping Peculiars was still against the law. Lena ran a trembling finger down a length of lapis blue jersey.

"That's a color I fancy myself." Lena met Margaret Flynn's black-fringed eyes. "But it would look better on you, bring out the blue of your eyes. So, you've come into Knoster for a little shopping."

It felt to Lena as if she had retreated so far inside herself that she had forgotten how to talk. She muttered and coughed. "Just window-shopping."

"Are you sure you're feeling all right? You look peaked to me." Margaret peered closely at Lena's face. Lena tried not to pull away. "Could do with a tonic," she added, nodding. The green feather in her hat bobbed. "Let's have a sit-down and a cup of tea."

Lena did not want tea. She did not want a sit-down, nor

did she want the company of Margaret Flynn. But there was something in Margaret's eyes. Lena's lip quivered. She blinked back tears.

"Oh my, is it an affair of the heart? I know all about those."

But Lena couldn't speak.

"Don't matter none. You could use some mothering. Thomas has broken more hearts than one in his time." Margaret took command of Lena's arm, and before Lena knew it, she was seated at a small table in the back of the dry goods store, tucked behind a giant barrel of dried beans and another of loose tea.

"Take your time. I've got all day. Well, at least until opening." Margaret stretched out her stout legs in a most unladylike manner. "Let me ask you a question. Why are you really going to Scree?" Her eyes, Lena noticed, glittered as bright and sharp as a bird's. In Lena's chest the bird ruffled its feathers as if in recognition. "Don't give me that cockamamy answer about business."

"I'm going to find my father." Lena snuffled.

Margaret produced a lace handkerchief as big as a man's. "Now we're getting somewhere." She patted Lena's hand without any hesitation. "I knew your father at one time. Saul Mattacascar."

Lena looked up over the lace edge of the hankie. "What?"

"Oh, he was a regular customer at the Parasol on his travels north. Could charm the skin off a snake, old Saul."

"But—" Lena began.

"Knew him before that, too. First time I met Saul we were both up in Scree. I was traveling with my husband and we were staying in a little settlement, couldn't even call it a town. There was some trouble while we were there. Why do you want to find your father?"

The question was so direct, it caught Lena off guard. Wouldn't anyone want to find a father who had left? Margaret's eyes still glittered, making it impossible for Lena to lie. "I want to know why he left. I want to know if what people say about him is true."

"Some parents are better left unfound. It sounds hard, but it's true. Some of them will only bring you heartache. What do people say about Saul?"

Lena pleated the now-soggy handkerchief. "Nana Crane says he's a goblin."

Margaret nodded her head. "A Peculiar. What do you say?"

"I don't know. That's why I need to find him. Maybe he's a good man, just misunderstood."

"And if he was, what difference would it make?" Margaret leaned forward so that her enormous bosom was resting on the tabletop. "Calling him a goblin is just one way of simplifying a man who has made good and bad choices. Saul made a few of both in his time."

"How did you meet him in Scree?"

"Are you sure it's the truth that you're after?"

Lena nodded her head, the bird inside levitating.

"Well, I suppose that it's better that you hear it from me

than from Thomas Saltre. Your father had to leave Scree the first time because he killed a man—a lawman."

The bird was trying to claw its way out. Flying against Lena's ribs, consuming all of her breath. Margaret grabbed her hand. Lena tried to jerk it away, but Margaret's grip was firm.

"Listen to me now. Saul was good and bad, just like all of us. He done some good things too. But for you to go rushing off to Scree without knowing the truth would as likely destroy you. You need to know what you're getting into."

But Margaret's words were slippery. Lena could not grasp hold of them except the phrase "your father killed a man." Her father was a murderer. "Was it his goblin blood that made him do it?"

Margaret snorted and released Lena's hand. "Who can say what demons anyone has to fight unless we're inside the person's skin?"

But Lena knew. It was his goblinishness. Who knew what horrid things any of them were capable of? Thomas was right. Peculiars had no place in society, and neither did she. Oh, she'd get the marshal into Zephyr House. And when he rounded up any Peculiars he found there, she'd have him take her, too.

CHAPTER 21

LENA PLANS AN ESCAPE

LENA DID NOT WANT TO RETURN TO ZEPHYR HOUSE. BUT AFTER spending a restless night at Margaret Flynn's florid apartment, she decided that she owed Jimson an explanation. She would tell him the contents of the letter she had left with Margaret for Thomas. Then Jimson and Pansy could leave the house before the marshal and his men descended on it. Mr. Beasley might be kind, but he was misguided. The law was the law and put in place to protect the citizens. She sincerely hoped no harm would come to him. And she, too, would be gone when the marshal arrived. She wasn't ready to turn herself in, not until she had confronted her father.

Lena caught the early coach north and rode with an odd assortment of travelers who were bound for the borders of Scree. The night's frost had created a white and sparkling landscape. The pumpkins no longer rolled through green fields to the sea. The fields had returned to brown earth, striped with the black of dying vines. She had planned to travel before winter set in. It appeared as it was arriving early this year. Now with whatever guide the marshal provided, Lena would be making her way across Scree just when the first snows were falling. She would no longer delude herself that the marshal would be her private escort. How could he fancy a Peculiar? Well, there was no helping it now. She unfolded the letter from her father that she kept pinned to her chemise. Once she crossed the border to the north, there would still be miles of mountainous terrain to conquer. And she would need to know, as well, where her father had last been sighted.

Lena crunched her way up the gravel drive to Zephyr House. The early sun gilded the widow's walk. The weather-vanes spun slowly in a light breeze from the north. She would need a heavier coat for traveling. The apple trees, now mostly harvested, were dropping their russet leaves. Despite everything, it was going to be hard to leave this place. One more day and the marshal should be prepared for the raid. He had said four days. Lena tried to picture it, but Mr. Beasley's face with his ridiculous painted eyebrows kept getting in the way. What would happen to him? That was something she tried not to think about. How could someone who was good make such bad choices?

She caught movement from the corner of her eye. Mrs. Mumbles emerged from under the laurel bushes, stepping daintily across the frost-tipped grass, stopping periodically to shake a paw. Behind Mrs. Mumbles came Mrs. Pollet, a woven basket over one arm and a thick shawl over a wooly sweater. She was tall and gaunt as a scarecrow in the garden. Lena's eyes flew to her bony shoulders where she knew the scars from wings were hidden. Beside her walked the young woman Lena had glimpsed at the funeral. Hardly a woman, Lena realized; younger than she first appeared. Just a teenager.

"Well, I see you've come back." Mrs. Pollet's voice held no welcome; it was dry and empty.

Lena nodded.

"You set the house upside down when you left. I hope you're satisfied with that."

Lena stopped a few yards from the door. "I didn't mean—"

"You don't know what you mean, because you don't understand anything. You think what you see is the whole story."

Lena took a step closer. "I thought he was hurting you."

Mrs. Pollet shifted the basket to her other arm. "Tobias Beasley saved my life and the life of my daughter Merilee." She gestured to her silent companion. "He risked his own life to help us. But maybe you don't think our lives are worth saving." In her quiet wrath she seemed to grow taller. "Do you think wings make us any different from you with your strange feet and hands, or from anyone?"

She took a step closer, and Lena took a step back, almost tripping over Mrs. Mumbles, who had come to rub against her legs.

"Do you know what it's like to work in the mines twelve

hours a day? You never see sunlight. You go down when it's dark and come up after the sun has gone down. Children, too. You hear children crying and coughing. And you know that it will never change one day to the next, all because you're different and they need someone to work their mines for them, to get their precious coal and copper."

Lena was feeling faint. Blood pounded in her head. Why didn't Jimson come out and save her?

Mrs. Pollet was close enough that Lena could feel puffs of breath as she spoke, see the mesh of lines surrounding eyes, the way one front tooth slightly lapped the other. "And some of us don't make it out, like my little Arabelle. Arabelle got a lung sickness and died."

"Arabelle died because of the mines?" Lena's mouth was dry.

"We tried to come back and have a normal life, but there is no normal once your child dies. Then we heard about Tobias Beasley. We stayed here and worked until Merilee was old enough to need his help. Her wings came later than her sister's, but they came just like we feared they would. Mr. Beasley gave Arthur a job. Arthur, who loved us and didn't care what we were." Her eyes brimmed with tears. "What do you know about our pain?" Merilee put an arm around her mother's waist.

Lena wanted to say that she knew pain, that she knew what it was to be different, to grow up without a father, to grow up not knowing who she was, but she had no words. "I thought most Peculiars were just sent back to Scree to live." Her voice sounded small and tinny even to her own ears.

Mrs. Pollet threw back her head and laughed. "Peculiars aren't human. Didn't you know? That's what the law says."

"Hush, Mama." Merilee tried to draw her mother away.

But Lena could only think of Arabelle Pollet, who died in the mines of Scree because she had wings.

Despite Merilee's grip on her arm, Mrs. Pollet took a step closer to Lena. "Do you believe what the law says about us, you with your funny hands and feet?"

Lena didn't hear the front door open until Jimson cried out, "She's back! Lena's here!"

Jimson was down the steps in a flash, followed by Mr. Beasley. He stopped just short of Lena. "We thought you might not come back."

Mr. Beasley rested a hand on Jimson's shoulder. "Why don't we let Lena come inside, Jimson? I think we could use a second breakfast."

Lena, Jimson, and Tobias Beasley sat around the dining table, and Milo refilled their cups with tea and served up toast and jam while Mrs. Pollet and Merilee cleaned up the kitchen from the first breakfast.

"Jimson and I had a talk last night, one I wish that you could have been here for as well," said Mr. Beasley. "I suppose I should have explained everything to you from the start, but I truly believed that not knowing about my side occupation might keep you safe. At least, I thought that about Jimson.

I thought I'd hired someone who would be content sorting books." He passed Lena a pot of raspberry jam. "But Jimson turned out to be more perceptive than I ever anticipated. And then you came along, Lena, and it was obvious that you were in some distress. I thought that I might be of some help to you as well. At least, give you a place to sort things out." He sighed. "I didn't expect either of you to be so . . ." He paused, then said, ". . . curious."

Lena shifted in the chair. She couldn't meet Mr. Beasley's eyes, didn't want his words to confuse her decision.

He continued. "Once I got to know both of you, I suspected that you would be people I could trust, but keeping you ignorant as long as possible seemed the safest thing. Try the marmalade, Jimson. Leticia made it herself.

"I have been assisting Peculiars for several years. Some decide to stay here at Zephyr House. Others want to continue living in the towns they came from. So, I do what I can to make them as inconspicuous as possible, so they can blend in. Others want to go to Scree, but for obvious reasons do not want to end up working in the mines. I have ways to get them the necessary papers to freely cross the border." He spread his hands. "Now you know my secret. I'm afraid my little operation has been discovered."

"Now that I've met Mrs. Pollet and Merilee, I can't deny Peculiars exist. But I can't pretend it wasn't a shock," Jimson said as he looked from Mr. Beasley to Lena. "Last night Mr. Beasley explained a few things to me. Did you know that there have never been any true medical studies on Peculiars? All this talk about them not having souls and being predisposed to violence is just talk. Nobody knows much about them. Anyway, I'm in. What I mean is that I'll do anything I can to help Mr. Beasley with what he's doing. What about you, Lena?"

She looked at Jimson's eager face. Mr. Beasley said nothing, but watched her with sympathetic eyes. Lena covered her face with her hands, fingers curving over her brows and digging into her hair.

"Lena?"

She shook her head without looking up. "I've done a terrible thing." A dreadful certainty filled her. Even if Peculiars were dangerous or criminals, as the marshal believed, they didn't deserve death in the mines of Scree. She thought of Mrs. Pollet and Arabelle and pictured the marshal as a steam train churning toward them. Lena raised her face and looked Mr. Beasley in the eye. "We need to prepare for a raid on Zephyr House. It should be tomorrow—October thirty-first."

It took her only a few minutes to explain about her meetings with the marshal and about the letter she had left with Margaret Flynn.

Mr. Beasley locked Lena in his gaze. "Thomas Saltre is obsessed with the elimination of Peculiars. It has been his single-minded pursuit for years, ever since his father was killed in Scree. That's why he trained and became a marshal at such a young age. Despite what he says, he has no intention of letting them return independently to Scree." His next words made the tears spill. "You did what you thought was best, based on the truth you knew. That's all anyone can do." He pushed away from the table. "Even if you hadn't left the letter for the marshal, we were already at risk. He's had his eye on me for some time. Now it's just sooner rather than later. And we'd better prepare ourselves. Fortunately, Pansy left early this morning. At least that's one person out of harm's way."

Lena turned to Jimson.

Jimson's face, usually so open and easy to read, was shuttered. Only his lips moved as he spoke. "She said she couldn't stay with people who were breaking the law. That if Peculiars weren't bad, the government wouldn't be arresting them. She stayed only one night." He looked away.

"But most people would agree with her," Lena said.

Mr. Beasley nodded. "You can't blame her. She's had no evidence to the contrary. It was wise, Jimson, to think of her safety. However, I'm afraid Pansy will feel compelled to share what she witnessed here at Zephyr House."

"I'm so sorry." Lena snuffled.

Jimson shrugged, and to Lena it looked more like a shrug of defeat than a shrug of indifference.

"We have twenty-four hours to get prepared. Leticia, Merilee, and Abel are my main concerns. And there are things that need tending to." Mr. Beasley rose and dropped his napkin on the table. "Be available." And he strode from the room.

"Abel?" Lena crinkled her brow.

"He's your red-haired man from the train. Abel Guthrie.

He's been helping Mr. Beasley refine titantum. That's what I saw in the laboratory."

"He's a Peculiar? Isn't Guthrie the name of the family who used to live here?"

Jimson nodded and slurped the last of the tea, still avoiding Lena's eyes. "Yes and yes. Do you have any conception of what you've done? How many people you've put at risk?" His voice was cold and remote. "Come on, there are some things we need to do in the library."

Lena followed silently, muffling her sobs.

The sun shone weakly through the lead-paned windows of the library. Gray flannel clouds gathered on the horizon to meet a flint and choppy sea. Even in this weak light the library was the most magnificent place Lena had ever seen. "What will happen to the library?" She pictured the marshal and his men ransacking the bookshelves, pawing through files looking for clues, thumbing through the jewel-encrusted books with pages fragile as old skin. And at that thought there was suddenly not enough room for her heart in her chest.

"That's why we're here. We've got to save as much as we can." Jimson surveyed the room. "What would interest them the most?"

Lena's eyes flew from display to display. Irreplaceable objects. How could they choose? Then her gaze settled on the wooden box. "The book from Cloister. It must be important."

Jimson nodded and retrieved the key from his desk. "We'll

take the book and leave the box. It will be easier to carry that way." He placed it in his canvas knapsack. "Whatever it is, Mr. Beasley thinks it's valuable." He picked up a book of early medical illustrations and thumbed through it. "What about that sketchbook? You gave it back to Mr. Beasley, didn't you?"

Lena twisted a lock of hair. "It's still in my room." And then, in the spirit of confession added, "I showed it to the marshal."

"You what! Lena, don't you ever think before you just rush out and do something?" Jimson ran his hands over his face.

"I didn't know—"

"No, I'm sorry. Why don't you just go get it, so we can be sure we don't leave it around? I'll go through the files." Jimson's voice was deliberate now, as if he were speaking to a child, as if he could barely disguise his disgust.

And he was right, Lena thought. She had been impulsive. But he hadn't done much better. He was so caught up in being a man of science that he hadn't been able to see what was staring him right in the face. She stalked down the hall. All that mattered now was getting everything and everyone out safely.

The low ceiling of gray was closing in quickly. Lena paused at her window looking out over the apple orchard. The trees, almost leafless now, stretched their twisted limbs. Beyond, the sliver of sea was churning with whitecaps. She reached under her mattress, closing her fingers over the slim sketchbook. Next she retrieved the money she had saved from her work at Zephyr House, then sat on the bed to think. Would it be enough? She couldn't work the extra weeks. Circumstances had changed, but not her plans for Scree. She would be crossing the border without the hoped-for guide, and she would have to do it quickly, before the marshal realized she had betrayed him. Perhaps he had never intended to provide her a guide. It wasn't immoral to lie to a Peculiar. She was nothing but a liability at Zephyr House. Jimson and the marshal both would be glad to be rid of her. She tapped her fingers against the cover of the sketchbook. A young single woman traveling alone would hardly go unnoticed, especially if that woman was traveling into Scree.

She pinned the money inside her chemise, next to the letter from her father, and thought longingly of the money and papers left inside her stolen purse. Then she selected her warmest garments and stuffed them into her valise. It would raise even more suspicion for a woman to travel without a bag or trunk. Perhaps she could claim that she was a teacher, volunteering to work in the remote lands of Scree—but she would need a letter from a school board. She recalled the missionary ladies from Miss Brett's. They probably had no trouble crossing the border to minister to the heathens. She would leave tonight before the raid, before the marshal rounded her up with the others and forced her into the mines of Scree. Before her departure, she'd do whatever she could to help Jimson and Mr. Beasley prepare. Hurrying, valise in hand, she descended the stairs.

CHAPTER 22

THROUGH THE LIBRARY WINDOW

JIMSON SAT FORLORNLY ON THE TOP RUNG OF THE LIBRARY LADDER. "They'll shut Zephyr House down, you know. I guess I can go back to Northerdam and work in my father's store."

Lena propped her valise against her desk. Jimson's bulging knapsack lay next to it. "Is that what you're going to do? Pansy will be glad to have you back in Northerdam."

Jimson mumbled something that Lena didn't catch.

"And what about Mr. Beasley?"

"He's got plans. He's going to make sure he gets everyone else out, and then he'll disappear into Scree." Each word dropped as heavy as lead.

"But what about the library? And all his inventions?"

Jimson shook his head. "You didn't think they'd let him go free, did you? It's now a federal crime to help Peculiars. They aren't going to just let him promise to be good and stay on here. And he's just discovered how to work with titantum!"

Lena ran her fingers over the keys of the gleaming typing machine, wondering if she could possibly feel any worse.

"What about you, Lena? Where will you go? You can't go to Scree." Jimson climbed down the ladder. His voice grew kinder. "The marshal's not going to give you a guide now that you've tipped us off."

Mrs. Mumbles leapt from the floor onto Jimson's desk, turned around twice, and curled into a ball.

"I can't go home. I still have to find my father. Besides, I don't fit in anywhere else." She looked out the window. "Look, it's starting to snow and it's still October!"

The sky had met the sea. A wall of white was moving toward the house, the first individual flakes skittering on the windowpanes.

A sharp clattering and banging reverberated overhead.

"It sounds like someone is on the roof!" Jimson opened the window, and a cold blast of air rushed in. He craned his neck out as far as he could. "It's coming from the widow's walk. But I can't see it from here."

"Where's Mr. Beasley now?"

"I dunno. I haven't seen him since breakfast."

Someone was pounding on the front door, almost as if they wanted to knock it down. At the same time, the whistle on the side door shrilled. Jimson and Lena ran into the hallway with Mrs. Mumbles at their feet. The heavy library doors clicked shut behind them. Jimson's hand closed over Lena's arm. "Wait. Let's see what's going on first." They peered around the corner into the entryway, where Leticia Pollet stood, hands on hips, blocking the way of the marshal and two deputies, who had their guns drawn.

Lena pressed her hand over her mouth before a gasp could escape.

Thomas Saltre was flashing a piece of paper. "We have one warrant to search the premises and one for the arrest of Tobias Beasley. And who may I ask are you?"

He stood directly under the gaslight, strong and formidable, close enough that Lena could see flakes of snow glittering on his mustache and on the shoulders of his tan trench coat. Behind him, on either side, two deputies in pin-striped jackets were pointing Colt Peacemakers at Mrs. Pollet. Their boots left pools of water on the wood floor.

Leticia looked down on the marshal. "Mr. Beasley is not in. I'm Mrs. Pollet, the housekeeper. Your men are ruining the floor." Her voice never quavered.

The marshal straightened up to his full height, but he was still a good three inches shorter than Mrs. Pollet.

"They weren't supposed to come until tomorrow!" Lena's wail was a whisper.

Jimson put a hand over her mouth. Lena considered biting it.

"Ma'am, if you'll just step aside so my men can conduct their business, we'll try to be as careful as we can." Thomas Saltre gestured for his deputies to lower their guns and begin the search.

Two more men rushed in from the side door. One of them carried a shotgun.

"Quick—let's go!" Jimson nudged Lena, but her feet felt as if they had been nailed to the floor. Jimson grabbed her hand and pulled her behind him down the hall and away from the men.

"We need to find Mr. Beasley and warn him. But first I need my knapsack." They flew to the library and tumbled through the great doors. Jimson grabbed his pack, and Lena reached for her valise. "Leave it," Jimson said. "It will slow you down."

"But—" She unclasped the lock and grabbed the sketchbook and a pair of gloves. She shoved the gloves deep into the pocket of her jacket, but the sketchbook was too large. Lena reached for Jimson's pack. He nodded and she slipped the sketchbook inside.

"We can lock the library from the inside, but it means going out the window." Jimson looked at her.

Lena could hear footsteps rushing up the stairs. "Do it."

Jimson set the locking mechanism while Lena ran to open one of the leaded glass windows that faced the sea.

The narrow sill was slick with icy white flakes. Tiny crystals spun from the sky. The temperature had fallen. Some four feet below the window was the basalt edge of the cliff. The cliffs dropped thirty feet to the water below. Just beyond the windows to the south was the brick terrace where Lena had enjoyed such happy dinners during her first days at

Zephyr House. To reach it, they would have to balance on the window ledge and jump. Lena drew back, dizzy with the thought.

"You can do this, Lena." Jimson's voice was next to her ear. She could feel the warmth of his breath. "It's five feet at the most to the terrace. We balance on the ledge and jump."

Lena looked at the ledge, and then she looked down at her impossibly long feet.

"I can't do it. You go and get Mr. Beasley. I'll be safe in here."

Jimson climbed onto the window ledge and heaved the knapsack to the far side. "For how long? No, you're going with me, Lena. We'll do this together." He held out his hand to her.

Lena stood on his desk chair. She had never been good at climbing. Her feet were too long and inflexible.

"Give me your hand." Jimson's voice was firm, commanding.

Lena stretched out her gloved hand, and Jimson grasped it. "Step up on the ledge. Turn your feet sideways so they're pointing toward the terrace. I'll hold you. You can't fall." He braced one hand on the window transom. Lena placed one foot on the sill. She put all her weight on it as she lifted her other leg. Her foot skittered. Jimson braced her with his leg. "Watch your skirt."

She nodded because she could form no words, and then she gathered the skirt up with her left hand, leaned heavily on Jimson, and lifted her left leg. The snow stung her face as it blew in from the ocean. She angled her feet, clutching Jimson's hand in a death grip. "Hold on to the window frame. I'm going to jump first so I can reach for you."

Blood was rushing in her ears. Jimson had to pry her fingers from his hand. Lena grabbed for the frame and dug her fingers in. And then he was jumping out into the white. He landed easily on the brick terrace, sliding some when his feet touched down.

"OK, now it's your turn. I'm going to reach out as far as I can. Jump and I'll steady you. It's not far."

But his voice sounded as if it were coming from a million miles away. Lena stood frozen, snow crystals icing her hair. There was pounding on the library door, followed by raised voices she could hear faintly.

"This one's locked."

"What the hell kind of doors are those?"

"Shoot the lock off if you have to."

Mrs. Mumbles sprang lightly onto the sill next to Lena and without a pause leapt into the snow. Lena closed her eyes and followed. As she pushed off, her feet lost traction. For a minute she felt as if she were running in the air. Her eyes popped open. Jimson was reaching out for her. She leaned as far forward as she could, but her jump was not as powerful as Jimson's. Her feet landed half on the brick terrace and half on rock. She slid back. Jimson lunged; his hand dug into one shoulder and he was pulling her toward him. Pain shot through her feet and she tumbled into Jimson's arms, knocking him onto his back, her long skirt tangling around her legs just as a shot rang against the library door.

The fall took her breath and then she was laughing with relief, laughing to still be alive. Jimson was buried somewhere underneath her, but she could hear him laughing too.

She struggled to her feet. "They'll see how we escaped!"

"Come on! We're going to the south wing." Jimson grabbed his knapsack with one hand and took her hand with the other. Lena stepped forward and winced; needles pricked the soles of her feet. But she ran, slipping across the terrace toward freedom.

CHAPTER 23

THE AEROCOPTER

THEY RAN OVER THE THIN CRUST OF SNOW ALONG THE SEAWARD side of Zephyr House. Mrs. Mumbles ran by their side, appearing and disappearing as she streaked behind bushes. The snow continued falling.

"We can get into the laboratory through the back door. That's my best guess where to find Mr. Beasley." Jimson kept a tight grip on Lena's hand.

"He must know what's happening by now." Lena's words were ragged. The cold bit her lungs.

They plowed through the messy winter garden, trampling old heads of lettuce and stepping on blackened tomato vines, running down the length of the south wing to a small door.

Jimson pulled a ring of keys from his pocket. The damp sea air made the door stick. He shoved with his shoulder until it gave way, and he had to strain to push it open. They stumbled inside—and found themselves face-to-face with a single-barrel shotgun.

Redheaded Abel Guthrie waited on the other end.

Jimson spoke first. "Where's Mr. Beasley?" he demanded.

"I heard she was the one who brought the lawmen in." Abel pointed the gun at Lena.

Lena's legs trembled and threatened to buckle. "I made a mistake. I didn't understand."

"Didn't understand that they'll kill us all one way or the other?" He was short and bandy-legged, just as Lena remembered him from the train. "Get inside and close the door."

Jimson and Lena eased through the door, almost closing it on Mrs. Mumbles's tail as she dashed back outside.

"Abel, does Mr. Beasley know the raid's begun?" Jimson was speaking very slowly and Lena wondered if that would anger Abel even more.

"Of course he knows. Best thing for us is to use traitors as a hostage, a bargaining chip. Get against the wall."

Lena, never taking her eyes off Abel, inched back until she could feel the wall of the laboratory against her shoulder blades.

"You used to live here before, when it was a farm, before you went to Scree," said Jimson.

He's babbling, Lena thought. This crazy Peculiar is going to shoot me, and Jimson is making conversation.

"My daddy's farm. He died in Scree because of what they

said he was. Shot him dead in his own mine right in front of all of us."

Lena gulped. "I'm sorry."

"That's not gonna happen to me. Mr. Beasley's going to get us all out of here. We were almost ready, and then you opened your mouth." The eyes that flicked over Lena were a flat brown, as if there was no life behind them at all.

"Lena and I are helping Mr. Beasley. We've got everything from the library that might be incriminating." Jimson held up the knapsack. "We need to get anything out of the laboratory that could be used against him."

But Abel never took his eyes from Lena. "Don't matter. By then we'll be gone, flying away. We'll give 'em the girl in exchange. Or I could just shoot her now."

Lena slid a few inches down the wall. Inside her gloves, her hands grew damp.

Jimson spoke faster. "What do you mean 'flying away'?"

"Beasley's flying machine. It's ready to go. We've been working on it for months. I helped build the frame . . . If they try and stop us, I'll shoot her." His voice was so calm that Lena began to think it was all some terrible dream.

Without turning his face from Abel, Jimson looked at her from the corner of his eye. But Lena had no idea what Jimson wanted her to do.

"Is that what you are working on in here? Something for the flying machine?" Lena asked.

"Titantum. Pure titantum. Mr. Beasley's a genius, you know. It's gonna save us."

Jimson jumped in. "How's titantum going to save you?"

"It's a magic metal. Boiler's made from it, so the machine's not too heavy to fly."

There were footsteps in the hallway outside the door and a voice. "Open up in the name of the law!"

Abel giggled and cocked the hammer.

Lena closed her eyes and sank all the way to the floor.

A shot.

The door flew open. A deputy, black bowler cocked on the side of his head, burst into the room and pointed his revolver at Abel.

"I'm going to kill her unless you put your gun away," Abel announced. "Maybe I'll kill her anyway!" Again, he giggled.

Lena opened one eye. Jimson was directly in her line of vision. He was white, both fists clenched.

"Drop your gun, you filthy Peculiar." The deputy didn't waver.

"I can kill her now." Abel sounded way too eager. Lena put her hands over her ears.

The deputy countered. "The marshal won't care. He said she's one of them too. It will be one less Peculiar for us to round up for Scree."

Lena choked.

"You—" The word exploded from Jimson just as the back door burst open. Cold air rushed in.

Milo stood in the doorway with Mrs. Mumbles at his side. "What's going on here?"

Abel started at the sound of the door, and as he turned, one of the deputies fired. Abel jerked, his arms spread wide as he tumbled backward. The shotgun, still clutched in his hand, fired as it hit the floor.

As the deputy dodged the random shot, Jimson grabbed Lena's hand and dragged her through the door to the outside.

"Wait, Milo's still in there!"

But Jimson didn't wait. Mr. Beasley called from the roof. "Up here! Use the stairs past the garden!"

The snow had stopped falling, but the stairs to the widow's walk were still covered with a fine powder. Jimson, with Lena in tow, ran through the garden to the base of the wooden stairs. They began to climb two steps at a time toward Mr. Beasley. From the north wing of the house, the other three deputies rounded the corner. Lena's feet, numb with cold, slithered on the narrow treads. Her breath came in ragged gasps. Jimson supported her by one arm. Three floors to the roof, and there, just a few steps above them, was Mr. Beasley. He was leaning out from the most remarkable contraption Lena had ever seen.

"It's the aerocopter!" Jimson shouted, but the words made no sense to her.

Mr. Beasley hung out the window of what appeared to be a gleaming red Concord coach detailed with yellow trim. A metal pole like a ship's mast topped the roof with a circle of wooden blades. Another, smaller, rotor was attached to one end of the coach. Crates and boxes were stacked inside and tied to the sides.

"Get in. Quickly now." Mr. Beasley, in top hat and tails, reached for Lena's arm.

Below, the three deputies had reached the base of the stairs. The laboratory door crashed open. Thomas Saltre appeared behind Leticia Pollet. She pointed toward the roof and raised her voice. "There they are! He's escaping with the rest o' the bad ones!"

Jimson hoisted Lena though the door of the coach and scrambled in behind her.

"She's already fueled and waiting to go!" Mr. Beasley lowered a pair of goggles over his eyes. The blades on the end rotor began to whirl. Lena dropped onto a leather-tufted bench and found that Merilee was already seated, leaning against one wall of the coach. Once inside, Lena realized that what appeared to be the walls of a Concord coach was really painted fabric stretched over an interior frame. The snug interior space was filled by two leather benches that faced each other, with a metal boiler in between. It had been installed in place of the middle bench and radiated delicious heat.

"It's the same coated fabric used by dirigibles," Jimson told her proudly. "But Mr. Beasley modified the frame by using titantum."

The coach rumbled and shook as the rotor blades whirred faster and faster. On one wall a gleaming instrument panel displayed a variety of brass levers and knobs. "What do those do?" Lena asked.

"Altitude indicator, boiler-temperature dial, fuel gauge, steam-pressure valve." Jimson pointed from one indicator to another so quickly it made Lena's head spin.

Mr. Beasley spoke. "If my calculations are correct, when we reach the end of the ramp we will become airborne and experience sustained flight. Of course, there was no time for a practice run."

Lena stuck her head out the window. A wooden ramp sloped all the way from the widow's walk down onto the roof of the south wing. Lena had never noticed it before. It must have been installed when she heard the clattering and pounding on the roof.

Then she had a terrible thought. She turned to Mr. Beasley. "What about Mrs. Pollet?"

"The marshal believes she's nothing more than a house-keeper. And that's what she is. She'll be fine until we send for her. That's been the plan all along. It's why she's playing at turning us in." His voice was pitched to a shout above the whirring blades. As the spinning rotor accelerated, Mr. Beasley used two hands to pull up on a lever.

The aerocopter lurched forward. Lena grabbed on to the window frame. Jimson braced his arms on the window opening as he leaned the entire top half of his body out one window.

"We're moving. It's takeoff!" he shouted.

"Get yourself back inside," Mr. Beasley shouted in return. "They may not be the best shots, but it's better not to give them a clear target!"

Mr. Beasley's last words were drowned when, with a sudden lurch, the coach rolled forward and shot down the ramp on rumbling wheels. As they hurtled forward, Lena stuck her head out the window just in time to see the end of the roof approaching. Beyond, the ramp dropped off into nothingness. At Lena's side, Merilee Pollet worried a wooden rosary as she mumbled prayers. Merilee's eyes were shut, but Lena couldn't look away. They were about to shoot straight off the roof!

Mr. Beasley held on to his top hat with one hand. "Don't worry! The upper blades are spinning as a result of the head wind! That should keep us aloft! But it may be wise to brace for impact just in case."

A shot rang out from the marshal's gun below and glanced off the roof of Zephyr House. Lena dropped flat on the bench and peered over the window frame. Freezing air stung her face. Far below, Thomas Saltre threw his head back, the bowler tumbling behind. Above the noise of the wheels, over the faint roar of the sea, Lena could have sworn she heard him laughing.

And then the clattering of the wheels stopped. There was another terrible lurch, and they dropped. Lena's stomach rose. She pressed her hand to her mouth. Never mind the marshal and his deputies; they would be crushed on the ground like insects.

Merilee screamed.

And then the rotor caught. With a jerk their descent stopped as wind spun the blades. The coach shuddered side to side, and Lena found herself on top of Merilee.

Jimson whooped and hollered.

Mr. Beasley gave a grunt of satisfaction. "I believe that the titantum was the key. It kept the frame and the boiler light enough, but I really didn't know for sure."

CHAPTER 24

THE BORDERS OF SCREE

EVERYONE WAS SILENT. WITHOUT THE CLATTER OF THE WHEELS, Lena could hardly believe they were moving. But when she gathered her courage and looked down, she discovered that they had gained altitude and were traveling south at a shocking rate of speed. There was nothing supporting them other than air. And that thought made her feel so funny that she pulled her head back inside.

"Aren't we going the wrong way?" Jimson asked. He had not, Lena noticed, stopped smiling since they took off.

"Not for long!" Mr. Beasley was adjusting a brass-and-wood handle that protruded from the instrument panel. "We steer by a rudder. A nice wide arc and we'll be heading north. This device"—he gestured to a long brass lever—"is the cyclic control. It lets me adjust the pitch of the blades."

"But what makes the top rotor spin?" Lena asked. "It looks like the steam pipe only goes to the rotor in the back."

"Smart girl! This"—he pointed—"is the fuel tank. It's filled with kerosene. It heats the water in the boiler. The water turns to steam and powers the rotor. The top rotor spins by aerodynamic forces. It doesn't need a motor, only enough air moving through it. That's why we needed a running start."

"It's amazing!" Jimson eyed Mr. Beasley's hand on the rudder. "May I fly it?"

"All in good time. You'll be doing everything from manning the gauges and filling the fuel tank to steering."

Lena noticed that Merilee hadn't said a word. The general ebullience seemed to have missed her, and Lena wondered if she feared for her mother. "Merilee, it's just like Mr. Beasley said, the marshal and his deputies have no idea that your mother is a Peculiar." She hesitated. "They believe she's just a housekeeper who was willing to help them."

Silent tears spilled from Merilee's hazel eyes, and she shook her head from side to side. "And what about the others?"

Of course Merilee wouldn't know that Abel had been shot. Lena darted a quick look at Jimson, who was suddenly subdued.

"One of the deputies shot Abel when he was holding Lena hostage. Abel was threatening to shoot Lena." Jimson's tone was bald, matter-of-fact, but his eyes, Lena noticed, were clouded with trouble.

Mr. Beasley's sigh was deep and ponderous. "I've been afraid something like that might happen."

Merilee made a small whimpering sound.

Mr. Beasley continued. "Abel was a bitter man. After his father was killed in the mines, he let his bitterness take hold and it grew until there was little else left. He wasn't the boy I once knew. I hoped I could help him, but he was never able to contain his impulses, most of which were violent. It's a terrible tragedy." He paused and removed his goggles, dabbing at his eyes. "I do believe that he would have been happier in Scree. He always volunteered for the most dangerous jobs, like helping the prisoner on the train escape."

"Was he a Peculiar?" Lena felt strange saying the word out loud in front of Merilee.

But it was Merilee who answered. "Abel and his brothers are goblins."

"But—"A cold wave of nausea passed over Lena. She felt Jimson's eyes on her.

"And what about Milo?" Jimson asked to change the subject. "He came just in time to save us."

"Milo has been around the world a time or two. He knew all about my business at Zephyr House, but he managed to keep himself apart from it. If anyone can land on his feet, it's Milo."

"And what about Mrs. Mumbles?" Jimson continued. "Do you know, I think it was the cat that brought Milo to us at the right time!"

Mr. Beasley laughed. "Never underestimate a feline. They understand much more than we give them credit for. Especially

Mumbles. She'll be company for Mrs. Pollet. She likes the cat more than she lets on."

Despite the warmth from the boiler, a cold wind whisked in through the glassless windows. Merilee shivered.

"If we draw the curtains, it will be a little warmer," Lena offered.

"Not yet. I've stashed blankets under the seats." Mr. Beasley reached under his bench and pulled out a plaid wool blanket. "There should be one for each of us . . . Well, what do we have here? A stowaway!" Along with the blankets Mr. Beasley lifted up Mrs. Mumbles by the scruff of her neck. "I guess she's more of an adventurer than I thought!"

"Mumbles!" Jimson exclaimed, reaching for the animal. But the cat ignored him and jumped from Mr. Beasley's arms to Merilee's lap, where she contented herself by circling once and settling down in a tight coil.

Lena handed a blanket to Merilee and then wrapped herself up as if she were on a familiar carriage ride rather than sailing through the sky.

She covered Merilee's hand with her own. The tall girl was tentatively looking out the window as the aerocopter banked into the wide turn that would bring them northward. "Where will we be going?" Merilee asked.

"Now, that part of the plan hadn't quite been finalized." Mr. Beasley looked abashed. "I did hope we had at least another day. Thomas Saltre will have a watch over all the borders. Crossing the border away from the road is my first plan. Then we need to proceed deep enough into Scree to be away from search parties. All my mining interests will be watched, so we can't go there."

He reached under the seat again. "I do have one more provision for our journey. Miss Mattacascar, your purse!" With a flourish he held aloft Lena's purse that had been stolen on the trip to Knoster. "Abel gave it to me some days ago. With all the brouhaha, I never had time to give it to you."

Lena reached for her bag. "I can't believe it." She opened the drawstring and looked inside. The money was gone, but she had expected that. She felt for the slit in the silk lining and inserted two fingers. The papers were still there. With a great sigh of relief she pulled them out. Then she removed her shawl. She looked at Jimson and Mr. Beasley. "Please avert your eyes."

Jimson's eyebrows rose, but he did as he was asked. And Mr. Beasley followed suit.

Lena unbuttoned her jacket and opened the small jet buttons on her dress. She reached inside and found the folded letter pinned to her chemise. She withdrew it, leaving the money in place, and did up the buttons. "Perhaps this will be of some help." She extended the letter and then the folded papers from her purse to Mr. Beasley. "For my eighteenth birthday, my father left me a letter, which I've kept close to my heart. He also left me a small inheritance, which I kept in the lining of my purse. They are a map and a deed to the Mattacascar family mine."

Jimson whistled and looked over Mr. Beasley's shoulder.

Mr. Beasley quickly scanned the map. "This is farther than we can travel by air without refueling, but the area's remote enough that I doubt we'd be discovered. I am somewhat familiar with this part of Scree. The nearest outpost is Ducktown. Does anyone still work your family mine?"

"I don't know anything about it. I didn't even know there was a family mine," Lena answered.

"Interestingly enough, the deed doesn't mention what type of ore is mined there, but the claim looks genuine. Yes, Lena. I think this will do very nicely." Smiling, he carefully refolded the deed and letter, returning them both to her. "We'll use the map and my wind triangle to help with navigation. Of course, dead reckoning depends on estimating our speed. It's not completely accurate, but it should get us close to your mine."

It was so cold that Lena longed to draw the heavy curtains, but her longing to watch the landscape sail by was stronger. The only sounds were the rushing of the wind and the whirring of the propellers. They had turned inland from the coast, and below them the frosted clumps of evergreens grew closer and thicker. Farmland gave way to forest, punctuated by outcroppings of rock.

"The main border crossing is on the coast at the rail line. We'll be crossing farther to the east, over an area that's difficult to traverse. By now the marshal will have sent a telegram to alert the border guards. They'll send an arrest warrant with the Pony Express across Scree. We can only hope that we're well ahead of him and that he has no idea where we're headed. Jimson, we need some kerosene added to the tank to fuel the boiler."

Jimson unscrewed the cap of the metal fuel can and used a funnel to pour the liquid into the tank.

"How far are we from the border?" Merilee asked. She had the blanket pulled up to her nose and well tucked in at her sides. Unlike Lena, she seemed less interested in the view than in staying warm.

"We'll be there in another thirty minutes if my calculations are correct. Of course, it's always difficult to tell where one country ends and another begins without a marker of some sort. The trick isn't the crossing. It's how we'll eventually land."

"How does she land?" Jimson lovingly stroked the fabric walls of the aerocopter.

"I am not precisely sure, but I do have theories."

Jimson sighed. "This is the best day of my life."

CHAPTER 25

THE BORDERLANDS

LENA FOUND THAT TRAVELING BY AEROCOPTER SUITED HER.
She tried not to think about what Nana Crane would say. It
would, to Lena's reckoning, be the final confirmation of her
own goblin blood. She also tried not to think about poor
Abel with his flat brown eyes. Was that what it meant to be a
goblin? She shuddered.

She let her mind settle on the image she had held at
bay, the marshal standing at the base of the widow's walk,
head thrown back looking up at her and seeing only another
Peculiar. All that time he had been using her, and she had
allowed it. More than allowed it, she had envisioned traveling
with him as her guide to Scree. And she had betrayed Mr.
Beasley and his work at Zephyr House. She had betrayed
them all. She burned with shame, feeling the hollow place
inside her, the place where her soul should reside, open
wider.

Across the coach Jimson laughed at something Mr. Beasley said. They both examined the wind triangle as Mr. Beasley explained his calculations. Jimson certainly did not seem to be pining for his missing Pansy. As she watched, Lena could feel his excitement catch like a flame to kindling. Despite the marshal, despite almost being shot by flat-eyed Abel, it was impossible to stay solemn when she was traveling in an aerocopter. If she was doomed to be wild, as Nana Crane had predicted, she would enjoy every minute of it.

Merilee, on the other hand, didn't seem to be faring half so well. She alternated between looking seasick and terrified. Which, Lena thought, was not in keeping with the reality of her wings. While Jimson and Mr. Beasley discussed the necessary terrain for a smooth landing, Lena whispered the question that had been nagging at her ever since she first saw the drawings of Annuncius syndrome in Mr. Beasley's sketchbook. "Could you fly? When you had your wings, I mean." And then she blushed, wondering if her question was too presumptuous.

Merilee looked at her with a small frown puckering her broad brow. "No, of course not. The wings were never strong enough. But I did try once when they first grew in. I jumped off a fence . . . and ended up on my face in the dirt." For the first time Lena saw laughter in Merilee's eyes.

"Were they heavy?"

"A bit. But the worst part was the itching—day and night as the feathers came in."

Then she looked shyly at Lena. "What's wrong with your hands and feet?"

Instinctively, Lena's feet crept under the hem of her skirt. "I don't know. Nobody does. But I was born this way." The next words were very hard to force out. "Some people say my father was a goblin."

Merilee looked at her directly with her wide hazel eyes. "They're not all like Abel, you know."

Lena leaned in closer. "You've known other goblins?"

"In Scree. There were others in the mines. I was very small, but I remember playing with a family of them. They were some of my best friends." She shrugged her thin shoulders.

"But did they look like me? Did they have hands and feet like mine?"

"No, not that I remember. They looked just like anyone else."

A gust of wind buffeted the coach. Merilee turned very white and closed her eyes again.

"It looks like we're headed into some nasty weather," Mr. Beasley announced. "I suggest drawing the curtains to preserve warmth." He was holding a compass and a brass spyglass. "We are on course. The border is just ahead. The land changes to rock and shale, but we may miss seeing it in all this weather. The clouds might work in our favor by adding some cover, but they will make navigation more difficult."

They were entering a wilderness of gray. Clouds clustered together like fleecy animals in a herd. It looked to Lena as if she could step outside and be carried away on their soft backs. But with the clouds came a chilling damp. It swamped the coach, forming small ice crystals on the window frame. They drew the curtains and leaned into the warmth of the boiler. Lena rubbed her hands together, glad this time for her gloves. If it was this cold now, how would they bear it in the middle of the night? There was a small hiss, and a light flared in the darkness of the coach. Mr. Beasley lit the kerosene lantern that hung from the ceiling. As the light swayed, shadows played across their faces, and Lena recalled her trip on the train to Knob Knoster.

Merilee leaned her head back against the tufted seat and closed her eyes. Mrs. Mumbles splayed across her lap like a cat fur muff. Mr. Beasley steered and scribbled in a small notebook, but Jimson's eyes, solemn now and deeply shadowed, were fastened on Lena as if he too was remembering the long-ago train ride. When she met his eyes, Lena found herself blushing and short of breath. Then she thought of Pansy and deliberately averted her gaze. The coach jarred side to side, the curtains fluttered and, with a sickening jolt, they dropped.

"It's just the air currents. Turbulence. We've flown into a pressure differential. We'll be fine if we can keep our stomachs." Mr. Beasley's confidence was reassuring, but for the first time Lena realized how vulnerable they were, sailing unsupported through vast miles of sky. "I'm going to drop us down a little to see if we can get below the storm. Jimson, I want you to pull this lever until the gauge reads minus ten degrees. Here." He pointed to a small brass handle. "I'll try and keep her steering straight. You might feel another sudden drop. Nothing to be alarmed about."

Lena clutched the edge of the bench as Jimson scooted forward and gripped the lever. With a ratcheting tick, they dipped, suddenly enough to make Merilee reach for the empty bucket under the seat. Lena felt her own stomach roil. Looking up, she again found Jimson's eyes. This time she didn't look away.

Then they were mercifully steady again. Jimson dropped his gaze as Mr. Beasley parted the curtains. "We're below the clouds. Any lower and we'll be brushing treetops. We should have crossed the border a good ten minutes ago. I suggest we look for a place to land."

"You mean we're not going to fly all night?" Lena felt strangely disappointed.

"Too difficult to navigate in the dark! We can't see the landmarks. And there are mountains just ahead. We don't want to risk flying into one. The trick is finding the right landing spot. We need a smooth landing area, but also a place with enough grade to aid in takeoff."

Lena peered out the window. In the dim light of October's end, sparse evergreens rose like ghosts. As far as she could see, in every direction, there were no smooth places for a landing.

"We're not quite as far as I thought. We're crossing into Scree now!" Mr. Beasley exclaimed.

Below, the trees gave way to rock, layers of dark gray shale like shingles on a roof.

Once more Jimson was leaning halfway out of the aerocopter. "The stony borderlands. What a view!"

All four of the passengers gazed over the wide band of shale and flint that ran along the border. A brown-and-gray world opened below them, as if cloud and fog had sucked all color from the landscape. Sailing low, they just barely cleared the tops of giant spruce and cedars, the ghostly sentinels to this rocky kingdom.

"We'll have to land soon, before the mountains," Mr. Beasley warned.

"But all I can see is rock." Lena wondered if Mr. Beasley really knew what he was doing.

Jimson held the brass spyglass to one eye. "I believe there's water just ahead. It looks like a lake on the flank of a hill."

Layers of rock gave way to wide swatches of bony earth. Boulders erupted through the thin skin of soil. Trees were still sparse, but in the fast-approaching distance evergreens ringed the feet of snow-blanketed mountains.

Jimson handed the glass to Mr. Beasley. "I don't suppose we can land in water."

"We have no idea how deep the lake is, but the land just above it may be our best option. It appears to be an open meadow and high enough on the hillside to facilitate our takeoff." Mr. Beasley considered the situation, then handed the spyglass to Lena. "The trick will be to not land in the middle of the lake but above it, in the meadow. I want you all to follow my instructions precisely. We will drop as gradually as possible."

Jimson was in charge of reducing fuel to the boiler. Merilee secured everything in the coach as well as possible, and Lena, who was longing to have some real part in flying the aerocopter, was allowed to help Mr. Beasley steer. "We want the rotor tilted into the wind, to maintain autorotation. We'll gradually drop, and at the last minute we'll slow our descent by angling up the top rotor. At that point, we should be traveling about seven miles per hour. When we land, I'll apply the brake."

Lena, with one hand on the rudder lever beside Mr. Beasley's, watched their descent toward the lake. It grew larger—a pale glacial blue oval surrounded by a gravelly shore. Suddenly, the drop was precipitous. The water of the lake came rushing toward them.

"Hold off, Jimson!" Mr. Beasley barked. He pulled on the lever. The aerocopter listed sideways and then straightened, but they were too close to the water. One wheel caught the surface of the lake, spraying water, tipping the machine perilously to one side. Lena slammed against the hot pipe of the boiler, shrieked, and landed hard on Jimson. Mrs. Mumbles tumbled in an undignified heap to the floor. The machine righted, jolted a few yards, and bounced to a grinding stop on the lake's beach as Mr. Beasley firmly applied the brake lever.

Everyone was silent. Lena could hear Mr. Beasley

breathing. A trickle of sweat had run down his face, causing one painted eyebrow to melt. Jimson carefully lifted Lena off his right hip and rubbed at the welt on the side of his face where it had smashed into the bench. "Are you all right?"

"I will be. It's a good thing I'm wearing two layers of skirts. I didn't get burned at all."

With her tail curled in the air, Mrs. Mumbles yowled, shook herself indignantly, and began to preen. Then Merilee began to laugh, and once she started they all joined in. It was a relief to be alive, to have finally made it into the wilds of Scree.

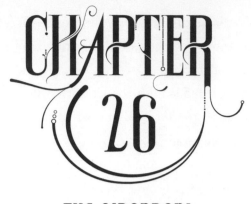

CHAPTER 26

THE GIRANDONI

LENA WAS THE FIRST TO STEP FROM THE COACH ONTO THE SOIL OF Scree. The ground at the edge of the lake was a fine gravel. A few lone pines, like point men from the northern forests, dotted the shore. The wind whipped at her hair, tearing it from its twist, and she staggered at the feel of solid ground beneath her feet. Even on the ground, she could still feel the sway of the aerocopter. Upon landing, one wheel had come loose, and the copter listed sideways. Other than that, the machine had performed admirably.

"We need to christen her!" Jimson said fondly, running a hand over her gleaming red paint. "It has to be something magnificent."

"Well, then, I can't think of it," said Merilee. "I don't know any magnificent names." She scooped Mrs. Mumbles up in her arms and dropped from the door of the aerocopter to the ground. But the cat wriggled from her grasp and jumped to freedom as if she was eager for solid ground under her paws.

For a few minutes all was silent as they pondered an appropriate name.

"I've got it! Why not Aeolus, god of the winds?" Lena suggested.

Mr. Beasley removed his top hat and goggles as he ducked out through the coach door. "Thankfully there's no damage inside. It's unfortunate that we didn't make it farther up the mountain. Aeolus it is, then! Welcome to the free land of Scree."

"It smells the same, like I remember it, like pine and snow," Merilee said. "Even in the summers here there was always a faint smell of snow." She wrapped her thin arms across her chest. "My father always said it was the wind carrying the scent from the glaciers in the north. Whatever causes it, it smells like home."

"We don't have much light left, and I'd like to look the Aeolus over before we lose what little is left," Mr. Beasley said. "But first there are a few things we must discuss. So gather round." He drew a circle in the air with one arm; Lena, Jimson, and Merilee drew in closer. "Having broken the laws of our country and fled the consequences, we are now officially outlaws. That means we must be constantly on the alert. Already federal marshals and lawmen are looking for us. News spreads fast. Telegraph lines run as far north as the train."

Jimson nodded. "I heard that, but we're some hours in from the coast."

"The Pony Express still carries news throughout the rest of Scree. There aren't any telegraph lines in the interior yet. Any lead we have may be swallowed up in the night. Because Scree is technically still a free land, our laws should have no jurisdiction here. However"—and here he cocked his one eyebrow—"it is an occupied land, and lands that are occupied follow the laws of the occupiers. That means that if we are caught, we are subject to the laws of our own country. Be vigilant. Watch out for each other."

"But—" Jimson interrupted.

Mr. Beasley held up one hand. "I have not quite finished. Scree presents its own problems. There is no infrastructure. Travel in winter can be difficult, and some say Scree is a lawless society. The people who have come here for quick profit are risk-takers and opportunists; many are used to living outside the law. Don't give your trust too easily. I have taken some precautions for all of us." He unlatched one of the leather trunks secured to the Aeolus. Reaching inside, he removed a rifle, which he held aloft. "The Girandoni! A forty-six caliber, twenty-two shot repeating air rifle! I got it from Meriwether Lewis. It was made by an Italian fellow, and the Austrians used these quite effectively against Napoleon."

"It's beautiful," Jimson said breathlessly. "A real jim-dandy."

It was the longest gun Lena had ever seen. The butt was covered in black leather. An eagle with scrollwork was carved into a brass plate that ornamented one side, just above the barrel. The narrow barrel was overlaid with polished wood. If guns could be beautiful, she thought, this one was.

"The chamber holds twenty-two round balls, which are expelled by air pressure." Mr. Beasley reached back into the trunk and removed a small hand-operated pump. "It takes fifteen hundred strokes to build up enough pressure in the gun so that it can fire forty times." He flipped a latch to open the chamber and dropped in the small round balls. "Each time I press the lever, one ball drops into place in the chamber." Then he removed the butt of the rifle. "This is where the pump attaches to the valve. I pumped it up before takeoff." He handed the rifle to Jimson for inspection.

"Fifteen hundred strokes! That must have taken forever." Merilee gave it an experimental pump.

"Between Milo and me it took thirty-four minutes exactly. But it gives us eight hundred pounds of pressure per square inch." He looked at Lena and Merilee. "I want you each to understand how this rifle works. I'm planning on leaving it loaded tonight in the aerocopter in case it's needed. Jimson and I will have the pistol."

"I've never shot a gun before," Lena said.

"Rifle," Mr. Beasley corrected. "You'll find that it's heavy but accurate. The butt fits into your shoulder here." He tapped the space below Lena's collarbone.

"I did shoot a gun once," said Merilee. "It was only a pistol. And when it went off, I closed my eyes."

"Let me demonstrate." Mr. Beasley reached for the rifle, and Jimson reluctantly handed it back.

"When you cock the hammer, it's ready to fire. You always pull the hammer toward you. If you push it the other way, air escapes and—" A loud shriek pierced the air.

Lena covered her ears.

"So, always *toward* you," Mr. Beasley continued. "Then you aim and pull the trigger." He raised the gun, letting the butt nestle into the hollow of his shoulder.

Prepared this time, Lena again covered her ears with her hands while Mr. Beasley sighted down the length of the barrel and pulled the trigger. Bark and pine needles splintered from a tree limb some yards away. Surprisingly, the shot was not as loud as Lena expected—not nearly as loud as the high-pitched squeal when air was released from the rifle. And there was no puff of smoke or flash.

"We never used guns. We just stuck close with the other miners," Merilee said. "And we never were out after dark if we could help it."

Mr. Beasley nodded approval. "Very wise. But I believe that this rifle might just serve us well. Now, we should get busy cooking some food and setting up accommodations for the night. If we have a small fire before it gets completely dark, it will be less noticeable. Goodness, where has that cat gotten to? Here, kitty, kitty!"

Lena formed a strong impression that Mr. Beasley was trying to distract them from Merilee's words. What would be the problem with being out at night? She looked at the giant pines and solemn boulders surrounding them. She was a city girl; she had never spent a night outdoors in the country before. Perhaps there were animals to be worried about. Mrs. Mumbles was not responding to his calls, but Mr. Beasley didn't appear alarmed. He continued giving them directions.

"The water from the lake is fresh. I suggest we boil that rather than use up our own supplies, and that we refill our own water tanks. Jimson, there is a small tent I would like you to set up. The ladies will be sleeping in the aerocopter; you and I should find the tent quite adequate."

Merilee had helped her mother gather the provisions for the journey. Because they had left sooner than expected, only some of their supplies had been crated and brought on board the Aeolus. "If you slice and cook up some of them apples, Lena, I'll cook up some cornmeal cakes. We've got some strips of dried venison from Milo that will be mighty tasty."

Lena marveled at how competent Merilee was with cooking. Nana Crane had done all the cooking at home, and whenever Lena had tried to help in the kitchen, she had been shooed out from underfoot—much to her relief. Cooking had never interested her very much when there were books to read. Now she was all thumbs as she tried to cut up and roast the apple slices over the small fire.

Jimson managed to set up the small two-man tent and

then joined Mr. Beasley in inspecting the Aeolus and the fuel supplies. Lena could feel rather than see Jimson's glances as he busied himself with work. Whenever she looked up, he quickly averted his eyes.

There was something cheerful about a fire, even in the enormity of Scree. The sky turned a blue so deep and rich that it was almost painful to look at, and in the north the first faint star peered shyly down. For her first night as an outlaw, Lena felt uncommonly content.

"The food's ready, such as it is." Merilee's cheeks glowed with the heat from the fire, and she wiped her hands on the folds of her skirt. "It looks like we're without plates, but I guess it tastes just as good out of the pots."

"Better," Jimson said as he sniffed the apples and corn cakes.

A movement in the shadows caught Lena's eye. She froze. A small, dark shape slunk into the firelight. "Mumbles!" The cat deposited her contribution to the evening meal—a fine big mouse that she dropped at Mr. Beasley's feet. "Ah, Mumbles, resourceful as ever." He scratched one ear, and she rumbled a purr in response, then settled down with the mouse between her paws.

Even though the night was chilly and they were forced to sit on the ground or rocks by the fire, it was a festive meal. Perhaps, Lena considered, being an outlaw wasn't so bad after all. She tried to envision her mother or Nana Crane eating out of a communal pot by an open fire, but her imagination failed at the attempt. Perhaps it was her goblin blood that made it so easy to adapt to this new life.

Jimson gnawed on a strip of venison. "I wonder what type of mine your family owns. Gold? Silver?"

"I wonder too. I didn't even know there was a family mine until I opened my father's letter."

"The majority of mines in Scree are coal or copper." Mr. Beasley warmed his hands over the open flames and popped another apple slice in his mouth. "Of course, the opportunists hope that this will be another gold rush like the one they had in California. This is new territory; there could be anything in the mines."

"But I thought your family had mines in Scree," Lena said.

The deep blue was giving way to an inky darkness, and millions of stars freckled the sky.

"The Beasley fortune was made in the mines—coal mines. But it was before our government decided that Scree was *terra nullius*. My grandfather was a man of extraordinary vision, and he was restless to boot. So when he was exploring this vast Northern Province, he befriended some of the indigenous peoples and learned about their mining practices. My father continued with the mine. I developed other interests—medicine, exploration—and the mine was eventually sold. But not until my father had made a considerable fortune."

The cold crept in with the dark. Merilee shivered as she scraped the remains from the pot. "I wouldn't be surprised if there was snow before morning."

Mr. Beasley nodded and stood. "I believe it is time we retired for the evening. I'd like to get an early start, considering we're on the run. And we need to put that fire out."

Jimson used one foot to scrape dirt on the flames and then stomped out the remaining embers. Without the fire, the dark drew closer. The cold grew biting and Lena looked longingly at the coach. As she brushed dirt and twigs from the back of her skirt, the night was split by a long, lonely cry. The cry was taken up by another and then by another. Mrs. Mumbles, claws extended, leapt to her old perch on Mr. Beasley's shoulders. He soothed her with a stroke.

"Wolves. We used to hear them most nights," Merilee said.

Her words were casual, but Lena detected something in the pitch—the slightest inflection, a reverberation of fear. A sliver of ice caught in her chest. Again the cries came, ringing them on all sides. "Don't we need fire to keep them back?" Lena's question dropped into the dark.

"Wolves are not usually interested in attacking people, despite what the stories say. But Jimson, Mrs. Mumbles, and I will be keeping watch." Mr. Beasley tickled the cat under her chin.

Once Lena and Merilee were inside the coach, the night eased back into itself. The close walls and the lingering warmth from the boiler conspired to keep threats at bay. Lena felt a twinge of guilt as she looked at the tent Jimson and Mr. Beasley would be sharing. She drew a wool blanket over her heavy shawl, shimmied the petticoat off from under her skirt, unlaced her boots, and curled up on one of the tufted benches. The plush fabric was soft against her cheek. She could hear Merilee settling in across from her.

"We're safe here," Lena sighed.

"I wouldn't be so sure. Wolves in Scree are different."

"Different how?" Lena propped herself up on one arm.

"Well, for the first thing, they're larger—almost the size of a pony. And they're cunning. We heard stories, time and again, of wolves working together to steal livestock or people."

"But Mr. Beasley said they don't attack people."

"These wolves do. We knew a family that had their daughter stolen by wolves, and an old man who worked the mines with us disappeared one night on his way home from a friend's house. Both times there were wolf prints. Big as your hands, Lena."

A cry rose, farther away this time.

"Wolves—they aren't the worst of it. There are things in Scree people have no name for, 'least no name most people know."

"You're not talking about Peculiars?" The word stuck in Lena's throat, and then it was out hanging in the air between them.

"'Course not. And don't be afraid to say it. Scree is full of different folk, people like me. But there are others—drifters and bounty hunters. The bounty hunters are the worst. They'd kill you for a dollar and not think a thing of it. And then there are the ones no one really knows, people who lived here time out of mind."

The ice sliver was back, dislodged this time, shivering its way through Lena. "If Scree's so dire, why did you come back?"

Merilee snorted. "I didn't have much choice. I need what Mr. Beasley can do. The operation's still too fresh. The wings'll come back without treatments." Her disembodied voice sounded conspiratorial in the dark. "But that's not the only reason. There are hundreds of people who need doctoring in Scree. Peculiars who work the mines don't have anyone to care for them. I know a little about nursing sick folk, and thought I could learn some things more from Mr. Beasley. I'll stay and help them some."

Lena heard Merilee rustling as she struggled to find a comfortable position. In the distance the wolf cries rose again. Lena tried to scrape Merilee's description from her mind.

"And what about you, Lena? Why'd you come north in the first place?"

The boiler ticked as it cooled. Lena drew her legs up to her chest to conserve the warmth. "For an adventure, I guess. To find the mine my father left me." Even in the dark, she couldn't be as open as Merilee; there were some things better left unsaid.

"I thought you might mean to find out if you're like me— half Peculiar."

"Your father wasn't a Peculiar, was he?" The word kept

sticking in her throat, left a sour taste in her mouth. "How then were the wings passed on?"

"No, he wasn't. But he loved us just the same. He didn't have to go to Scree with us when we were sent, but he did. Did your father get sent away?"

Lena felt like a piece of fruit, each question peeling part of her away, exposing more of the apple-white flesh beneath. "No. He left because he wanted to." It was the first time she had spoken that truth out loud. "He said that he had no talent for normal life."

Merilee was silent for some time, but Lena could hear her breathing on the other side of the coach. "I'm sorry for that. Maybe you'll find him up here. Maybe there's some reason he left, that he didn't tell you."

"I don't think so. I think he just grew tired of us."

CHAPTER 27

TRAVELS TO DUCKTOWN

SOMETHING REELED LENA IN FROM HER DREAMS. SHE SAT UP, aware of a stiffness in her neck and of moonlight on snow. Merilee had been right. A thin white blanket now stretched across the rocky soil. The world was eerily silent, the drone of the wind gone, and into that silence came a faint noise—a snuffling, a slathering that made Lena's heart grow cold. She parted the curtain. In the distance the silhouette of a large beast loomed black against the snow. It was the wolf of nightmares or fairy tales, twice as large as any wolf should be. But the snuffling and pawing came from somewhere closer.

"Merilee!" There was no response from the seat across from Lena. She raised her voice. "Merilee, wake up!"

A rustling and murmuring in the darkness.

"The wolves are here!"

"Where?" Merilee's voice was alert now.

"I can see one in the distance, and I hear one right outside."

"Right outside?" Merilee's voice was rising with panic.

As her words hung in the air, a howl rose like a summons.

Through the window Lena saw a great wolf no more than a foot from the Aeolus. The creature's muzzle was pointed skyward. On the far edge of the clearing, three more wolves trotted into view. And as the howl continued, the wolves began to run, bounding across the vast expanse of white toward the Aeolus and the small tent pitched just yards away. Frozen with fear, Lena watched their progression. The flap of the tent lifted. Jimson's tousled head protruded, followed by Mr. Beasley's, a striped stocking cap pulled over his bald head.

"Here, Lena." Merilee thrust the air rifle at her. "I'm no good with guns. It's already loaded."

With shaking hands Lena gripped the long rifle, butting the stock into her shoulder as Mr. Beasley had shown.

She watched as Mr. Beasley stepped out of the tent, a revolver grasped in two hands. At her side, Merilee trembled. The wolves were just yards from the tent now. As Mr. Beasley raised the gun to fire, a streak of orange flew from the tent. Mrs. Mumbles launched herself at the head of the lead beast.

Lena heard the crack of a shot. The second wolf faltered, but the others didn't slow. Mrs. Mumbles clung to the wolf's head. Lena sighted down the rifle, knowing she had little chance of hitting the wolf and that if by luck she did, she might hit Mrs. Mumbles as well. Her arms shook. Then she remembered Mr. Beasley's demonstration. As the lead wolf shook Mrs. Mumbles from his head, jaws snapping, Lena rammed the lever on the air rifle forward. An earsplitting squeal pierced the night. As if they had hit an invisible wall, the wolves tumbled to a stop, turned, and fled into the distance.

Lena's own ears felt as if they might bleed. Mrs. Mumbles lay like a cast-off fur coat in the snow. Jimson rushed from the tent to scoop her up. Lena turned to see Merilee's lips moving, but her ears were not working. Instead of words, Lena heard a strange whining.

With a blanket wrapped around her, she struggled from the coach. Had the cat really tried to defend them? And had she survived? The cold bit at Lena's cheeks as she ran forward, trying not to stumble over the draped blanket. Jimson cradled the cat. As Mr. Beasley reached his side, Mrs. Mumbles stirred in Jimson's arms and then leapt nimbly to Mr. Beasley's shoulder.

"Brilliant! You were brilliant!" Mr. Beasley had to shout before Lena could hear him above the persistent whine. "I never would have thought of that solution!"

"I've never shot anything before, and I was afraid of hitting Mrs. Mumbles. This seemed the easiest thing to do!" She didn't add that there had been something exhilarating about using the gun, even if she hadn't actually fired it. Nana Crane's face rose in her mind, nodding smugly. Lena felt her heart sink, but when she looked at Jimson, his face was split by a crooked grin.

"You are the bravest girl I have ever met!" Jimson's words

spread a rush of warmth through Lena, and she felt her face flush with pleasure.

"And I've never seen a cat do anything like that. Aren't normal cats supposed to be afraid of dogs and wolves?" Jimson asked as he reached to scratch Mrs. Mumbles behind her ears.

"She's not your ordinary cat," Mr. Beasley said, a note of fondness creeping into his voice. "She's a Scree-cat. One of my patients at Zephyr House left her as a parting gift when Mumbles was still a juvenile. I'm not sure I appreciated it at the time."

Merilee cocked her head and squinted at Mrs. Mumbles, who was pressing her head into Jimson's scratching fingers. "Scree-cats don't tame easy. You can't pick them; they have to pick you. We tried to tame one once when I was little. Wouldn't have anything to do with us, and then we found it living with a family down the road. They're fierce, loyal, and not afraid of anything."

"We've always had cats to keep the mice away. Never paid much attention to them," Jimson confessed. Mrs. Mumbles pulled her head away from his hand and twitched as if she understood everything that had just been said.

"It's only two a.m.," said Mr. Beasley. "I suggest a bit more sleep for us all. We'll need to be well rested for today's journey."

Back in the Aeolus, Lena was sure that she was done with sleep. The Girandoni lay on the floor within easy reach. Merilee's breathing grew easy and regular, but behind Lena's closed eyes, wolves snarled. She bunched her shawl into a makeshift pillow under her head. She never felt brave, but Jimson's words made her smile in the dark.

Overhead a crow clicked from the branches of an Austrian pine. A burst of pounding echoed off the mountains. Lena leaned out the coach window. Scree was silver in the early-morning light. Snow crusted the pine boughs and capped the boulders on the lake shore. Mr. Beasley and Jimson were bent over the loose wheel, whacking it back into place with a large rock.

Lena seemed to be the last one up, even though the sun had barely breached the horizon. As she made her way to the lake shore, she was stopped by the sight of giant paw prints. A surge of adrenaline brought her fully awake as she recalled the wolves' fearsome howls. But there was nothing to be seen in the distance now, save for the snow-draped mountains of Scree. Running a tortoiseshell comb through snarls of hair, Lena clipped the locks back away from her face. Then she cupped icy water in her bare hands and buried her face in it. A crow landed overhead, dislodging a tumble of snow. It fell in an icy clump on her neck and Lena straightened, shaking it off like a dog rising from the water.

"There's hot water for tea and some bread and jam. But we need to move quickly. I want us to be on our way before the sun's completely up. And it will take some work to get the Aeolus into the right positioning for takeoff." Even though Mr. Beasley had stayed awake the rest of the night watching over their camp, he now moved with energy and purpose.

"We've enough kerosene to get us some miles east by nightfall. One more night and we should be nearing the location on your map, Lena. We'll stay well away from the outposts." He dipped a chunk of bread in his tea. Lena noticed that even though their conditions were primitive, his eyebrows were again carefully painted in place.

"What if the mine is being watched?" Jimson tipped the tin cup high to drain the last of his tea.

"That's a chance I'm prepared to take," Mr. Beasley replied. "I believe it's remote enough that even the Pony Express would have a difficult time making it there before us. I seriously doubt anyone knows exactly where we're headed. They're more likely to search the outposts."

"But what about the marshal, Lena? Does he know about your father's mine?" Merilee's faced was scrunched with worry.

Lena considered before answering. "I've wondered about that too, but I don't think so. At least, he never let on that he did. He seemed genuinely surprised I was going to Scree. Even my mother and Nana Crane never mentioned a family mine. I don't think my father ever told anyone about it." She absently rubbed one hand down the length of her thigh and stared into the distance. "There's a chance the marshal's father knew. The marshal said his father tracked mine for years. But there's no way to know for sure."

As they finished the makeshift breakfast, Mr. Beasley

described the process they would use to launch the aerocopter. "We have enough open field and slope to build up the necessary speed for launch. If we can reposition the Aeolus near the top of the meadow facing southward, we can take advantage of the natural slope of the land."

Lena eyed the hill above them and noted how close they were to the edge of the hillside. If the Aeolus didn't stay on course, they would never be found among the sharp rocks below. Jimson was on his feet in an instant. "If we all help push, we can be off right away, before we have to worry about the Pony Express. We'll have to push her at least a hundred yards."

With the four of them pushing and tugging, they managed to move the aerocopter higher up the hillside and then stood panting in the thin meadow grass. Below them the small lake sparkled, reminding Lena of one of Nana Crane's glittering rings.

"All aboard!" Mr. Beasley called as he donned his top hat and goggles.

Despite a healthy dose of fear, the journey secretly thrilled Lena. Looking at Jimson, she suspected he felt the same way. Of course, no normal woman would relish sleeping in her clothes or flying in a homemade contraption into a land of criminals and opportunists. She tried to smooth the wrinkles in her skirt. Jimson hadn't once tried to catch her eye that morning. Perhaps being brave was not highly desirable in women. Normal women would have fled, like Pansy. And that, she was sure, was exactly why Jimson was engaged to Pansy. She was dainty; she was conventional; she would make a fine wife. She was everything Lena was not.

Lena stepped into the coach and dropped onto the bench. Already the boiler pipe was putting out a comfortable amount of heat as water gurgled into steam. She watched from the window as a V of black-throated geese glided onto the lake, sending up a spray of silver. The rotor whirred faster. Mr. Beasley checked the steam-pressure gauge and adjusted the tilt of the top rotor.

Jimson climbed in last, settling next to Mr. Beasley. Mrs. Mumbles sat upright at his side, her long tail switching slowly back and forth.

"On the count of three." Mr. Beasley looked over at Jimson. "One . . . two . . . three."

Jimson released the brake lever, and the coach began to move, wheels bumping over the uneven ground.

Lena hung her head outside the coach window. They picked up speed, faster and faster. The air stung her cheeks. Mr. Beasley clenched the steering rudder with two hands as they clattered down the shallow grade.

"There's someone in the trees!" The words had barely left Merilee's mouth when the geese lifted from the lake flapping and honking.

"Two someones!" Jimson leaned across Merilee to the window. "And they've got—" A shot cracked the air, followed by another.

"Get down!" Mr. Beasley held tightly as the coach shuddered. "We're almost up. Are they in uniform?"

"No, they're in buckskin coats and—"

Again the crack of gunshots as the coach wobbled into the air with a great roaring.

"Bounty hunters, most likely," Mr. Beasley stated.

Crouched down, Lena snuck a look out the window. They were eight or ten feet up; already the lake was yards behind them. The two men were quickly diminishing. But something was pouring from the side of the Aeolus. "We're leaking!" A smell strong enough to make Lena's eyes water filled the coach.

"We're what?" Mr. Beasley leaned over her. "Drat! It's kerosene. Our fuel barrels have been hit!"

The liquid continued to rain down at an alarming rate.

"Can't we do something?" Lena's voice rose to a squeak.

"I'm afraid there is nothing we can do unless we want to land and have the bounty hunters upon us. If they hit the boiler, it would explode, boiling us all like lobsters."

Merilee held a handkerchief over her nose.

"Maybe I can patch it if I can climb out and if you hold me—"

"Don't be ridiculous, Jimson," said Mr. Beasley. "We need to move to our alternate plan."

"We have an alternate plan?" Jimson asked.

"We always have an emergency plan. But it's risky." Mr. Beasley consulted the map. "We have enough fuel in the tank to make it to the Ducktown outpost."

"But I thought we had to stay away from outposts." Lena's mouth was dry.

"It is the best we can do under the circumstances. I just hadn't counted on exposing ourselves so soon."

For a while no one talked. It was too easy to imagine landing at the outpost and being greeted by the sheriff or marshals. Just what was the penalty for assisting a Peculiar to escape and for attempting to shoot a federal marshal? Lena wondered. Could it be worse than being sentenced to work the mines? She glanced at Merilee, who looked even whiter than usual and was worrying her lip with her teeth. Jimson began to whistle to himself as he looked at the map.

Whistling, Lena thought, must be a very useful habit. One could do it anywhere and it could express so much. Of course, no lady would ever whistle. Lena puckered her lips and blew a tentative puff of air. Nothing.

"Ducktown"—Mr. Beasley broke into her thoughts as if he was starting a history lesson—"is one of the first outposts established by our government in Scree. It's called Ducktown because the government provided settlers with ducks and geese for food if they were willing to come and work the mine. Each family that came was given a house, rented from the mining company, a brood of ducklings, and a small stake in the mine."

"What kind of mine is it?" Lena asked.

"Coal. One of the largest coal mines now operating in Scree. The settlers who came are mostly foremen, while most of the workers are Peculiars or felons."

Merilee perked up. "I've heard of Ducktown before. That's not where our family lived, but it isn't far. They said that if you married a girl from Ducktown, her babies would hatch out of eggs. That there are more ducks than people in the town."

They were dipping low over the trees now and Mr. Beasley was checking the fuel levels more frequently. "It's one of the best-producing and deepest mines, with a six-hundred-foot vertical shaft and tunnels that run horizontally under the outpost."

When Lena tried to imagine being more than six hundred feet belowground, a bubble of panic rose in her throat. She turned to Merilee. "How far down did you go?"

"Our mine was only four hundred feet, but the littlest kids like me didn't go down. We'd follow the coal trains with gunnysacks and pick up any coal that dropped. Our families needed it for heat and cooking." She looked at Lena's drawn face. "That part wasn't so bad. It was like a treasure hunt. We were always squabbling to see who could find the most. I only went down in the mine itself a time or two. But that was enough for me to know I never want to do it again."

Jimson broke his silence. "Were those bounty hunters after anything they could find, or did they know to expect us?"

"That's the question now, isn't it?" Mr. Beasley rubbed his face, removing a section of eyebrow. "I expect we'll know if we have a welcoming committee."

Great flannel clouds had gathered in the west, turning Scree into a gray, shadowy land. The mountains were steeper here and the hidden valleys darker. Snow had not yet softened this part of the landscape but soon would by the looks of the sky. Lena sat wrapped in a blanket as close to the boiler as she dared. Her thoughts had turned as bleak as her surroundings. An adventure that ended six hundred feet below the ground in Scree was a lot less appealing than the daring adventure they had embarked on yesterday. She hated close spaces, dark spaces, places where she couldn't see the light of day. She'd be no good in the mines. And then what would they do to her? She looked at Jimson. He was still half leaning out the window of the coach.

"I see something ahead. A building of some sort. It's—" Jimson's words failed him.

Lena joined Jimson at the window. At the foot of a bare and distant hill stood a patchwork castle topped by a hodgepodge of metal rooflines. Blue and gray, streaked red with rust, they intersected with a circular tower that rose from the center like a corrugated turret.

"The Ducktown Mine," Mr. Beasley said. "It's the largest building in the outpost. We're going to land in the first open field I find just to the west."

Smaller buildings, fashioned from a muddle of stone and wood, appeared between the trees.

"Last time I was here, there were thirty-two homes—all owned by the mining company, Great Northern Improvement—a general store, stables, a brewery, a warehouse, and a wash house."

The trees became sparse, and the landscape opened to grassy, stone-pocked fields.

"It's time we landed the Aeolus. The fuel's almost out, and I don't want to get any closer in. Look for the first good slope."

Jimson lowered the spyglass. "This isn't much more than a village. Will they have enough kerosene?"

"Oh, the only kerosene would be too scant and precious for us. We'll need coal to fly out of here. Coal and a firebox."

The descent was smoother than the previous time, but the ground, more pitted with rocks, was a less hospitable landing surface. The slope of the rocky field was not ideal, but their landing area was screened from the town by a thick border of trees. Every bone in Lena's body vibrated as the Aeolus bumped its way across the field.

"We may have knocked a few things loose!" Mr. Beasley shouted over the noise of the wheels and rotor.

As they trundled to a stop, Lena tried to prepare herself for various scenarios—marshals, bounty hunters, curious miners. But she was not prepared for the total silence that greeted their arrival. Even the mine was silent.

"Have we landed near a ghost town?" Jimson cautiously climbed from the coach. Mrs. Mumbles leapt daintily to the ground right behind.

"There's something not right here," Mr. Beasley said as he drew the small revolver from the inside pocket of his coat. "Lena, take the air rifle."

Lena's heart thumped so hard that it was difficult for her to get her breath. Someone must have heard their descent, or at least their clattering approach across the field. Weren't mines raucous places, loud with machinery? She crouched low in the coach, the air rifle in her hands. Merilee trembled nearby.

"The entrance to the mine isn't far from the outpost. There should be the sound of the headframe working, the winch lowering carts into the ground, and the pump removing water. This bears some investigation."

"I'll go and scout it out." Jimson rolled down his shirt-sleeves and ran fingers through his disorderly curls. "No one knows who I am and there's nothing to make me stand out." He did not look at Lena.

"Well, you're about the right age for an adventurer. Hmm." Mr. Beasley ran a hand over his face, considering. "It would be helpful to know what was going on, and of course we'll need to purchase coal. But I think I should go with you."

"No, if the Pony Express has gotten here, it will be your picture on the notice, not mine."

Lena had never seen Jimson contradict Mr. Beasley before, but she was sure he was right. In a mining town, Jimson would be the most invisible of all of them.

"You'll need a story, and you'll have to be able to stick to it," Mr. Beasley cautioned.

Lena's mind raced. Stories were something she could contribute. After all, she had spent much of her time reading amusements. "You're here as an engineer or surveyor. No, that would take specialized knowledge. You're here to try your hand at mining. You were looking for work and you heard about Ducktown." It was harder than she thought.

"Then what's he need the coal for?" Merilee asked. "Besides, not many folks travel alone way out here." She chewed her lip. "How 'bout this: You heard there was work here, and you and your wife sold everything and came north. You're headed farther, to a smaller mine just starting out. You need coal for heating your place, but the new mine isn't producing yet, so they sent you down to Ducktown for supplies. I'll go into town with you as your wife."

"That's not bad." Mr. Beasley considered. "You could pick up food supplies as well, but there's considerable risk."

"I could go with him," Lena said, feeling unexpectedly annoyed with Merilee's plan. "You might run into someone who knew you from before."

"I was six years old. Don't think anyone would recognize me from those days. Besides, you can't let yourself be seen." Merilee looked pointedly at Lena's gloved hands and at her feet. "They're suspicious of everything up here."

"I believe Merilee is right. We'll wait for you here. I can start the modification of the firebox. First find out about the silence. Don't take any unnecessary risks, and that means don't give away any information that you don't have to. Order the coal and say that you'll be back to pick it up. We'll have to find a way to transport several sacks."

Jimson looked only too ready to go. "We'll be back before you know it. Ready, Merilee?" She straightened her shawl, slipped her arm through his, and they sauntered off toward the outpost.

Jimson, Lena thought, appeared much too pleased.

She scanned the miserable sky. Bleak. The clouds were low enough for their bellies to rest on the ridgeline. The only color was in the rusted hues of the roof of the foundry. She set the air rifle against the side of the coach. Why had she come on this adventure? She could be home safe in the City with her mother and grandmother, helping at the library, spending quiet evenings reading at home. But that picture felt no better.

It was intolerable to be sidelined like this. Even Mrs. Mumbles had darted away into the underbrush—to hunt rodents, Lena presumed. She watched the receding backs of Jimson and Merilee with envy. She wondered what the marshal was doing now in their pursuit. Had he really planned to treat her like any Peculiar? Perhaps she'd misunderstood. She tried to recall his touch on her face, but when she did, she shuddered.

Mr. Beasley was already tinkering with modifications for the firebox. What harm could it do to wander a little closer to the outpost? Just close enough to get the sense of a mining town. She would be stealthy, just like the stories Jimson told of Stanley searching for Dr. Livingstone.

CHAPTER 28

BOUNTY HUNTERS

A STAND OF PINE AND BRUSH SEPARATED THE LANDING FIELD FROM the edge of the outpost. Lena found that if she walked carefully enough to avoid twigs, she could move almost silently through the low bushes. Besides, no one appeared to be out and about, and Mr. Beasley was occupied. She had slipped the spyglass into the pocket of her jacket and, once positioned behind a large boulder, she employed it.

The outpost was a slipshod town of wood and stone. Most of the buildings were clustered along one muddy street. Lena recognized the saloon from the crooked sign O'GILLIGAN'S, and next to it a small, squat building with a smokestack in the middle bore the words WASH HOUSE in crude letters. At one end of the street was a steepled building that had to be a church, and at the other end was Gunter's General Store. They were connected by a wooden boardwalk that would keep people a foot or two above the mud. She could see Jimson and

Merilee from behind as they ambled along the wooden planks toward the store.

The houses she could see were little more than shacks sprinkled among the pine trees. And sure enough, each had a wire-fenced duck yard, where muddy-feathered fowl squawked and strutted. A little girl ran into one of the pens with a bucket of something that she cast on the ground. She was the first person Lena had seen, and as she watched her, the child disappeared just as quickly back into the house. So, not completely deserted, Lena mused.

Beyond the store, and beyond the mine itself, a dark pile towered to a height that almost matched that of the church steeple. Lena crept forward a few yards more. The pile was made of rubble and black clumps that must be coal. A waste dump for the mine. She had expected the mine to be a large hole in the ground with rails running down into it. But this building with its roofs, smokestacks, and scaffolding was more like a tattered castle watching over the meager town.

She caught movement and turned in time to see two things happen at once. Jimson and Merilee emerged from the general store just as the doors of the church opened and a line of miners came out. They were dressed in black and carried long pine box after long pine box. Women in black with children in their grasp followed. A funeral, Lena realized.

Jimson and Merilee stood to one side as the funeral procession passed down the center of the muddy street, veering left behind the wash house and saloon. How many of them had died? Lena crept to the edge of the tree line. Mourners were passing within a few yards. She drew back. They were a solemn lot, pale-faced and obviously wearing their Sunday best: jackets with vests and bowler hats. There was hardly a smooth-shaven face in the crowd. The women wore black shawls over their heavy dresses and black lace coverings over their heads. A group of men at the rear of the line struck up a mournful tune. A French horn wailed side by side with a trombone, and a short man built like a fireplug banged on a drum.

Snow began to fall—thick, white flakes that pirouetted to the music. They frosted the handlebar mustaches and caught in the black lace covering the bowed heads. A man stopped and spoke with Jimson and Merilee, but they were too far away for Lena to see clearly through the snow, even with the spyglass. Feet squelched through the mud; the musicians droned a solemn rhythm. A boy turned his face skyward, stuck out his tongue, and caught white stars.

These seemed to be people accustomed to grief. They marched as if they had done this many times before. Lena looked for signs of otherness. Which of these miners were Peculiars? But they looked like any gathering of poor folk, mourning their dead. She watched an old woman with a hunched back. Did the shawl cover a pair of furled wings? She gazed so intently that she was startled by the snort of a horse just behind her.

"I think we caught us one!" A horse and rider suddenly appeared at her side from between the trees. They towered over her.

"Look at those hands. That's a freak if I've ever seen one." The face that bristled down at her was as round as a moon, one cheek distended with tobacco. The man's eyes were red-rimmed and watering.

"Excuse me. I must be going," Lena babbled, fear burning her throat. She slid the spyglass into the pocket of her jacket.

Another voice came from behind. "Looking for others of your kind?"

Lena spun.

He was an Asian in a buckskin jacket, and he had a pale scar running the length of one cheek. Lena, who had never seen anyone from Asia up close before, suddenly remembered Nana Crane's warnings about the dark alleys of Chinatown and young girls sold into white slavery.

"Look at her feet." The moonfaced man spit a stream of brown liquid close to Lena's boots.

Lena tried to draw them in under her skirt. She was trapped on both sides. Sweat prickled her armpits. She ran her tongue over dry, chapped lips. Why hadn't she stayed near Mr. Beasley?

"What's your name, girlie?" Moonface spat again, and a trickle of saliva caught in the stubble on his chin.

Lena pressed her lips together.

"Hey, she don't understand English. Why don't you try some Chinaman talk on her?"

Scarface grumbled low in his throat but did not reply.

Jimson and Merilee were too far away for her to call out. The end of the procession was passing now. She called out anyway. "Help!" If only she could whistle!

Her voice was drowned out by the French horn. Before she could call out again, the scar-faced man was dropping a rope over her head. She was slammed to the ground as the rope slid down her legs to her calves and was pulled tight.

"You been lassoed," Moonface cackled.

Her breath came fast now and shallow. "I have a birth disorder. That's all. And if you need proof you can talk to—" She realized she was about to give her friends away and cut off her words.

"A whole nest of Peculiars? Everyone knows they live like roaches. Find one, find an infestation," Moonface said.

Scarface remained silent, the rope in his hands.

"How much can we get for her, do you think?" Moonface bit off another chunk of tobacco.

Scarface finally spoke. "Maybe fifty dollars. Maybe more." He bent over Lena, pulling her arms behind her back and tying them at the wrists.

Sticks and twigs poked into her side. The rope was cutting off the circulation in her legs. Her wrists were chafed. The snow was falling harder. She would not plead. "You won't get anything but trouble when they find out you've taken a citizen captive."

"Fifty dollars is good money," Scarface said. "And we will get even more because you are so unusual."

"Wait a minute. I hear someone. Might be more of 'em Peculiars!" Moonface lifted a rifle from his saddle and pointed it hopefully into the trees.

Lena heard a low murmuring in the trees, the snap of breaking twigs. But she saw no one. "Come out of there with your hands in the sky or we shoot this girl!" Moonface cocked the trigger.

The murmur of voices grew louder, came closer.

Lena looked up from the cold ground. If Mr. Beasley was coming with help, she needed to warn him. "He's got a gun!"

Scarface pulled the rope tighter. It bit into her calves.

A flash of movement caught her eye.

"I said show yerself!"

A scrabbling in the underbrush and Mrs. Mumbles launched herself, spitting and hissing, at the man with the rope. He threw up one arm to protect his face; the other hand still clutched the rope. The cat's surprise attack, her weight, and her sharp claws all caught Scarface unprepared and off balance. He teetered, flailing one arm at the cat.

Mrs. Mumbles sunk her claws into his neck, bit at his flailing hand.

Scarface's feet scrabbled for traction on the slick new snow. They shot out from under him. Cat and man tumbled to the ground in a spray of snow and curses. "Get it off me!" he cried.

"Why, it's nothing but a cat! Han-jee, we've been fooled by vermin!" Moonface swung the gun toward Mrs. Mumbles.

Lena scrambled to her feet. The now-loose rope dropped to her ankles. Scarface's shout was muffled by the cat: "Don't shoot! You'll hit me, you fool!"

With numb fingers Lena tried to slip the rope off over her feet, preparing to flee.

"Think I can't shoot?" Moonface pulled the trigger. The shot splintered a fragment of rock.

Mrs. Mumbles fell and lay still.

Scarface knocked her away.

Lena screamed. She couldn't leave Mumbles! But she hesitated a moment too long.

Moonface grabbed her, clamping a hand over her mouth. She bit it.

Cursing, he jerked his hand away and twisted Lena's arm behind her back.

"Music's too loud for anyone to hear her, but that shot may bring a few folks." He dropped the rifle to his side. "Han-jee, better truss her up again."

Han-jee, his face raked with fresh cuts, tied her hands and secured the rope around her waist.

Lena stared at Mrs. Mumbles's still form through a film of tears.

Moonface spat into the snow. A small brown circle spread into the white. "We're only upholding the law." He gestured toward the back of the retreating funeral procession. "Townfolks in enough trouble already. Peculiars being buried in a churchyard when everyone knows they got no souls."

CHAPTER 29

LENA JOINS THE CRIMINAL CLASS

IT WAS DIFFICULT TO MUSTER ANY DIGNITY AT ALL WHEN SHE WAS lassoed around the waist with her hands tied behind her back, but she tried to keep her voice calm. "Just who do you think will pay for me? And how dare you, how dare you shoot that cat!" Tears coursed down her cheeks, but she had no way to wipe her eyes or nose. Where was Mr. Beasley?

Moonface squirted a long dark stream of tobacco juice onto the frosted ground. "Money comes from the gov'ment. But we get paid by the town sheriff. Now, it looks like he may be otherwise occupied at the moment, but we can wait."

"I refuse to wait in this cold, Thaddeus. We will take her into the saloon." Scarface walked over to his horse, boots crunching on the thickening ground.

"I told you not to call me that, Han-jee."

Han-jee ignored him. "We'll go slowly enough that you can walk." Without a backward glance he vaulted onto the horse's back and coaxed it to a slow pace.

Lena was forced to follow. Her thoughts raced and her heart ached as she looked at Mrs. Mumbles lying in the snow. By now Mr. Beasley should be wondering where she was. Perhaps he'd come in time. If not, when they led her into town Jimson and Merilee would surely see her and get help. But Lena had no idea where they were at the moment.

The funeral procession had left the main street of the outpost. Lena could hear a few cacophonous notes in the distance. The bounty hunters stopped outside O'Gilligan's saloon. Thaddeus dropped from his horse with considerably less grace than his partner and tied the reins to a hitching post. Lena was dragged inside, but not unwillingly. The new wet snow had brought a chill that had begun to seep into her bones. It took a moment for her eyes to adjust to the dim light of the interior. The air was warm with the smell of tobacco and alcohol. Despite the shabby exterior, someone had taken considerable effort to produce a long wooden bar that glowed with polish and an ornate gilded mirror that reflected back the faces of the patrons.

The saloon was nearly empty. A barkeep and two patrons were clustered together at one end. Not a single one of the small round tables was occupied. Lena's heart sank. She had been hoping . . . but why would she expect Jimson and Merilee to be there? The three at the bar looked up when they came in.

"Caught us a Peculiar here!" Thaddeus called out. "And we need a little celebratory drink!"

The two patrons—men who looked as if they might have slipped out from the line of the funeral procession for a quick refreshment—returned to their conversation, heads bent so close that the tops of their bowlers nearly touched.

The barkeep made his way toward Lena and her captors. "You'll find most of the town at the funeral. Mine explosion two days ago, seventeen killed." He shook his gray head.

"We're truly sorry to hear that news. Nevertheless, we have business to attend to." Han-jee pushed Lena forward as if to illustrate the point. "Perhaps you could tell us where to find the sheriff of this outpost."

"Not till we get a drink first, Han-jee. I'll take a whiskey straight." Thaddeus edged onto a bar stool, his face expectant.

Lena felt the barkeep's eyes on her. She looked up. His gaze was sharp behind his steel-framed spectacles. He gave her the briefest nod. "The sheriff is overseeing the funeral. They're in the outliers' graveyard, lowering the caskets even as we speak."

"Thank Jesus for that. Thought they might be trying to unload a bunch of 'em Peculiars in a Christian cemetery. 'Course, that could have advantages for us. Lots of money in reporting towns that don't follow the law." Thaddeus shot a practiced stream of brown into a brass spittoon at his feet.

"Oh, I think you'll find this outpost quite law-abiding." The barkeep poured amber liquid into a tumbler and passed it to Thaddeus and then offered the same to Han-jee.

A woodstove roared in the center of the room. Lena began

to thaw. She flexed her fingers, wishing they would loosen the rope that tied her hands behind her.

"Fifty dollars will come in handy about now." Thaddeus lifted his drink and contemplated the amber liquid. Then he tossed it back.

"I am not a Peculiar, and you won't see fifty dollars on my account." Lena decided that the best thing to do was to brazen it out. The barkeep looked friendly enough; perhaps she could persuade him to her side.

Thaddeus didn't even look her way. "Not a Peculiar," he mimicked. "Did you ever see hands like those? Puts a chill right through me. Untie her hands, Han-jee, so everyone can appreciate their beauty."

Han-jee grunted and released the tight cords. Lena almost swooned with relief. He kept a tight rein on the rope around her waist, however.

"Take the glove off'n it. You know mebbe we could get more money selling her to a sideshow."

Lena curled her hand into a fist. They would *not* remove her glove. Han-jee looked uncertain. The other two patrons moved down the bar for a better view of the commotion. Lena could feel their eyes, hot with the thrill of seeing something titillating. Tears stung her own eyes.

"Philosophically speaking, I am opposed to humiliating a female." Han-jee crossed his massive arms.

"Not your philosophy'n again, Han-jee. Don't matter what you think. We don't stand for no freakishness here." Thaddeus was so close that Lena could smell the whiskey on his breath. He grabbed her right hand and pried the fingers back, and Lena shrieked in pain. Her black gloves fit snuggly. Thaddeus tugged. The glove clung to her hand. He grunted and pulled harder. "Oh, for the love of Pete." The patrons and even the barkeep crowded in close. Their breath was hot and noisy. Thaddeus split the glove wide across the palm and jerked Lena's hand out. A collective intake of breath as he lifted it high and waved it in the air. Lena cringed. The tears spilled down her cheeks.

The door flew open. "What is going on here?" The female voice was strong, authoritative. The men drew back. Lena's head spun. The two missionary ladies from Miss Brett's stood hands-on-hips in the doorway of the saloon. Red poppies still bloomed on the larger woman's hat. "We heard you outside! What are they doing to you, dear?" She moved forward swiftly. "This is no way to treat a lady!"

"This ain't no lady. She's Peculiar," Thaddeus said with some satisfaction.

"I wouldn't even let you two handle a dog." The woman with the red poppy hat whose name Lena could not recall put her thick arm around Lena's shoulder and looked down at the exposed hand. "I recognize her from Knob Knoster. My, my. So, a Peculiar." She drew away just the slightest bit. "Well, I suppose you must do your duty, but I'll not have you treating her poorly. We're to respect all living things, even those that are soulless."

Lena gulped. She would not sob in public. The men moved away and the barkeep with them. Thaddeus and Han-jee began to discuss the weather report with the two missionaries. Lena curled her exposed hand into a ball. The glove was beyond saving. Perhaps she was as well.

"Snow's not supposed to let up for three days. You fine ladies may want to delay your travels. I'm sure we could find a family to put you up." The barkeep handed them each a mug of something steaming hot.

The second missionary woman spoke. "Our work will not be delayed. We have been called to the interior of this wild land to serve those laboring in the mines."

The barkeep shrugged. "Just a suggestion, seeing how the weather can turn right nasty this far north this time of year."

Lena edged away from the bar. If she could somehow slide free of the rope by loosening it bit by bit . . . But even as she planned it, she realized it was hopeless. The rope encircled the narrowest part of her frame. She'd have to widen it considerably to slide it down over her skirts.

Footsteps on the boardwalk. Chatter. The funeral must be over. The door swung open, ushering in the cold, and the room swelled with men.

"Guess we should be getting back to business." Han-jee looked meaningfully at his companion. "Sheriff will be back in his office by now. We can get paid and out of here before the snow gets too high."

Please, please, Lena begged silently, let Jimson and Merilee arrive with the crowds.

The throng of miners seemed eager to quench their thirst after the solemn funeral. Not a single woman came through the door, and the missionary ladies had taken a table in the back of the room. Had the women all gone home to their little shacks? In her experience, Lena had found women to be more sympathetic to the plight of someone in need, and she felt sure she could make her case if she could only find one.

"That's the sheriff there. Jack Spaulding." The barkeep nodded toward a large bear of a man who had just swaggered into the room. His hair and mustache were flaming red; his face was weathered and freckled. He stood a good head taller than most of the miners.

"Jack! Over here. These fellows have some business with you."

The sheriff elbowed his way through the crowd, speaking with one person, commiserating with another. He stopped to laugh at a joke someone told, throwing back his head and hooting loudly. Lena tried to sink into the floor. Surely in this crowd there must be some way to escape before she was placed in the hands of the redheaded monster. She straightened her hair, then put her hands behind her back. If she couldn't escape, she would put on the best face she could.

"What you got for me, boys?" The sheriff's voice, like everything about him, was larger than life.

Thaddeus turned obsequious. "Sir, we're bounty hunters,

and we found us a Peculiar. She was hunkering on the edge of the outpost. There might be more like her nearby."

The sheriff turned his gaze to Lena. His eyes were deep-set, a rusty brown. He didn't say anything.

"You can see she is very different. An unusual specimen." Han-jee looked at her bare hand with distaste, then picked up her gloved hand. He also pointed at her feet.

"Hmm. I can see there are some abnormalities."

This was her chance, Lena thought. "Yes, chromosomal abnormalities. Just a genetic problem I was born with." She tried her most convincing smile.

"Aw, you can see she's a Peculiar. You can smell it."

The sheriff turned his back to Thaddeus. "Now, Miss . . . ?"

"Mattacascar."

"Miss Mattacascar. The law says that we must provide protection for anyone of a Peculiar nature. It's for their own safety. You can appreciate that. Otherwise, folks like these two gentlemen here might try and take advantage. Peculiars in Ducktown have guaranteed work, food, and shelter. But what's a young lady like you doing traveling alone?"

Lena had expected the question. If she was to be sent to the mines, she would not incriminate her friends. Best to tell a half-truth. "I am traveling to join my father who owns a mine east of here."

"A mine owner, is he? What's his name?"

"Saul. Saul Mattacascar. It's just a small family mine; I doubt you would have heard of it."

"Well, can't say the name Mattacascar rings any bells for

me. But we can't be too careful these days, so you'll understand if we hold you overnight. Besides, the weather's not fit for travel."

"But I'm expected—"

He now turned his back on Lena. "Boys, I'm taking her in till this gets sorted out. I suggest you cool your heels in town overnight if you want your reward."

"But by tomorrow the roads may be impassable." Han-jee gave the rope a yank, causing Lena to wince.

"You wouldn't want to argue with the law, boys," was all the sheriff said as he removed the rope from Han-jee's hand. "If she's Peculiar, you'll get your reward."

"Where are you taking me?" Lena's voice came out in a squeak.

"Why, to the jail—to our finest accommodations, Miss Mattacascar." And he made a mock bow as he led Lena toward the door.

The crowd parted to let them pass. Were any of these patrons Peculiars, Lena wondered, or would they not be allowed in? There was so much she didn't know. And what could she expect in jail? Her father had been in jail, and Nana Crane had always talked about it as a wicked place. Her heart quickened in panic. Jail was the domain of thieves and murderers. She'd be lucky to survive. As she was led through the crowd, she felt a hand settle on her backside. She pulled away. The press of people closed around her, but there in the back was a face she recognized, a face that looked curiously blank without eyebrows. Mr. Beasley winked.

CHAPTER 30

IN WHICH JIMSON AND MERILEE DISPLAY ACTING ABILITIES

LENA WAS A SPECTACLE. CROWDS PARTED AS THE SHERIFF LED HER through the door of the saloon, and on the narrow boardwalk women gave them a wide berth, pulling children close, away from any possible contamination. There were two reasons a woman might be taken into custody in Ducktown: if she was Peculiar, trying to pass herself off as a citizen, or if she was a woman of entertainment who had overstepped her bounds. Women of questionable character were expected in the saloons of Scree. When they plied their trade on the streets, they risked running afoul of the ordinances of the outpost. It was a double standard no one was eager to explain; without working women, miners who came to seek their fortune, leaving home and hearth behind, grew restless. Brawls broke out. Lawlessness increased. But these same women who civilized the miners and helped keep the peace were not to be seen in the day-to-day life of the outposts.

Lena did not care to be thought of as either type of woman. If she was Peculiar, she would learn to live with it on her own terms. She would not be flaunted before the entire community. But to be thought of as *that* type of working woman was almost more than she could bear. A deep shame spread from the tips of her alligator boots to the crown of her bare head. So she walked with her eyes down, listening to the tap of her shoes along the boardwalk, reciting some words her mother had repeated when life's complications abounded: "All will be well, all will be well, all manner of things shall be well." Mr. Beasley had seen her. Surely he'd be there any minute.

The Ducktown jail was a cheerless place attached to the small office of the sheriff. Its most common use was to corral drunks until the fight went out of them and they could be released back into town. Occasionally, a fight broke out over mine claims, but rarely was a Peculiar held. The Peculiars knew their place, and when they weren't working the mines, they socialized only with one another and kept their distance from the citizenry. Peculiars were allowed to shop at the mine store and at the general store but only on Saturday afternoons from four to five p.m. Their homes were on the farthest outskirts of Ducktown in a subcommunity known as the Trenches.

Lena was led into a small, dank room with stone walls. A single barred window faced east toward the mine works. An iron gate separated the cell from the sheriff's office, and a wooden pallet with a thin mattress offered the only comfort in the place. Lena again felt tears brim, but she was determined not to let the sheriff see her cry. He had not spoken one word to her on the humiliating march through town, and he led her to the tiny cell with an almost apologetic speech. "I know it may not be what you're used to, but it's where you'll be till we get this sorted out. There's a physician comes by once a week who specializes in identifying Peculiars. Due here on Wednesday, but with this weather who can tell?" He shrugged.

Lena's heart sank even further.

"'Course if you want to confess up front, we can get you moved into the Trenches, which are more comfortable accommodations than this. We've got a boardinghouse of sorts for single Peculiars." His size dwarfed the already small room.

Lena shook her head. "I'm a citizen, raised in the City. The sooner I'm released, the less this outpost will have to apologize for. The people at my family mine will be expecting me, and when I don't arrive on schedule, I'm sure they will send out an expedition." The simple speech exhausted her, but she was loath to sink onto the thin, questionable mattress that topped the wooden pallet.

"So be it, then. There'll be soup at sundown." The sheriff shrugged his massive shoulders again, placed a toothpick in his mouth, and closed the gate. The iron clanged with such finality that the tears finally did spill, and Lena sat gingerly on the mattress wishing she had never left home. Her only consolation was that Mr. Beasley knew what had happened, but even his wink offered her no cheer.

Outside, the noise of the mine works began again as the miners returned to work. There were still a few hours left in the day and they couldn't afford to let the work stand despite the increasing swirl of snow. Lena could hear the roar of the steam engines, the clanging of rail carts, and noises she couldn't identify. If she stood on the bed, she could see the falling snow and the roof of the foundry. She tried the spyglass, but there was nothing to see except snow-covered branches and the patches on the foundry roof. The window was set securely in stone, and the thick metal bars made the hope of any escape that way ludicrous. She sat on the bed, leaning her back against the stone wall. The noise of the mine droned in the background. In the other room she could hear the shuffling of papers and an occasional door open and close.

The vision of Mrs. Mumbles lying in the snow haunted her. The cat had been trying to save her! Hot tears leaked from her eyes. Jimson would come to her rescue, she was sure of it. She would let her eyes rest . . . only for a moment while she planned the next move.

The clang of the metal door startled Lena awake. Her neck was stiff and her head sore where it had rested against the wall. The sheriff ducked into the cell. "You've some visitors—Mrs. Fortinbras and Mrs. Fetiscue," he said and then withdrew.

The two missionary ladies pressed into the cell, faces crinkled with distaste. Lena recognized their names from previous meetings but couldn't remember which was which. She sat up straight and buried her hands in the folds of her skirt.

"We were compelled to see that you are being treated fairly. All creatures deserve that." The lady sporting red poppies sniffed and pressed a lace handkerchief to her thick nose. "I am Mrs. Fortinbras, and this is my sister, Mrs. Fetiscue."

"I remember. My name is Lena Mattacascar, and I'm on my way to join my father at the family business."

"But Peculiars don't run businesses, dear. Is your father working in a mine?" Mrs. Fetiscue lifted the hem of her black skirt a few inches from the ground so as not to soil it on the floor of the jail cell.

"My father owns a mine. And I am being held illegally." Lena stood to face the two women.

"Well, well, I guess the sheriff knows what he's doing. But he hasn't mistreated you?"

Lena could feel her face growing red and her voice rose. "I would call being held illegally mistreatment!"

Mrs. Fetiscue took a step back. Her sister fixed Lena with a stern eye. "Please control your temper, young lady. After all, we have come at our own will to make sure that you are not being abused in some manner."

These women could speak in her defense, but they were of no use. Lena stomped one foot. "You're not listening."

The outside door banged open. Lena could hear a high, insistent voice—a familiar voice.

"And I will see my sister right now!"

Merilee appeared in the doorway with Jimson at her side. Lena was so relieved, she felt her legs grow limp.

"See here. The prisoner already has visitors." Baffled, the sheriff looked from one set of visitors to the other.

Merilee cut through his words. "Lena was always the black sheep of the family. When James and I were married, Mama told me to keep a careful eye on her. She's always been trouble, probably 'cause of the way she looks." Then she leaned toward the sheriff and hissed in a stage whisper, "Birth deformities. No man would marry her. So my husband and I"—here she poked Jimson in the ribs—"we took her under our wing. And what do we get? She's always trying to run off. We'll just take her home and—"

"You mean she isn't a Peculiar?" Mrs. Fortinbras's eyes grew round with puzzlement.

"Is that what she told you?" Jimson smiled his most charming smile. "Little sister, you could get yourself in a passel of trouble pretending like that."

Passel, Lena thought. Where he did ever learn a word like "passel"? It didn't matter; she could hug them both. "Well, I wanted a little adventure." She could play the part as well.

"We'll just take her home with us—" Merilee's voice was commanding.

"Now, wait a minute here. What proof do you have that this lady is your sister?" The sheriff blocked the doorway to the cell with his massive frame.

"Birth certificates." Miraculously, Merilee reached into her purse and pulled out two official-looking documents and thrust them under the sheriff's nose.

He grabbed them in his meaty hands and studied them carefully. "Lena Mattacascar and Gina Mattacascar Quiggley. Well, I . . ." He unlocked the door, and the two missionary ladies rushed out, followed by Lena, head held high.

"I'm very sorry, Miss Mattacascar, but you can see that it was a natural mistake." He looked at her feet.

"My family will hear about this," Merilee said. She grabbed back the certificates, then took Lena firmly by one arm and Jimson took the other. They propelled her toward the door.

Never had fresh air been so appealing. Lena took a deep breath. It took the greatest effort to keep from running. As the three of them stepped onto the boardwalk, followed by the two missionaries and the sheriff, a horse pounded up. Despite the cold, his coat was flecked with sweat. The rider, in his blue jacket with brass buttons, also shone with perspiration. His fair hair dripped with melting snow. "Pony Express with an urgent message for Sheriff Jack Spaulding." He jumped from his horse, gathering the reins in one hand and thrusting a large envelope toward the sheriff with the other. His breath made little puffs of steam as he spoke.

Lena looked at Jimson, who pinched her arm and continued to drag her from the boardwalk. Beyond, the steam from the wash house mingled with the heavy fall of snow. The entire world was white and swirling.

The sheriff laid a hand on Jimson's shoulder. "This might be important, son, something you might need to know to protect your family. I don't want you leaving until I've read it."

With that, he unfolded the single sheet of paper and read out loud.

WANTED: Tobias Beasley, for collaborating with Peculiars and for the death of Abel Guthrie. Escaped October 30th in a flying machine with three other persons of interest, one young male and two females—maybe Peculiars. Consider all four armed and dangerous.

The two matrons punctuated the message with shocked exclamations. The sheriff took another look at Lena. "How'd you say you arrived in Ducktown?"

"I—we—" Lena's brain felt sticky and slow. She thought she might faint, but her name wasn't mentioned in the telegram.

Jimson breathed into her ear, "Go. Go now." He looked at the sheriff. "My wife and her sister have suffered a terrible shock. They need to get out of this cold. If you could use my services in any way to help capture these scoundrels, I will do everything in my power to assist you."

Lena let her head fall onto Merilee's shoulder as if completely exhausted. Sheriff Spaulding looked at Jimson's tense face and then at the downcast gaze of the girls. The wind picked up, whipping the snow into a frenzy. "Don't leave town. I'm not through with you yet. Where are you staying?"

Jimson blew on his hands to stall. Lena tried to imagine a reasonable place to stay in the mining outpost. Nothing came to mind. She couldn't very well say they were staying in an aerocopter in the woods. If she invented an accommodation, the sheriff would be sure to check it out.

"We just arrived and haven't secured accommodations yet," piped up Merilee.

Mrs. Fortinbras was not about to let this opportunity pass. "We found rooms with one of the Great Northern Improvement foremen and his family. I'm sure I could put in a word for you."

The streets of the outpost were emptying. Everyone was fleeing the cold and night was approaching fast. Jimson nodded. "Thank you. We appreciate it."

The two missionary ladies beamed and then, arm in arm, headed back toward their accommodations.

The sheriff looked as if he would like to return to somewhere more hospitable as well. He turned up the collar of his jacket and stomped his feet. "I'll be in touch, but if this storm comes in, I doubt you'll be going anywhere." And he lumbered back to the warmth of his office.

"Can you point me in the direction of the stables?" The Pony Express rider brushed a dusting of snow from the arms of his jacket.

Jimson indicated down the main street toward the church.

"Can you imagine? A flying machine. I've heard about 'em. But wouldn't I like to ride in one! You bet! Have you ever seen one?" He stroked the nose of his mount.

"As a matter of fact, I have," said Jimson.

The rider looked at him with envy. "That's the wave of the future, you know—steam-powered flying machines. In a few years they'll be as common as trains. I hear the army's got dirigibles now. Won't be long before convicts got nowhere to run."

The boardwalk was deserted, and the noise from the mine was drowned by the rising wind. Jimson had rescued her! Lena felt an overwhelming desire to laugh. *Hysteria*, she thought, but it didn't seem to matter.

"This way." Jimson plunged into the snow in what Lena hoped was the right direction.

"Why wasn't my name in the message?" She spoke close to Jimson's ear before the wind could snatch away the words.

"The marshal's crafty. If he left your name out, he had a reason. We've got to get out of here before the sheriff figures it out."

The wind stung Lena's face and snow sifted into the top of her alligator boots. Was the marshal trying to protect her, after all? She could barely feel her hands. Merilee trudged along in silence, her face determined, one arm still linked with Jimson's.

Despite the snow, Jimson's sense of direction prevailed. But it took them twice as long to make their way back to the clearing, where Mr. Beasley was waiting with the aerocopter. He had worn a path smooth with pacing. When they came into view, he bounded forward. "I knew you could do it!"

All four hustled into the coach of the aerocopter, where

Mrs. Mumbles sat washing her fur. One leg was splinted, but the cat purred with contentment.

"Oh, Mrs. Mumbles, you're alive!" Lena threw her arms around the cat, who drew back from the undignified embrace. "I saw the bounty hunter shoot her. I was sure she was dead!"

Mr. Beasley lifted the cat onto his lap. "She dragged herself back to the clearing with a broken leg. The shot must have missed her. There wasn't any bullet hole, but something must have hit her."

"A rock splintered. I remember that." Lena reached over and stroked the cat's fur. "She tried to save me. The bounty hunters heard her and thought someone had found them."

"I'll never berate felines again," Jimson said.

"I can't thank you enough for rescuing me." Lena looked from Jimson to Merilee.

"It was Merilee's idea. Mr. Beasley had already made the fake certificates before we left in case there was trouble crossing the border." Jimson beamed at Merilee.

The press of bodies in the small space made it almost comfortably warm. Mr. Beasley handed around tin cups so they might draw from a pot of soup.

"Wait a minute—it's warmer than it should be in here," Jimson said, looking suspiciously at the boiler.

"That's right! While you were having your own adventures, I was able to get a little help at the foundry. I've modified the old firebox—for coal."

Mr. Beasley looked as delighted as a child, Lena thought.

"The good news is that the storm will keep us hidden a while longer," he continued.

"The Pony Express arrived." Jimson filled a tin cup from the pot. "And you were mentioned by name. The rest of us were just described."

"Just as I feared. But I do have a solution." He climbed out of the Aeolus. Then reappeared at the window.

The three looked at him quizzically.

Mr. Beasley held up a single pair of long wooden skis in triumph.

CHAPTER 31

STRANDED IN THE SNOW

"BUT THERE'S ONLY ONE PAIR." MERILEE'S BROW FURROWED. "AND they're longer than any skis I've ever seen. When we lived in Scree, we used snowshoes."

"Snowshoes would never work for our purpose. These are for the Aeolus. I had them made at the foundry as well."

"So we'll strap them on instead of wheels!" Jimson's face was ruddy with excitement.

"These will allow us to leave despite the snow, unless the visibility keeps us grounded, which just may be the case."

The warm soup and coal heat made it difficult for Lena to concentrate. She closed her eyes just for a minute. Her head slumped against Jimson's shoulder. They would have to sleep sitting up all night. Voices blurred, a great heaviness infused her limbs. Just before falling asleep she thought she felt the brush of lips against her cheek.

In her dreams, they were gliding through the snow on

long skis pursued by the sheriff and the two bounty hunters, who were riding the fearsome wolves of Scree. Ahead was the entrance to a darkly gaping maw. They were swallowed, and Lena awoke.

She and Merilee were alone in the coach. Merilee still slept, her head thrown back on the stem of her long neck, her mouth open. Lena's own neck was stiff, and her long feet ached in the confines of her boots. First light revealed a world buried in snow, but the whine of the wind had stilled. Jimson and Mr. Beasley were loading the tent and a shovel onto the Aeolus.

"Nothing like a snow fort to keep one warm! We were quite snug!" Mr. Beasley shouted. Without his eyebrows, his smooth face reminded Lena of an overgrown baby.

"Didn't sleep a wink; he and Mrs. Mumbles snored all night." Jimson leaned in the coach window. "You got the best deal."

But Lena wasn't so sure. She was unaccustomed to sleeping in her clothes and boots. Her hair needed brushing and her face washing. A handful of snow to wash the sleep from her eyes would have to do.

"My plan is to leave immediately," said Mr. Beasley. "The wind is still, and the visibility good except for a little fog. It's November first. Who knows how long our luck will last."

Excitement and expectation permeated the air. There was nothing quite like the start of an adventure, Lena thought. No matter how bleak the situation looked, each beginning promised new hope; expectations rose like mist from the snow and carried them until the next complication arose. A little thrill of anticipation shot through her. That was the problem with most people, she mused, they were so busy planning for the complications that they missed out on the anticipation.

Merilee was up now, braiding her hair into a single plait. There would be no time for tea. Mr. Beasley urged them on, as he explained what was needed for them to become airborne.

"We have to have a running start. The Aeolus needs a bit of a downhill while the rotors get fired up. Then she'll glide with much less resistance than when we relied on the wheels."

"It will give us a lower roll-resistance coefficient!" Jimson added.

"Exactly. But there is one task before we leave. Merilee, it's time for your injections. Lena, if you will assist me. Jimson, go outside and make sure everything is secure for takeoff."

Merilee turned a bit pale, but she obediently turned her back to Mr. Beasley and Lena. "They were itching something fierce last night," she said. She unbuttoned the top of her wool dress and slid it from her shoulders.

"That's because the wings will keep trying to reassert themselves until the entire root is killed."

Lena found that her squeamishness was overcome by a strong curiosity. From the top of the scapula a track of red scar ran, ending just under the shoulder blade. Merilee's skin was very white, her shoulders thin and sharp. In the center of the scar, where it stretched tightly over swollen tissue, the buds of new wings were about to poke forth. Why, it reminds me of a baby's gums when the teeth are about to poke through, Lena thought.

Mr. Beasley removed a precious syringe from a pack of medical supplies. "This is a hypodermic syringe used to inject a chemical to kill the fledging," he explained.

The only time Lena had seen a syringe before was in Mr. Beasley's laboratory at Zephyr House. Now she examined the instrument carefully. She marveled as she looked at the long, thin needle.

"I'll inject each side. Lena, please clean the area with this cloth dipped in alcohol. The nuns at Cloister had quite good success with sterilization techniques that involve alcohol. It prevents infection from bacteria." He stuck the tip of the needle into a vial of liquid and drew back the plunger until the cylinder was almost full.

Lena carefully poured alcohol onto the clean cloth and, taking one thin shoulder in her hand, blotted the scar. Merilee trembled under her grip. "Does it hurt?"

"Not now, but it burns when the medicine goes in."

Lena expected to turn her eyes away when Mr. Beasley stuck the needle into the swollen skin, but she found that she could not.

Merilee shuddered and gave a little hiccup.

"You're doing just fine. Things look just the way they should. Only one or two more rounds of injections and you'll be done until they reassert themselves again—but that may not be for years." Mr. Beasley carefully repacked the syringe while Merilee slipped her dress back over her shoulders. "If there had been any infection, the swelling would have been aggravated. Now, Lena, in case anything untoward should happen on this adventure, you know how to carry on in my place. Just be sure to sterilize the syringe before using it. Germs are the enemy."

"Oh, but I don't think—"

"You've seen me do it. It's really quite simple. The amount of serum is listed in the notebook." Lena saw that the notebook was identical to the one she had hidden in her own suitcase, the one she had found with illustrations. Guilt washed over her. How could she have ever suspected Mr. Beasley?

As a patch of blue appeared between the clouds, they turned the Aeolus until it was facing down a gentle slope. Mrs. Mumbles came bounding through the snow despite her splinted leg.

"This is it. Be prepared. Unless the mine starts up at the same time to cover our noise, we'll have everyone and his brother down here." Mr. Beasley looked at his pocket watch. "Mine works start at seven a.m., in ten minutes."

They all boarded the Aeolus.

Jimson stoked the firebox. The rotors turned, whirring loudly. The Aeolus slid forward slowly, then picked up speed.

The coal was messier and smellier than kerosene, but they had a good supply—enough, Mr. Beasley assured them, to take them to the Mattacascar mine. Even now he was examining his compass and showing Merilee how to tell the direction of their flight.

Lena studied Jimson's face. He appeared distracted, lost in his own thoughts. There had been very little time to talk to him since fleeing Zephyr House. She wondered if he missed Pansy and how his flight from Knob Knoster would affect the status of their relationship. Pansy didn't seem to be someone who was particularly adaptable. Perhaps he regretted leaving so abruptly, but if so, he disguised it well. And had she really felt the brush of lips last night? Were they his?

"I don't like the look of those clouds," Mr. Beasley said as he leaned from the coach and pointed eastward. They had been flying into a headwind for several hours, but now the weather was growing more severe. Lena stuck her head out the window. The air bit her cheeks. The wind drove a heavy mass of gray, as solid-looking as concrete, in their direction.

"I've no experience flying blind, but we may have to. It looks like we're in for more snow. At least we're off the ground, even if the wind means we're traveling no more than five miles per hour."

"Can we fly under the clouds?" Jimson asked as he joined Lena at the window.

"Perhaps, but we'd have to be much lower than I'd like."

Regardless, Mr. Beasley dropped the Aeolus so that the thick clouds would form a ceiling overhead.

The first snow started as a sleety rain that tap-danced on

the roof and then turned to white. The heat from the boiler kept the snow from building up on the roof and propeller blades. As the wind increased, the snow came in hypnotizing swirls from every direction. It seemed to Lena that they were barely moving.

"Hold on—we're going lower!" Again the Aeolus dropped, this time so that it barely cleared the tops of the tallest trees.

Below them, the ground was already thick with snow from the day before, the trees heavy and bent. It reminded Lena of being inside a snow globe that had been vigorously shaken. Snow fell as far as the eye could see.

"There's someone down there." Jimson pulled his head back into the coach. His dark curls were white with frost. He handed the brass spyglass to Mr. Beasley.

"Who would be fool enough to be out in this weather?" Mr. Beasley asked aloud.

Lena could see dark shapes moving, although they were obscured by the falling snow. She couldn't see any road they might be following. If there had been, it was covered now by drifts. Her cheeks were wet and flakes clung to her lashes.

"I can't be sure, but it looks like there are two women out there and at least two men. Their wagon is up to its axles in snow. They won't be going anywhere," Mr. Beasley said.

"I think there's something familiar about them . . . Let me see." Merilee reached for the spyglass. "Yes, it's the missionary ladies. I can tell by the red poppies in the hat."

"And the men?" Jimson asked.

"I don't know. I can't see their faces under their hats, but one of them has a shovel."

"Even a missionary must have more sense than to try and travel in this." Mr. Beasley's voice was impatient. "Even they have to abide by the laws of nature. I hope they have enough food to last several days."

Lena thought of Mrs. Fortinbras and Mrs. Fetiscue trapped in the snow. They had probably thought more of the souls they had planned to save than of how to survive in the wilds.

"Can we help them?" Merilee asked.

Jimson scratched his head. "They don't even believe that Peculiars have souls. Why would you want to help them? Besides, what could we do?"

"If we land, there's no guarantee we'd get up again." Mr. Beasley looked at his three traveling companions.

"But we can't just leave them there, no matter what they think."

Lena felt no particular fondness for the ladies. In fact, during every encounter she had found them abrasive and narrow-minded. But that didn't mean that she wished them harm. She wished the decision were as clear-cut for her as it was for Merilee. For one thing, they would be putting themselves at risk. Even now the long arm of the marshal had reached Scree. People knew about her, about all of them. On the other hand—

"We've come about twenty-one miles and there are at least

ten more to make it to the mine. We have no idea who the men are with them. If we don't decide immediately, we'll be too far past them to do any good." Mr. Beasley kept his hand firmly on the rudder.

"I say let them work it out. Either they'll survive or they won't." Jimson leaned back against the seat, arms folded across his chest.

Merilee thrust her jaw forward. "That's not the way I was raised to treat people."

Indecision still ruled Lena. She bit her lip. Jimson was undoubtedly thinking of his Mr. Darwin again, and maybe he was right. They were just past the group on the ground now. A small clearing appeared between the trees. Lena opened then closed her mouth. "Merilee's right. We should go down."

Mr. Beasley didn't say a word as he engineered their descent, but Jimson rounded on Lena. "You do know that we aren't likely to get away again, not until the storm's over? If we survive that long. I just got you out of jail before you could be sent into the mines. If you'd think occasionally, you'd realize how ridiculous most of your notions are!"

Tears stung Lena's eyes. This was a Jimson she hadn't seen before.

"It was my idea," said Merilee. "You can blame me, but if you were any kind of gentleman at all, you'd have thought of it first." Her cheeks were flushed and her breath came in little gasps.

Mr. Beasley's voice was calm. His eyes darted between Jimson and Lena. "I suggest we try not to destroy each other. We will need all the cooperation we can muster in this situation."

They were descending quickly, almost straight down. Lena glared across the coach at Jimson, but his eyes were now closed. Why had he turned on her that way? She rested a hand on Merilee's shoulder, and Merilee covered it with her own.

The wind buffeted the Aeolus in her descent. They were too close to the trees. A long branch pushed its way in through the window of the coach. Merilee screamed.

The whine of the rotors made the group on the ground look up. Mrs. Fetiscue began waving her arms overhead. One of the men pointed a rifle skyward.

"It's the bounty hunters," Lena said flatly. "They must have left Ducktown yesterday." Jimson had been right, but it was too late to change their trajectory now.

The whine changed to a scream. "We've caught a branch in the rotors." Mr. Beasley was leaning so far out the window that Lena thought he might fall.

The Aeolus shuddered and tipped, ramming against a tree. It listed sideways. Lena clung to the bench. Beyond the scream of the rotors she could hear the cries of people below. And then they were falling from the sky. Jimson was saying something that she couldn't hear.

• • •

Mr. Beasley and Mrs. Fortinbras were bending over Lena and talking, but their words made very little sense. What she did know was that she was warm, warmer than she had been in days. Her head ached slightly as she rose up on her elbows. She was still inside the coach of the Aeolus. It was canted badly to one side. There was still heat from the firebox. It was apparent that the machine was badly damaged.

"Sit up slowly. You've a fine bump on the head." Mr. Beasley supported her back. "You've been out for half an hour."

"Where are Jimson and Merilee? Mrs. Mumbles? Are they all right?" Lena winced as she spoke, and her hand felt for the knot on her head.

"Jimson's got a cut down the side of his face, and Merilee's seeing to it. That cat has used up another of her lives. She's fine. We're all in better shape than the Aeolus."

"You came just in time, just like angels descending from on high," Mrs. Fetiscue said, fluttering. "We've been out here for hours trying to fix an axle on the coach. The driver had no idea what he was doing." She ran her words together in one breathless string.

"My dear lady, what about the bounty hunters?" Mr. Beasley's voice was an oasis of calm.

"Them!" Mrs. Fortinbras joined the conversation, the red poppies now sadly askew, bobbing with each word. "Said they would accompany us and that they knew a shortcut. When they saw your flying machine, they skedaddled all the faster. They are no gentlemen."

Mrs. Fetiscue nodded in agreement. "Our driver went with them. Said he'd come back with help, but I don't trust him, either. He left us the horse. Medrat, he calls it. But my sister and I never learned to ride. Without you, I don't know what would have happened to us."

"It was the decision of my companions to offer assistance, even in the face of personal peril." Mr. Beasley indicated the battered Aeolus.

"Well, we owe them our lives." Tears threatened to spill from Mrs. Fetiscue's eyes. She pressed a sturdy hand on Lena's shoulder.

"The important thing now is to assess the damage and make a plan for survival. I doubt we'll be flying anywhere." Lowering his voice so only Lena could hear, he continued. "I suspect the bounty hunters left in a hurry to claim a reward for directing the law to us. I would like to move as quickly as possible, but with two of our party injured and with the extreme weather, I believe we are done for the day."

Merilee appeared at the door to the coach. "Jimson should have sutures if the wound's going to stay closed." Then she noticed Lena sitting up. "You're all right, then. I was praying you would be."

"What's happened to Jimson?"

"When we crash-landed, just about the time you hit your head, Jimson got thrown against the firebox. It sliced a nasty cut on his cheekbone. There's a superficial burn. He's lucky it isn't worse," Merilee said, sounding like a doctor.

"Let me take a look at him," Mr. Beasley said. "We can find suture material, but it will have to be sterilized, as Dr. Lister says in his books."

Merilee dragged Jimson to the coach, where the entire group inspected the gash that sliced from the outside corner of his right eye across his cheekbone. The flesh under his eye was swelling and purpling as well.

Lena remembered his angry rant when she agreed that they should land the Aeolus. He did not meet her eyes.

"Well, I have just the thing." Mrs. Fetiscue hurried over to her coach and returned with a small needlepoint bag. "My sewing kit. One should always be prepared." She reached in and removed a spool of black thread and a packet with two silver needles. She reached for the straight needle, but Mr. Beasley requested the curved upholstery needle.

Jimson blanched.

"Yes, that should work quite nicely. I'll just soak the needle and thread in a little carbolic acid." Mr. Beasley looked at Merilee and Lena. "You girls can do the work. I need to establish a bivouac with the assistance of the ladies."

"But how will they know what to do?" Jimson winced and touched his face.

"I assure you that ladies have much more practice at sewing than I, and will do a neater job. And you really should put some snow on that eye before it swells shut."

Lena looked around the coach. "I think you should lie down. It might be more comfortable that way." Privately she was thinking that this would not be comfortable at all and that she could use snow to help numb the cheek before they started stitching.

In the end it was Lena who threaded the needle and prepared to seam together the open wound. Merilee had applied snow until Jimson stopped wincing and declared he was quite frozen.

It was so cold that Lena's fingers felt stiff and clumsy. It had taken her three attempts to finally thread the needle. Then, hoping that Jimson couldn't see she was trembling, she used two long fingers to press together the sides of the wound. There was something awful about sticking a needle into human flesh and pulling a thread through it. It felt nothing like what she had done countless times before while hemming handkerchiefs and darning stockings.

Jimson glared at her through his one good eye. "I hope you know what you're doing. After all, it is my face."

"Not that your face is any great beauty." Lena pinched the skin tighter and prepared to make the initial puncture.

"Here. You can bite on this, so you don't scream and throw her off." Merilee stuck a twig in his mouth. "I'm going to hold your hands down."

Lena clenched her jaw and jabbed the needle through the flesh, making the tiniest stitch that she could. The twig snapped between Jimson's teeth. She hesitated. Then she decided it would be better to go fast and get it done. She tried not to respond to Jimson's grunts but to imagine one of her mother's fine silk handkerchiefs. Nana Crane had made her practice over and over until her stitches were small and perfect. Merilee gripped both of Jimson's arms and held them down while Lena worked. Seven stitches and she finished with a perfect knot. A sheen of sweat coated Jimson's face.

Lena examined her work. It wasn't her best; Jimson had wiggled too much for that, and it was too bad that the only thread available was black, but other than that, it looked as good as could be expected. "I hope it didn't hurt too much."

"You about killed me." He talked through one side of his mouth, not wanting to move his face.

Merilee held out a small silver flask. "Here. Mr. Beasley said you're to take a swig of his emergency brandy."

Jimson took a long swallow, shuddered, and wiped his mouth on the back of his hand.

He really did look quite dreadful, Lena thought, with one black eye swollen closed and the black stitches looking like a many-legged beetle on his face.

"Well done!" Mr. Beasley had returned with Mrs. Mumbles perched on one shoulder to examine the work. "It will give your face a bit of a story. Now, I suggest we wait out the worst of this weather. As soon as there is enough visibility, we move, but that won't be until morning. No telling what the bounty hunters have planned. We're about ten miles from the mine, according to the map."

"Ten miles?" Lena could barely feel her feet.

Jimson nodded painfully as if he was following every word. "A storm's good. The snow will cover our tracks." But his words were slurred.

"I suggest we burn a little coal to keep us warm while we wait and that everyone rest if they can."

Lena looked around the inside of the battered aerocopter. Already it was diminished in size. How would they all ever fit?

"I've brought the coach over as close as possible," Mr. Beasley said, as if he'd heard Lena's thoughts. "We should be able to share some of the heat between the two. Mrs. Fetiscue and Mrs. Fortinbras are already inside. I'll get a fire started here and join them. Then try to sleep if you can."

Merilee busied herself distributing apples and bread while Lena helped Mr. Beasley stoke the firebox. She draped a blanket across Jimson.

"I'm sorry I yelled at you like that," Jimson said. "I didn't want you to have to go through another experience with those bounty hunters. You don't always think things through." His eyes were unfocused. Lena pulled the blanket up to his chin. He had already fallen asleep before she could reply. His mouth hung open. A thin line of drool ran from his mouth to his chin. Green and blue bruises bloomed on his cheeks. Lena found herself almost feeling sorry for him.

She brushed the coal from her gloves, but they were hopelessly stained. Merilee had settled herself in the opposite corner from Jimson, leaning her head against the wall, eyes closed. There was nothing for Lena to do but wedge herself in between. She tugged at the blanket on both sides. It was so cold that she could see her breath. Outside, the wind shrieked. Gradually, the warmth from the firebox seeped into the coach, but much of it dissipated quickly. She shifted positions, trying to keep herself erect. There was no way to get comfortable.

She tried to imagine the Mattacascar mine. She pictured her father there waiting for her. Then what would she do? Would he be as crazy as Abel Guthrie? She moved Jimson's leg out of the way. And what about the rest of them? Once Jimson had his adventure, would he go back to Northerdam to work in his father's store with Pansy? She tugged the blanket harder. At least he *could* return. But what about her? The run-in with the bounty hunters made it clear that someone with her characteristics would no longer be tolerated. Merilee began to snore. Lena pulled the blanket over her head and tried not to snuggle into the warmth of Jimson—after all, he was still an engaged man. If being a goblin meant feeling cantankerous toward the world around you, then her transformation had begun.

CHAPTER 32

THE QUESTION OF GENETICS IS RAISED ONCE MORE

IT WAS COLD . . . SO VERY COLD. LENA BURROWED CLOSE TO something warm on one side of her. From the other side, cold air rushed in, and a voice, a very annoying voice, was forcing itself on her consciousness.

"Get up. Mr. Beasley wants us to leave now while the snow will cover our tracks."

Lena opened one eye. Merilee's face was hanging over her own. She was holding the blanket back. Lena tried to snatch it from her hand. The one warm side of her body was pressed against Jimson, who was starting to shift into wakefulness. His face looked even worse this morning, if that was possible, Lena thought. She sat up fast, glaring at Merilee and brushing the hair out of her face. She felt wretched. Her neck was cricked, her mouth felt as if it had been filled with paste, and it wasn't even light outside yet.

"What's all this about?" Jimson's good eye popped open.

"We're going to start off as soon as possible. The snow's not so heavy now, and we need to leave while it will cover our trail in case the bounty hunters come back." Merilee handed Lena a tin cup. The water was cold. "Mrs. Fetiscue and Mrs. Fortinbras are up and almost ready to go."

"Are they now?" Jimson touched his purpled face tenderly and winced when he tried to whistle. He managed a single note repeatedly.

It was the most annoying sound Lena could imagine hearing so early in the morning.

So it was in that undecided time—not still night but not yet morning—when they set out. Mr. Beasley insisted that the missionary ladies sit together on Medrat's broad back. Since neither lady had ever been on a horse before, there was a great deal of slipping, sliding, and praying for mercy.

"We'll change off riders periodically," said Mr. Beasley. "Mrs. Fetiscue, please stop pulling back on the reins. It tells Medrat to stop when we actually want him to go forward. I'll be leading him. You're perfectly safe."

"I've filled the packs with food." Merilee shrugged a knapsack onto her back and handed one to each of her companions.

"Remember that hypothermia is our enemy," Mr. Beasley warned them. "There are about two feet of snow on the ground. We'll move as quickly as we can through it and hope that more doesn't fall, or even Medrat will have a hard time. We don't know when the bounty hunters will return, but you can be sure they will." Raising his voice, for the benefit of the missionaries, he added, "And I fear it is thievery, not help, that they will bring. Our saving grace is that they have no idea where we're headed." With the compass in one hand and Medrat's bridle in the other, he turned to look at Lena and Jimson. "Jimson, you bring up the rear. Lena, as soon as your feet cause you too much discomfort, we'll put you on the horse."

"What about Mrs. Mumbles?" Lena asked. "How will she manage with her injured leg?"

"For now she'll be fine following in Medrat's tracks. Remember, she's a Scree-cat, at home in the snow. If the snow deepens, one of us will carry her."

Lena gave a last look at the Aeolus. It was almost unbearable to leave her like that, listed to one side, her fine frame dented, the rotors bent and broken. Lena hunched her shoulders against the cold and silently thanked Nana Crane for the sturdy wool skirt and the wool shawl she wore over her traveling jacket. Her feet already complained, but she didn't want to be a liability.

They trudged forward silently, Mrs. Mumbles bounding, despite her splinted leg, from hoofprint to hoofprint, while a fine white snow floated down as if a baker in the sky were sifting powdered sugar over a plain brown world.

Lena looked over her shoulder. Jimson lagged behind. She paused to let him catch up. "Is your face bothering you?"

"No, I think it's your feet that let you go faster."

"My feet?"

"They work like snowshoes. The more surface area, the easier it is to stay on the surface."

Lena looked down at the length of her feet.

"I didn't mean to offend you. I wish mine were as long." A red wash spread across his cheeks. "I'm making it worse, aren't I? What I mean is—"

Lena cut him short. "I know exactly what you mean, Jimson Quiggley, and for once I don't mind my feet at all." She threw a handful of snow in his direction and for a minute it felt like old times before all the awkwardness of Pansy and the marshal.

She wondered if he had ever forgiven her for telling the marshal about Mr. Beasley's work. She wouldn't blame him if he hadn't.

The trees were thicker here, spruce and pine soldiering next to each other on the uneven ground of the hillsides. They puffed up one hillside and slipped down another. Mrs. Mumbles took up her perch on Mr. Beasley's shoulder. The snow had stopped, and their footprints were blue shadows in the snow, an easy trail to track. None of them had much energy to talk. Even Mrs. Fetiscue and Mrs. Fortinbras had stopped grumbling about being carried off on a runaway horse. Dawn touched the snow, turning it rose and then gold. Overhead two ravens clicked and cawed the sun up. It was a cold beauty unlike anything Lena had seen before.

"I believe it's time to take a little nourishment." Mr. Beasley lowered his knapsack to the ground. "We'll change riders after we have a meal."

The meal was better than Lena expected. Although there was nothing warm, there were apples and a good sharp cheese and Mrs. Pollet's homemade bread. When they had finished, Mr. Beasley produced two bars of chocolate, which he carefully divided.

After the meal, he insisted that Merilee and Lena take a turn on the horse. Like the missionary ladies, Lena had never ridden a horse before. She clung to Merilee and wrapped her legs tightly around Medrat's broad back. Merilee dozed, her head bobbing onto her chest, but Lena's thoughts ran ahead, imagining the mine and her father and trying to decide what exactly she would say.

They stopped well before dark. They unloaded the shovel from Medrat's pack and searched for a place where the snow had drifted against a ledge, deep enough to build two snow caves for the night. Mrs. Fortinbras and Mrs. Fetiscue would share the tent. While the others took turns digging, Mrs. Fetiscue built a small fire and produced a pouch of dried meat that she added to a pot of boiling water, along with a handful of potatoes.

"A missionary is always prepared. We didn't venture out with nothing for the journey."

"It smells wonderful," Lena said as she crouched close

to the warmth of the fire. Mumbles rubbed herself against Lena's leg and purred.

"Do they get extra cold, those long hands and feet of yours?" Mrs. Fetiscue was using a stripped stick to stir the pot.

"Well, they're cold, but I don't know if they're colder than anyone else's." Lena stared into the fire rather than meet Mrs. Fetiscue's curious gaze.

"I've always believed that regular folks—people like me, I mean—were created in the image of God, whether we know it or not. It must be horrible to be accused of being Peculiar. Peculiars have always seemed like a mistake—something gone wrong with the design, something not quite human." She continued to stare at Lena's feet. "But you can understand why the bounty hunters and the sheriff mistook you. I hope you don't mind my speaking my mind like this."

Lena bit her lip very hard, but still she couldn't hold back the words. "How do you know what God's design was? I *am* Peculiar. Maybe it's people like you who are the mistake! Maybe God's a Peculiar."

"Why, that's heresy! You're lucky you don't get struck dead on the spot." Mrs. Fetiscue's nostrils flared; her chin quivered. She backed away. "Do you mean to say we've been traveling with . . . with a Peculiar all along? That you've been lying to decent people?"

Now Lena couldn't stop the words from rushing out. She leapt to her feet, startling Mrs. Mumbles. "What do my hands and feet have to do with who I am? I don't know who I am.

But do you know who you are? Does anyone really? What makes a decent person? Does being the same as everyone else mean being better than other people or does it just make it easier to look down your nose at them?"

"The apple falls close to the tree, my dear. We can't escape our genetics. A goat may want to be a sheep, but it's a goat all the same." Mrs. Fetiscue had regained her composure. She dipped a cup into the soup and took a noisy slurp. "Just about ready. You seem to have done remarkably well for yourself, even if you haven't got a soul and even if that temper is a bit of a problem."

Tears of rage blinded Lena's eyes. She opened her mouth, but no words came out.

"Charles Darwin would say we all came from the same ancestors, but that some of our traits disappeared over time," Jimson interjected. "I'd say that anyone who still has some of the old traits is a survivor." His voice was calm and steady.

"Charles Darwin is a godless man," replied Mrs. Fetiscue, straightening and fixing Jimson in her sights. "He has removed God from the universe."

Now Lena watched Jimson's eyes dilate in the firelight. "Darwin never says that. God may have created the laws that put natural selection in place. Any man of science knows that."

"Are we having philosophy with our supper this evening?" Mr. Beasley looked from Lena's pinched face to Jimson's and then let his eyes settle on Mrs. Fetiscue's rosy cheeks.

"The soup is ready, Mr. Beasley. I can see that you have your hands full managing these young people . . . Mrs. Fortinbras,

Merilee!" Mrs. Fetiscue wiped her hands on her skirt and began ladling out hot mugs of soup.

Lena found a rock to sit on just outside the circle of the fire. Night was creeping in. Mrs. Fetiscue's words had reopened a wound she was trying her best to ignore. For the first time in many weeks she longed for her home in the City, longed to see her mother's face frowning over a missed stitch or hear her voice reading from the newspaper. She even missed Nana Crane's lectures. Merilee was laughing, telling a story about growing up in Scree. Mrs. Fortinbras and Mrs. Fetiscue thought she was a miner's daughter. Because they couldn't see the scars from her wings, they never suspected she was different.

Jimson crunched through the snow to where Lena sat. "She's rude and ignorant, and I've brought you some bread."

"Thanks." Lena dipped the thick slice in her soup to soften it.

"I heard you stand up to her. You were right. No one really knows who they are. Why, I bet even the two missionaries wouldn't be feeling so high and mighty if we hadn't rescued them."

Lena took a bite of the sopping bread and felt the juice trickle down her chin. She was too tired to even wipe it away. "I just said those things without thinking. I don't even know if I believe them. Remember the book from Cloister? Do you still have it?"

Jimson nodded and drained the last of the soup from his mug. "What's that got to do with anything?"

"I'm not sure, but maybe everything."

CHAPTER 33

THE FAMILY BUSINESS

MR. BEASLEY HAD THEM UP BEFORE DAWN AGAIN. THE TEMPERATURE had dropped overnight, but no more snow had fallen. Lena walked alongside Merilee. Snug last night in the snow cave, she had told Merilee about her conversation with Mrs. Fetiscue. Surprisingly, Merilee hadn't been angry. "I've heard it all before. You've spent most of your life living as something else. I've always known I was half Peculiar. People like them— I just feel sorry for them."

"How can you even know there is a God?"

Merilee had just shaken her head, laughing until her long hair covered her face. "Oh, Lena, that's something you just know. Not something you have to prove."

And with that unsatisfactory answer still ringing in her ears, Lena had fallen asleep.

This morning, Merilee was the only cheerful one of the bunch. Mrs. Fetiscue and Mrs. Fortinbras were so sore from riding the horse that they could barely walk, but they were on Medrat's back again at Mr. Beasley's insistence. He was convinced that the bounty hunters would be returning, and he hurried them all along in an unusually brusque manner. Even Mrs. Mumbles was loath to walk and rode imperiously on Mr. Beasley's shoulders. Jimson in the rear was brooding over his own thoughts, which Lena suspected had something to do with being out of communication with Pansy. Merilee's chatter at least kept her distracted from her aching feet and the cold that none of them could escape.

As the morning wore on, the low, flat sky felt burdensome—a weight Lena longed to discard. Mr. Beasley was consulting the map and his compass more frequently, and at times they were forced to double back on their tracks to find a turning they had missed. The hem of Lena's skirt was stiff with snow, and she longed for the freedom that men had wearing pants. Overhead the ravens watched their progress and chattered about it among themselves.

Then the skies opened, dumping a fresh fall of snow. Mr. Beasley stopped in his tracks, one hand gathering up Medrat's reins. "I thought we'd have been there by now, but the mine appears to be well concealed. I plan to aim for downhill of where I think it's located. If we go too high, we may miss it completely. If we find a stream, we'll know we're close."

"How will we find anything in this snow?" Mrs. Fortinbras's voice was querulous.

"Consider it a blessing, dear lady. No one will be able to find *us*. Follow me; we're headed downhill from here."

Lena could see little but Merilee's narrow back in front of her. She was plodding through white into white. Somewhere behind her, she knew Jimson faithfully brought up the rear, but he may as well have been in a separate universe. They were all locked in the world of their own footsteps.

Then a strange noise intruded into that world, a whirring noise that grew louder, closer. For a minute Lena imagined the Aeolus had been resurrected. She looked up, but the snow stung her eyes.

"Get down!" Jimson pushed hard on her shoulders.

Lena crouched into a ball, Jimson by her side, one arm across her back. "I can't see what it is."

"Hopefully they won't be able to see us, either."

The others crouched down as well while Mr. Beasley guided Medrat under a nearby tree's branches to hide. The noise vibrated through Lena's body. She peered up into the falling snow. "I can see something, but it's just a big dark shape—a *huge* dark shape."

Something long and dark as a ship's hull glided over them. Lena looked up like a swimmer from under the water.

"Jeez! It's a dirigible!" Jimson almost stood, but Lena tugged sharply on his topcoat.

They stayed hunched in the wet snow until the monstrosity passed over them.

"Only the army has those. I've always wanted to see one!" Jimson obviously felt none of the terror that shook Lena.

"It's quite possible that the dirigible was sent on our behalf," declared Mr. Beasley. "We need to find shelter in case it returns." He sounded only slightly less excited than Jimson. "A marvel of engineering, but dangerous for us. Ladies—" He extended a hand to Mrs. Fetiscue, who had dropped from Medrat when the dirigible approached.

"I am not getting back on that animal, even if you have to leave me to freeze to death here. My backside can't take it another minute."

"If you understood our predicament—"

Then Merilee's voice came through the snow from several yards beyond. "There's water here. It's frozen, but I think I've found the stream!"

Several yards above them an outcropping of basalt rock was layered with branches of pine trees. Jimson bounded uphill.

"Wait!" As the words left Mr. Beasley's lips, a dark shape pounced, knocking Jimson flat. The two figures tumbled head-over-heels in the wet snow.

And then a voice: "Don't move."

It came from above them, from the branches of one of the spruce trees.

Looking up through the falling snow, Lena glimpsed a wizened face staring down, and saw a bow and arrow pointed at Merilee, who was standing right at the base of the tree.

Jimson struggled, but the small man sat on his chest,

pinning his arms into the snow. From inside the rock two more people emerged: a man, slight of build with a thin gray beard, and a woman, old and wrinkled as a walnut. They pointed rifles at the travelers.

The woman stepped forward. She was dressed in furs, her hair covered by a hood. She kept her eyes focused on Mr. Beasley. But it was her hands clutching the rifle, one finger on the trigger, that caught Lena's eye: long, spidery hands, each finger with an extra joint.

A small noise escaped Lena's mouth. The thin man veered his gun toward Lena.

"What's your business?" The woman's voice was deep and harsh.

Mr. Beasley and Lena spoke at the same time. "I—we—"

"I've come because my father left me a deed to the Mattacascar family mine," Lena managed. "These are my friends."

The old woman crept forward lightly on the snow. Her feet, long and slender, kept her well supported. She peered closely at Lena's face. "And your father is?"

"Saul. Saul Mattacascar."

Mr. Beasley held out the map. The man snatched it from his hand. Mrs. Mumbles leapt to the ground. Lena could hear Jimson's ragged breathing as he lay captive in the snow.

"A Scree-cat as a companion. And one with an injured leg." The woman raised an eyebrow. She picked up Lena's gloved hand in her own gnarled one.

Lena stared into the old woman's face. It was not familiar. The eyes were a faded brown. Nothing but the hands and feet were familiar. Snow stuck to the fur of her hood, to her thick lashes. "Where is my father?"

Instead of answering, the woman gripped Lena's arm and turned to the rest of the group. "Bring them in. Don't keep them standing here in the snow."

Jimson hung back, scowling, brushing the snow from his arms and legs until he was encouraged at rifle point to move. Mrs. Fortinbras asked in a loud voice, "But what kind of people are they, pointing weapons at us?" She grew silent when one of their captors took Medrat from Mr. Beasley, tied the horse to a tree, and nudged Mrs. Fortinbras and her sister forward. Mr. Beasley and Merilee quietly followed Lena into the mouth of the mine. Mrs. Mumbles padded at her side.

The passage sloped downward. Lena could feel hard stone beneath her feet. Lanterns along the narrow passage threw just enough light to keep her from stumbling on the uneven floor and to illumine rivulets of water that glistened on the walls. They were being led into the bowels of the earth. The old woman's firm grip on her arm and the slap of footsteps behind were the only things that kept Lena from panic. Just when she thought she could bear it no more, the passage opened into a wide, high-ceilinged chamber, all flickering light and shadows. Hundreds of lanterns hung like stars in the dark; Lena felt as if she had walked into the night sky.

Slowly she became aware of other people in the chamber. At first they were merely moving shadows, but as her eyes adjusted in the glimmering light, she could pick them out— men, women, and children, thin and ragged, all watching her. She looked over her shoulder and found the reassurance she hoped for: Mr. Beasley and Merilee and, behind them, Jimson, still scowling, with Mrs. Fortinbras and Mrs. Fetiscue, both of whom for once had nothing to say.

"Welcome to my home. This is where we have been living for some time, since your government declared our land *terra nullius*. The mine supports seventy-three of us Peculiar people. Thirty of us live inside."

"Ah!" Mrs. Fortinbras swayed as if she might swoon, and Jimson grabbed her arm.

The old woman laughed. "Ah, yes. We are all Peculiar, but I think you will find us hospitable as well, as long as you obey our rules. First you must get warm and eat. We'll go into the eating room."

Mr. Beasley stepped up to Lena's side. He looked, Lena thought, absolutely delighted, not terrified as she felt.

"This is marvelous," he said to the old woman. "You live in a working mine!"

"We do not live well, but we manage to survive."

They were led into a smaller room in which there were three long tables. The lanterns' light reflected from the nearby walls, walls with a strange purplish cast. The slab tables and benches almost filled the space.

"Sit," the old woman said. "We'll bring food and we'll talk, and then we will decide what's to become of you."

For the first time in two days, Lena began to feel warm. A cooking fire blazed in the back of the small chamber, the smoke disappearing up a fissure in the rock. A young boy ladled out bowls of a thick stew. A dish of water was placed on the floor for Mrs. Mumbles. Jimson slipped a chunk of meat to her under the table.

"Roots and rabbit. The best we have. And strong mead. It keeps the cold at bay."

They were given cups of a dark liquid that burned Lena's throat as she swallowed. Mrs. Fortinbras pressed her lips firmly together. "We do not partake in spirits."

The old woman shrugged, turning her attention to Lena. "Why have you come here?"

"But I showed you the map," Lena began. "My father—"

"So, you have a map," the woman interrupted. "And you have the hands and feet of a goblin."

Lena blanched.

"Does it trouble you for me to say it out loud? And that other girl"—her eyes glinted toward Merilee—"has the long bones of an Annuncius."

"I knew it!" Mrs. Fetiscue mumbled through a mouth full of stew.

"I am asking what your intentions are. You'll have to forgive me if I'm suspicious, but I've found that most visitors do not have our best intentions at heart."

"I've come to find my father." Lena spoke quickly before Mr. Beasley or Jimson could say anything.

"And why do you want to find him?" The old woman leaned forward across the narrow table. Lena could see hairs bristling on her chin and along her upper lip. Her breath smelled strange, both sweet and musty.

How could Lena answer this question when she didn't know herself? She stared at the old woman's spidery hands, thick with veins. Her words echoed deep in the empty space Lena carried inside herself. *You have the hands and feet of a goblin.* There was no escaping it now. She was the same as the wizened woman across from her.

The table was silent, waiting for her answer.

"I need to find him because he left when I was five. I need to know why he left me." Embarrassingly, her eyes flooded with tears. "I want to know if I'm like him."

The old woman was silent, considering. She ran a long finger down the ridge of her nose.

"Tell me how you got the map."

So Lena took out the letter and handed it to the old woman. She explained her mother's reluctance to let her leave, and she told her about Nana Crane's predictions that Lena was as wild as her father.

"And the rest of them?" The old woman nodded toward the others at the table.

Lena caught Jimson's eye, and it gave her courage. "Mr. Beasley has been helping Peculiars escape or change, so they wouldn't be captured. Jimson is his assistant. He works in Mr. Beasley's library." She looked questioningly at Merilee, unwilling to give away the secrets of her friend.

"You're right. I'm half Annuncius," Merilee said. "Mr. Beasley removed my wings."

Mrs. Fortinbras let out a small shriek. Lena was sure she heard the man with the bow hiss and others watching from the entry grumble low in their throats.

"He removed them at my request. My sister died in the mines here."

"And these fine ladies?" The old woman rose and walked toward Mrs. Fortinbras and Mrs. Fetiscue. "What about them?"

"We are missionaries. We've come to help the heathens of Scree. Peculiars are none of our business." Mrs. Fetiscue's chin trembled as she spoke.

"None of your business, you say?" The old woman made her way around the table to Lena's side. Again she raised Lena's hand in her own and looked at it.

"Your father, Saul, is dead." Her faded eyes grew dark and glittered.

Lena felt the room recede. She struggled to release her hand, but the old woman gripped it firmly with her own sharp fingers. All this way, all for nothing. The empty space inside her expanded until she was hollow.

The woman was speaking. Her words circled like birds. How many times she repeated them, Lena never knew, but eventually they landed, whispered in her ear.

"I am your grandmother, Saul's mother. I am Lavina Mattacascar."

But Lena only stared. The emptiness consumed her.

Lena and her grandmother sat long by the fire. Merilee had fallen asleep at the table, her cheek pressed to the wood plank like a small child, and Mrs. Fortinbras and Mrs. Fetiscue had been led to an alcove where they could rest. But Jimson and Mr. Beasley, with Mrs. Mumbles twitching her tail, remained alert nearby. My guardians, Lena thought.

"He died this past summer, here in Scree. But I know he thought of you and your mother every day."

Lena had found a voice again, but it was flat and empty, not her own voice at all. "How do you know?"

"Because he told me so. He wasn't a monster, no matter what other people want you to believe. He was a man who made his own bad choices and reaped what he sowed. He was my son, and I loved him."

"How did he die?"

"He was shot in a brawl, which he started." Her voice was neutral, contained. "I'm sorry you didn't get to see him again."

Lena shook her head. "I was so little, I don't know if I ever knew him. I only remember bits and pieces." Pausing, she phrased her next words carefully. "I need to know if I'm like him. What it means to be a goblin." She looked down at her hands.

"He was brilliant and charming, but also selfish and rash.

You were the one choice he made that wasn't completely selfish. He courted trouble all his life."

"I heard he killed a man." Lena's voice was almost a whisper.

Her grandmother nodded. "He liked nothing better than a good fight. But this time he picked the wrong man. He killed a federal marshal, a man named William Saltre. But the truth is if he hadn't killed Saltre, the marshal would have killed him. After that, his life was never the same. He was always on the run."

William Saltre. Lena's head reeled. *Her* marshal's father? Margaret Flynn had said her father killed a man in Scree. She never mentioned it was Thomas's father. Is that the only reason the marshal had sought her out? Her grandmother was watching her intently. "But my father couldn't help himself; he was a goblin."

"Is that what you think? That being a goblin predisposes you to selfishness and trouble?" Lavina snorted. "Being alive does that. We're all selfish, Peculiar or not. But Saul made the kind of choices that changed him into a bitter, angry person. It wasn't because he was a goblin." With one pointy finger, she tilted Lena's chin up so that their eyes were level. "It's not your family who defines you; they're an influence, all right, but they don't have the final say. We answer for that ourselves."

Lena should have felt relief, yet she felt nothing but a great sadness and weariness. The marshal had used her all along. Jimson was watching her too closely. The room was too small;

the purpled stone was pressing in on her. She wanted to be out, above the ground with the cold stinging her cheeks.

Mr. Beasley spoke. "Perhaps Lena could use some rest?"

"Perhaps she could, but you and I still have much to discuss, Tobias Beasley."

When he raised the empty space that should have been his painted eyebrows, Lavina added, "Oh, yes, I've heard of you. I know you were once a medical man, and my people have been without medical care far too long. Kroll, take Lena somewhere to rest, and take her friends as well."

The last words Lena heard her say were directed to Mr. Beasley. "I need to know if you've been followed."

CHAPTER 34

PORPHYRIUM

DESPITE EXHAUSTION, LENA WAS UP EARLY, ALTHOUGH IT WAS impossible to tell time within the perpetual gloom of the mine. If she didn't get outside, she thought, she'd go mad.

She tiptoed past the still-sleeping Jimson, but the small man called Kroll stopped her before she was able to leave the large chamber. From a greater depth she could hear the sound of the mining operations. Shadowy figures moved purposefully in the dimness, already going about the daily operations of the mine. Lena noticed something that had escaped her attention in the dark. A large water wheel turned slowly, fed by an underground stream.

"Our ventilation system." Kroll's voice was full of the creaks of rusty hinges. "It draws fresh air down the shaft."

"Why is the stone purple?"

"This is a porphyrium mine. We mine the rock for its purple color and for its heat-storing properties."

Lena wondered if Kroll was also a goblin. Although short and wiry, his feet and hands were of normal length, but his teeth were odd—widely spaced and pointed as if they'd been filed.

"I've never heard of porphyrium."

"That's because the only mines are here in Scree, and your government isn't interested in 'em. Leastways not the way they're interested in silver and copper and coal. We grind the stone for purple dye, and we cover our cooking pots in porphyrium dust to hold the heat longer."

Lena ran a gloved finger along the stone. The finger of her glove came away stained with a fine purple dust. She looked at her gloves in disgust. They were streaked and dirty. Why would she need them here? Deliberately, she removed one and then the other. She flexed her hands, goblin hands. Then she balled the gloves tightly and dropped them in the pockets of her skirt.

"Your grandmother asked to see you when you woke up," Kroll said. He led Lena back to the eating area, but even before they arrived, she could hear the demanding voice of Mrs. Fortinbras asking if there were any "normal people" she could speak with.

Lavina Mattacascar ignored Mrs. Fortinbras's request and welcomed Lena to the table, where Merilee and Mr. Beasley sat. "Good morning, Lena. Join us. We were just discussing the properties of porphyrium."

Mr. Beasley was wiggling on the bench like a schoolboy.

Mrs. Mumbles sat next to him at the table as if she were part of the conversation. "Why, this is remarkable!" he said. "Porphyrium. I've heard rumors of the stuff for years." He got to his feet and rubbed one hand along the wall. "But I never expected— Do you know what this could mean?" He turned to look directly at Lavina.

She looked even more stooped and wizened than she had the night before, Lena thought, as she watched her fold her sinewy arms on the table.

"It means that we scrape by. The market for purple dye is almost gone, and Peculiars leave to work in other mines. It means we can't support the ones who've escaped and come here for refuge."

"No, no." Mr. Beasley held up his hands as if warding off blows. "Its heat-storing properties—"

"We've dyed clothes with it for years." Now Lavina was on her feet too. "I have mined here my entire life and my parents and their parents."

"But technology has changed, Lavina; heat storage is invaluable. It goes way beyond cooking pots. Why, we could coat boilers for steam power. We must go outside into the sun. We need to take a chunk of this marvelous porphyrium with us for a demonstration."

Looking at Mr. Beasley as if he'd gone quite mad, Lavina reluctantly led the group, including Kroll, along the lengthy passage to the mouth of the mine. Outside, the sun was glinting. Medrat stood contentedly munching a breakfast of grain. Lena's heart sped up. It was all she could do to keep from running toward the light. Mr. Beasley carried a large chunk of purple porphyrium in one hand. Holding out an arm to stop them before leaving the mine, Lavina nodded at Kroll, who scooted out and returned immediately to say all was clear.

They trooped into the sun, blinking against the bright day. The sun danced off snow and rocks. Lena squinted to shield her eyes. She had never felt so happy to be out of doors. Mrs. Mumbles was already there, eyes closed, her body stretched long as she warmed herself on a rock. Following her example, Lena leaned into a warm rock and her shoulders relaxed.

"I shall put the porphyrium in the direct sun against an already-warm rock and I'll put another type of rock next to it," Mr. Beasley said, describing his experiment. He grabbed a piece of basalt that had been shaded by the overhang of the mine entrance. "Now we wait."

Merilee caught her hair up with one hand and let the sun warm the back of her neck, and Mrs. Fortinbras washed her face with a handful of snow. Lavina squatted nearby, watching skeptically. In the bright light, Lena could see that her grandmother's hair was thin and silvery white. She saw that Kroll's bones jutted beneath his pale skin. As they waited, Mrs. Fortinbras and Mrs. Fetiscue excused themselves from the group to attend to women's business.

"Don't go far. It isn't safe," Lavina warned.

Jimson appeared in the mouth of the mine looking tousled and rubbing the sleep from his eyes.

"Put your hand on this rock. It's slightly warm." Mr. Beasley was almost shouting in his excitement. "Now here— put your other hand on the porphyrium. It's hot. Porphyrium absorbs heat very efficiently. Instead of radiating the heat away, it transfers the heat through conduction."

Lavina laid a hand on each stone. "That's why we've used it on our cooking pots."

"Yes, but there are so many new applications. You could coat a solar collector with porphyrium and it would be a very efficient way to capture heat. You could coat a steam boiler— the options are endless!"

"And to think you have a whole mine of this stuff!" Jimson transferred the hot chunk of porphyrium from hand to hand. "I can't believe nobody ever tried to exploit this before."

"Not many people know about the porphyrium mines, and Peculiars aren't about to broadcast the news," Lavina said. "There're only a few working porphyrium mines left. This may be the largest." She turned to Lena. "Besides, it's Lena's mine now."

Lena startled. She had been enjoying the sunlight, hardly focusing on the conversation at all. She saw that all eyes were turned on her. "But I don't know anything about mining."

"Nevertheless, your father has left you a lega—" Lavina stopped suddenly as a loud swishing sound cut through her words. A shadow slid over them.

Lena shivered.

"It's a dirigible!" Jimson shouted. "Get inside!"

Mrs. Fetiscue and Mrs. Fortinbras, still several yards away, screamed.

Lena looked up.

A voice boomed directly overhead, amplified by a megaphone. "We've found their nest. Shoot them all!" A face appeared in a window of the dirigible. Lena squinted up into the sun.

In one leap, Jimson knocked Lena into a bank of snow. She sputtered and twisted up her face, cold and pocked with snow.

"But he can't mean us! We're not Peculiar!" Mrs. Fetiscue cried, her hat askew. She stood in a clearing of snow, looking upward.

"Why, I suppose he does, my dear," replied Mrs. Fortinbras, shaking her fist at the dirigible.

The sun glinted off the barrel of a revolver.

"Get down!" Merilee dove toward the missionary ladies, arms outstretched, just as a gunshot from the dirigible split the air. She landed in a belly flop, her arms at their feet, as if beseeching. The snow bled.

There was a second shot, and then another. The horse screamed and struggled against his tether. Lavina pointed a rifle at the underbelly of the now listing dirigible and pulled the trigger a third time. "I think I managed a few good hits."

The dirigible was already obscured by trees. Instantly, Mr. Beasley joined Mrs. Fetiscue and Mrs. Fortinbras at Merilee's side. Lena sat up, caked with snow from chin to knees. Jimson was on his feet beside her. Mr. Beasley straightened slowly. "We have to get Merilee inside now." The snow grew redder.

Lena rushed to help Mr. Beasley, but he had already lifted Merilee in his arms. Her body was limp and her hair spilled almost to the ground. Lena's heart hammered wildly. She had known the voice as soon as she'd heard it.

The marshal had found them at last.

Mrs. Fetiscue seemed to have recovered her wits more quickly than Lena. "Hurry! We need to set up a place where he can work." She pulled Lena by the arm. They moved quickly into the mine.

Lavina, rifle at her side, was giving orders. "Use the eating table." She turned to Jimson. "Make sure some water is boiled. We've got clean rags and more lanterns."

They laid Merilee on the table. Her mouth was still open as if caught in mid-shout, and her face was an ashy gray. Her eyes flickered briefly.

Mrs. Fetiscue blew her nose forcefully. "She was trying to save us. Her being a Peculiar and all, she was trying to save us."

"We should pray for her." Mrs. Fortinbras swiped her eyes with the heel of her hand.

Lena felt as if something within her might erupt. "Why bother if she doesn't have a soul?" The words escaped from her lips like steam from a kettle. "Do you know that's why we saved you the first time, because Merilee said to? She couldn't bear to think of harm coming to anyone. She wasn't a mistake any more than you are."

"Lena." Mr. Beasley's voice was as hard as stone. "Get the scalpel from the medical bag."

Lena was glad to have a task. She blinked away tears of frustration. Jimson handed her the bag. She sorted through its contents.

"I think you'll be in need of this." Lavina Mattacascar set an earthenware jug on the table. "It's a hundred and twenty proof."

Mr. Beasley nodded. "Jimson, I want you to help me turn her over. Lena, clean the scalpel with the alcohol."

Merilee's breath was fast and shallow. Lena felt her own hands slippery with sweat. She tried not to think about the pain Merilee must be feeling and tried instead to concentrate on the task. Mr. Beasley kept talking calmly. "Merilee, I want you to swallow some of this drink; it will help with the pain."

Obediently, she opened her white lips, swallowed, sputtered, and coughed.

"The bullet entered right below the shoulder, through the site of the old wound," Mr. Beasley said. "I'll need two people to help me."

Mrs. Fetiscue stepped forward. "I've done some nursing before."

"Lena?" Mr. Beasley's voice was more command than question. "Everyone else, please leave. But remain within earshot in case I need you."

"They could be coming back for us at any time," Lavina said. "Jimson, I want you and Kroll to be lookouts. Come on. Stop gaping—we've got work to do." She hustled the others from the room. "And bring that cat with you!"

It was eerily quiet all of a sudden. A ring of lanterns had been set on the table, but still the light was spotty. Merilee seemed to be resting more easily. Lena's mouth was dry. She had never assisted at a real operation before. And it was worse because it was her friend. Mrs. Fetiscue seemed comfortable enough, and Lena tried to draw strength from her calm.

"I will make the incision here," Mr. Beasley said. "You'll both need to hold her. When I've removed the bullet, I'll stitch her up just like you did, Lena, with Jimson's cheek. I'd like you to sterilize the needle for me."

Despite the alcohol, Merilee screamed and writhed when Mr. Beasley sliced the flesh of her back. Mrs. Fetiscue made no comment when she saw the long scars where the wings had been removed. She worked calmly and competently. Lena concentrated on breathing slowly so that she wouldn't throw up as Mr. Beasley dug about for the bullet, which he extracted and dropped into a cup.

Mrs. Fetiscue gave Merilee more alcohol while Mr. Beasley turned to Lena. "Your stitching is neater than mine. I'm sure Merilee would appreciate having the smallest scar possible."

"No, I—" But he was already handing Lena the needle and thread.

"I'll hold the skin closed while you work."

On the first prick, Lena felt Merilee flinch, and she almost stopped. Her hands shook so badly that it took all her concentration to steady them, and that was what ultimately let her work. She concentrated on making each stitch small and perfect.

"She's lost a great deal of blood, but she'll recover. We need to let her rest now, somewhere comfortable."

Lavina reappeared and offered a warm bed space near the fire.

Lena walked stiffly toward the mouth of the mine, every muscle screaming its displeasure; she had been clenching them the entire time. Now she was eager for the sting of cold air on her cheeks. But she was exhilarated too. It had felt good being able to help Mr. Beasley and help Merilee. In the end, she had been able to forget about the blood and just do her work the best she could. And she did it well. Mr. Beasley said so.

A shape was hunched against the rock wall: Jimson, with a rifle resting across his knees, his eyes closed, head thrown back. The scar on his cheek was healing. His eyelashes created shadows on his cheeks. Unfair, Lena thought as always, those eyelashes should belong to a girl. "I'm glad you're protecting us!" she said.

Jimson's eyes flew open. "I was just resting my eyes. I—"

Lena laughed. "The bullet's out and she's sleeping." She leaned against the entrance to the mine, and let the warmth of the rock seep into her back, then sank slowly down onto a log next to Jimson. "How soon do you think the marshal will be back?"

"Soon. Even if the dirigible was damaged and he's slowed down, there will be others looking for us. We need to leave, all of us."

"But there's no law about Peculiars working in a mine. What can the marshal do?" She turned and looked into Jimson's face. Freckles dusted the bridge of his nose; her own face was reflected in the depth of his eyes.

"The law says a Peculiar can't *own* a mine. I don't know if the marshal has any jurisdiction over us here," Jimson answered.

"You mean," Lena said, "that he may not be able to arrest us just for running away."

Jimson nodded. "I'm sorry about your father, Lena. I didn't get a chance to tell you."

Lena looked away as her throat tightened. She shrugged. "My father killed the marshal's father. No wonder he hates Peculiars . . . So, I really am part goblin. I'm half Peculiar, just like Merilee."

"What does it matter if—"

She cut him off. "It matters because I can't go back." It was the first time she had spoken aloud what she had been thinking, worrying over in her mind, like a dog with a bone.

"Do you want to?" Jimson's usually mobile face was very still.

"Do you?" Lena asked. "Pansy won't want to wait forever."

"Pansy? Pansy doesn't want anything to do with me now. Her last letter made that pretty clear."

"I'm sorry," Lena mumbled, but she felt surprisingly lighter.

"Don't be. I feel as if a huge weight has been rolled off my back. I can do what I want now."

Lena closed her eyes. "It's strange. Suddenly, you're freer and I'm not. Even if I wanted to go back to the City, I'd be sent back here to work in the mines. And all the answers I thought I'd get from my father—" She shrugged again, feeling the warmth of the sun on her face. "I'm not who I thought I was. Everything is different now. I don't know how to be part goblin."

"It doesn't change anything, Lena. That's what I've been trying to say. You're still the same person today that you were a week ago—the most interesting girl I've ever met. It doesn't change the way I feel about you."

Lena opened her eyes. Jimson was staring at her earnestly. She stood up. "Maybe I'm interesting because I'm half Peculiar, something collectible."

"That's not what I mean, and you know it." Jimson was on his feet too, a scowl shading his face.

But Lena couldn't stop herself. How could Jimson care about her when she didn't even know who she was anymore? "What did you mean about my ridiculous notions?"

In one stride Jimson was closer. "When you were arrested, I was terrified. Terrified that I might lose the most amazing girl

I'd ever met. And then when you agreed to landing again—"
He shrugged.

Lena looked at his familiar face. One eye was still purpled;
the black stitches gave him the look of a desperado. She
reached up and traced the black threads with one long bare
finger.

"Not just the most amazing girl . . . the most dazzling
woman." He cupped Lena's cheek with a warm hand. Lena
eased back against warm rock. There were flecks of green in
Jimson's blue eyes. Why hadn't she noticed that before?

Jimson traced her lips with a finger, leaned closer until
his eyes, framed with thick black lashes and the sprinkling of
freckles, were all Lena saw.

"We're having a meeting in the eating room. Now. Kroll
will take over as lookout."

Jimson pulled back.

Lavina was standing in the mouth of the mine. Turning
her stooped back, she clearly indicated that she expected them
to follow.

Lena felt a laugh bubble up from somewhere deep inside.
Jimson took her hand.

Mr. Beasley, Mrs. Fortinbras, and Mrs. Fetiscue were
already seated on the benches. Mr. Beasley looked tired,
Lena thought. It was funny how a lack of eyebrows made
his expressions so difficult to read. Mrs. Mumbles lay draped
across his lap. Meanwhile, the missionary ladies had managed
to keep their air of competence. Fortitude, Nana Crane would

have said. Mrs. Fortinbras and Mrs. Fetiscue were both blessed with an unusual amount of fortitude.

"Very soon, I should think, we'll have visitors," Mr. Beasley said. "Lawmen, who will want to shut this mine down and take it over. They won't be interested in the porphyrium—at least, not at first—but they won't allow a mine to be owned and operated by Peculiars. Lena, your deed gives you ownership, but your genetic heritage may not allow you to *claim* ownership. I don't know if the law applies to half Peculiars. Lavina and I have discussed a plan that we hope meets with your approval." Here he paused.

Lena looked at Jimson, then back at Mr. Beasley as he continued.

"Lena could turn the deed over to me, which I would agree to hold and operate in trust for her until a time when these laws have been replaced with more equitable ones. I would continue to employ the entire colony of Peculiars already working the mine. With expanded uses for porphyrium, we would be able to fund decent housing for the employees. And that's what the Peculiars would be, employees who each receive a salary."

When Lena started to interrupt, Mr. Beasley held up his hand.

"Let me finish. Merilee needs to return to her mother at Zephyr House. She needs time and a place to recuperate, and the work here will be strenuous. Leticia Pollet has already had enough tragedy in her life. But Merilee can't travel alone. I'm suggesting that Jimson escort her back and, still in my employ, care for my library until I can return." He looked around at the faces of his companions. "Mrs. Fortinbras and Mrs. Fetiscue?"

"But—" Lena interrupted again.

Mrs. Fortinbras cut her off. "My sister has decided to stay here. As I see it, she's been enchanted, blinded by the devil and his works. But she's my sister." Lena noticed that she never met Mrs. Fetiscue's eyes while she spoke. "I will be leaving as soon as possible to report to the mission agency that our work has been a failure."

Mrs. Fetiscue pushed away from the table. "Not a failure, Irene Fortinbras. You can't say we failed. We may have a difference of opinion, but we have helped innocent people."

"That is the point, isn't it?" her sister argued. "They are *not* people, no matter what you say, Mrs. Fetiscue. They have no souls."

Lena's heart pumped harder. She felt a hand on her shoulder.

"What about the book, Irene? Can you explain that?" Mrs. Fetiscue threw up her hands. "It seems that Peculiars"—here she darted a glance at Lena and then away—"may have the same Creator. Last night Lavina showed us a most unusual book." And amazingly, she put a broad hand over her mouth and emitted something that sounded like a cross between a strangled sob and a giggle.

Lena looked at Jimson, willing him to think of the book from Cloister buried in his pack.

"A very ancient book with pictures of the creation story.

And there was a creature with hands and feet like hers," Mrs. Fetiscue added, pointing at Lena. "Right from the start."

Mr. Beasley smoothed his hand over his strands of hair. "A companion book came into my possession from the sisters of Cloister. I believe it was saved from my library when we left so hurriedly?" He looked at Jimson.

Jimson blushed. "It's in my pack, sir."

Mr. Beasley smiled. "I hoped so."

Mrs. Fortinbras crossed her arms over her ample bosom. "The book is blasphemy."

"And what if you are wrong, Irene? I would rather err with charity, as we were shown charity."

But Mrs. Fortinbras pursed her lips and shook her head. The soiled red poppies dangled wildly from her hat.

A deep note interrupted further conversation. It was like the bellowing of a bull elephant.

"It's Kroll. Alerting us." Lavina rose.

Mr. Beasley turned to Lena. "Lena, the mine and its people are at your mercy. I have drawn up some papers—"

Voices were at the door—angry, threatening voices—followed by shouts.

CHAPTER 35

LEARNING TO WHISTLE

THE THREE MEN WHO STOOD IN THE MOUTH OF THE MINE WERE uniformed marshals. Thomas Saltre was the youngest one of them, even though he was the most senior. "This mine is now under federal protection." The man who spoke was short and thin, but his bass voice boomed and echoed from the rock walls. He continued. "Under section 17c of the proclamation of *terra nullius*, it states that all unclaimed natural resources are now owned by the government."

"And I say that this mine is *not* an unclaimed resource." Mr. Beasley held up the papers in his hand. "These people have owned and worked this mine for generations."

Thomas Saltre was growing red in the face. Lena wondered how she could have ever found him attractive.

"A criminal who colludes with Peculiars is trying to interpret the law." Saltre turned and spat on the ground. "Arrest him and send this batch of vermin away. The mine will be shut down." He turned to Lavina. "Get the rest of your kind up here, old woman. Production stops immediately."

Something was building inside Lena, a fierceness that was not familiar. Legs trembling, she surprised herself by stepping forward. "The Mattacascar mine has been deeded to Tobias Beasley unconditionally. As a citizen, he has every right to own and operate this mine. Give me a pen."

Mr. Beasley reached into his jacket pocket and then handed over the papers and a pen to Lena. He looked at her. "Are you sure, my dear? This mine has been in your family for generations."

"I have never been surer about anything." And as she said the words, she realized they were true. With a few quick strokes, she signed the deed to the mine into Mr. Beasley's ownership.

"And I wish to add a codicil." She hoped that was the correct term. "That ownership requires Tobias Beasley to keep the same workforce and that any profits from the mine will be distributed at Tobias Beasley's discretion. Will you agree to that, Mr. Beasley?"

He nodded solemnly.

Thomas Saltre exploded, "Peculiars cannot sell property, because they can't own property! And there's no doubt what she is—look at her!" His eyes raked her body. "Such a waste!"

Reflexively, Lena moved her hands to the folds of her skirt. Then slowly she pulled them back out and held them up on display. "Half Peculiar, Mr. Saltre. My mother is a citizen and not a Peculiar, despite what you see here." Then she lifted her hands and wiggled her long, spidery fingers.

"Will you look at that!" The second marshal, whose mustache was a few sparse bristles on his upper lip, leaned forward. "I ain't never seen nothing like them before."

"These things are criminals. He colluded with Peculiars and broke federal law." Thomas Saltre, his finger shaking with rage, pointed at Mr. Beasley. "And arrest the old bags, too." He gestured inclusively at Mrs. Fortinbras and Mrs. Fetiscue.

"Excuse me, sir." One of the marshals had been shuffling through the papers Mr. Beasley had passed to him. "But everything here seems to be perfectly legal, even if we don't like it. Mr. Beasley now does legally own the mine, and we can't arrest them for crimes as long as they're here in Scree."

Lena let a small breath escape. She was aware of Jimson, hands clenched, by her side, of Lavina on her other side standing as tall and proud as her four feet eight inches would allow, but Lena never broke contact with Thomas Saltre's ice-blue stare.

"I believe everything is in order, then." Mr. Beasley's words were more statement than question. "As sole owner of the mine and as a citizen, I have the right to choose my own workforce."

"The minute you step foot on federal ground again, you'll be under arrest. I'll be waiting. And you"—the marshal turned to Lena—"will be deported to whatever service I see fit."

"I'm afraid we're all remaining here," Mr. Beasley said. "Except young Jimson, who will be accompanying an injured girl back to her mother in Knob Knoster. Her mother works for Jimson at Zephyr House."

"You crafty bastard." Thomas Saltre stepped toe to toe with Mr. Beasley. "Are you going to tell me that you sold that big house of yours?"

"I didn't sell it. I gave it free and clear, as a gift for services rendered."

Lena heard Jimson suck in his breath, but she didn't turn her head.

"He was in on the whole thing, harboring Peculiars," the marshal protested.

"Prove it, Marshal Saltre. Jimson was employed as my librarian. His parents are store owners in Northerdam. His work was solely in my library."

Thomas Saltre raised his pistol, pointed it at Mr. Beasley's head, and cocked the trigger.

One of the other marshals put his hand on Thomas's shoulder. "Come on now, Thomas. We need to leave before there's trouble."

He shrugged him off. "I'm not going to be taken in by a bunch of Peculiar-loving vermin."

Lena could see beads of sweat on his brow. His left eye twitched, but the hand that was pointing the gun held steady.

"But I'm afraid you have no choice." The voice from behind was flat, devoid of emotion. It was the sheriff from Ducktown. Beside him stood Kroll. "I heard there was a marshal overstepped his bounds. Commandeered an army dirigible. Now I hear from a mine employee that he shot a girl and she almost died. That goes beyond the authority of the law, marshal."

Thomas Saltre turned, still pointing the pistol, and was met by a rifle.

"Who the hell are you, a sheriff, to be telling me the law? I don't answer to anyone but the attorney general."

The sheriff's voice was still calm, flat. "Seems you have a misunderstanding of the law. Marshals serve their communities and the gov'ment. They don't shoot to kill unarmed folks, and they don't steal army property. Isn't that right?"

The second marshal swallowed. His Adam's apple bobbed up and down. "Maybe we need to be going, Thomas. I think he's made his point."

"Drop the gun, Marshal, and I'm sure this can be resolved," the sheriff said. "I've come a long way to make sure justice is being done in my territory. Some bounty hunters told me where they had last seen these missionary ladies. Though I lost them a time or two in the snow, it wasn't hard tracking them all from there."

But Thomas Saltre did not move. A trickle of sweat was running from his brow down the side of his face and into the curve of his mustache. "You're no lawman, Sheriff. You're a namby-pamby, afraid of doing your duty. We don't need men like you."

The distraction was enough. Lavina sprang. From behind, she threw all her weight against Thomas Saltre's right leg. The knee buckled. For one crazy second he wobbled, the pistol veering wildly in his hand. As he went down, he fired. The bullet echoed loudly and lodged in the rock wall.

The two other marshals held him down and, over loud curses and promises of retaliation, tied his hands behind his back.

The sheriff lowered his gun.

The second marshal straightened. "I'd like to plead guilty to commandeering a dirigible, sir."

"No need, son. No doubt you were pressured by your senior officer."

The sheriff looked at the ragtag group but spoke to Lavina. "Don't ever let me hear of a Peculiar going against a lawman again." With that, he turned to leave. "Now get this marshal out of my territory and that dirigible back where it belongs."

Lavina leaned close to Lena. "Your father never would have given the mine away. He would have wanted to keep the profits for himself, even if it meant sacrificing his own people." Then straightening herself as tall as she could, she took Mr. Beasley's arm. "I think I'd like to rest."

He led her to a bench in the eating area, where Mrs. Fetiscue brewed tea for everyone.

"I meant what I said about Zephyr House, Jimson," Mr. Beasley said. "Someone has to take care of it, make sure the books are properly looked after."

For once Jimson was at a loss for words.

"We'll have to arrange transport for you and Merilee in the next few days. Lena, my dear, I'm sorry, but it looks as if you might not be able to return home for the foreseeable future."

But her grandmother's words were still ringing in her ears: *Your father never would have given the mine away.* "I would have chosen to stay anyway. After helping you with Merilee and after working on Jimson, well, I know I have a lot to learn, but I like medicine. I'd like to stay and learn from you if I can."

Mr. Beasley nodded. "I suspect there are a number of people here who could use some medical attention, and I'd be proud to offer it as well as run the mine if you, Lavina, would continue as forewoman."

"I don't know that I'm up to the task anymore, and since my granddaughter has her sights set on medicine, I might suggest Kroll as foreman. He's been with me a long time. It seems my granddaughter, unlike her father, has an altruistic streak. She's becoming her own woman."

Lena's eyes grew bright. "Maybe being a goblin isn't what I thought it was."

Mr. Beasley turned to Jimson. "Your Mr. Darwin, Jimson, addresses only biological change. He never addresses bitterness or forgiveness and how that choice can change the course of a life. I was a medical man for many years. I've seen how people's choices influence the course of their lives. I know some things are right and some are reprehensible, but where that sense of right and wrong comes from, I dare not think about."

"But altruism is advantageous to the species," Jimson said with certainty.

"Only if I help someone in my own tribe or community," Mr. Beasley countered. "Helping someone else in a different group isn't advantageous to me at all. And there's another danger on this road. Random replication means there is no purpose to the emergence of humans or Peculiars. That's the sticking point for me. I cannot live a purposeless life."

Lena felt as if her head were spinning, and there was no time to sort out all of Mr. Beasley's words. Even Jimson remained silent.

"You and Merilee must be prepared to leave as soon as she is strong enough—in the next day or so, I think," Mr. Beasley continued.

"I'm not sure I'm ready to go back." Jimson's face was hidden in shadow.

"I'm asking you to go back to help Merilee get home."

In the shadow, Lena could see Jimson's head nod.

Jimson stood and changed the subject. "I don't suppose I'll have another chance to see a dirigible anytime soon. Lena, do you want to come?"

Lena looked at her grandmother drinking tea with Mrs. Fetiscue.

Mrs. Fetiscue spoke. "I just checked on Merilee. She slept through the whole commotion."

Lena nodded and followed Jimson out of the mine.

They walked out into what should have been the afternoon

sunlight, but the dirigible cast a broad shadow as it lifted off. The sheriff, mounted on his horse, watched the ship begin its journey home. "Still listing a bit, but it looks like they can fly it all right." He clicked his horse to a trot in the direction of Ducktown.

Lena watched the giant ship, thinking how much it looked like a whale sailing the skies.

But Jimson wasn't watching the dirigible; he was watching her. His eyes traced her face as if asking a question.

His was the most honest face she had ever seen, Lena decided. There were so many things she wanted to say, but there were also many things she wanted to do and to learn. They all required time. When she spoke, her voice was breathless but sure. "It's a long road home, Jimson. Take care of Merilee and Mrs. Pollet. I'll send a letter with you for my family." Mrs. Mumbles wound herself around Lena's ankles.

"It looks like the cat plans to stay with you and Mr. Beasley. I'll be back for you, Lena Mattacascar. Just see if I'm not."

Lena imagined the snow-covered miles through Scree, the train ride from the border to Knob Knoster. She pictured Zephyr House and the library she had come to love. She would miss it all, but she had a purpose here, and there was something new stirring inside her, the wild heart Nana Crane had always feared. She scooped Mrs. Mumbles into her arms and smiled.

"You'll know where to find me. Jimson, will you teach me to whistle?"

HISTORICAL NOTE

The Peculiars is a work of fiction set in an alternative late 1800s. I've included historical references from that time period, but I've also taken some liberties. For example, the Pony Express was short lived—it lasted only eighteen months (although in legend it lasted much longer). The first rider traveled from Missouri to Sacramento, California, in 1860, and the last ride was made in 1861. The Pony Express delivered the mail to the West Coast in just ten days! In *The Peculiars*, the Pony Express is still operating in 1888—and traveling a much greater distance.

The following list should help sort some fact from fiction.

An **aeolipile** is an engine that spins when heated. Hero of Alexandria described the device in the first century AD, and many sources give him credit for its invention. That's how it came to be called "Hero's engine." You can see a video of how an aeolipile works on YouTube.

Cayley (1773–1857) and **Stringfellow** (1799–1883) were early pioneers of winged flight. George Cayley, a British engineer, is considered the father of aerial navigation. He encouraged his friend John Stringfellow, who designed lightweight steam engines, to build and fly three steam-powered aircraft, one of which was still flown by Stringfellow's son, Frederick Stringfellow, in the late 1800s. Of course Mr. Beasley would have known about that!

The **Colt Peacemaker** was a .45 caliber handgun that held six rounds of ammunition. It was one of the most common guns in the West. Designed for the U.S. cavalry, it was adopted by the army in 1873.

The **Concord coach** was the finest overland stagecoach of its day. It was built in Concord, New Hampshire, by the Abbot Downing Co. throughout most of the nineteenth century. Despite its popularity, it was quite uncomfortable by today's standards. The windows had leather curtains that did little to keep out the elements. The interior, which held up to nine people, was only about four feet in width. However, in 1861, Mark Twain traveled west in a Concord coach and said it rode "like a cradle on wheels." The exterior of the coach was painted in bright colors with gold scrollwork.

The **Girandoni** was a remarkable pneumatic weapon—a twenty-two shot .46 caliber air rifle that produced no smoke and very little noise. However, to operate it, one had to pump it by hand (more than 1,500 times). It was made in Austria in the late eighteenth and early nineteenth centuries and was used during the Napoleonic wars (1803–15). It was later used by Lewis and Clark on their famous western expedition. You can see video of the Girandoni on YouTube.

Meriwether Lewis (1774–1809) was an explorer and the official leader of the Lewis and Clark expedition, which began in Missouri in 1804. In 1805, the members of the expedition reached the Pacific Ocean. They returned to St. Louis on

September 23, 1806. As an explorer himself, Mr. Beasley would of course take a keen interest in Lewis and Clark's journey.

Joseph Lister (1827–1912) was a surgeon at Glasgow University in Scotland in the 1860s when he began using carbolic acid to kill germs and make surgery safer. He also insisted that doctors wash their hands using calcium chloride. This was met with skepticism, especially because the acid burned patients' skin. Lister refined his techniques for preventing infection and introduced a carbolic acid spray that didn't have to be applied directly to a patient's skin. But it wasn't until the 1880s, when he was chair of surgery at King's College Hospital in London, that others began using his methods.

David Livingstone (1813–73) was a British missionary and explorer best known for his explorations of Africa. He was a popular national hero noted for saying, "I am prepared to go anywhere, provided it be forward." He received the gold medal of the Royal Geographical Society of London and was made a fellow of that society. When he lost contact with the outside world for six years, **Henry Morton Stanley** (1841–1904) was sent by the *New York Herald* to find him. Stanley set out in 1869 but didn't find Livingstone until 1871. By the late 1800s, the explorations of Stanley and Livingstone had reached mythic proportions.

Joseph Norman Lockyer (1836–1920) was an English astronomer who, at the same time as Pierre Janssen, discovered helium. He also invented a method to observe solar prominences using a spectroscope. Between 1870 and 1905, he headed eight government expeditions to observe total eclipses of the sun.

A. A. (Albert Augustus) Pope (1843–1909) imported European "penny farthing" bicycles into the United States but soon began manufacturing them in Hartford, Connecticut. He founded the Pope Manufacturing Company in 1877, and it became the largest and most successful bicycle business in America at the time. As usual, Mr. Beasley was at the front of the curve.

Steam-powered carousels were very popular in European fairs in the early twentieth century. I set the Pleasure Dome in Knob Knoster in the late 1800s. The animals and gondolas were in enclosed tents that often had tables and dance floors surrounding the rotating platform.

 ACKNOWLEDGMENTS

Each book has its own peculiar journey to completion, and I have been lucky to have many friends on this journey. I could not have traveled far without them.

Thanks go out to the Monday Writers for their insights, laughter, and faithful slogging through drafts: Lenora Good, Jeff Copeland, and especially Stephen Wallenfels, who is owed gallons of tea and a fair share of October. To Randy LaBarge, for unfailing encouragement. And to all my other early readers, for sharp eyes and kind hearts.

Most of all, my thanks to my family, who are my greatest fans: Dennis, whose patience and ideas rarely fail and who has read more drafts than a person should ever have to; Brennan, who champions everything I do; and Claire, who loves words.

Sandra Bishop, my agent, believed in me from the start. I've had the best of editors in Howard Reeves. Thanks to the entire Abrams/Amulet team.

ABOUT THE AUTHOR

Maureen Doyle McQuerry is an award-winning poet and teacher. She has taught for many years, specializing in young adult literature and writing. Her poems appear regularly in *The Southern Review*, *Atlanta Review*, and other publications. She is a founding member of Washington State's Young Adult website, www.ya-wa.com. She currently lives in Richland, Washington.

This book was designed by Meagan Bennett and art directed by Chad W. Beckerman. The text is set in Adobe Caslon, a typeface designed by Carol Twombly. It is a variant on the original Caslon typeface, which was created by William Caslon, an English gunsmith and typeface designer. This font was made in 1990, and is specifically based on Caslon specimen pages printed between 1734 and 1770. Its versatility and its friendly, round letterforms make it a popular font for a variety of books and publications.

KEEP READING FOR A SNEAK PEEK AT MAUREEN

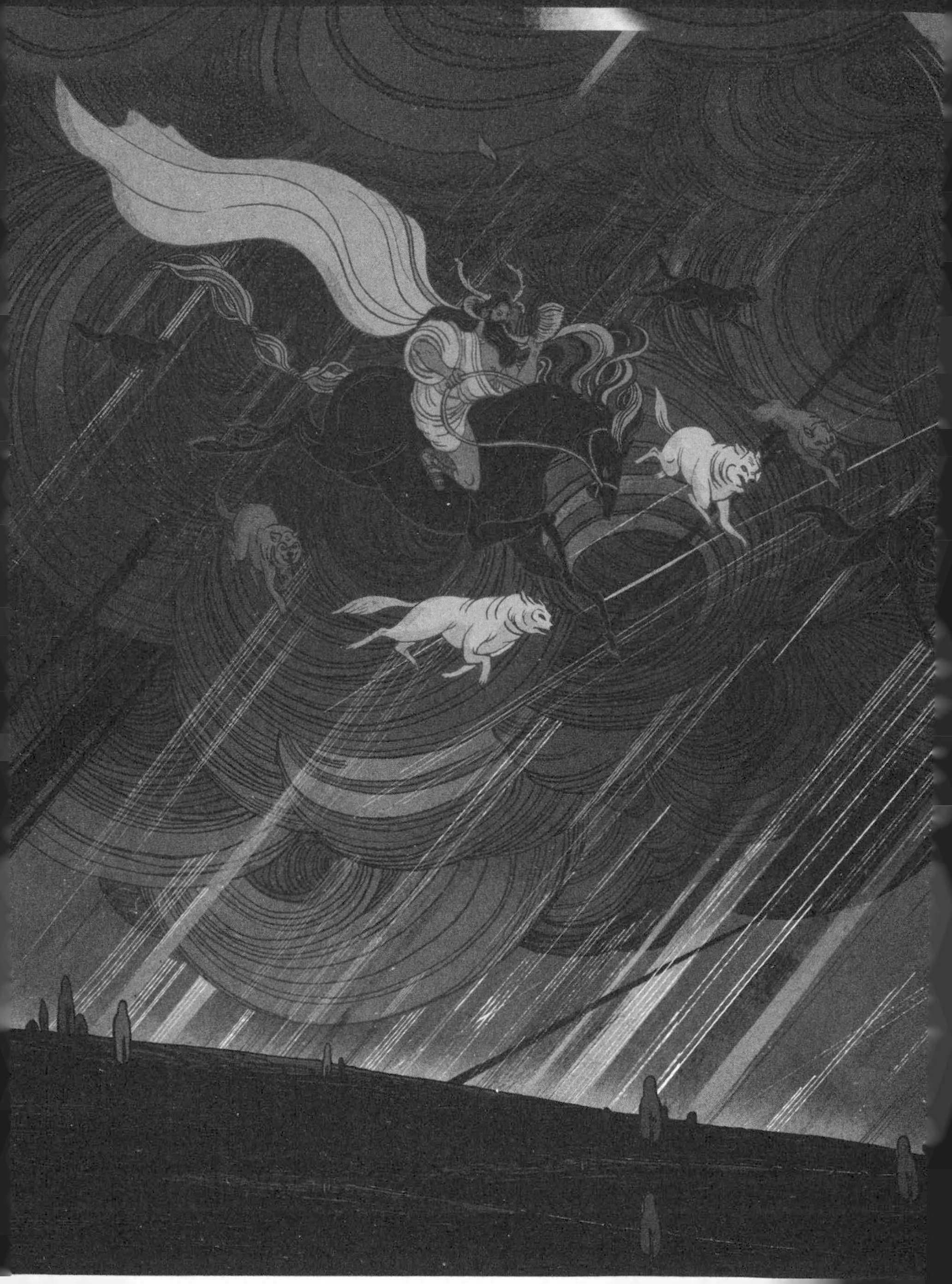

DOYLE McQUERRY'S EXCITING NEW FANTASY NOVEL

TIME OUT OF TIME

BEYOND THE DOOR

STORMS RISE,
EVIL LURKS,
HOPE SWELLS,
AND
COURAGE TRIUMPHS!

AT THE DOOR AND INTO THE HOUSE

A STRAY GUST OF wind howled down the chimney, sending a spray of last fall's leaves out of the hearth and scuttling across the living room floor. Timothy James Maxwell jumped up with a start from the book he had been trying to read. It wasn't a windy night. Leaves had never blown down the chimney before. He went to the fireplace and peered cautiously up the chimney, but all he could see was the blackness of the flue. A puff of air blew directly in his face, and he pulled out his head, smacking the back of it on the bricks. "Ouch!"

Fortunately, neither the leaves nor his cry awakened Mrs. Clapper, who had fallen asleep in the recliner at least half an hour ago. She slept soundly, with her legs, thick as tree trunks, sprawled in front of her, head thrown back, mouth gaping like a trap. Her nose whistled with each deep breath and her full lower lip quivered. She wasn't really too bad, as babysitters went, Timothy thought, but the fact that she was a babysitter was a problem. At eleven and three-quarters, he was quite sure he no longer needed a babysitter. Unfortunately, his parents didn't agree. And even though they tried to pass her off as a companion, he wasn't fooled. So when they had taken his older sister, Sarah, to a ballet audition in the city, Timothy was left, alone, with the Clapper.

"We'll be home Sunday night as soon as we can—promise," his mother had explained. Timothy looked down at the carpet and drew his eyebrows together.

"Buck up, son. Clapper's a good sort, and she'll probably play Scrabble with you to your heart's content." Timothy considered this to be nothing more than bribery because his father knew how much he loved Scrabble: the smooth wooden tiles, the random surprise of letters, and, of course, the fact that he usually won.

"I don't think I need a babysitter anymore, now that I'm almost twelve," Timothy replied with dignity. "I can take care of myself just fine. What could happen? Nothing ever happens here. If you really don't want me left alone, then one of you should stay. It doesn't take two people to see an audition." He knew he was being unreasonable, but he couldn't stop the words.

"We know that you're very capable," his mother had replied, bending close so that he caught the minty fragrance of her soft brown hair and a faint whiff of turpentine. "We just want you to have some company, and Mrs. Clapper has already agreed. Do be kind to her, Timothy."

At that point, Timothy had known the battle was lost. He thought of the word conquer. A handy word to use in Scrabble, but a miserable word when it was directed at him.

Over the years, Mrs. Clapper had stayed a number of times, but always when he and Sarah were home together. He didn't like the idea of having Mrs. Clapper to himself. He'd always counted on Sarah to divert most of the babysitter's attention. And he was still haunted by some of the strange stories she had told them, stories about people who shape-shifted into animals, about changeling children or creatures that came in from the dark if you left a door or window open.

The evening hadn't passed as slowly as he had feared. They had played Scrabble, and he'd won every game but one, and she'd let him play WarGames on the computer for an hour. But even this couldn't make up for tolerating a babysitter. Then Mrs. Clapper had made a batch of ginger cookies and begun one of her stories. It was about a stone that had been missing for many years, a stone that cried out loud when the right person put a foot on it.

"How can a stone cry out?" Timothy popped a warm cookie into his mouth.

"This one has a voice, but it's not a human voice. A cry rings out when a just leader places a foot on it. Of course, there are those who'd rather the stone was silent."

"Why?"

"Because they're not interested in justice."

"Are you sure there isn't a sword in this stone?" Timothy asked, thinking of the story of King Arthur.

"No, there is no sword in this stone. But there is a missing sword in the story, and a missing spear and cauldron as well." She handed Timothy a dish towel and the wet mixing bowl. "Like Arthur's stone, one specific person is intended to find it."

Timothy considered. "A good story should have battles."

"Oh, there are battles, fearsome battles, and if the Dark wins them, the Dark grows stronger."

"The Dark?"

"Of course, the Dark. The Dark wants the stone and is willing to do all kinds of terrible things to prevent anyone else finding it. That must never happen. Just as the Light longs for everything to be free, the Dark longs to control everything."

The story was definitely getting interesting, Timothy thought. A chill passed up his arms. "What kind of things?" He set the bowl aside and bit into another of Mrs. Clapper's ginger cookies. Crumbs cascaded to the floor.

"Things that are better left unspoken. They'd give you worse nightmares than the wolves you're afraid of."

Timothy cringed. He never should have told Mrs. Clapper about the wolves in his nightmares.

"Before I say anything more, close the drapes. You never know who might be watching us. And lock the door. You never know what might wander in." She barked out a laugh, and went into the living room. Settling into the leather recliner with a sigh, she pulled the plaid tartan throw over her legs and closed her eyes.

"This throw is from your mother's family, isn't it? The O'Dalys."

"Yes, I guess so, but who would be looking in here? There's nothing very interesting in our house."

"Sometimes ordinary things turn out to be more interesting than you think."

Timothy drew the drapes. "So where is this stone?"

Mrs. Clapper opened one blue eye and peered up at Timothy. "Only the Stewards of the Stone know that, and maybe not all of them. But the stone is meant to be found. By the right person, of course . . . If he survives."

Her words hung in the air. Timothy breathed them in. "It's a quest, isn't it?"

But Mrs. Clapper's breathing had become deep and regular. She had fallen asleep. Timothy had picked up his book on magic tricks and tried to read, but the story of the stone distracted him. A talking stone would definitely be spectacular.

That was when the leaves had blown down the chimney.

Now rubbing the knot forming on his head, he took one more careful look up the chimney. Nothing. Too bad real adventures were so hard to come by. He looked at the snoring Mrs. Clapper. Once she was in bed for the night, he could spend more time on the computer. He could stay up all night if he wanted to.

He grasped Mrs. Clapper's sweatshirt-clad shoulder and shook: no response. This time he grabbed her shoulder more firmly and spoke directly into her ear. "Mrs. Clapper, I'm going to bed now."

She snorted loudly. "Oh, my goodness, it's past eleven. At least you don't have school tomorrow." She pushed up her reading glasses to the top of her head. "Time for you to get ready for bed, and I think I'll be heading that way myself." Easing herself up out of the overstuffed chair, she cocked her head to the side and her clear blue eyes peered sharply at Timothy. "Is there anything you need?"

For a moment Timothy felt as if she knew he was planning to stay up most of the night. "No." He feigned a yawn. "I'm just really sleepy."

"Well, good dreams, then, Timothy. Good dreams." And she wandered down the hall to the guest bedroom. "And turn off the lights on your way to bed."

Timothy set off in the direction of his bedroom. He stopped in the bathroom and made sure to let the water in the sink run at least three minutes to simulate brushing his teeth. Then he flushed the toilet and checked the hallway. No Mrs. Clapper in sight, and the door to the guest bedroom was firmly closed. Now for the computer.

As he passed the front door, Timothy couldn't resist opening it and peering out into the dark. The night was warm for mid-March, and the wind that had blown the leaves down the chimney seemed to have completely disappeared. And, of course, there was nothing waiting to come in as Mrs. Clapper had suggested. If only life were more like the stories she told. He could hear the night noises, the shuffle of trees getting comfortable, the soft trill of a screech owl, and could smell the mustiness of the river a few blocks off. Maybe he should try an experiment. What if he kept the door open a few inches and waited to see if anything came in? He had all night to get to the computer.

Timothy left the door open just a crack, grabbed his book, and climbed halfway up the stairs to wait.

Scientists had to be open to all possibilities. This was a data point. He didn't believe any of Mrs. Clapper's stories, but it was best to be objective. He opened his book and began the chapter about sleight-of-hand tricks. Every few minutes he looked up. Nothing happened. Timothy finished the chapter and stood up, feeling foolish. What had he expected? He'd never tell anyone about this little experiment. Time for the computer.

Two steps down the stairs and the door moved. A strange thumping began in Timothy's chest, as if his heart was trying to escape the cage of his ribs. Slowly, the door swung inward. Timothy drew back into the shadows of the stairs and held his breath. He thought of Mrs. Clapper's words, *Things that are better left unspoken.* A long face followed by a long, spare frame sidled into the living room. Beneath his shaggy black hair, the man's face was as pale as moonlight, his eyes the startling green of new leaves. Timothy froze. Should he call out and try to scare him off? He checked his pocket for his cell phone. Empty.

He leaned forward and let his breath out slowly, quietly,

so he wouldn't be heard. He'd watch for a few minutes and see what the man was after before calling Mrs. Clapper.

The man grabbed at the air. The light in the hallway dimmed. As Timothy watched, the man stuffed his hand into a large pocket of his coat. The pocket glowed.

It was impossible! No one could grab light as if it were a solid object; all the laws of physics were against that happening. But that is exactly what the man did. When one pocket was full, he filled another, and the light in the room grew dimmer. Timothy could see light spilling out over each pocket's edge like a moon just brimming above the horizon. If the man moved too quickly, the light would spill on the floor.

Timothy crouched down and concentrated on keeping his breath quiet. Now that his initial terror was gone, he felt . . . He wasn't sure how he felt. Intrigued, he thought to himself . . . no, mesmerized. Scrabble tiles popped into his mind. Mesmerized, twenty-four points, a good choice because of the z.

The man continued filling his pockets. The light in the living room dimmed even more. Something rustled in the doorway. Timothy clenched his hands.

A girl came in, and with her came the smell of snow. She was a little older than his sister, Sarah, and moved with the grace of a dancer.

Timothy was leaning so far forward now that he almost lost his balance and tumbled down the rest of the stairs. The girl, shining with a faint light, walked through the living room, picking up books, flipping the pages, and setting them down again. Every now and then, she ran her fingers through her white hair—hair even longer than Sarah's—and Timothy heard a faint tinkling sound. Wherever she walked, she left footprints of silver-white dust on the blue carpet. Timothy bit his lip. This really couldn't be happening.

By now, the man's pockets were full of light and the room was almost dark. Timothy inched farther down the steps. What should he do next? Suddenly, dogs howled in the yard.

Timothy didn't move. Mrs. Clapper must hear them. She'd be here any minute. She didn't come. His heart beat wildly.

A large head thrust itself into the room, a man's head with thick curly brown hair and a disorderly beard. The rack of antlers that sprouted from his hair scraped across the door lintel. A silver hunting horn swung from his belt. His eyes roved back and forth. Timothy made himself as small as he could. A cold sea sloshed in his stomach. Something about the man felt dangerous, unpredictable. Timothy shuddered and tucked his chin into his chest.

The howling was closer; he could hear claws clacking on the porch. The wolves of his nightmares, rangy beasts with glittering eyes and snapping mouths, popped into his mind. Timothy began to sweat. Why didn't Mrs. Clapper wake up? The situation was definitely out of control. The dogs were sure to have very large teeth!

The horned man spoke in a rumbling voice. "You've summoned the hunt early this year." Once more, his eyes raked the shadows. Then he leaned forward and sniffed.

Adrenaline surged through Timothy. If he moved, he'd be discovered. With every clenched muscle, he wished for the horned man to go away.

"There are rumors that Balor and the Dark are on the move again. Events are unfolding that require haste. The Filidh must discover his role and his strength. Cerridwyn assures me he is ready." The pale man's voice rustled like the branches of trees in the wind.

Timothy ran his moist palms down his jeans. What he was hearing made no sense at all. The Dark? Was this the same Dark from Mrs. Clapper's story?

The horned man nodded his great head, the antlers knocking a lamp shade sideways, clattering a picture to the floor. "Dark or Light, you know that the hunt takes no side in the battle. Who is the prey?"

At the word prey, Timothy flinched. Why did the man ask Who instead of What?

"It remains to be seen," the pale man answered. "I don't know what choices will be made, but you and your hounds are free to hunt lawful prey. Know this: I will do whatever it takes to defend the Filidh. And Balor will do whatever it takes to destroy him." The pale man was standing taller now. He opened one of his pockets. The light inside glowed. "I have captured some of the light of his house. It will call him to me."

The girl said nothing. She watched and listened.

The horned man turned to leave, ducking his antlers under the door. The baying of the hounds receded. Then the glowing girl followed him out the door, trailing the fine silver dust like the tail of a star.

Timothy pressed his face against his hands. He didn't like the word prey. The pale man looked around. His pockets bulged with light, and his green eyes peered into the shadows. They settled on the stairs where Timothy hid, as if he sensed his presence. Then the man turned and left, taking most of the light from the room with him.

In the dimness, Timothy leapt from the bottom step. He slammed the door shut and locked it. He leaned against the familiar solid wood while his breathing slowed. Should he get Mrs. Clapper, or call the police first? But what would he tell them? No one would believe his description. What did the man plan to do with the light? And how could light call someone?

He ran one hand through his hair and looked around his perfectly ordinary living room: a layer of fine silvery dust powdered the carpet, the lamp shade hung askew, and a picture lay on the floor. Nothing else, except the dimness, gave a clue that anything out of the ordinary had occurred.

If he woke Mrs. Clapper, he'd have to explain. She'd tell his parents. The questions would never stop. And he'd be doomed to having babysitters for the rest of his life. Nothing had been stolen. Timothy straightened the lamp shade, hung the picture back on the wall, and looked at the footprints with dismay. He'd sweep the silvery dust up. But first, he scraped some of it from the floor into a plastic bag, which he slipped into his pocket. Evidence. He'd save it to show Sarah. She could keep a secret. Then he hurried to the broom closet. In the distance, the dogs bayed. Timothy thought he could still smell their damp doggy odor. The silvery dust came up easily, leaving the floor just as it was.

For a long time Timothy gazed out the living room window, his heart still tap-dancing in his chest. Question after question bubbled up. He felt like a shaken bottle of soda, about to explode. If only Sarah were home!

Reluctantly, he climbed the stairs to bed, but it was many hours before he fell asleep.

Rosemary Clapper sat on the edge of the guest bed, looking at her watch. March 15, way too early for the horned man to be out and about, she thought, unless there was something unusual, something worth hunting. She had watched Timothy and Sarah grow over the years and now it appeared the time had come. She got up and pushed her feet into a pair of pink slippers. She shivered and tightened the flannel bathrobe. The temperature always dropped by at least ten degrees after a visit from a star.

AVAILABLE SPRING 2014